WHERE THE BIRD
SINGS BEST

WHERE THE BIRD SINGS BEST

Alejandro Jodorowsky

Translated from the Spanish by
ALFRED MACADAM

RESTLESS
BOOKS

Originally published as
Donde mejor canta un pájaro, Grijalbo, 1992;
2nd edition Ediciones Siruela, 2002

First English edition published digitally by Restless Books, 2014
First English hardcover edition published by Restless Books, 2015

ISBN: 978-1-63206-028-0
eISBN: 978-1-63206-007-5

Cover design by Richard Ljoenes
Set in Arno by Tetragon, London

Ellison, Stavans, and Hochstein LP
232 3rd Street, Suite A111
Brooklyn, NY 11215

publisher@restlessbooks.com

www.restlessbooks.com

CONTENTS

Prologue

1

—

ONE

My Father's Roots

3

—

TWO

My Mother's Roots

41

—

THREE

The Farthest Land

89

—

FOUR

The Promised Pampa

183

—

FIVE

Jaime and Sara Felicidad

243

A bird sings best in its family tree.
JEAN COCTEAU

PROLOGUE

WHILE ALL the characters, places, and events in this book are real, the chronological order has been altered. This reality was further transformed and magnified until it achieved the status of myth. Our family tree is the trap that limits our thoughts, emotions, desires, and material life, but it is also the treasure that captures the greater part of our values. Aside from being a novel, this book may, if it is successful, serve as an example that all readers can follow and, if they practice forgiveness, they too can transform family memory into heroic legend.

—ALEJANDRO JODOROWSKY

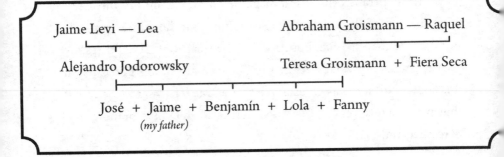

Jaime Levi — Lea

Abraham Groismann — Raquel

Alejandro Jodorowsky

Teresa Groismann + Fiera Seca

José + Jaime + Benjamín + Lola + Fanny
(my father)

MY FATHER'S ROOTS

I N 1903 TERESA, my paternal grandmother, got angry: first with God and then with all the Jews of Ekaterinoslav (now Dnipropetrovsk, in Ukraine) who still believed in Him despite the deadly flood of the Dnieper. Her beloved son José perished in the flood. When the house began to fill up with water, the boy pushed a trunk out to the yard and climbed on top, but it didn't float, because it was stuffed with the thirty-seven tractates of the Talmud.

After the burial, carrying all the children she had left, four toddlers—Jaime and Benjamín, Lola and Fanny—who were conceived more out of obligation than passion, she invaded the synagogue ferociously with her husband hot on her heels. She interrupted the reading of Leviticus 19: "Speak to the entire assembly of Israel and say to them—"

"I'm the one who's going to speak to them!" she bellowed.

She crossed into the area forbidden to her as a woman and pushed aside the men who, seized with childlike terror, covered their bearded faces with prayer shawls, silken tallises. She threw her wig to the floor, revealing a smooth skull red with rage. Pressing her rough face against the Torah parchment, she cursed at the Hebrew letters:

"Your books lie! They say that you saved the entire nation, that you parted the Red Sea as easily as I slice my carrots, and yet you did nothing for my poor José. That boy was innocent. What did you want to teach me? That your power is limitless? That I already knew. That you are unfathomable? That I should test my faith by simply accepting that crime? Never! That's all well and good for prophets like Abraham. They can raise the knife to their sons' throats, but not a poor woman like me. What right do you have to demand so much of me? I respected your commandments, I thought of you constantly, I never hurt anyone, I gave my family a holy home, and I prayed as I cleaned, I allowed my head to be shaved in your name, I loved you more than I loved my parents—and you, you ingrate, what did you do? Against the power of that death of yours, my boy was like a worm, an ant, fly excrement. You have no pity! You are a monster! You created a chosen people only to torture them! You've spent centuries laughing, all at our expense! Enough! A mother who's lost hope, and for that reason doesn't fear you, is talking to you: I curse you, I erase you, I sentence you to irrelevance! Stay on in your Eternity, create and destroy universes, speak, and thunder, I'm not listening any more! Once and for all: out of my house. You deserve nothing but contempt! Will you punish me? Cover me with leprosy, have me chopped to pieces, have the dogs eat my flesh? It doesn't matter to me. José's death has already killed me."

No one said a word. José wasn't the only victim. Others had just buried family members and friends. My grandfather Alejandro, from whom I inherited part of my name—because the other half came from my mother's father, who's name was also Alejandro—dried the tears that shone like transparent scarabs on the Hebrew letters with infinite care as he bowed again and again to the congregation; his face crimson, he muttered apologies that no one understood and led Teresa out, trying to help her with the four children. But she wouldn't let go and hugged them so tightly against her robust bosom that they began to howl. A hurricane blew in, the windows opened, and a black cloud filled the temple. It was every fly in the region fleeing a sudden downpour.

For Alejandro Levi (at that time our family name was Levi), his wife's break with Tradition was just one more nasty blow. Nasty blows were a fundamental part of his being: he'd put up with them stoically throughout his life. They were like an arm or an internal organ, a normal part of his reality. He wasn't even three when the Hungarian maid went mad. She walked into the bedroom where he slept, hugging his mother Lea, and murdered her with an axe. The hot spurts dyed his naked little body red. Five years later, in an outburst of hatred over the libel that Christian children's blood was used to make matzo, a swarm of drunken Cossacks poured into the streets of Ekaterinoslav: they burned the village, raped women and children, and beat Jaime, Alejandro's father, to a bloody pulp because he refused to spit on the Book. The Jewish community of Zlatopol took him in. They gave him a bed in the yeshiva. There they taught him two things: to milk cows (at dawn) and to pray (for the rest of the day). That milk was the only maternal scent he knew in his childhood, and to feel a feminine caress, he taught the ruminants to lick his naked body with their huge, hot tongues.

Reciting the Hebrew verses was torture until he met the Rabbi in the Interworld. It happened like this: Alejandro davened so much, chanting passages he didn't understand, that his feet went numb, his forehead was boiling, and his stomach filled with acid. He was afraid he would gasp like a fish out of water and faint right there in front of his classmates, who understood the texts (unless their fervent expressions of faith were just an act to earn them a good supper). He made a supreme effort, and, leaving his body to its davening, he moved outside himself and found himself in a time that didn't elapse, in a space that didn't extend. What a discovery that refuge was! There he could languish in peace, doing nothing, only living. He felt intensely what it was like to think without the constant burden of the flesh, without its needs, without its various fears and fatigues, without the contempt or pity of others. He never wanted to go back, he only wanted to remain in eternal ecstasy.

Piercing the wall of light, a man—dressed in black like the rabbis but with Oriental eyes, yellow skin, and a beard with long, slack whiskers—floated next to him.

"You're lucky, little man," he said. "What happened to me won't happen to you. When I discovered the Interworld, there was no one there to guide me. I felt as fine as you do and decided not to go back. A grave error. Abandoned in a forest, my body was devoured by bears. And then, when I needed human beings again, it was impossible to go back. I was doomed to wander perpetually through the ten planes of Creation. A sad bird of passage. If you let me plant roots in your spirit, I'll return with you. And to show my thanks, I'll be able to advise you—I know the Torah and the Talmud by heart—and you'll never be alone again. What do you say?"

What do you think this orphan boy was going to say? Thirsty for love, he adopted the Rabbi, who was from the Caucasus and steeped in Kabbalah. And seeking out the wise saints who, according to the Zohar live in the other world, he got lost in the labyrinths of Time. In those infinite solitudes, he, a contumacious hermit, learned the value of human companionship, understood why dogs long for their masters. He discovered that others are a kind of sustenance, that men without other men perish from spiritual hunger.

When he regained consciousness, he was stretched out on one of the school benches. The teacher and his classmates were gathered around him, all pale, because they thought he was dead. It seems his heart had stopped. They gave him some sweet tea with lemon and sang to celebrate the miracle of his resurrection.

Meanwhile, the Rabbi was dancing around the room. No one but my grandfather could see or hear him. The joy of the disincarnated man to be once again among Jews was so great that, for the first time, he took control of Alejandro's body and recited (in hoarse Hebrew) a psalm of thankfulness to the Lord:

Thou hast been our dwelling place in all generations.

Everyone panicked. The boy was possessed by a dybbuk! That devil would have to be flushed from his gut! The Rabbi saw his blunder and leapt out of my grandfather's body. And no matter how hard Alejandro protested that his friend promised never to enter his body again, they went ahead with the exorcism. They rubbed him down with seven different herbs; they made him swallow an infusion of cow manure; they bathed him in the Dnieper, whose waters were many degrees below zero; and then, to warm him up, they gave him a steam bath and thrashed him with nettles.

Even though they considered him cured, they still had their superstitious doubts for a while. But as my grandfather grew, they got used to his invisible companion. They began to consult him: first about Talmudic interpretations, then about animal illnesses, and then, seeing the positive results in the first two instances, they moved on to human maladies. Finally, they made him a judge in all their disputes. The entire village praised the Rabbi's intelligence and knowledge, but they had no regard whatsoever for Alejandro. Timid by nature and essentially humble, he had no idea how to capitalize on his position as an intermediary. People invited the Rabbi, not him. Whenever he came into the synagogue, they'd ask for the Rabbi, because from time to time the man from the Caucasus would disappear to visit other dimensions, where he'd commune with the holy spirits.

If the Rabbi accompanied him, they'd seat him in the first row. If not, no one bothered to speak to him or offer him a chair. The man from the Caucasus had said that what he liked most was to see children. So whenever people came to consult him in Alejandro's modest room next to the stable, they brought along their offspring, bathed, combed, and dressed for the Sabbath. This display was all the pay he got. No one bothered to bring an apple pie, a pot of stuffed fish, a bit of chopped liver.

Nothing. Only the Rabbi existed; my grandfather was the real invisible man. From the cradle he was never accustomed to being indulged, so this made him neither sad nor happy. He milked the cows, prayed, and at night, before sleep overcame him, he had long conversations with his friend from the Interworld.

One day, at the first light of dawn, Teresa approached him. She was small but had strong legs, imposing breasts, and an iron will. She fixed her dark eyes, two coals swimming feverishly in sunken sockets, on him and said:

"I've been watching you for a while. I'm of age to have children. I want you to be the father. I'm an orphan like you but not as poor. You'll come to live in the house my aunts left me. We're going to organize these consultations so that we can feed the children. You will be paid. The Rabbi needs nothing because he doesn't exist. He's the product of your madness. Yes, you're crazy! But it doesn't matter: what you've invented is beautiful. What you think he's worth, that's what you're worth. That knowledge only comes from you. Learn to respect yourself so others will respect you. Never again will they speak directly with the phantom. They will tell their problem to you and will have to come back later to hear the answer. They will no longer see you entranced, talking to an invisible being. I'll set the prices, and we will not accept dinner invitations where they try to take advantage of you. The Rabbi will stay home. He will never go out on the street with you, and if he doesn't like that, he can leave—if he can. But as soon as he leaves you, he'll dissolve into nothingness."

And without waiting for an answer from Alejandro, she kissed him full on the mouth, stretched out with him under the udders of the cows, and took permanent possession of his sex. He, after gushing forth his soul in his seed, squeezed the udders and bathed the two of them in a shower of hot milk. When they married, she was pregnant with José. The community accepted the new rules, so never again did the family table lack for chicken soup or fried potatoes or a fresh cauliflower or a plate of porridge. Ten months after José's birth, they had twin boys. The year after that, twin girls.

In the corset shop, in the presence of her neighbor ladies, Teresa would brag about living with a holy husband who never stopped praying, even during his five hours of sleep. Moreover, he would always eat, no matter what the dish happened to be, with the same rhythm so he could chew without ceasing to recite the psalms. And when he wasn't praying, he only knew how to say two words: "Thank you."

Everything was going so well and then, catastrophe! José dead! An extraordinary son, good among the good, obedient, well mannered, clean, with an angelic voice for singing in Yiddish, of resplendent beauty. Yes, his natural joyfulness brightened sorrows; he was a dash of salt in the tasteless soup of life, a wash of color for the gray world. Whenever he strolled past the trees at night, the sleeping birds would awaken and start to sing as if it were daybreak. He was born smiling, he blessed anyone who crossed his path, he never complained or criticized, he was the best student at the yeshiva. Why did a ray of sunshine have to die?

Teresa clung violently to her grief. Forgetting it, she thought, would be a betrayal. She refused to accept that he was gone, and she held him there, swallowing muddy water, blue from asphyxiation, an incessant victim, a lamb in eternal agony. This she did to justify her hatred not only of God and her community but also of the river, the plants, the animals, the dirt, Russia, all of humanity. She forbade my grandfather from solving the problems of others and demanded—otherwise she would kill herself—that he never mention the Rabbi again.

They sold the little they had and went to live in Odessa. There they were taken in by Fiera Seca, Teresa's sister, who was two years younger. Their father, my great-grandfather, had been married and widowed three times. His three previous wives had died giving birth the first time, and the children in turn had never lasted more than three days in the cradle. According to the old gossips, Death was in love with him and out of jealousy snatched away the wives and their fruit.

Abraham Groismann was a strong, tall man with a curly red beard and big green eyes. He made a living through apiculture. And while all that business about Death's love was just an old wives' tale, the love of his bees, on the other hand, was a clear fact. Whenever he harvested the honey from the hundred or so little multicolored hives, the bees would cover him from head to toe, without ever stinging. Then they would follow him like a docile cloud to the shed where he bottled the delicious honey. Many nights, especially during the glacial winters, they would gather on his bed to form a dark, warm, and vibrant blanket.

Teresa's mother, Raquel, was thirteen when she gave birth in the cemetery. The old crones put her in a grave and wrapped her in seven sheets so Death wouldn't see. There, in the cool earth, surrounded by dark bones, my grandmother bore her first child, whose mouth was filled quickly with a fragrant nipple to maintain the silence that was essential: Death had a thousand ears! Abraham, convinced that once again he was going to lose mother and child, prepared his heart for the tragedy by repressing any feelings. Their survival wouldn't generate either heat or cold. He just went on submerged in his sea of bees, speaking with them in an inaccessible universe. But when Raquel, now fifteen, became pregnant once again, hope blazed in his soul.

Though he'd been warned that the Black Lady, as faithful and loving as the bees, would follow him anywhere, he went to the cemetery, pushed aside the ladies who were holding up the seven sheets, and looked into the deep grave. He saw exit the bloody temple the most beautiful of girls. A strange wind whipped the white cloth and carried the sheets toward the mountains as if they were immense doves.

The mother was now dying. "Fool!" the women shouted. "Why did you come? You've brought your ferocious lover. She's already devouring the mother. The daughter is next." They poured salt and vinegar over the child's head and baptized her with a name that would shock and disgust Death: Fiera Seca. Then they put her in a basket, swaddling her in clusters of grapes, and carried her off to a secret place the father could never know, to hide her from the Enemy. Fiera Seca had to live as a prisoner in a barn until she was thirteen, when her menstruation began. When childhood came to an end, the danger disappeared. Death was looking for a girl, not a woman. Fiera Seca was led home by one of the old gossips. As she walked along the streets, the terrified townspeople closed doors and windows. To scare off Death, in case she discovered the child's hiding place, they'd taught Fiera Seca to make horrible faces, one after another. Her face, like a soft mask, passed from one ugliness to another. If you looked at her for more than ten seconds, your head would ache.

When Fiera Seca entered the room, which was simultaneously kitchen, dining room, and bedroom, Teresa ran out to the garden with the dogs, which began to howl, and the cats, which began to hiss. Fiera Seca was alone. She heard footsteps. It had to be Death! Out of her hiding place she felt more vulnerable than ever. Besides contorting her face, she'd also begun to deform her body. She bowed her legs, twisted her spine, and made her hands look like claws. She drooled and foamed at the mouth, tinting that wretched mess with blood she sucked from her gums. The door opened with an insect-like screech. Abraham saw a monster, a kind of giant spider, but he did not run because he was covered with bees. To Fiera Seca, the buzzing of that dark mass seemed like the song of the Black Lady.

There they stood, face to face, sweating in terror. Perhaps the only beings that understood the situation were the bees. They began to fly in a circle that became larger and larger until it surrounded father and daughter. Within that living cordon, the girl saw the most beautiful man she could have imagined. In the depth of his green eyes, she found an ocean of goodness. That sublime spirit became a world where, if she could make herself small, she would have wanted to live. Little by little, she stopped making faces and stretched out her body, revealing herself as she was—a beautiful woman. Abraham realized that all the others, those who died giving birth, had been nothing more than sketches of the thing that, without knowing it, he'd sought forever: standing erect before him, like a tremendous miracle, his own soul was calling him. They submerged one into the other, they spoke words of love to each other, they wept, laughed, sang, and fell into the bed. The bees formed a curtain that separated them from the world, and there they remained, two bodies transformed into a single bonfire, not thinking of the consequences.

Teresa felt superfluous. Her father and sister disappeared forever, transformed into lovers. She put what little she had in a sack and went to live with her aunts. Two years later, she received news from her sister, a letter:

Forgive me, Teresa, for having neglected you all this time. Dad is dead. You are the only one who knew our secret. I hope you'll understand. It was stronger than we were, a passion we couldn't control. No one in the neighborhood dared to imagine anything like that. Whenever I went out to shop, I made my faces and contortions so that no one would speak to me. My father, my lover, only showed himself covered with bees. Our real bodies were a miracle we only enjoyed in the intimacy of the house. To ward off spies, Abraham taught the insects to rest on the roof and outer walls of the house until they covered it like a thick quilt. We made love inside a gigantic honeycomb, drunk on pleasure, unable to stop, again and again, wishing we could fuse and become one being. That insatiable quest, that impossible dis- solution; mixed in with the pleasure was a constant pain, a dagger piercing our string of orgasms. A short time ago, I became pregnant. We thought we were angels, beings from another world, unaffected by human phenomena: we had to return to reality. After five months, my stomach began to bulge. In dreams, Abraham received a visit from the Black Lady. She was insane with fury and jealousy. When he awoke, he said, "I am going to be responsible for your death. She will not listen to my pleas. Her cruelty knows no limits. You will never be able to give birth and survive. Understand me, my daughter, my wife, I must sacrifice myself, hand myself over to Death, let her carry me off to her palace of ice. That way her love will be satisfied, and she will not devour you."

I wept for days, but I could not convince him that it was I who should disappear. He filled a bathtub with honey and submerged in the golden syrup. He died looking at me. He never closed his eyes. A tranquil suicide—he was smiling, and the bees flew, forming a crown that slowly circled over the yellow surface. Under the mattress, I found a note: "I shall never stop loving you. Please look after the bees. Don't abandon them. They are my memorials."

I fell into the bed. I spread my legs, and as my stomach shrank I expelled an interminable sigh from my sex. Nothing remained of our child. It turned into air.

Teresa never answered that letter and hadn't returned to her paternal home until the day she went to live in Odessa with Alejandro and the four children. An obscure shape came out to meet them. When they walked into the room, the bees separated from Fiera Seca and went to suck at little plates filled with sugared juices. Crying out, Fiera Seca threw herself into Teresa's muscular arms. She did not seem to notice the presence of my grandfather and the children.

"Oh, sister! No one knows about Abraham's death. I still make the atrocious faces when I go shopping, and I receive those who come here to buy honey covered with insects, so they go on thinking it's Abraham. I never buried our father."

As the family was moving in, she led Teresa to the barn. Among the honeycombs, from which came a buzzing similar to a requiem, was the honey-filled bathtub with the smiling corpse beneath its yellow surface.

"Honey is sacred, sister. It preserves flesh eternally. He never wanted to leave. I feel him stuck to me. He's waiting for me."

As she said that, Fiera Seca took off her clothes. She revealed her naked body, a delicate structure with a skin so fine that the pattern of her veins, like those of a leaf, could be seen. A thick, animal-like pubis contrasted with that angelic delicacy: it was so black it sparkled blue and covered her belly up to her navel.

"I shouldn't abandon the bees. They are the reason I remained in this world. That's what he asked me to do. But now you've come, and I can leave. I'm leaving these wise animals in your care. If you look after them carefully, they will feed your whole family."

And with no further explanation, she leapt into the tub, embraced her father, and allowed the honey to cover her. She made no signs of drowning and seemed neither to suffer nor to die. She simply became immobile forever; her eyes wide open, staring into the open eyes of the other cadaver.

Teresa felt as dead as her father or her sister. Only her obligation to her family kept her alive. And hate as well. Especially hate. It was a source of energy that allowed her to tolerate the world only so she could curse it. In all things she saw the presence of a cruel, despicable God. There was nothing that didn't seem absurd, impermanent, or unnecessary to her. The plot of life was pain. She could detect the incessant fear hidden in laughter, in moments of pleasure, in the stupid innocence of children.

For her the world was a prison, a charnel house, the sick dream of the monstrous Creator. But what infuriated her most (a rage that made her curse from the moment she awoke until the moment she fell asleep) was knowing, without wanting to admit it to herself, that this hate disguised an excess of love. In her childhood she learned to adore God above all things, and now, in her absolute disillusionment, she had no idea what to do with that immense feeling. She could not channel those fervent oceans toward her husband or children because they were condemned to die prematurely.

Just as the Dnieper flooded its bank and carried José away, some accident or other would exterminate them. Security was fragile. Nothing lasted. Everything shrank to nothing. Unthinkable evils were possible. A rock could fall from the sky and crush her family; an ant could lay eggs inside their ears, where armies of tiny beasts would be born that would devour their brains; a sea of fetid mud could slide down from the mountainside and cover the city; mad hens could become carnivorous and peck out the eyes of the children; anything could happen.

What was to be done with that unclaimed love building up in her bosom, shaking her heart so violently that its pounding could be heard up and down the street at night, drowning out the chorus of snores? Suddenly, without being able to understand why, she discovered the only thing deserving of her love in this world: fleas! She remembered a circus act she'd seen in her childhood and decided to train those insects. She always carried out her tasks as wife and mother. She provided her family with a clean home, she cooked and ironed, all the while hurling insults. Before her four children went to bed, she made them get down on their knees and recite: "God does not exist, God is not good. All that awaits us is the cat who will urinate on our grave." And when they slept under the huge quilt next to the brick stove, she, hidden in the cold basement, dedicated herself to domesticating her fleas.

When she fled her father's house, Teresa stole his pocket watch, the only souvenir she wanted to keep. Now she emptied it of its movements, removed the white dial with its Roman numerals and hands like a woman's legs, and pierced its cover with holes so that her acolytes could get the necessary oxygen. There were seven of them. To each she gave a different territory to suck blood: her wrists, behind her knees, her breasts, and her navel. She bought a magnifying glass and other necessary instruments and made them costumes, decorations, tiny objects, furniture, and vehicles. She reduced her sleep time and spent entire nights teaching them to jump through hoops, to fire a miniature cannon, to play drums, to swing, to play ball. Little by little she got to know them. They had their own personalities, subtly different bodies, individual forms of intelligence. She named them. She communicated better with them than she had with dogs. The link was profound. After a long while, she could speak and plot with the fleas against God.

She compared the affection of fleas with what she got from the Jews, and her revulsion intensified. She wanted to change her race, to go off and live with the goyim. But her last name, Levi, was like a six-pointed star carved into her forehead. My grandfather—who was still seeing the Rabbi from the Caucasus, though he never admitted this to Teresa, wishing to forestall those flights of rage that were so strong they shifted the furniture—found some nobles of Polish origin who did not want their only son to do his military service with peasants. The family supplied him with official papers bought from a venal functionary so he could join the army in the place of their delicate heir. It happened his name was Jodorowsky. With that Polish last name, he and his family could move to another country, cross borders without major problems, dissolve among the non-chosen races in just five years, when his enlistment was over.

While waiting for her husband to return, Teresa supported her family by selling honey and sweet rolls shaped like moons, towers, and crabs. At night, she relieved her solitude by working with the seven fleas to create—by reading the lines they traced while dancing on a dusting of flour—a method that would allow her to read the future.

The Rabbi was not much help to Alejandro in the army. The soldiers' world seemed impure, and when he saw my grandfather in the mess hall devouring pork chops or other forbidden foods, his face became even yellower and from his slanted eyes poured tears as immaterial as his body.

"If you don't understand me, Moisés will, bless him. I have to eat this Russian garbage because if I don't, they'll figure out who I am. It's hard enough to cover up my circumcision. Leave me in peace. What do you know about the pain in my gut when your intestines aren't even solid? If all you want is to add more suffering to my sorrows, I'd rather you stopped speaking to me."

During those arduous five years of military service, the Rabbi said not one word more.

Alejandro had other problems. Whenever he held a rifle he went white as a sheet, fell to the ground, and vomited. Tired of trying to cure him with kicks and whippings, the officers made him a kitchen helper and bootblack for the squadron. He also had to clean the latrines and stables. Instead of feeling depressed, he decided, accustomed as he was to the blows of life, to turn his disgrace into an apprenticeship. God had put him here to peel stunted vegetables, to polish smelly boots, to clean up human and equine shit in order to teach him something important.

Amiable, calm, smiling, he peeled tons of potatoes, carrots, and cucumbers. Though what was demanded of him was quantity and not quality, he tried to do it all rapidly but well, taking care that the food was clean, the potatoes free of eyes and rot, the vegetables not dried out. He was constantly honing his skill in eliminating skin without sacrificing the slightest bit of meat. And it was in this constant separation of dirt-covered surfaces that he ended up seeing himself, as if in each day's work he were pulling old skins, pains, rancor, and envy from his own memory. Every vegetable that sparkled naked and clean in his hands gave him the sensation of an internal birth. During his final months of military service, he carried out this task singing with the innocence of a child.

Also with innocence, but that of a thousand-year-old man, he cleared the excrement. Horses and men were one in those evacuations. An immense pity that transformed into tenderness filled his spirit when he purged the latrines. That fecal matter was a testimony to the animal nature of the soul, of the soul's ties to the flesh. And he marveled when he thought about how in those bodies that produced this fetid magma, faith also could manifest itself, as well as love and so many other delicate feelings. He learned to respect excrement, to consider it his equal, to see things from that humble level. He opened his heart as he emptied the receptacles, trying to be a true servant, one who sees the work of God through misery and who works to make it shine. He recognized in himself the presence of the Divine Superior and desired, with ecstatic joy, to obtain the blessing of being useful to Him. It was there, in those places of defecation, where he learned to pray sincerely for the first time. If a being like him, an excrement gatherer, was worthy of a relationship with the Supreme Being, the door was opening for other men who had—all of them—more merit than he.

After shining boots and shoes for almost five years; scraping off thousands and thousands of filthy crusts; applying polish, oiling, using a cloth; patching soles; flattening rebellious nails; over and over, hour upon hour, he began to like the work. "The feet," the instructors would always say, "are the most important part of the military. A soldier with badly fitting boots is a soldier lost." During cold weather, on the incessant marches, during the many combat maneuvers, the infantry needed its lower extremities very well protected.

Alejandro imagined life as a spiritual war and felt an almost unbearable sorrow for the poor men who trudged barefoot or suffered from shoddily made boots. Being a shoemaker was a profession that fit his modesty. If he were meant to serve, he would transform his labors into works of art. Those who previously only walked would dance in his shoes. This he decided the day that a captain, loudly guffawing through aromatic waves of kielbasa and vodka, gave him a pair of boots stained with Jewish blood. For an hour he polished them, not to make them shine but to erase that painful image. He swore he would only make fine shoes that would be as soft and durable as faithful animals, to give health to the body. A man who dances can sing, and all songs, human and animal, exalt God.

As soon as they were liberated from military service, the Rabbi smiled again. After five years of silence among uniformed goyim, he went merrily along with Alejandro toward the Jewish neighborhood. His joy made him fly quickly like a grand crow above the rooftops. When he saw the sparrows flee, my grandfather realized that they could see the phantom. That lifted a weight from his mind because, for him, it proved he wasn't insane.

He shouted to the Rabbi, "Hey, my friend, come down here! Now I know that you are not a hallucination! Let's resume our conversation."

The man from the Caucasus left the company of a dead leaf that was being wafted about, landed, and spoke to his companion: "Mr. Levi— pardon me, I mean Mr. Jodorowsky. During these past years, not being able to speak with you, I dedicated myself to reviewing, within myself, the sacred books I know by heart. I had the idea I should summarize them in a single volume. Then, in a single chapter, then in a single page, and finally in a single sentence. This sentence is the greatest thing I can teach you. It seems simple, but if you understand it, you will never have to study again." The Rabbi recited it. And life, from that moment on, changed for Alejandro. "If God is not here, He is nowhere; this instant itself is perfection."

Teresa received my grandfather shyly, hugging the twins to her body. Shorn of moustache, beard, without curly payot hanging by his ears, without long hair, wearing goyish clothes, Alejandro was unrecognizable. His smile had become a meaningless contraction. His wife had put on weight, and his children had grown. The boys were almost seven, the girls around six. Benjamín was completely bald. Fanny had curled her hair and dyed it an aggressive red. Jaime and Lola, he muscular and she spectrally thin, were as alike as two drops of water. My grandmother, aside from being three times her original size (the result of eating only honey in order to save money, she said later), boasted a skull covered by a thicket of gray hair, which contrasted violently with her round, young face with its ruddy cheeks.

Alejandro burst into tears, sobbing loudly. He fell to his knees. My grandmother recognized him. She pushed the boys into his arms and ran from the room. The children wriggled out of their father's embrace, flailing their arms every which way, and ran to a dark corner, cringing like frightened chickens. Under no circumstances would they ever accept this intruder.

The Rabbi spoke to him: "Hold back your tenderness. Wait. It's one thing to give it, but quite another to force someone to accept it. Little by little, they'll come to you."

Teresa came back wearing a clean dress and a black, well-combed wig, carrying some pieces of honeycomb in a clay bowl. With a single shout, both fierce and kind, she sent the twins to the barn. While Alejandro ate voraciously, spitting out bits of wax, Teresa got into bed.

With her brow deeply furrowed, she said, "Tell you-know-who he should also leave."

Alejandro, with great dignity, retorted, "I don't have to. He left with the children." And with that, he jumped on top of her, tearing her dress and underwear to pieces. They possessed each other with such passion that the bed collapsed. When it fell, it knocked over a brazier. The burning coals scattered over the floor. The wood began to burn. Enormous flames devoured furniture and walls. My grandparents noticed nothing.

Not for an instant did they interrupt their caresses. Perhaps because the sweat from their bodies soaked the sheets, perhaps owing to divine intervention, the fire never touched the bed. After the final orgasmic explosion, they returned to reality and found themselves resting in a house reduced to smoking ruins.

"No regrets," said Teresa to my grandfather. "Things happen when it's time for them to happen."

"That I know," he answered, "because when you've got faith, all things happen for the better."

"Well then, follow me. I've got a surprise for you."

In the stone barn at the far end of the yard, the children, who were pretending to be statues of salt under a cloud of bees, hadn't noticed a thing. Teresa clapped her hands three times like a circus ringmaster, and the children, grimly, began to bottle the honey as the bees resumed their duties within their little cells.

"Take a good look at the hives, Alejandro. Do any look odd to you?"

No matter how hard he looked, my grandfather could find nothing unusual.

"Ask you-know-who."

Obeying his wife, he thought of his friend from the Interworld. The Rabbi, who was floating around in the shape of a tiny cloud, recovered his human form and walked over to point to a hive much like the others.

"Something tells me it's this one, Teresa."

"And in what way is it different from the others, Alejandro?"

My grandfather swallowed hard and glanced obliquely toward the Rabbi, who told him, "There are fewer bees entering and leaving through its door."

"You're right! You're a great observer! It took me four years to realize it."

"Can you tell me why?"

"Because it has a false bottom, Teresa."

"Bravo! Congratulations, Alejandro! That is the case."

This praise was a painful blow to my grandfather's humility. Embracing her judgment as his own, his eyes filled with tears and his throat with sobs.

"You're more of a child than the children," said my grandmother. "When will you learn to accept your merits? Being righteous serves only to make you oblivious to those who humiliate and take advantage of you!" And to console him, Teresa sank his face between her bosoms.

To him it seemed that his nose traced a mile of cleavage before it touched the warm depth that vibrated with each beat of her enormous heart.

"Come along with me!" she said.

My grandmother led him by the hand to the hive. She pulled out a few nails and freed up the rear door. Within the hiding place was a leather coffer. When she opened it, Alejandro stopped weeping, lost control of his facial muscles, and opened his eyes so wide that his eyeballs nearly popped out. The jewel box was filled with gold coins!

Teresa burst into a nervous giggle. "Yes, my friend, this cramped neighborhood, filled with bearded fanatics and bald witches, is finished! We're going to a free world where we don't have to believe in that cruel God who demands our absolute adoration and rewards us with massacres!"

"But Teresa, where did all this wealth come from?"

"I'm going to read you a letter from my father that I found under the coins."

I'm writing this in case someday you find this treasure, which for me has been useless. For three generations or more we've been building it up by making huge sacrifices. Moisés, my father, received a large part of it from David, my grandfather, who was a state tax collector in Hungary. That was the only position the gentiles allowed Jews to occupy, because for them it was despicable to debase oneself by charging money. He lived, destroying wealth, between the hatred of the people and the contempt of the aristocrats.

One day, after counting up his savings and looking at himself in the mirror, he was so disgusted by his reflection that a tumor sprouted in his left eye. In less than a month, he was blind in that eye. Then his hands became covered with warts, his back with sores. He stopped eating until he died, skinny and white, like a paraffin candle. My father received the leather coffer, two-thirds full, as his inheritance. After burying David, he fled toward the Ukraine and settled down in Odessa as a moneylender. The gold coins multiplied at the same rate as the rancor of his debtors. Finally, a nobleman who refused to pay had his hounds bite my father and his servants daub him with hog excrement. Moisés, naked, foul smelling, and bloody, reached the synagogue looking for consolation. In despair, he recited Psalm 102: *I am like a pelican of the wilderness: I am like an owl of the desert.* The rabbis chanted along with him: *I watch, and am as a sparrow alone on the roof. Mine enemies reproach me all the day.* Moisés, counting on the support of his coreligionists, who covered him with a tallis, bellowed out the end of the psalm, straining his vocal chords, while the white silk became blotted with red. Just at that moment, a bee flew through the window and, after fluttering around the sacred candelabra, landed on the chest of the wounded man and for no apparent reason—he made no abrupt movements, concentrated as he was on communicating with God—buried its stinger in his heart. My father felt that all his blood had settled in that organ, then that his chest was exploding, and then that a boiling flood washed over his brain. He fell to the floor, trembling like an epileptic. For half an hour he howled and then lost consciousness for three seconds. When he awoke, he was a different man. His narrow personality split open, allowing a sensitive, much vaster being to appear. He announced that

God had given him a message by instilling in him a love for bees. The filthy money he obtained from loans would be exchanged for perfumed honey. He forgave all debts and became a beekeeper. He hid the jewel box full of gold in a hive, promising himself he would never use it as long as the honey business made enough for him and his family to live on. His wife, Ruth, could not accept the change, felt terrified about the future. After converting to Christianity, she ran off with a Cossack, leaving her only child, me, in the cradle. The brutish Cossack, during one of his drinking sprees, realized that she was drunk on a Saturday and cut off her head with a slice of his saber. I think it was then that Death put on my mother's face as a mask. And from then on, Moisés lived covered with bees in order to erase his body from the world. For me, he was only a blur of vibrating insects. I can't even tell you what color his eyes were, so hidden were they by the shimmer of beating wings. When did he die? I never knew. One day, I realized that the human form composed of bees was empty. Perhaps when he felt himself dying he asked the bees to eat him. I went among them, filling the space my father had left and taking my turn. I never had to use a single one of those coins.

—Abraham Groismann

Alejandro and the Rabbi were moved. They could not imagine how my grandmother clung to the leather coffer.

"Let's just leave things as they are, Teresa. We'll use only a few coins to rebuild the house and put the rest back into the hive. Let's live off the honey, the miracle of these bees, organized and peaceful as perhaps human beings will one day be if they learn to work together."

"Enough!" interrupted Teresa. "I am not a professional victim. If we stay here, they're going to slit our throats, with Adonai's good wishes. The Union of Russian People is accusing Jews of stealing blood from Christian children, and *The Protocols of the Elders of Zion* is being published in every city. The whole country is sharpening sacrificial knives. And what is it you're defending? A black suit? A fur cap? A beard and side locks? A rest on the Sabbath? A few festivals based on fairy tales? A few prayers in a dead language? A severed foreskin? Is that what it means to be a Jew? Bah! We're just as disgusting as everyone else! So, why not blend in? We'll move to the United States. There, all citizens live in palaces and have their teeth plated gold. Nobody pays attention to your name, and no one asks you where you're from. Their only interest is how much you have. And we have a fortune. We will be welcomed. We can apply for permits to leave today. Let's sever our roots!"

That afternoon, they brought the tub with the two enraptured corpses down to the Dnieper and slipped it into the water. Like a small white ship, it was carried by the current toward the reddish sun. The bees, in a compact black cloud, went along with it.

Alejandro, Teresa, and the four children abandoned the empty hives and left Odessa with the clothes they were wearing— and the jewel casket my grandmother hung between her breasts. Then they rented a hotel room in Elisavetgrad. Thanks to Alejandro's Polish name and the magic of a few gold coins, they had no trouble acquiring an exit visa.

"I grant the present certificate to the subject Alejandro Jaimovich Jodorowsky, thirty-six years of age, native of the district of Zlatopol, Administrative Department of Kiev. This certificate confirms that there exists no impediment with regard to the Municipality of Zlatopol to the aforementioned Alejandro emigrating along with his wife, Teresa Jodorowsky, maiden name Groismann, thirty years of age, and their children Benjamín and Jaime, born on July 25, 1901, and Lola and Fanny, born on July 4, 1902. In accordance with the protocols of the municipality, it has been determined that the aforementioned Alejandro Jodorowsky and his family have committed no crimes, criminal or civil. I, Vladimir Grigorievich Shevchenko, notary, in my offices located on Upenchaya Street, number 27, in Elisavetgrad, delivered the original and the copy of the aforementioned document to the Jodorowsky family, who reside in the vicinity of the third commissariat of Elisavetgrad. On this day, the 14th of March, 1909."

What immense joy! With that scrap of paper they could get to the other side of the world! A series of stamps, seals, signatures, and sonorous words that conferred freedom: Code, Document, Certificate, Subject, Power, Family, Crimes, Commissariat, Administration! "This Vladimir is a ridiculous madman," Teresa observed after an attack of happiness, and she led the family into a large store to dress her entire family in the style of the goyim.

They bought third-class tickets and, after filling a couple of baskets with food, they boarded a train that would leave them in Paris. There they would obtain visas for the United States and take a ship leaving Marseille. On the ship, they would learn English and forget Yiddish and Russian forever.

They ate creamed herring, blinis, pickles, and apple pie. Only when their stomachs were full did they raise their eyes to observe the other passengers, the goyim. What they could plainly see, and the fact upset them, was that the car was filled with miserable-looking Jews. Pretending that the emigrants didn't exist, Teresa belched, sighed with satisfaction, and hugged the precious coffer even more tightly against her chest. She first made sure the children were asleep, and then, to attract her husband's attention, she pinched his leg.

"It's going to be a long night, Alejandro. Now that we're well on the way, I'll have time to tell you what your children have been up to these past five years."

It took my grandfather an hour before he could concentrate his wife's stories. Seeing so many Jews piled up on the narrow benches, carrying packages wrapped in faded shreds of cloth, dignified in their misery, some with bandaged heads, others with their arms in slings or with black eyes or broken noses, doubtlessly fleeing some pogrom—it all filled him with an overwhelming sadness. Oh dear! Those maternal women with huge, wrinkled hands, licking the wounds of their children with dog-like love! Oh dear! Those underfed and beaten men with their eyes burning with religious zeal! Oh dear, those children dressed in black, still and wise, wrapped up in their Bibles, which they already knew by heart! All of them like a tribe of the just, suffering for the crime of loving God above all things! The Rabbi lamented not having a real body so he could warmth the fugitives with his embrace, so he could kiss the wounds on their feet. He flew from one place to another, emitting heartbreaking moans at the sight of his compatriots' plight.

Alejandro, repeatedly pinched by Teresa, was absorbed little by little by her tale. The personalities of Benjamín and Jaime were exactly opposite. Each felt a strange need to differentiate from the other. Jaime (the one who would become my father at twenty-eight) was interested in manual labor, in violent games, in killing sparrows, cats, and ants. He became an expert in stamp collecting and in smashing the faces of the neighborhood brats. Benjamín observed the life of the bees, collected fairy tales, and made great efforts to learn how to read them as soon as possible. He liked to water flowers, always slept with a burning candle beside him, and did not play with boys; the slightest contact with harsh cloth wounded the fine skin on his hands.

The same thing happened with the twin girls. Lola was taciturn, so much so it seemed she knew just two words: "yes" and "no." She ate little, liked to bathe every day, even in cold water, and painted beautiful land-scapes on the honey labels. She hated helping her mother in the kitchen, but she adored setting the table, lighting the candles, and embroidering tiny birds on napkins. Fanny was violent, funny, and voracious. She hap-pily twisted the necks of chickens and peeled potatoes with astounding speed. Her pudgy fingers worked the darning needle with disgust. But doing carpentry work, digging, clearing the chimney, and, in summer, robbing fruit from the neighbors' trees—all that, she adored.

The boys got along badly with each other, as did the twin girls. They formed two mixed couples: Benjamín, the delicate boy, was fond of the company of the mischievous Fanny. She quickly took control of the duo and protected her brother in street fights. She knew how to punch and kick better than the scamps wearing trousers. When he was with Lola, the vigorous Jaime would change. The nervousness that caused him to move around ceaselessly—little leaps, wiggles, rough-housing—would disappear, and he would stand there observing his younger sister in a state of astonishment. Contact with that feminine refinement revealed in him unimagined desires, subtle feelings, delicate tendencies that anguished him. He would finally bellow to break the spell and run for the street, where he would give a bloody lip to the first boy he met.

Teresa, half asleep, half awake, went on talking as the train sliced through the rough wind—snorting like a dying bull, emptying itself of steam clouds—and stopped for eternities in dark stations. More emigrants got on. Fat policemen passed through checking passports and cutting open packages, treating the Jews with a mocking disdain. If they found even the slightest error in the papers, they would order entire families off with rifle butts and kicks. Other groups would quickly fill the empty spots.

All around the Jodorowskys, who passed as goyim under the Administrative Code thanks to the Certified Document, was an aura of respectability. The fugitives, fearful of abuse, did not dare look at them. The soldiers, seeing that magic document, clicked their heels noisily, saluted energetically, and grimaced sympathetically, apologiz-ing for the abject neighbors such honorable passengers were obliged to put up with. Throughout the third-class cars dialects echoed from all parts of Europe: the Yiddish of Lithuania, Poland, the Ukraine, Crimea, Bulgaria, Austria, and Hungary. Poor people with no homeland, fleeing to who knew where.

Teresa made a point not to acknowledge any of this. Speaking Russian slowly and carefully so she wouldn't reveal her Jewish accent, she made her words into a shield that separated her family from a reality that had become, for her, a familiar nightmare.

Tugging on Alejandro's left earlobe, she whispered:

"If you want to survive, you'll have to change. Forget the others and watch out for us. They are to blame for whatever happens to them because they're going around disguised as the righteous, believing in superstitions. God gives them bad luck. Death feeds on good fools. Follow the example of the goyim: everyone works for himself, and the one with the wettest mouth swallows the most beans. Stop daydreaming and listen to the story of how Benjamín lost all his hair.

"One spring morning, a circus wagon painted like a carriage from the funeral parlor pulled by two skeletal horses decorated with black plumes passed along our street, heading for the town square. A man wearing a skeleton costume held the reins. Next to him sat a female dwarf dressed as the Angel of the Last Judgment, playing a sad melody on an old trumpet. Attracted by their sinister looks, we ran to see the performance.

"Those trapeze artists really knew how to seduce the audience. A show that was merely jolly could never compete with Nature, which was emerging exuberantly from its winter lethargy. Between the invasion of multicolored butterflies and the blossoming of lascivious flowers, the abject levity of a few acrobats couldn't have interested anyone. But decked out this way, gloomy and toothless, miserable remains of the glacial cold, they gave us the chance to feel healthy, well fed, and safe.

"The starving clown fighting with a rag-doll dog over a piece of kielbasa made us shriek with laughter, as did the rubber man disguised as a worm, who was making all sorts of contortions inside a coffin and threatening us in a ferocious voice that one day he'd eat us. The female dwarf unrolled a carpet in the center of the square and put a basket down on it. A thin black man, probably the one we'd seen dressed as a skeleton, decked out in a turban, a robe, puffy trousers, and slippers whose toes curled upward, all in a golden-red color, kneeled before the basket and began to play a flute that was long and had a ball at one end.

"We'd never seen human skin like that, as black and shiny as the boots the Cossacks wore. Nor had we ever heard a sound like that. It seemed like the hooting of an owl combined with the wail of a woman giving birth, plus the screech of a metal door. He spoke an incomprehensible tongue, which the dwarf lady said was Sanskrit, the magic language of Hindustan. For the first time in Russia, the illustrious public would witness the taming of a cobra, queen of venomous beasts. To encourage the Hindu prince, she asked that we fill her trumpet generously with coins.

"As we dug into our pockets and shed, with difficulty, a bit of money, the melody resounded continuously, without silences, drawing us closer to the land of dreams. When the collecting was over, the dwarf lady, causing her paper wings to chatter, opened the basket. Out came a huge serpent hissing like an angry cat. It flared its hood and struck at the black man, who expertly dodged it and intensified the undulating rhythm of the flute. The snake, like us, fell under his spell and just stood there, stiff, erect in a terrified beatitude.

"I have no idea what happened to Jaime. I still don't understand. We were all frozen with terror, hypnotized by the Hindu and his serpent. We practically didn't even dare to breathe. Then Jaime stepped forward into the empty circle, and with a big grin he stretched his hand out toward the cobra and began to pet its head.

"The lady dwarf tensed up, and signaled to us not to move. The animal, hearing the slightest whisper, could reassert its aggressive nature. The flautist, terror on his dark face, went on playing the same phrase again and again. Jaime kissed the serpent's snout. Then he picked it up and, staring at it with tender eyes, danced delicately while hugging the snake to his bosom. Since the serpent was much longer than he was, its tail dragged along the tiles of the kiosk's floor, making a metallic sound. It sounded to me like the chattering of Death's silver teeth.

"Jaime stopped opposite Benjamín and, with innocent cruelty, offered him the snake. Benjamín was covered in sweat from head to toe, but since his brother had brought it so close that he'd actually put the serpent's snout next to his mouth, he held back his tears and his nausea and took hold of the cold animal. 'Dance! Dance!' cried Jaime. Benjamín, awkward, his legs stiff, his mouth wide open, his breath short, tried a few steps. The lady dwarf made more and more signals to us not to move. Our desperate silence spread to the entire neighborhood—you couldn't hear a cart, the birds stopped singing, the wind left the leaves still. The whine of the flute filled everything. Benjamín made slow circles, staggering like a fatally wounded bear, with the deep gaze of the cobra fixed in his eyes. A yellow liquid ran down his legs and a coffee-colored stain marked the seat of his short pants.

"Jaime pinched his nose shut and burst into laughter. The snake went mad. It began to smack its snout against Benjamín's forehead. Transfixed by terror, he didn't let go. Luckily, as we found out later, the cobra had no venom and no teeth. But the blows it gave as it tried to bite were as hard as a hammer. With his face lowered, Benjamín took the punishment on his skull.

"The Hindu tossed aside the flute, ran to the boy, and tried to tear the snake out of his frozen hands. The cobra, feeling strangled, tried to get free by striking harder and harder, not only with its snout but also with its tail, dangerous lashings that kept us from getting too close. The rubber man took out a knife and prepared, at great personal risk to himself and the child, to cut off the snake's head. I didn't know what to do. Once again, God was stealing one of my children. I began to curse Him. Lola, with a calm like Jaime's, picked up the flute and started to play.

"Even though the cobra, as we found out later, was deaf, it instantly calmed down. Benjamín finally opened his fingers. From his hairy scalp, marked by a lattice of cuts, poured a red cascade. The Hindu brought out some powdered clay, added water, and covered Benjamín's head with the greenish paste. The blood stopped flowing, and we all calmed down.

"Fanny was clinging to one of the black man's legs and began to cry, saying 'Papa!' He took her in his arms and rocked her. She immediately fell asleep, smiling.

"The black man said to us, 'In a former life, far off in time, I really was her father, a good king. She was a wise prince named Rahula. One day, I decided to test his filial love. I summoned two thousand soldiers, whom I transformed with a mantra into kings, identical to myself. The vizier gave my son a ring and, pointing to the multitude of identical monarchs, among whom I was standing, ordered, "Majesty, go and put this ring on the finger of your father's right hand." Without a moment's hesitation, Rahula entered the group and came directly toward me. His true love could not be beaten by two thousand illusions.'

"The black man had a coughing fit. When he recovered, he returned Fanny to me and went on talking: 'Now we must leave. Soon, sick as I am, I will give up the ghost. When this little girl turns seventeen, she will be my mother. But I, worn out after so many reincarnations, will only live nine months in her womb. I shall be stillborn.'

"During many mornings, Fanny would run off, go to the plaza, sit down in the center of the kiosk and start to cry, whispering 'Papa.' Her hair began to curl and take on a reddish color similar to the Hindu's costume. I had to buy Lola a wooden flute. She discovered that the only thing that interested her in life was music. When we finally removed the clay shell from Benjamín's head, we were dismayed to see that he was completely bald. We thought he would be sad, but to the contrary, he was happy.

"'Mama, when I grow up, I don't want to have a single hair. I want my eyebrows and lashes to fall out, I want nothing to grow in my armpits or on my pubis, and I don't want teeth or nails. I'll be happy when I have no animal traces on my body.'

"The only comment Jaime made was the promise that when he grew up, he'd be a tamer of lions, tigers, panthers, and elephants in a circus."

Teresa, with great difficulty, finished her last sentence with a long and soft "ciiircuuus" and fell asleep next to the twins. The Rabbi took that as an opportunity to show Alejandro a grandfather, father, and young son praying, wearing the black horn of the tefillin on their foreheads. Next to them a ravaged woman gave her breast to a fretful baby. Just beyond, to the right, to the left, throughout the car, men were imploring God. From each one of those genuine families, all sharing in the suffering, emanated a peace bestowed by everlasting contact with the Truth.

Alejandro, deeply moved, followed the Rabbi's adamant counsel and very carefully removed the coffer from between Teresa's breasts and replaced it with one of his shoes. Then, limping along, he went over to one of the religious Jews, opened the box, showed the contents, and whispered, "I will exchange gold coins for any kind of money." He went from group to group distributing his treasure and getting copper or nickel coins and banknotes of little value in return.

Weeping with gratitude, they tried to kiss the foot wearing the shoe, but he silenced the poor wretches out of fear my grandmother would awaken. He distributed the greater part of the gold, leaving only what was strictly necessary for the voyage, that is, the price of passage to the United States and the cost of living in France while waiting for the ship to sail. He checked the weight of the coffer. It was lighter now, so he put in a Bible he'd hidden away. When he pulled out his shoe, it almost burned his hands—that's how hot Teresa's huge breasts had made it. Then he put the jewel box back in its place.

33

His wife woke up a few seconds later, insulted God as was her custom, and went back to dreaming. It started to snow. It stopped snowing. It rained. The sun came out. They changed trains again and again until they lost count of the changes. Jaime and Fanny traded punches. Benjamín and Lola insulted each other. In Germany, a large number of Jews left the train. The remaining refuges were met in Paris by the Universal Israelite Alliance.

Alejandro, with deep nostalgia, watched his fellow Jews embrace and kiss, weeping with emotion, as if they'd known one another since childhood. He felt a pang in his heart when he realized he was no longer part of that family. Alone in that immense train station rocked by violent gusts of cold air, disoriented, he, his wife, their four children, the Rabbi: branches without a tree, swallows without a flock, severed hands floating in the void.

Alejandro regretted using the Holy Book to compensate for the weight the leather coffer had lost. He wanted never to move again, to become as immaterial as his friend, to sink his nose into the text and remain there, a deaf mute, reading forever. Teresa and the children, impressed by that monumental and horribly alien train station, clung to him. Where could they go without an address, without speaking a word of French? The Rabbi began to recite Psalm 22: "My God, my God, why hast thou forsaken me? Why art thou so far from helping me, and from the cries of my anguish?" And suddenly an answer came.

An elegant man—with a monocle and walking stick, a fur coat, gaiters, and a top hat—mopping the perspiration from his face with a silk handkerchief, trotted up to them and said in refined Russian, "Pardon my tardiness, dear compatriots. I am the envoy of the Russian Committee, whose mission it is to guide the subjects of our noble land through the Parisian labyrinth. A free service provided by the government. Here is a list of hotels, restaurants, museums, stores, theaters, money exchanges (with all prices clearly marked)." And, kissing Teresa's hand, he introduced himself, "Count Stanislav Spengler at your service. What is the name of the family with whom I have the honor of speaking?"

Alejandro began to cough, pursed his lips, and stared at his wife with pleading eyes. If he uttered a single word, his Jewish accent would betray him. Teresa made her mouth small to imitate the aristocracy, assumed an indulgent air, and, imagining herself as a countess—that is, wearing clothes dripping diamonds, emeralds, rubies, gold medals, and spangles—burst out in a high, nasal voice:

"We are the Jodorowsky family—Alejandro, Teresa, Benjamín, Jaime, Lola, and Fanny. We're from Odessa, honey merchants, but with noble Polish ancestors, people with lots of money!"

And moved by some obscure impulse, she extracted the coffer from her cleavage; tossed it around, making a huge sign of the cross; and then restored it to its refuge. The Count's monocle dropped from his right eye. An embarrassed silence ensued. Jaime broke it by walking over to the train to squirt out a yellow arc that splashed among the steel wheels. In a dry voice, the envoy of the Reception Committee asked to see their official papers. He examined them carefully, smiled, and said, "Well, I'll be frank with you. No matter how many Polish last names you may have, madam, by your manner of speaking it's obvious you're Israelites. I'd appreciate your not wasting my time by denying it. All we need to prove it is the penis of the boy we saw urinating."

Teresa shot a furious glance at Jaime. Fanny and Benjamín laughed. Lola looked at them all with disdain. Alejandro could only think about the Count's boots. He'd never seen footwear so fine, and that cruel perfection terrified him.

"You are all very lucky, because even though I'm of noble birth, I don't harbor anti-Semitic feelings. Quite the contrary, I think of Jews as old friends. My father amused himself in the desolate winters of White Russia studying dead languages, which led him to an interest in Hebrew. One day, he discovered that Jews kept that ancient tongue alive. From then on, a steady stream of rabbis, bankers, and Jewish doctors passed through our mansion. We received them with the respect the bearers of such a marvelous culture deserve. So don't worry. While this makes my task more difficult—you cannot be received by our committee, which is only for Russians—I'll put myself at your service. We will speak more comfortably in a private room in the restaurant next to the station. Come with me."

Relieved, smiling, they followed the Count, who for his part acted as a tourist guide and shared with them a thousand and one insignificant details of the great city. Then, seated opposite bowls of onion soup and a platter of fried potatoes in a discreet corner, they talked calmly. When Stanislav Spengler found out they wanted to live in the United States, he shook his hair-creamed head from side to side with a disdainful sigh. "Because of the legend, now spread all over Europe, that three hundred Jewish magnates secretly dominate the world, hundreds of thousands of Israelites have been forced to flee to America. It's almost impossible to get visas. Nevertheless, I have a good friend in that consulate, the secretary general, who can do us that favor. But it will cost a lot of money, perhaps more than you have!"

Teresa, a smile on her face, answered, "Your price is our price." And she placed the leather coffer on the table. The Rabbi fled out the window. Alejandro's face took on a greenish tinge. With great pride, my grandmother raised the lid.

The Count peered into the interior and said, "A Bible? Perhaps, madam, you're confusing earthly goods with cultural treasure?" Teresa, utterly wild, clutched the book in her tremulous hands, threw it to the floor, observed the filthy banknotes and copper coins, and emptied the contents of the box onto the table.

She separated the few gold coins from the miserable rest. She bellowed, staring at my grandfather, "Who did it? You or the ghost? Or was it the two of you together? What did you do with the bulk of the gold? Don't tell me! I can guess for myself. You gave it away to that pack of mangy beggars! Oh dear, oh dear! Why did I ever marry a righteous man? A lunatic, an idiot! He protects strangers before his own family! But he's innocent. It's all the fault of that damn book!" She picked up the Bible, ripped its pages, spit on it, threw it toward the street, and began to cry in her husband's arms. Unable to say a word, he covered her face with kisses.

The Count, pushing around the gold coins with the corner of his monocle, counted them. "Well, we have enough for your passage and something more for the hotel. And if we pick one of the lowest quality, we might even have a little bit left over for a gift to my friend. The secretary general owes me a few favors. I'll try to convince him to be charitable this time and to help a family with a father of such saintly generosity." The Count dried his eyes with his silk handkerchief. "Let's not waste time. It's still early. We'll go straight to the American Consulate."

A streetcar dropped them opposite a luxurious building, where the venerable flag waved its stars and stripes. The aristocrat asked them to sit in the waiting room while he went to the offices on the second floor to speak with his friend. He went toward the stairway and stopped. He came back. "Madame Teresa, a good idea just occurred to me. I'll tell my friend the marvelous story of your husband's saintly generosity. Let me borrow the coffer for a minute, so I can show the secretary general the gold coins and the worthless money of the emigrants. That more than anything else will convince him. I'm sure he'll reward Alejandro's open-handedness toward his poor tribal brothers and give us the visas for nothing." Teresa ceremoniously put the jewel box in the Count's hands. He clicked his heels as a soldier would and, with all dignity, entered the elevator.

They waited and waited. The Count never returned. When the buzzer sounded announcing the imminent closing of the consulate, they ran up the stairs to the second floor. There were no offices, only a huge, empty salon for cocktail parties. They did see an emergency exit. They understood.

There they were, on the street, desperate, without a penny. My grandmother's world collapsed. She kicked the luggage, sat down on the ground, closed her eyes, and said, "Take care of yourselves the best you can. I'm no longer here."

"In that case," observed Alejandro, "if you're no longer present, then I've recovered my right to summon the Rabbi. He'll get us out of this fix."

"Bah! More stupidity. I've already told you the Rabbi doesn't exist. It's only your imagination."

"Imagination or whatever it is, the Rabbi is the Rabbi. If he doesn't come, there's nothing I can do."

"All right then, call that thing. I'd be surprised if he could do anything for us."

She must have been shocked, because the Rabbi gave them the only reasonable solution: "Look for a commercial street. Examine the stores. If any one of them belongs to a Jew, you'll certainly find some sign of our religion. Speak to them in Yiddish." And that is exactly what they did.

Walking aimlessly along, they found a street lined with shops. On a shelf in a jewelry store, they saw seven-armed candelabra. They walked in. Moishe Rosenthal clearly spoke Yiddish. Since Teresa hated to be Jewish again, she pretended to be mute. Alejandro only told part of his miseries and, ashamed, finished the tale with lies. Disguised as goyim, they'd fled a pogrom, and now they were lost in Paris, with no money, with no idea what to do, and hungry, especially the children.

The first thing Moishe did was feed them in the kitchen behind the shop. Then he left his wife in charge of the jewelry store and accompanied them to the Jewish neighborhood. After offering them a little money, which Alejandro accepted, kissing Moishe's hands, he presented them in the offices of the Comité de Bienfaisance Israélite, founded in 1809.

There they were treated with maternal care. They were housed for two days in a modest but clean and Kosher boarding house. From there they were sent on to Marseille, where they were put, along with other refugees, on a ship sailing for South America. They were given the only visas anyone could get—Chilean. Teresa knew nothing about Chile, but she was sure that in such a country, located at the end of the world, the citizens did not live in palaces and did not have gold teeth.

Alejandro I — Cristina Prullansky   Salvador Arcavi — Luna

Ivan Prullansky — Felicidad Arcavi   +   Sara Luz Arcavi — Salomón Trumper

Alejandro Prullansky   Jashe   +   Shoske

Sara Felicidad
(my mother)

TWO

MY MOTHER'S ROOTS

I F TERESA GOT MAD at God, it was God who got angry with Jashe, my mother's mother. And along with God, all the Jews in Lodetz, in Lithuania. Her periods began—with mathematical precision—on the same day as those of Sara Luz, her mother, and of Shoske, her sister. The power that regulated such a sacred phenomenon was the pride of Hasidic women, because it confirmed that their bodies obeyed the same laws as the stars. Far away from the men, they would dance without underwear under the moon to allow the plasma to run down their legs and fertilize the land. Jashe confessed, amid tears and cries of joy, her love for the goy.

While her mother, breaking the law, sold plum brandy to the Jewish bankers, Jashe would stroll the streets of Vilna. For her, the smell of the city was like the most exciting of perfumes. Purely by chance, she ended up in front of the Municipal Theater, where Swan Lake was about to be put on by the Imperial Russian Ballet. She'd never seen any theater. Something irresistible made her buy a ticket, the cheapest. Feeling the lecherous stares of beardless Lithuanians with curled side locks, she took her reserved seat in the last row without daring to raise her eyes from the floor. The music exploded, she heard the curtain go up, and then the pattering of steel taps like confused rain. Little by little, among those synchronized tapping feet, she distinguished different ones, rough and at the same time delicate, in some strange way familiar to her.

A heat wave overwhelmed her belly and made her look toward the stage. She did not see the sets, the lights, the dance troupe, or the audience in their seats. All she saw was a gigantic male dancer with skin whiter than marble, with long golden curls, and blue eyes so potent that she could feel them near her face even though he was so far away—thousands of miles from the last row in the balcony, but nearer, much nearer than her own father.

Her sex palpitated with such intensity that, obeying its demands, she got up from her seat and, like something between a sleepwalking angel and a burning tree whipped by an invisible tempest, she looked for the dressing rooms. She entered the one with a crippled Christ nailed to the door, caught the giant naked, and fixed on his member the miraculous gaze that comes only with total surrender. The Russian, enraptured, undressed her slowly. That small, perfect body (Jashe was under five foot four), that undeveloped sex—a docile line crowned by a triangle of savage shadow—engulfed him in such vertigo that for a few seconds the room turned upside-down, and he found himself hung like a chandelier on a floor transformed into a ceiling.

Alejandro Prullansky, without knowing it, had been waiting for this Jewish woman his entire life. Even though he had no experience, even though he had known only the love of men, he knew how to possess her, leading her many times to a state of frenzy on the flower-patterned sofa. Exhausted, he fell asleep in her arms. Jashe, observing his handsome, white foreskin with a tenderness that swelled in her like a river, and knowing she was a prisoner of the Law, ran away without leaving her name or address.

Luckily for the lovebirds, the success of the Imperial Ballet extended the season for several more weeks. My grandfather—first dancer, gold-medal recipient in every competition—was still there, circles under his eyes, desperate, waiting for her. Then Salomón, Jashe's father, deposited her, pregnant, without luggage or money, right in front of the Municipal

Theater. The traitor had been expelled from the village and symbolically buried in the cemetery, for which they filled a coffin with her clothes and personal possessions. Now for a week her family would toss ash on their heads, sit on the floor, and, with torn clothing, drink chicken soup. She would be wept over as if she were actually dead.

Alejandro thanked the icon of the Virgin for such a prodigious gift and married Jashe in an Orthodox church, the bride dressed in white and the groom in black, like any Christian couple. With one difference: the groom wore boots of a gaudy red. When my grandmother asked him why he was wearing such scandalous footwear, she learned that the union of their two souls, which seemed like pure chance, had been in preparation for centuries.

As her husband told her the family saga that led him to wear red boots, Jashe too sought out the roots of her love. Guided by the memory of her mother, she traveled through time and journeyed all the way to Spain, before the fatal year 1492, when because of that evil, ambitious, thieving witch, Isabel the Catholic—may she lose all her teeth in hell, all but one so it will ache eternally—Jews who did not accept conversion were expelled. Sara Luz, in the middle of the nineteenth century, listened to her father, Salvador Arcavi, lament his fate and curse the kings of Castile and Aragon every single day for depriving them of paradise.

Yes, Spain, before the marriage of those two anti-Semitic monarchs, before the State Police, before the Inquisition, was a paradise for Jews. Muslims and Christians tolerated them. Within the furtive zones of their ghettos, free as never before, they practiced their religion. They sought out new paths to satisfy their thirst for that unreachable God. They entered into the text like virulent lovers, and they made it explode, moving vowels around, going mad over numbers, giving an terrible meaning to every letter. They became visionaries, mad men, magicians. They opened interior doors and got lost in the labyrinths of Creation, making their contact with the Torah a personal adventure, assuming the right to interpret everything as they saw fit.

In those good old days, Salvador Arcavi, the first of a long series of Salvadors—traditionally all his descendants had the same name—though respectful of the Holy Book, decided he was not to going to be a prisoner to its letters. Following the prophecy Jacob made to his son ("Your hand will be on the neck of your enemy. Your father's sons will bow down to you. Judah is a young lion."), he became a lion tamer.

His way to draw nearer to God was to study those beasts and to live an itinerant life, giving performances in which his union with his animals surpassed the limits of reality and reached the miraculous. The lions jumped through flaming hoops, balanced on the tight rope, danced on their hind legs, climbed up on one another to form a pyramid, spelled out the name of a spectator by choosing wooden letters, and, the greatest test, accepted within their jaws the head of the tamer, without hurting it, then dragged him through the sawdust to draw a six-pointed star.

My ancestor had a simple way to make the beasts love him: he never forced them to do anything, and he made their training into a game. Whenever they wanted to eat, he fed them, and if they decided not to eat, he did not insist. If they wanted to sleep, he let them, and if they were rutting, he let them fornicate without distraction. He adopted the rhythm of the animals with care and tenderness. He let his hair grow into a mane, he ate raw meat, and he slept naked in the cage, embracing his lions.

One day he found a Spanish girl, Estrella. Drunk on his beastly aroma, she abandoned the Christian religion and followed him so she could give herself to him, lying supine, whenever the animals went into heat. Cubs were born at the same time as human babies. At times, the woman gave her bosom to the tiny carnivores, while her own children crawled toward the teats of the lioness to slake their thirst.

They forgot Hebrew and used a limited Spanish of only a hundred words. The great cats learned most of those words and in turn taught their trainers a wide range of growls. When rehearsals or shows ended, after dinner, at midnight, in the intimacy of the great cage, humans and animals would sit face to face to stare fixedly into one another's eyes. In those moments, the lion was the teacher. It was he who was there, present, concentrating, with no interest in the past or the future, united with totality. In his animal body, the divine essence became palpable. The lion taught the Arcavis about economy of gestures, strength in repose, the pleasure of being alive, authenticity of feeling, obedience of oneself. Finally, seeing the nobility of the beast, his majestic inner solitude, they understood why Jacob compared Judah to a lion.

The Kabbalist rabbis of Toledo understood that a new form of biblical interpretation had been born. In silence, with the greatest respect, they entered the cage protected by the miraculous touch of Salvador's hands. They meditated, staring into the lion's eyes. They asked permission to bring their brothers in study, and with them came handsome old Arabs dressed in white and pale Catholic monks with sunken, burning eyes. The Koran, the Torah, and the Gospels were eclipsed by those imposing beasts, capable of standing so still that fireflies fleeing from the cold dawn rested on their warm skin, transforming them into phosphorescent statues.

When the first Salvador Arcavi began to die, he asked not to be buried. Instead, his body should be cut into pieces and fed to his lions. Estrella wanted to do it by herself. After the last morsel of her husband disappeared into the animals' jaws, she went to the river to wash her reddened hands, undressed, stepped into the water, and let herself be carried off by the current. Her son Salvador kept the show going and soon married a good woman. On their wedding day, he changed her name to Estrella, his mother's name.

The mystics from the three religions continued meditating opposite the lions. The years passed. The political situation changed. Hordes of fanatics began to burn the ghettos. The mystics stopped visiting. The wagons of the lion tamers passed through cities where converted Jews, sentenced to death by the Inquisition, were burning. The thriving communities became sad streets walked by dark rabbis, as circumspect as shadows.

An enigmatic impulse made the Arcavis go to Valencia. As they drew closer to the city gates, they came upon hundreds of families, guarded by soldiers, marching along the road in file upon melancholy file. They could carry little, just a few packages wrapped in embroidered cloth, nothing more. Why more, in any case? They'd been expelled from the country because they refused to convert, and when they reached the gates, the state police stripped them of most of their treasure. Ah, what a terrible year 1492 was! God was punishing them for wanting to plant roots in a land that wasn't their own—these people whose mission was to wander and to plant the holy Word in all nations—by giving them thieves as their king and queen.

The gold they had honestly saved up for generations would flow into the royal treasury. The only wealth they could remove from the country, without fear of being despoiled, would be the Spanish language:

> *Holy language*
> *It is you I adore*
> *More than all silver*
> *More than all gold.*
> *Though my holy people*
> *Have been made captive*
> *Because of you, my beloved,*
> *It has been consoled.*

They reached Valencia. After ruefully handing over their money, the Jews were in no hurry to board ships. As tranquil as a black lake, they slept all squeezed together on the docks and sea walls, ceaselessly praying for the Messiah to come and blast Isabel and Ferdinand. But God's silence was the only answer received to their mournful prayers. That multitude could have massacred the few soldiers present, but none of the Jews showed the slightest hint of rebellion. All they did was rock back and forth, chanting their prayers, and staring at the heavens: to be humiliated and plundered was normal for them. They had to cut their beards and burn their Talmuds and Torahs. A mountain of burning books sent up sallow clouds.

To open a path through the impenetrable mob, the Arcavis released the lions from their cages and walked ahead, leading them as if they were domestic dogs. They reached the dock, where the customs officials were shaving the exiled Jews before allowing them to set foot on the precarious boats. Nearby, in the garbage, lay a venerable old man: the officials thought it useless to cut off his beard because he was dying of fatigue, hunger, or sadness. Salvador recognized him. It was the Kabbalist Abramiel, leader of the group who had followed them throughout almost all of Spain, meditating at night opposite the lions. He brought the teat of a lioness to the old man's mouth and squeezed in a gush of hot milk. Abramiel swallowed eagerly and then poured out a flood of tears that left white lines on his dirty cheeks.

"What sorrow, what shame, what despair! Sorrow because everything is gone with the wind. Even though we know our books by heart, it's terrible to see them burn. Not for the words within, since we will someday write them down again, but for the pages we loved so much. For centuries, we washed our hands before touching them. They were our intimate friends, our real mothers. How can the flames devour those angels? Shame, because of those who chose to convert, to eat pork, to work on Saturday, not to circumcise their sons—those people are losing the very meaning of life. Despair, because what we had achieved—peace among the three religions—has been destroyed, perhaps forever. The sacred books will become justification for murderers."

The old man opened a pouch of violet leather, then looked right and left. He took out a small package wrapped in a silk handkerchief that was the same color as the pouch, unfolded it carefully, and revealed a deck of cards:

"This humble game, which we've named Tarot, summarizes, without naming them, the three branches of wisdom—Judaism, Islam, and Christianity. We conceived it in the shadow of your lions. Thanks to their example, we were able to pass through the thicket of traditions to reach the single fountain. Staring at the beasts, who were neither asleep nor awake, we received the first twenty-two arcana. Each of their lines, their colors, was sent to us by God. Then we combined them in a game of fifty-six Arabic cards that we modified according to what was dictated to us. These cards are like your lions: you have to observe them in silence, memorizing trait after trait, tone after tone, to allow them to work from within, from the shadowy region of the spirit. The knowledge they will bestow on you will not be sought but received. Hunting is forbidden; only fishing is allowed.

"Salvador and Estrella Arcavi: look at the first card, the card with no number. It shows a fool followed by a kitten. This sacred madman walks with the kitten, is sought by it, but he pays it no attention because he's chasing an ideal located outside himself. Up ahead, on card number eleven, Strength, a woman with a huge head joins a luminous yellow lion. With her mouth closed, she listens, and he, with his jaws open, speaks, transmitting the message that pours into her the Infinite Profundity. The beast—that is, the body—and the woman (that is the soul) become a single being. Knowledge, the vision of God, cannot be found except within oneself. And finally on the last card, The World: just look at the lion crowned with an aureole, which indicates the sanctification of instinct. Which brings us back to the words of Jacob: 'Judah is a young lion: from the prey, my son, you have gone up.' This, the enlightened man sacrifices his material welfare and ascends, lion transformed into eagle, into pure spirit to give himself to the divine hunter and be devoured by Him."

The Arcavis did not understand Abramiel's symbolic language, but as they studied the drawings on the cards they felt possessed by an ineffable emotion that was a mixture of awe and terror.

"My children, your name is Arcavi, which means 'I saw the ark.' Take with you this last vessel, this temple that will pass through the flood, transporting sacred knowledge through the centuries. Copy the deck. Give it to common people. Scatter it throughout the world. Disguise it as a vice, so that people will take it for a mere game and not censor it. By way of thanks, the deck will supply you with food and keep you from catastrophe. Always remember you are carrying a Being who, little by little, overcoming ignorance, will allow the union of all human spirits."

While Salvador kept the animals under control, Estrella hid the Tarot in her bodice. The wise old man climbed up on the back of the lioness who had given him milk and asked that he be taken to the bonfire of books. The docile beast, carried him to the pyre, followed by the others. Abramiel, his face radiant, walked into the fire and recited a poem in Hebrew as the flames devoured him.

Every time Sara Luz Arcavi told her daughter Jashe about this sacrifice, tears would pour ceaselessly down her neck. Leaving a dark trail on her starched apron, they would finally fall among the cats, which would gather to lap them up with delight. There was no suffering in her. She would smile sweetly, knowing she was a conduit for sorrow that came from the past, sorrow that would pass before the eyes of countless generations to end up who knew where.

Perhaps she didn't weep out of sorrow but out of reverence. When the wise man entered the bonfire, memory broke into fragments and reality mixed with legend. Different versions of the event circulated within the family: Abramiel climbs up the burning books as if they were a ladder he gets to the top of the pyre, spreads his arms out like a cross and burns, blessing the world, cursing the world, giggling, until he turns to ash, ash that spits flames in the form of eagles that fly in a flock toward Jerusalem. Or, he opens a door in the smoke, walks through into another world, and disappears. No, he was an alchemist who created an elixir that allows anyone who drinks a few drops to live a thousand years. Abramiel, in his protest, sacrificed several centuries of existence. Before his immolation, he gave his precious drink to the lioness that carried him, which is why the animal went on working for a different Salvador Arcavis. No, Abramiel in reality was the philosopher Isaac Abravanel, who tried to commit suicide. The flames, out of respect for his holy wisdom, refused to consume him. He emerged untouched from the bonfire and sailed with Estrella, Salvador, and the lions on a ship whose crew was made up of Moors who promised to carry them to Morocco. This last version was the one Jashe preferred.

After paying the stipulated price—which, despite the urgency of the situation, was fair—they stored the cages on the deck, near the poop, with the help of the amiable crew. How many lions were there? My grandmother did not have exact figures. There may have been twelve, like the twelve tribes; or seven because of the sacred candelabra; or four, like the letters of the unsayable name of God. The family was never able to agree on any of this. They all agreed that the lions over time, because of their repeated incestuous couplings, began to be born albino. Their red eyes and white fur filled even the most hardened warriors with a hypnotic terror.

Isaac Abravanel, invigorated by the lion's milk and his passage through fire, accompanied the Arcavis. Enough families followed him to fill the hold and the rest of the deck. The Moors offered each passenger a glass of tea with mint. The ship set sail, leaving behind the coast of Spain in its wake. The women sobbed, the men squeezed their lips together, someone took out a guitar and, in a cracked voice, sang a farewell to the lost homeland.

Soon the passengers calmed down. Some yawned, and a general drowsiness made everyone stretch out and sleep as the ship cut through the water, pushed by a righteous wind. "Adonai seems cruel," said Isaac the Wise, "but in the moment of our greatest pain, He preserves us by making us sleep in broad daylight as if it were night. His love is as great as his severity!" Salvador, despite these words, was very nervous. Between him and the lions there never were differences. If they were hungry, he would eat; if they fornicated, he would mount Estrella; when, for no reason, the beasts, possessed by an irrepressible joy, started to roar, he could not keep from shouting at the top of his lungs, made drunk by a similar feeling. So, how was it possible that God sent him sleep but did not make the lions fall asleep? To the contrary, enlivened by the sea breeze, they wouldn't stop playing. He fought as much as he could until he fell, as if struck by lightning, next to his wife who was looking for him in a virgin forest, riding on a gigantic scarab, while she snored with her mouth wide open.

The passengers, thanks to the drug that the Moors dissolved in the tea, slept for two days. They woke up in chains. Without their friendly smiles, the sailors showed what they really were: slave traders. The prisoners would disembark in Constantinople, and from there their freedom would be negotiated with some Jewish congregation in Europe. If the ransom was paid, they ran no risk, but if not . . . An ominous silence ended the sentence.

Salvador, Estrella, and their lions roared angrily and refused to leave the cage. The Moors got out their harquebuses and swore to kill the beasts if they didn't. The Arcavis followed orders. The pirates tied up Salvador with his arms and legs open and then put a dagger blade into a brazier filled with hot coals. Laughing and drinking dark liquors, they began to pound drums and dance, pushing one another into Estrella, who defended herself scratching and biting.

Suddenly, they pulled off her dress, knocked her down, spread her legs, and before the very eyes of the horrified Jews started to rape her. Salvador began to howl. The pirates, out of their minds, stripped off his lion-skin tunic, exposing his genitals. A sweaty fat man, muttering curses, seized the red-hot dagger and burned Salvador's testicles. Seeing her husband castrated, Estrella sighed like a dying woman and stopped resisting.

One after another, the drunken men tried to possess her, but she squeezed her vagina with such force that none of them could penetrate it, no matter how hard they smashed their torsos against her. They would kneel before her, try, and then get up, humiliated by the sarcastic laughter of the others, their penises still erect. Salvador had fainted. They tossed Estrella like a bag of garbage next to Isaac. The pirates moved on to rape other women, and the party continued.

Abravanel, in a calm, deep voice, as if he were speaking to a little girl, said to her, "God will make you understand, my daughter. From the pack in your bosom, take out a single Tarot card and tell me what you see."

Estrella, numb with pain, dug into the package and extracted The Sun. "Two children . . . happy."

"Well seen, Estrella. Those two children are the ones you will have with Salvador."

Hearing that, Estrella was overcome with such unbearable grief that it became a fit of laughter. She laughed and laughed so much that her laughter spread to the Moors who, not knowing why, hooted like barking dogs. Estrella's convulsions stopped, and in despair she whispered, "He's no longer a man. My womb is dead. You're mocking me."

"No, my daughter. The Tarot never lies. Believe in the impossible, have faith." Pulling her toward his chest, he put out his tongue, drew a Kabbalistic sign with saliva on her forehead, and began to recite strange words. "*Hamag! Abala! Maham! Alaba! Gamah!*" He pronounced them with such intensity that the squeals, prayers, drumming, cruel laughter, and songs all ceased.

The sea suddenly became choppy. The ship began to waltz up and down. The waves grew bigger and bigger. Black clouds came down from the center of heaven, and a powerful wind whistled words that, even though no one understood them, left people breathless and crushed their hearts. A pirate leaped toward Abravanel, waving his scimitar. An invisible hand threw him against the mast with such brute force that his skull split and spit out his brains.

"Release my brothers or the ship sinks!" bellowed the old man, surrounded by a greenish mist and looking like a demon.

This part of the story, even though she heard it directly from her mother when she was small, always seemed incredible to Jashe. She wanted to know about the real lives of her ancestors, not a fairy tale or a Bible story. But Sara Luz, smiling, explained that the past was a continuous invention, that every character in her family tale was like a stone that with the passage of years, from telling to telling, piled up to the sky, a shining star that gives light sweeter than sugar.

"All the people in your family, my child, will, by the end of time, become champions, heroes, geniuses, and saints. Treat them as if they were and day after day deposit in them the treasure of your fervent imagination. Which would you like better, a miserable old man burnt to a crisp in a bonfire or a magician? Let him board the ship so that when the storm breaks, the Moors become terrified and beg on their knees for mercy! Accept the fact that the prisoners will disembark in Nice. Isaac the Wise, disenchanted with philosophy, will dress up as a clown and accept the wandering life of the lion tamers. Estrella will become pregnant and give birth to two boys. This time it's no miracle: Salvador attained the wisdom of the lions. When the red-hot blade touches him, he withdraws his testicles into his belly, so only the scrotum is burned."

Doing their lion acts and card readings, with comic interludes by Abravanel, they traveled the Mediterranean coast from France to Italy. When they reached Padua, the plague robbed them of one of the twins. The little boy, who did not know how to read or write, whispered in perfect Hebrew before yielding his spirit, "Get wisdom, and whatever you get, get insight. Prize her highly, and she will exalt you; she will honor you if you embrace her. She will place on your head a graceful garland; she will bestow on you a beautiful crown."

Isaac closed his eyes and mumbled with muted elation, "He recited from the last verses of the fourth chapter of the Book of Proverbs! This illiterate child died a saint! Hallelujah!" And with patient work, in short sentences and growls, he translated their son's message to his disconsolate parents. "Do you understand, my friends? The child asked you to learn to read our sacred books. It's time to stop speaking like beasts. Recover your human intelligence." After the lions ate the small body, Salvador and Estrella took their first Hebrew lesson. They stayed for seven years, putting on shows in Verona, Bassano, Rovereto, etcetera. By the time they reached Venice, they knew how to read and write. Like them, the lions also spoke Hebrew properly.

"Yes, Jashe," said her mother sternly. "The lions learned to speak Hebrew. If you want to draw some benefit from your history, you must accept not only this miracle but also many others. In memory, everything can become miraculous. All you have to do is wish it, and freezing winter turns into spring, miserable rooms fill up with golden tapestries, murderers turn good, and children who cry out from loneliness receive compassionate teachers who are really the children themselves, sent back from adulthood to their early years. Yes, my daughter, the past is not fixed and unalterable. With faith and will we can change it, not erasing its darkness but adding light to make it more and more beautiful, the way a diamond is cut.

The Venice ghetto, which could only be entered from a bridge with doors guarded at both ends, looked from the outside like a great fortress, with all its exits blocked and its windows sealed. The Arcavis and Abravanel entered that dark neighborhood. They found clean streets populated by tranquil Jews, their heads covered with the obligatory yellow yarmulkes. The luminous color sticking out above their tallises made them look like a field of sunflowers.

The arrival of the albino lions was taken to be harbinger of the Messiah. Isaac Abravanel suggested that they might hasten his arrival by adding the voices and magic of the beasts to their daily prayers. They were given lodging, and after midnight, when the doors at both ends of the bridge were locked so that no Israelite could leave the ghetto, in the secret space of the synagogue, the rabbis rocked back and forth in a trance, more and more rapidly while the lions repeated in their cavernous and powerful voices the invocations and entreaties of the philosopher disguised as a clown. This ceremony was repeated for nine months.

The ghetto seemed to sleep, but in reality and without the guards realizing it, the fortress had escaped from Venice. Through the power of Kabbalistic words, its matter was frozen, and the astral substance arose out of the stones and human bodies. Invisible, the ghetto traversed the sky like a fleeing star and came to rest next to the Wailing Wall in Jerusalem.

"Yes, Jashe, my daughter," Sara Luz would say. "May that which we call God bless you. I beg you to believe this story and tell it to your future husband, to your children, and to your grandchildren. Every night, for years, the Venice ghetto visited the Holy Land, demanding the arrival of the Messiah. At dawn, when the Marangona, the largest bell in San Marcos, rang, the spectral neighborhood rejoined its empty stones and its cataleptic inhabitants. When the two doors on the bridge were opened, life returned to normal."

Isaac never lost hope and communicated his enthusiasm to the men and the animals: "Tomorrow the world will be fixed." The divine messenger would unite all religions, impart justice, give them peace, work, health, and felicity. He would lead them back to Israel.

One night, he made so many efforts to hasten the great event, invoked it with such exaggerated fervor, demanded so much of the superior planes, employed such potent enchantments, that an angel appeared before him flashing rays of fury: "Isaac Abravanel, you have upset the equilibrium of the angelic choruses, you have opened in your time and world the door of madness. Just look at what you've done!" The magus was transported to the heights, and from there he could see Jewish congregations invaded by divine madmen: David Reubeni, Moshe Chaim Luzzatto, Asher Lämmlein, Mordecai Mokiah, Yankiev Leibowitz Frank, Jacob Querido, Sabbatai Zevi, Miguel Cardoso, and many more. Armies of messiahs spread like the plague, in a holy war between fervor and rapacity, pride and fear of death, each one cheating his followers.

"Your punishment will be clarity," said the angel, just before abandoning him. Isaac collapsed on the pews in the synagogue as if struck by lightning.

"Magic is useless," he said. "I've opened the Fifteenth Arcanum and let the demons loose in our world. My search led me down the wrong road. The only hope is for us to reach ourselves, because God is hidden in our hearts. What isn't done here will not be done in the Beyond. No miraculous messenger will come to offer us a homeland. We were expelled from the land so that we would transcend it and inhabit pure spirit, not so that we go on clinging to the roots, to childhood, setting up the past as an ideal future. One day, all humans will be wandering angels who dance through the Universe in luminous freedom. Estrella, Salvador, you two were right, forgive me. I've led you away from the true path; I interpreted the words of your dying son poorly. He wasn't addressing them to you, but to my madness. Forget about the books, go back to being lions, go on traveling eternally through all worlds."

Abravanel, with superhuman effort, awoke from the illusion that is life and entered the reality of death, bursting into laughter that was heard many miles away. He died the way all true clowns die: standing on his head.

The Arcavis went back to their old ways, slowly forgetting Hebrew. As her only memento of Abravanel, Estrella kept the Tarot deck, while

Salvador held on to the wise man's red shoes. From then on, he and his son and his son's son and all his descendants wore them during performances as an important part of the lion tamer's costume. They traveled for two centuries through Italy and Greece, Sicily, Egypt, and Turkey. They did it surreptitiously, generation after generation, staying poor, using only their one hundred Spanish words. And in that way, as social outcasts, they could live in peace.

At first, Estrella's Tarot readings were answers to practical questions: Where is the stolen cow? Will the boyfriend be a good or bad husband? Will the harvest be affected by the weather? Will family members get sick? She kept silent about the rest. After so many years studying the cards, it was easy for her to see when and how the client would die. She hid that power. It was painful and useless to know the future, because nothing could be done to change it.

But despite knowing better, she read her own fortune. When the Thirteenth Arcanum turned up next to the Wheel of Fortune, Power, and The World, Estrella felt a chill. The moment they feared so much, the moment of the lions' deaths, had come. She turned over one more card: the House of God. It would be in an earthquake! They were in Smyrna. They fled to Constantinople. There was no earthquake in Smyrna, but there was in Constantinople, and a crevice swallowed the lions. It had been time. Their hides, stretched thin over their bodies, were almost transparent. Each time they breathed it was so labored the lions seemed to sob. They had practically no animal nature left. They were aged nobles with the humble serenity that comes with attaining self-awareness.

Without lions, the Arcavis had to become merchants, transporting cinnamon and camphor over seas infested with pirates. They sold furs, swords, eunuchs, export and import textiles, salt, wine, rice, honey, sheep, horses, pickled fish, perfumes—just about anything. The years went by, as did the births and deaths of Salvadors and Estrellas, but they could never free themselves from nostalgia for their lions. The red shoes, which the men never stopped using, aroused mistrust in their business associates. That outlandish footwear showed them the Arcavis were not normal Jews, and little by little they stopped dealing with them.

The Arcavis found themselves obliged to transport a cargo of prostitutes to China. They sailed from Constantinople intending to cross the Black Sea, disembark on the Caucasus coast, and march across the continent to Shanghai. Unfortunately a storm wrecked them. Salvador did not know how to swim, but since Estrella was a strapping girl of 280 pounds, he simply floated on his back and let her swim, pulling him along by the hair.

To keep despair at bay, Estrella mentally reviewed the seventy-eight cards, which she knew by heart. She swam for two days without stopping. Finally, they washed up on a Crimean beach. Salvador left the water with a thirst for God. He went down on his knees in the sand and tried to pray, only to realize he knew no prayers, that money left no room for Adonai. There was nothing Jewish left in him. He had no definition, no race, and the world was fading away, so much so that his penis was nothing more than a useless bit of skin: he'd been with his wife for more than ten years without producing a child that resembled him. Recognizing his infertility, he wept so passionately that he seemed to vomit up his liver.

Estrella was tossed among the rocks, almost dying of fatigue after her monumental exertion. She saw her husband drowning in himself, scrutinizing himself with the anguish of a castrato, not even bothering to see if she was alive. She used her last remnants of energy to extract the violet leather bag from between her bosoms and throw the Tarot, with perfect accuracy, at Salvador's head. The jolt restored him to reality. He ran compassionately to his wife, his homeland, his identity. He took her in his arms, licked the sand off her face, kissed her hands, caressed her icy body. She did not try to react. She let herself slip, sighing with relief, toward death.

"Now that you have been saved, Salvador, understand that I have to die. God brought me into your life for the sole purpose of showing you how deeply you'd sunk. You were an absurd repetition, a bone without marrow, a man without traditions. Study, seek the Truth, and when you find it, you will see next to it the woman who befits you, the mother of your children."

He buried the voluminous dead woman right there, along with what little money he had left. Without knowing why, he traveled by foot to Lithuania, as if pulled by a magnet, begging for food in Jewish communities. One dark night, covered with dust after having walked hundreds of miles, he knocked on the door of Elijah the Gaon of Vilna, a great teacher of the Talmud and of Kabbalah.

No one opened the door. He waited five minutes and knocked again. No answer. For half an hour more he knocked. A strong wind was blowing, rustling the leaves of the trees with a metallic whisper. Through all that noise, Salvador could hear another murmur, also unremitting, coming from within the school. It was the sound of human voices lamenting. He pushed the door, which opened easily, and made his way along a frozen corridor. The lamentations grew louder. He passed through several rooms with clean hearths, as if no one, despite it being winter, wanted to use them. The collective sobbing intensified. He went up a staircase and entered a vast salon with pews arranged in synagogue style, where a hundred or so rabbis, seated with their bare feet submerged in pails of icy water, were praying, weeping, tearing their black vestments. In the center of the classroom, so cold that vapor clouds came out of every mouth, on top of a pedestal made of books, there was an open coffin where the body of the great master lay, as if in sleep.

While they were moaning, the disciples enumerated again and again the merits of the Vilna Gaon:

"You, who were a teacher starting at the age of seven."

"You, who in order to study more only slept two hours a day."

"You, who in order to avoid laziness never lit a fire and kept your feet in a pail of icy water.

"You, who protected us from the Hasidim, that lying sect that believes in ecstasy and visions, you who studied seven thousand books and taught us to reason."

Salvador, with no one stopping him, made his way to the dead man; echoing in his ears was not the desolate chanting of the students but Estrella's last words: "When you find the Truth, next to it you will see the woman who befits you." Next to Elijah Ben Solomon Zalman, wearing a dress so white it seemed silver, was his daughter. Once and for all, his pounding heart revealed to him, repeating it myriad times even beyond the day of his death, the girl's name: Luna, Luna, Luna, Luna. Queen of night, sum of all the Estrellas, from woman to woman, the Salvadors had moved toward her, and now, face to face with the incarnate dream, he could do nothing but give thanks to God for leading him to the end of the road. He walked toward her, clasped her hands and removed them from the casket to draw them to his chest, which was bursting with each heartbeat. Luna immediately knew his name, and when she said it, erasing the pain caused by her father's death, there arose within her a tremendous joy that brought heat for the first time to that cold world: "Salvador!" In a single glance, their souls fused, and that meeting, sought after for a thousand years, changed the world.

Another chorus of voices flooded in from outside, bringing with it a jubilant song mixed with laughter and ecstatic shouting. More than two hundred Hasidim, smelling of alcohol and tobacco, followed by stout women and their children, made their peasant boots echo through the lecture hall. The glow from their torches chased away shadows, and the gray walls shone golden. A warm air dissolved the clouded breath emanating from the open mouths of the rabbis, who were paralyzed by this sacrilege.

A small but muscular old man, crowned with a huge fur hat, led the euphoric horde. Smoking a pipe and staggering, he stopped opposite the Vilna Gaon, waved his arms around, guffawed so loudly the pews shook, rolled back his eyes, and leapt into a kick that sent the coffin boards flying.

"Enough with this comedy, Elijah! Through my mouth the voice of Israel Ben Eliezer, the Baal Shem Tov, he who knows the secret name of God, speaks to you! I can do nothing; he can do everything. Riding on me, his mount, he has come to show you that you're mistaken."

This possessed man raised his hands: the coffin rose in the air and stuck to the ceiling. The peasants applauded, but a painful groan shook the rabbis. The chief of the drunken mystics paid them no attention whatsoever and went on hectoring the dead man.

"You cursed us, putting out the candles in your shul as the shofar wailed so that our spiritual life would be extinguished along with them. You cursed us, day and night, when we slept and when we got up, when we came and when we left. You asked God not to pardon or know us. You asked Him to erase our names from the Earth. You forbade people to speak to us or write to us, to help us, or to live under the same roof with us. You whispered that we should be denounced to the Christian authorities so they could eliminate us. You forgot that we were brothers. You shut the windows and sank into a frozen wakefulness. You murdered the language of dreams. You gained intelligence, but you lost love. For a month now, you've been lying here pretending to be dead. You don't rot because you are alive but overcome by indifference. Breathe again! Awaken and come dance with us! Joy! Joy! Joy!"

The coffin fell from the ceiling and shattered on the floor. The Vilna Gaon opened his eyes, looked at his audience, stood up, and in a fit of laughter ran to give his daughter a long embrace. He gave Salvador one too, blessed them both, danced with the old man and his Hasidim, dragged the rabbis by the beard and made them join in the round.

Violins and tambourines were played. Vodka moistened throats. The women brought a white veil and the men a tent and a velvet hat. They covered Salvador's head with the hat and Luna's with the veil. The Gaon, seconded by the drunken old man, paused in front of the couple and offered the Bible to the future groom.

"I cannot deny the feelings consuming my daughter. Show us you're worthy of such a flame. Tell us what you see in the seven words of the first sentence of Genesis."

Arcavi, bathed in sweat, trembling from head to toe, opened the Holy Book. He did not know how to read Hebrew and had no wisdom. In his soul, full of love for Luna, there was no room for God.

The old Hasid whispered with the voice of Baal Shem Tov, "The first and last letters of the Torah form the word heart. There is no greater knowledge than Love. You can do it. Be daring. You are a lion tamer, and each letter is a lion."

Salvador stopped doubting. Like his ancestors staring keenly at the lions, he fixed his eyes on the letters without trying to guess what they said. They were beings, not signs. The first word began with a descending arc, a horizontal base, and a period: ב. He watched the form empty itself out, allowing his eyes to see without the interference of his mind. Slowly, the arc and the line transformed into an open jaw and then, within it, the period vibrated like the roar of a beast, a complete, generative scream.

He focused with such force that the small stain grew and deepened to become an endless tunnel, an insatiable gullet that began to swallow all the other letters. Finally, all that remained on the page was that enormous period. Salvador felt that its voracious center was absorbing him, extracting him from his body. He let himself be swallowed with no fear, and his soul entered that dark passageway. He felt he was dissolving, but he went further and further with faith.

At the far end, an immense sphere of light awaited him, a sun that did not scorch. Entering into it, he began to lose his memory, but his heartbeat continued to echo: Luna. His chest was a golden temple with an altar of living flesh at its center. Above him was a fiery cup filled with holy water. He knew he would never be thirsty again, that his mouth was the arc, the line, and the period, a divine fountain, and he allowed love to overflow and felt the pleasure as his cup ran over. And the water filled the world, and he awoke preaching in Spanish or Yiddish or Hebrew (he never found out) among the rabbis who wept, the Hasids who danced ecstatically as they listened, and the women who kissed his hands and placed them on the heads of their children so that they might be blessed.

The great Vilna Gaon kneeled before him and sang with a voice like a deep river as he married him to his daughter. When he finished the ceremony, he handed over the keys to the school, asked forgiveness for his errors, bade farewell to everyone, and set out on a trip to Palestine. Luna never heard another word about him. Sadness was forbidden. Solemn occasions became festivals, where never-ending joy was offered as thanks to God. Salvador and Luna had the same reveries and visions, which they shared with the poor. Together they cured a host of illnesses.

For the first time in the history of the Arcavis, a girl was born. Since she was the fruit of a year spent in matrimonial bliss, they named her Felicidad. They tried to have a boy so he could be baptized Salvador, according to custom, but two years later another girl was born. She was named Sara Luz, given for her luminous gaze and in the name of Luna's deceased mother. She was a saint who in one fervent day devoured a complete volume of the Talmud. Unfortunately, she could not digest the thick sheets of parchment and died with the swollen stomach of a pregnant woman.

The first girl was given Abravanel's red shoes as a talisman and the second, the violet leather bag containing the Tarot. Thirteen years went by. The two little women, despite the difference in age, had their periods on the same day, at the same hour. Luna woke them at midnight and led them out of the house while Salvador pretended to be asleep. A group of ladies was waiting for them. Their mother ordered the girls to remove their nightgowns, and then she undressed as well. Other women who were also menstruating joined them. They began to dance in the fields among the fresh furrows so their blood would flow down their legs and make a good crop of wheat.

They were having the time of their lives, beating drums and singing, when they saw in the distance a group of husbands waving torches. They quickly put their clothes back on and waited anxiously. Until then, no men had ever interrupted that womanly ritual.

Pale, Salvador spoke to the women: "We're very sorry, but you have to return to the village immediately. There's been a new eruption of anti-Semitism. Over in the next village, they first raped Rabbi Shlomo's widow, then cut her into pieces and burned down her shack."

As they all ran their houses to lock themselves inside, Felicidad said to her mother, "Papa should take up a collection so we can buy weapons!"

"Weapons? How can a daughter of mine talk like that? God will punish you! If we deserve to be defended, He will do it. The sacred commandments forbid Jews to spill human blood."

That night they had trouble falling asleep. The moon tinted the sky red. The dogs never stopped barking. Sara Luz got out her Tarot, shuffled the deck, and picked three with her eyes closed. When she opened them, she screamed. She refused to tell what she saw. The hours passed. Just before dawn, cloaked by the sound of heavy rain, ten black shadows opened the door of the school with expert skill.

On the second floor, they found three families who shared the farm work with the Arcavis. In minute they bound and gagged the men, who made not the slightest gesture to defend themselves. They stripped the women—three adults and four children—and locked them in the bathroom. They then left, only to return genuflecting behind a corpulent man wearing a leather mask and a bearskin coat.

In despotic fashion he stretched out his enormous hand, and a shadow, saluting the whole time, handed him a well-sharpened kitchen knife. The masked man took off his overcoat and revealed his erect phallus, itself of extraordinary size. His henchmen pulled a woman out of the bathroom, kicking her and dragging her by the hair. As soon as she saw the monster, she ran for the door, out into the rain, and began to shriek. The attacker caught her there, and with one blow cut off her head. He took hold of her body and drank the steaming spurts of blood from her arteries. Then he threw himself on the headless corpse to penetrate her while he grunted with pleasure. Staggering like a drunk, he went back into the school. Making brutal gestures, he shook the knife. They let loose a little girl. He chased and cornered her. The child fell to her knees and showed her face, bathed in tears. The first thrust of the knife hit her in the eye. Ninety-nine more followed.

Upstairs, on the third floor, Salvador, Luna, and their two little girls heard everything: the cries of the women, their bare feet scrambling over the cold floor, the deep panting of the murderer, the weapon slicing the air, the slippery sound of bodies being sliced open, the guts spattering against the walls, the blood falling onto the floorboards like a fountain of thick water, the heavy body of the beast wallowing in the viscera, and his triumphant shout in orgasm.

They counted the victims: seven. And now the thirsty monster was climbing the stairs. Salvador, impotent, trembled as he prayed. Luna took off her clothes to offer herself as a sacrifice, hoping to spare the girls. Sara Luz ran and hid under the bed, kissing her Tarot again and again. Felicidad, with anger so great that it seemed like it would explode her little body, slowly and carefully put on the red shoes and lit the candles in the menorah.

A violent blow opened the door, smashing against the wall and breaking off chunks of plaster. The criminal entered the room, his body soaked with blood and the mouth of his mask overflowing with chewed-up intestines. Reflecting the candle flames, his knife threw off a web of golden rays. Salvador opened his arms, desperate. Luna walked toward the blade, offering herself resignedly. The murderer hunched over to give his stab more force, and for fractions of a second the world stopped in an eternal silence.

Then everything accelerated. Felicidad shouted an order so loudly that the roof beams creaked and a curtain tore open: "Halt!" Raising her right hand, she stopped the criminal. She completely cut off his movement. There was not the slightest speck of fear in her attitude, only perfect self-control. A superhuman will inhabited that fragile little body. Through that will, the spirit of all the lion tamers revealed itself. For Felicidad, descended from so many Salvadors, dominating a ferocious beast was a natural, necessary act. She'd never felt better.

The monster stopped short, fixed his gaze on the burning eyes of the tiny woman, roared, and clutched his stomach as if his liver had just exploded. He dropped the knife, fell on his knees, and sank his enormous head on the girl's chest. In a sweet voice, saturated with love, he whispered in Russian, "Forgive me." The mob of assailants climbed the stairs and tried to enter the classroom. A single gesture from their master stopped them. Another made them bow, and a third compelled them back downstairs and out of the school.

The girl took the belt from her robe, tied it around the giant's neck, and led him like a pet toward the patio. The rain had stopped. Salvador, Luna, and Sara Luz heard the galloping of horses that faded into the distance. Felicidad disappeared from their lives forever. Never again were murders like that committed in the villages.

From that moment on, the lives of the Arcavis were no longer the same. On the one hand, the congregation praised the girl's heroic sacrifice, but on the other they could never forget her triumphant smile as she tied the belt around the murderer's neck. Also, he did not try to kidnap her. It was she who forced him down the stairs like a dog and then disappeared into the darkness. What happened after that? The madman could have shaken the spell and cut her to pieces as he did the others. But why had the murders stopped?

One morning, at first light, Luna awoke screaming. Hugging Salvador, her breath short and eyes wild, she told him, "What I'm thinking is atrocious. The night of the seven murders, I saw in the encounter between the monster and Felicidad something similar to what happened to us: in her eyes there was love—a huge, sudden love that survives beyond death."

Sara Luz never wanted to hear another word about magic. She locked the Tarot in a coffer and tried her best to forget it. All three widowers asked for her hand in marriage. Together with her parents, she chose Salomón Trumper, much older than she but simple and tranquil.

On the way home from the wedding ceremony, the coach carrying Salvador and Luna crashed down a ravine because a yellow dragonfly flew into the horse's ear. They both died. A year later, at the same time, on the same day, in the same month, Sara Luz gave birth to Jashe. And a year later, also at the same time, on the same day, and in the same month, she gave birth to Shoske. Jashe and Shoske, two common names with no greater significance, deliberately chosen to bring an end to all miracles.

The two sisters were brought up the same way: they slept together, dressed identically, and learned to embroider, cook, plant wheat, and clean the house so that each Shabbat everything would shine. Shoske was happy with that life and hated anything out of the ordinary. Jashe began the same way, but one day, as she raked the garden, a yellow dragonfly began to fly around her, getting closer and closer until it entered her head through an ear and buzzed as if trying to give her a message.

Jashe imagined that the same insect that had caused the death of her grandparents came to pay its debt. She thought she understood what it was saying: "Forgive me, my child. I never wanted Salvador and Luna to die. In exchange, I'm going to give you the most valuable treasure in the world." The insect flew to the school. The girl followed, all the way to the attic. The dragonfly landed on the old coffer then flew out the window. Jashe opened the box and found the Tarot. For years, in secret, she studied the cards, and they became her Master, teaching her to See. Everything changed. She could see the madness in which they were submerged; religious law seemed like a prison; and she tried to escape, to abandon her many absurd obligations, all superstitions, and arranged marriage. She wanted to live the holy life every day and not just on Saturday, to love freely and without tribal limits, to eat whatever she wanted, to travel the world, to live not just one life but thousands, to recover magic. She was in that effervescent state when she found the door, the light, the road: she found him, Alejandro Prullansky.

As soon as Jashe finished telling him the story of her ancestors, the Russian dancer took her in his arms, hugging her so tight it was as if he wanted to absorb her through his skin and said, "Chance is a subtle form of Destiny. My mother's name was Felicidad. She was Jewish and was stolen by my father. My family history doesn't go back as far as yours for a simple reason: my grandmother, Cristina Prullansky, burned all the documents and pictures that tied her to the past."

An only daughter with six brothers, much older than she, descended from nobility, Cristina had been educated by governesses brought from Germany. During the maudlin afternoons, these women would stroll among the pines on the estate, stomachs swollen, having been raped by Cristina's father Ivan, a hunchbacked widower who could not restrain himself when drunk. After a few months, a black carriage would bring a new governess and carry away the old one, who was never seen again. She had fifteen governesses in ten years.

In that secluded place, more than thirty miles from Minsk, with her brothers in the army and a father who never spoke, the only possible entertainment was beating the maids—for any conceivable reason. She pulled up their skirts, pulled down their linen underwear, and with her short, hard whip left crimson furrows on their milky buttocks. In her family, there were only invisible women and dead soldiers to defend Peter the Great, Catherine I, Ivan VI, Paul I, Peter III, and other czars in their wars with France, Turkey, Sweden, Great Britain, and many other nations. Her grandfathers, her uncles, and her brothers all gradually metamorphosed into portraits, medals, and posthumous decoration that covered the walls in the enormous hall. Only her father, stinking of vodka, urine, and vomit, would walk there, ashamed of his monstrous body, which would not allow him to take part in the continuous massacre.

When Cristina was fifteen, the French governess, imported as a birthday present, was raped the night she arrived. Ivan, poisoned by alcohol, his buttocks filthy with excrement, howling like a dog, smashed the door down with an ax, threw himself on top of the young woman, squeezed her breasts until they burst, and, at the moment he reached orgasm, bit off her nose. The piece of flesh choked him to death. The governess' heart stopped, and Ivan suffocated. Cristina was left alone, surrounded by myriad attendants, servants, and serfs.

Her father was buried in the family mausoleum and the governess next to some boulders in the forest. That year, the winter was harsher than ever. On three occasions, the wolves dug up the victim's body. In the long corridors of the manor house, Cristina saw the noseless woman floating like a silent ship. She was beginning to bite her nails to the point of ripping off bits of flesh, when she received the message inviting her to the coronation of Alexander I.

She wasn't even aware that the previous emperor had been assassinated. In the governess' trunk, she found a nightgown with a stylish European cut that excused the modest fabric quality. Her grandmothers' jewels more than made up for whatever was lacking in her costume. During the entire voyage, dressed up like a lady, in that Spartan coach built to carry military men, she—accustomed to letting days pass without bathing, clad in the trousers and boots of her brother, killed in the Swiss Alps fighting the French—felt strange.

As the powerful horses carried her toward Moscow, she had the feeling that those bracelets, necklaces, and earrings, that light cloth, those silk undergarments were awakening her body. She began the journey flat chested, and now her breasts were growing, hard, big, with nipples so sensitive that the rubbing of her brassiere with each lurch of the carriage gave her a pleasure she had to admit despite her shame. The pores of her pubis opened to make way for an exuberant triangle of hair, and for the first time she felt the heat from her labia. She slowly spread her legs, and with her face red and her eyes tight, she understood that she was going to the Czar's coronation in search of a man.

Cristina's virginal beauty dazzled the court. That petite, delicate princess whose eyes radiated a savage power attracted a flock of nobles prepared to love her unto death. She remained unmoved. None made her flutter. There were young men as handsome as battle stallions, intelligent and possessive forty-year-olds, august old men willing to offer the intoxication of power. They seemed paltry. Her newborn femininity wanted a total lover, perfection incarnate.

When the bells rang, when the trumpets blared, when the coronation began, Cristina saw the object of her desire enter in the person of Alexander I. He was an impossible ideal, but her heart would hear no objections. She pledged her hymen to the emperor—or to no one. Standing before that Christ-like adolescent, delicate and tense, much more shadow than body, unfettered like all serene hearts but also an implacable warrior capable of transforming his soul into a saber of ice, all other men became mere cadavers.

As soon as they approached, the stench that arose from their mouths made her deaf to their advances. She saw them eaten by invisible worms. The Russian nobility was a charnel house sustained by a living fountain. She knew that loving the Czar was like loving the Sun: a consuming dream. She didn't care. She stretched her soul until it became a thread wrapped around Alexander's ring finger, like a wedding band. She left the court knowing she was forever married to the emperor. She forced her driver to wear out several horses because she wanted to reach her estates as quickly as possible. There she would begin to share, isolated from the world, the life of her beloved.

She had the portraits of her ancestors taken down and burned along with their uniforms, diplomas, medals, letters, and any other document that might preserve the slightest particle of their existence in her memory. "When you know the ocean, you're not interested in the rivers flowing into it." Every night, without exception, for years, she dreamed the Czar came and took her from her bedroom, carried her through the air to the top of a century-old oak tree and there, in a nightingale nest, possessed her, depositing a gold coin bearing his bearded likeness deep in her vagina.

Following the axiom of a Chinese sage, taught to her by one of her many governesses, "The well-ordered desk of a good notary is worth as much as the well-ordered country of a good Emperor," she began to follow, on her estates, the policies of the Czar. When Alexander I saw the ignorance of the Russian people he put education at the forefront of government programs, she transformed the right wing of her mansion into a school and forced her servants to learn Greek and Latin. She struggled, not sparing the whip, but the brutes were incapable of learning more than three words. Then, when the Czar's councilors thought of creating a new constitution, she spent whole months dictating laws. She wanted the servants to learn self-government. To give them a taste for freedom, she decreed two days of independence per week, when her employees could make decisions as they thought proper. As a result, they all got drunk, fornicated, fought, and burned down a few cottages. Cristina felt lost. She lacked her idol's wisdom in solving social problems.

Where her property ended, the vast hunting grounds of the imperial family began. To reach that frontier, she had to gallop nine miles, which she did every morning, hoping to see the Czar in person. Her wish was never fulfilled. Occasionally she would hear the barking of a distant pack of dogs, but nothing more. She had to accept the nightly lover who filled her womb with gold coins.

Napoleon's invasion created a better opportunity to commingle with the Emperor. The night of the battle of Borodino, Alexander I visited her, accompanied by 42,000 dead Russians. Her bedroom had to expand a few miles in length and breadth to accommodate them all. On their knees, the dead observed their habitual coitus, whining like pathetic dogs. The Czar tossed his gold coin into her weakly, and within her his image looked blurry. Cristina begged him not to lose faith, to never give in to the enemy. She arose from the bed and used her whip to cast out the tearful ghosts. Her beloved swore to carry on the struggle. Then Cristina spread her legs and let fall into those noble hands a stream of coins, all she'd accumulated on those connubial nights. That was her contribution to the Emperor's war effort.

When Napoleon sacked the Kremlin and the Russian army retreated, she decided to fight the invading troops on her own. She ordered three barrels of vodka loaded onto her carriage and told the driver to go to Moscow. She proceeded through devastated fields, saw skeletal children wearing army overcoats and cutting chunks of meat off dead horses, passed right by drunken French soldiers busy raping peasant women. No one tried to stop her.

She made her way through the great capital city, looking for a neighborhood where the wind was blowing in the right direction. The carriage stopped at a solitary corner. Cristina breathed in the smell of all the wooden houses. She shed many tears, and ordered the coachman to soak as many walls as possible with the vodka. All she had to do was touch them with a torch. In seconds the entire neighborhood was on fire. The flames galloped on the wind toward the opposite end of the city. No Russian tried to fight the fire. Moscow turned into a rose of flames.

After Napoleon's defeat, Cristina lost all sense of time. She sewed a military uniform exactly like the one her idol wore and began to speak in a man's voice. One night, the smiling Czar appeared naked, his pubis streaming blood. He offered her his severed member so she could carry it between her legs. Cristina awoke screaming. Someone was knocking on her bedroom door, a messenger: "Alexander I is dead!"

Foaming with rage, she called the servants and whipped them across the mouth until they cried. Later, in the court, the rumor circulated that the Czar, exhausted by power, had fled to Siberia to live as a holy hermit. The corpse with the rotten face that was seen in the imperial coffin belonged to his syphilitic cousin. To go on living, Cristina forced herself to believe those tales.

Five years after the perhaps false death of Alexander I, the murder of sheep began. With each full moon, female sheep appeared on the farms near the imperial forest, their sex and anus destroyed and showing traces of sperm identified by a doctor as human. The animals were raped, their throats bitten through, their stomachs ripped open, and their intestines scattered in an attempt to form letters.

One night, when the moon was at its fullest, Cristina tied up a flock of sheep at the entrance to the forest and waited, hiding in a ditch. After a few hours, a naked man covered with mud and grunting like a savage beast appeared. He raped the animals, pulled off their heads, yanked out their intestines and used them to write, "Forgive me, my God." Then he fled into the brush.

Cristina, with the skill of a hunter, followed his tracks to an enormous oak. Her heart was pounding so hard she thought it would break her ribs. The tree was identical to the one in her dreams. How many times, at the top of the old tree, had she given herself to her beloved? She'd lost count. The man, standing under a small waterfall, began to wash himself with a surprising delicacy. Soon the cold stream cleansed him of mud and blood. In the silvery light, Cristina, hidden in the thicket, could make out some details of that firm body, which seemed to be about fifty years of age. By piecing together the shape of his nails, the arc of his eyebrows, his protruding lower lip, his marbled skin, the beauty mark on his left ear, his blue eyes, his slight limp, and the horizontal wrinkle that furrowed the nape of his neck, Cristina concluded that the man was His Majesty Alexander I, Emperor of Russia. Holding back a scream, trying to be silent, she knelt in exaltation.

The Czar entered the oak tree through an opening in the trunk and did not come out. Cristina waited for several hours, immobile as a statue. Raucous snoring from within the tree startled her out of her stillness. She walked cautiously through the opening and found seven stairs that led down to a cave. On a straw pallet with neither blankets nor pillow lay Alexander I. Wearing a white cassock and a crippled Christ that hung from a bone necklace, he was deeply asleep, lit up by a candle.

Aside from three dead serpents on a hook and an icon of the Virgin surrounded by sheep, offering her bosom to the Child, the place was empty—movingly so in its voluntary poverty. The Czar, master of immense Russia, was living there, solitary, eating reptiles, transformed into a saint, a degenerate. Cristina bowed over the bridegroom of her nightly dreams, made the sign of the cross, and left without turning her back on the Czar. She galloped back to the manor. A hurricane-like rain soaked her to the skin, but she never noticed; her body and soul were burning.

She shouted to wake the servants. She had the furniture from the grand salon thrown out into the yard and installed a herd of sheep. She lived for a month among the animals with the windows closed, never leaving, not caring that the animals' dung was staining the sumptuous Turkish rugs. She suffused herself with animals' odor. When the full moon came, she drove the sheep to the edge of the forest, tied them up at the foot of a tree, and killed one in order to skin it. Then, naked, she covered herself with the still-warm skin and got down on all fours, her backside toward the oak.

She'd chosen a corner covered by a thicket so the moonlight wouldn't expose her. The bleating of the sheep attracted the Czar who, transformed into a monster, threw himself on top of the most appetizing sheep. Cristina felt the impact, stifling a shout of happy pain. Her hymen, hardened by so many years of waiting, exploded into fragments that cut her like shards of glass. None of this kept her from pushing toward the testicles, squeezing out the long-awaited liquor. The hermit ejaculated with monumental spasms and then sank his teeth into the Cristina's neck, trying to sever her aorta. Cristina had developed manly muscles in her legs from so much riding: they were as strong as tree trunks. She slipped free and fought her attacker, squeezing his torso between her thighs and cutting off his air. Then she tied him on his back to some roots. Paying no attention to his howls of fury, she sat on top of him, making herself seven times the repository of his sperm. At the end of the final orgasm, the man wept, muttering, "Forgive me, my God!" and fainted.

Cristina carried him in her arms to the great oak and, after bathing him in the cold water, brought him over to her flock, dressed him in the white cassock, and put him to sleep. Soon fever made the Emperor delirious. He was seeing lascivious sheep coming to devour his testicles, all wearing his mother's velvet and ermine dresses. At dawn, when his fever dropped and he regained his senses, he kissed Cristina's hands to show his gratitude. Nothing had ever been easy for him. Dominated by his family, forced into marrying a woman he did not love, unable to make her pregnant, obliged to be an accomplice to his father's murderers, overwhelmed by power, unsuccessful in leading his people to freedom, he abandoned everything, trying to become a saint. But his soul was rotten.

As a child, he was often sent to study with his grandmother, Catherine the Great. On her lap, he learned military strategy, politics, and many other things. As she spoke to him about her battles, court intrigue, and the engagement of her granddaughter to King Gustav of Sweden, the old woman slid her arthritic hand into his trousers and played with his penis. Then on her knees before him, with a rapacious, imperious look on her face, she sank her rotten teeth into his foreskin. He didn't dare move, for he feared amputation. Later, after an interminable moment, she released him and laughed like a crow, showing the stinking depths of her throat.

He hated his grandmother, his mother, and his wife. Three women, but at the same time one woman. He sought refuge in the Virgin Mary. He thought that in the solitude of his arboreal hideaway, he would attain sainthood, but one night, when the moon was full, the nightmare began. Possessed by a bestial desire, he was forced to rape and slaughter herds of sheep. Now, after what Cristina had done for him, he realized that beneath the skin of those animals he was seeing the naked bodies of the women who smothered and corrupted his youth: Catherine, Maria Feodorovna, and Isabel.

Cristina, her eyes wet with tears, listened without a word. It wasn't an emperor speaking to her, but God. Alexander I picked up a shepherd's crook, kissed her on the forehead, and bade farewell to her and the world. He would walk to Siberia, and beyond, reaching the polar ice where he would die in the whiteness and purifying cold. Cristina watched him drift away among the trees. The green leaves that hid him also made him disappear from her life. Feeling herself to be pregnant, she returned to her manor; gathered together servants and administrators to announce that she would be living in the forest as a hermit. She promised to visit them every lunar month to see to the proper functioning of the estate, and then she returned to the oak of her dreams.

There, dressed in a white cassock, she prayed, bathed in the waterfall, ate snakes, gave birth to Ivan, cut the umbilical cord with her teeth, and devoured the placenta. She went on living that way for fifteen years. She sprouted a white moustache and a beard of fine, translucent hair. She didn't teach her son to read or write. When the boy's pubis blackened and he started to get erections every time he looked at the icon of the Virgin, Cristina offered him a sheep so he could vent his passion.

For many days the boy didn't touch the animal, but when the full moon came, he threw himself on top of it, penetrated it, bellowed angrily, ejaculated, bit open its stomach, and enjoyed himself while pouring out its guts. His mother thought it was a miracle. She believed that within Ivan's body lived the spirit of the Emperor. She brought him sheep until the boy, transformed into a powerful giant, rolled around in the mud and then leapt from tree to tree, making his way to the farms of her servants. At dawn, he returned, covered with blood. Then he slept, smiling and satisfied.

In the morning, when Cristina went to the manor house and delivered her monthly abuse to the servants, she heard talk of the night before, when eight women were raped and torn apart. Cristina took a knife from the kitchen and galloped out to the oak tree to castrate her son. She was caught in a blizzard. Dropping from fatigue, she reached the refuge, where a hungry bear attacked her. Hearing her screams, Ivan came out of the oak tree just in time to see the enormous beast bite off his mother's head.

He picked up the kitchen knife and buried it in the bear's heart. He felt happy as never before. He looked toward heaven and said, "I forgive you, my God." With the bearskin he made a coat and a mask. He then took possession of his mother's estate and chose ten of the most muscular servants. He cut off their testicles and made them his personal guard. So the authorities would suspect nothing, he committed his murders in the Jewish villages, under the guise of anti-Semitism.

One day, he attacked the school of the Vilna Gaon. When he saw Felicidad, he realized that his entire being, transformed into a beast, was seeking a tamer. That fragile woman was his soul. To destroy her would mean immersing himself in darkness forever. He gave himself to her as only an animal could. His ferocity was now obedience. Felicidad was the Law. If she unleashed him, he would eviscerate the world.

Felicidad, descendant of countless lion tamers, understood that only dominating that beast gave her life meaning. That beast was a part of her, her home, her foundation. If before she languished, far from the wetlands that could nourish her flower of fire, now, standing before that beautiful monster, she felt herself reborn. By dominating vice, she would bring virtue to the world. Virtue, which is nothing more than putrefaction transformed. In order for the man to become light, the woman would have to extinguish her lamp in the darkness. She would unite her life to that of the murderer to sate him, make him release the prey, convert his roars into prayers, teach him to give and receive at the same time, transformed him into a prism that would absorb colors and transform them into a single ray.

Ivan had all the furniture in the manor house piled up in the garden and set it all on fire. Then he ordered his eunuchs to paint the walls, ceilings, and floors white. White was the only color he could stand now; all others made him sick. Felicidad's spotless skin made even snow seem filthy. He locked himself up in that dazzling space with his tamer. She resolved never to go out again. Her mission, in this profound solitude, was to fabricate the stone that would transform base metals into gold: a prophetic son.

Ivan and Felicidad prepared for months, perhaps years, without speaking, staring into each other's eyes, stock still for entire nights. He only ate fruit; she, raw meat. When she felt the spiritual union had been consummated, Felicidad stretched out on the white floor and ordered Ivan to give himself over to the only sexual act either would experience in their whole lives.

Slowly, delicately, tenderly, the man entered the woman, who in turn opened wider and wider until she lost all boundaries and fused with the entire Earth. The semen descended to the core of the planet, fell into a dark abyss where the galaxies dance. The Universe absorbed the rain of fire. Felicidad was pregnant. Now Ivan could disappear.

"I want you to cut me into pieces and eat me," he said to his lover and softly expired in her arms. She buried his body in the snow, and for the nine months of her pregnancy nourished herself on it.

The child arrived in a breech birth. The midwife brought him, feet first, into the world in a single great pull. "His feet will be more important than his head," she declared. Felicidad understood: Alejandro Prullansky would be a great dancer, not a prophet. For humanity, art was more important than an unreachable God—art that transformed matter into soul. His family tree told of the struggles of sensitive souls in search of the beauty, the glow of the hidden Truth. Thanks to the sacrifice of the murderous instinct, violence could metamorphose into poetry. And there was no poem greater than a dancing body. When the boy was five years old, Felicidad sent him to the Imperial Ballet School in Moscow.

That morning, Felicidad opened the windows and let in the frozen, fragrant air from the snow-covered park. All the hair on her body had turned white. "You will never see me again," she said to Alejandro. "I'm not going to die, but I am going to dissolve into the whiteness. Always remember me." The boy saw his mother, so pale she looked like a plaster figurine, remove all her clothing, press against the wall and blend into the white stucco. When she closed her eyes (the only dark spots on her body), he could no longer see her at all. He ran to the wall, groping it desperately. All he felt was a smooth surface.

The giant dancer began to weep in Jashe's arms—for the lost maternal kisses, for the tortures of apprenticeship in classical dance, for the boys who had their sexes kissed in the dressing rooms, for that old choreographer who raped him behind the piano when he was eleven. Whenever he was given a room with white walls, he would hurl himself against them until his forehead bled. He could have died of sadness had it not been for Abravanel's red shoes. Those century-old, impervious boots that changed size, adapting to the child's feet and stretching as they grew, proved to him that he was the bearer of a collective soul that would allow him to reach the end of Time, beyond all space, where only Truth exists.

Jashe placed the red shoes on top of the violet bag containing the Tarot, and with those sacred objects next to her, coupled with her husband to give my mother, Sara Felicidad, the chance to incarnate herself in a place of love.

The alarm clock did not work. The newlyweds ran out of the hotel only half dressed and just managed to reach the station in time for the train that would carry them to the port of Bremen. There they boarded the *Weser*, an impressive ship whose first-class passengers included members of the Imperial Ballet, on their way to Buenos Aires for their debut at the famous Colón Theatre. The *Weser* boasted cabins in Chinese-French style, dinners enlivened by a string quartet, steam baths, spacious entertainment rooms, and long passageways with wood paneling that imitated ebony. In third class—that is, in the hold or on the poop deck—were packed 1,200 Russian Jews accepted by the Argentine government on the condition that they work on the pampa as farmers.

No sooner had Jashe set foot on the packet boat's ladder than she sensed a menace to her happiness. Someone, one of the of dancers who leaned on the railing of the upper deck, was watching them with a look that burrowed into them like a hateful maggot. Alejandro too felt the ominous glare. His face pale, he said between his teeth, "Walk behind me and carry the bags as if you were a servant. I'll explain later." When they entered the spacious bedroom assigned to him as a principal dancer, the giant embraced Jashe, muttering apologies.

The situation was complicated: in a sense, he belonged to the Imperial Ballet, and the members of the corps were not allowed to marry. This of course was not written in their contracts, but it was an unspoken rule. The Director General, whose real name no one knew, went by Vladimir Monomaque in honor of the ancestor of the princes of Moscow who, in the eleventh century, had distinguished himself with his talent as an organizer and administrator. He enforced a ferocious discipline on the dancers, making them rehearse all day long, never giving a thought to their emotional needs.

Monomaque's possessiveness kept outsiders from the inner life of the Ballet. Equally possessive was the sublime Marina Leopoldovna, the prima ballerina and the tyrant's pampered pet, whose many caprices were tolerated because the success of the tours depended on her. Her immense talent and technical perfection attracted crowds in every country.

Well, he was telling her all this because he had something very unpleasant to confess. One afternoon, yielding to the demands of the temperamental diva, Vladimir Monomaque entered Alejandro's dressing room and, after reminding Alejandro of everything he owed him and the school—a refuge for the orphan such as him—ordered him to satisfy Marina's sexual appetites, which seized her on the twenty-first day of every month. No one argued with the Director General. Unfortunately, because of the precipitous nature of events, Alejandro had not had the time to communicate to—let's call things by their proper names—his lover the news of their marriage.

The news—he was sure of it—was going to cause a lot of trouble. Knowing Marina as he did, he knew she would faint and then wake up a few seconds later, foaming with rage. Then she'd refuse to dance, and finally, forced by the steely Director, she would wage silent war by spreading animosity among the troupe until she made their lives impossible. All this could stop if Vladimir only found her another lover in the group—impossible, as they were all effeminate.

"I'm very sorry, Jashe. You have to eat and sleep in the servants' area. The crossing will be long; it will last thirty-five days, and the tour will last six months or more. Aboard the ship, we will make love when you bring me my breakfast, and on land, if they give us a day off each week, we'll go to some discreet hotel. When the tour is over, when we're back in Moscow, we can finally return to normal. But if the star of the show finds out the truth and we have a crisis, Monomaque will instantly find someone in the school to replace me."

Jashe held back her bitter tears, knowing she had no choice but to accept the arrangements for now. The only thing she couldn't understand was how her husband could have lied, insisting that she was his first. He lowered his eyes in shame for five minutes that seemed like five hours. Finally he whispered in a broken voice, "Tomorrow is the twenty-first. Marina Leopoldovna's desire comes on with mathematical precision. Any moment now she will walk into this cabin. You should leave without looking back and wait in your place until tomorrow. I suggest you not talk with the servants, because they will fill your ears with obscene gossip. Ah, Jashe, how we suffer! You have to believe that this repulses me and that I suffer as much as you."

Jashe's love knew no limits. They threw themselves into each other's arms and made love, more passionate than ever. A gong announced dinner. The liner was now rocking on the high seas. They said goodbye with a deep and furtive kiss, and Jashe, despite her seeming fragility, showed her impeccable moral strength. She picked up her suitcase, went to the servants' quarters, accepted the suspicious looks of the little old ladies in charge of costume, and did not argue when she was given a tiny cabin with no windows that smelled of rotten beets. Impassive, she turned on the faucet, ran water onto the floor, and set about cleaning until everything sparkled. Every once in a while, some stagehand would open the door and look her up and down obscenely or mockingly.

The foreman, a fat Ukrainian who breathed through his mouth with a slight but constant whine, escorted her to the dining room and gave her a place at the shared table. Barely able to keep from vomiting, she had just tossed a sack of gelatinous beets overboard. Now, as the only accompaniment to her breaded cutlets, she was served a few of those red tumors. A sour wine, made from powder and water, was passed around freely. Men and women, drunk, began to mimic a ballet. Showing their backsides, which they kept bare under heavy, long skirts, the assistants, the makeup women, and the seamstresses all spread their legs shamelessly so the workers could slip their calloused hands into the dark stains of their sex and lift them like awkward swans.

Up in the air, they imitated flying birds, erupting with crass squawks, and dropped onto the table chest-to-chest with their men. Trying not to call attention to herself, Jashe got up from the table and walked along the passageways to her cabin. Like an immense pelican, the Ukrainian, reeking of sugary sweat, fell on top of her. Staggering, he dragged her out on deck and laid her down under a lifeboat. She offered no resistance. She allowed him to raise her skirt and pull off her panties. She spread her thighs and took his fat member in both hands as if to show him the path. Then she delicately slid her fingers toward his testicles and crushed them with murderous intensity. The brute twisted and howled, but she kept squeezing until he fainted. Then she went to her pigsty of a cabin and slept peacefully.

The next morning she ordered breakfast at the first-class kitchen and brought it to her husband, to whom she said told nothing, to spare him grief. When he finished his tea with lemon, he gazed with anguish through the porthole, drew the curtains, and bolted the door. Then he undressed Jashe and took her to bed. After an hour, when the two of them had forgotten where they were, Marina Leopoldovna urgently knocked on the cabin door. Jashe had barely enough time to dress, snatch up the brush, kneel at the toilet, and pretend to be cleaning it.

Alejandro, without bothering to cover his nakedness, let her in. The diva stood in the center of the bedroom, stamping her little foot. Her steel toe smashed against the linoleum floor with a thunderous echo.

Jashe exited with averted eyes and closed the door, biting her lip. She felt the click of the lock like a knife in her heart; the ballerina's light steps were like bullets as she ran to throw herself into her giant's arms. She had difficulty making her way along the corridor, which seemed soft and sticky, back to her own dark room. She wanted to vomit, to expel blood from her sex in a violent gush. Her face became violet red, the soles of her feet were burning. Stifling a roar, she made a half turn and with bared teeth returned to the cabin and peeked through the window.

The ballerina was leaning back on Alejandro's broad chest with a despotic grin, tugging at his hair. She made him bite the nape of her neck, a task he performed with the face of a penitent. Jashe could no longer control her hatred for that lascivious, cruel woman, and a pain in her stomach kept her from seeing clearly. As if shrouded in fog, the Russian woman knelt before Jashe's man and swallowed the sacred organ, making little-girl squeals. Then, with the gesture of a tragic actress, she tossed aside the Japanese silk robe that covered her nakedness, and like a white, skeletal worm slithered to the bed and offered her buttocks, imitating the barks of a bitch in heat.

The fog cleared, and hatred gave way to indignation. She felt herself transformed into the Eighth Arcanum, Justice, with a scale in one hand and a sword in the other—no less implacable for being invisible. She decided that very day that Truth must control the world. Justice meant giving to everyone what he or she deserved, and Marina Leopoldovna deserved a scandal.

Jashe went to the rehearsal studio and hid behind the piano. Soon, Madame Teodora, an intense, efficient old woman, shook her tambourine, and in a few seconds, the entire corps de ballet assembled with military discipline in straight lines. With her eyes, Madame Teodora consulted Vladimir Monomaque, and he nodded his lustrous head affirmatively, satisfied with his inspection. The pianist played a mazurka. No one moved; they waited for Leopoldovna, standing before the first row, to take the first steps so they could then imitate her with admiration and envy.

The distinguished diva only managed a plié before Jashe emerged from behind the piano, pouncing like a furious cat and tearing her tutu. The ripped garment flew off, but the other dancers could not intervene; they were paralyzed by shock. But when the white panties fell and the pitch black of her pubis showed the animal within that body, which moved so skillfully that it seemed immaterial, they all shouted in horror. The Director, popping the buttons of his shirt as he tore it off, ran to cover Marina's unmasked body. Too late. The truth had come to light. The secret he'd kept for so many years, sharing it only with the first male dancer, had been exposed. Everyone saw that thin, flaccid, bright red penis hanging between the legs of the ballerina. Yes, the celebrated, sublime, lighter-than-air Marina Leopoldovna was a man.

Jashe took her husband by the hand and led him past the stunned Russians until they stood opposite the tyrant, who was calming his sobbing transsexual, hugging him with surprising tenderness. My grandmother understood what no one else had been able to imagine. Speaking with a Jewish accent full of majesty, she said in Russian, "You can't blot out the sun with a finger. That poor man is your son. Just look at what your ambition has made of him. You stole his manhood just to make him into a trained monkey. You deserve the contempt of the whole world. I want you to know that this man is my husband and that you no longer have any right to rule his private life. Alejandro Prullansky is no longer your slave!"

The Director General fixed his gaze on Alejandro's eyes, and for the first time, Alejandro stared back.

"Either that woman or me!"

With no hesitation, Alejandro shouted "Jashe!" Lifting her up in his powerful arms, he carried her out on deck to breathe the invigorating ocean air.

Dropping his usual domineering tone, Vladimir Monomaque spoke to the Imperial Ballet. The future of the entire corps depended on the silence of each and every one of them. A scandal would finish them off forever. With sincere humility, he begged them to erase what they had just seen from their memory. Very soon, this very year, when they reached San Francisco, where surgery was very advanced, Marina would undergo an operation to eliminate that annoying detail and make her a woman like all others. The company applauded. Alejandro Prullansky would be expelled immediately, but only after receiving a very significant sum of money to guarantee his silence. The company applauded again. Marina never stopped crying, seized by wild convulsions. His father slapped him and dressed him in a new tutu. Recovering his authoritarian voice, more severe now than ever, he ordered his son to go on with the rehearsal or he'd kick his ass to pieces. Marina blew her nose in the hands of her faithful dresser, Tito, and began to dance. Soon the mazurka was danced more enthusiastically than ever.

Jashe descended to third class, followed by Alejandro who was carrying the bags and had hidden a thick roll of American one hundred dollar bills in his underwear. None of the religious Jews bothered to greet that tiny apostate accompanied by such an enormous goy. Here, they were fleeing pogroms: what gave anyone the right to impose the presence of a Russian on them? It was like poking a thorn into their wounds. They didn't move to make room for the newcomers, and went on rubbing their delicate hands with pieces of harsh rope to create callouses—all so people would think they were farmers.

My grandparents had to take refuge in the wretched corner, the den of sin, a back room among crates of apples where Icho Melnik and his six prostitutes had been relegated. "Man does not live by the Torah alone," he said winking an eye and offering them a swig of vodka as the girls, making off-color remarks, set out the sacks they'd use as beds.

Jashe found a piece of soap and a pail of water. Instead of a sponge, she used a rolled-up cloth belt to wash the giant as if he were a little boy. "Don't be sad," she said. "Argentina is a grand country. There's lots of work. We'll invest the money they gave us and get rich. You will found your own ballet."

Alejandro let go of his sadness and began to laugh. They slept in each other's arms.

In the unheated storage space, the passengers were freezing. Slowly but surely, the whores got closer and closer to the couple to attach themselves to those bodies heated by love. Icho Melnik, a discreet drunk, opened a few crates and made himself a mattress out of apples. A group of old folks, rocking back and forth in exhaustion, querulously recited the last prayer of the night. Before he began to snore like thunder, the pimp muttered, "It's useless to ask God for something you can get for yourself."

THREE

THE FARTHEST LAND

FTER CROSSING the Atlantic and passing through the Straits of
Magellan, the ship rode icy Pacific currents along such a jagged
coast that the Rabbi, with an ominous look, exclaimed, "Oy vey!
This must be the ass of the world, and God has really kicked it!" Finally,
they dropped anchor at the port of Valparaíso.

Teresa had played the mute for four weeks, so now her mouth felt
heavy with the weight of stifled insults. Every single day on the rocking
ship, she'd been forced to hear the *shacharit* (morning prayer) and the
mincha (afternoon prayer), accompanied by the vulture screeches of
the seasick mystics as they vomited. No matter what, they always had
their *gartels* around their waists, those black silk cords used to divide
the body in two, the spiritual parts—the hands, the heart, and the brain,
worthy of serving the Most High—and the profane parts: the stomach,
the sex, and the legs. They could transform any place at all, no matter
how vulgar, into a synagogue just so they could drone their prayers to
God, hour after hour, all twenty-four: "Oh Terrible One, we carry out
our 613 commandments so You do not admonish us; we are righteous
because we are sodden with fear; You guide us with stabs, bullets, and
bites; teach us with Your fury and Your curses."

Teresa hated God more than ever. Just look where the Ancient Cruel
One had led them! What was the meaning of that port, devoid of flat
ground, with thousands of houses that didn't seem man-made, but like

89

abscesses spreading along the sides of the hills? The Russians may have been dangerous, but at least they didn't eat human flesh. But the Indians here, who knows? Maybe not cannibals, but thieves, all of them! Anyway, what did that matter when not even the crumbs were left of the few dollars Moishe Rosenthal had given them?

Now at least she wouldn't have to rub elbows with the Jewish wives (who didn't know how to live without swapping things—a wool vest for three sets of underpants, half a loaf of onion bread for six rotten oranges) invading the kitchen to fry their latkes, boil up some kasha, or bake matzo, slapping their children, dribbling out a constant stream of proverbs—"Spare the rod and spoil the child," "The answer is always in the question," "God punishes those He loves"—and scaring off *sheidim* from every spoon, knife, fork, plate, and casserole. Teresa paid a waiter from the second class to bring them goy food in pots. Seeing these renegades devour impure food, the immigrants kept their distance: they preferred being even closer to one another so they could leave a six-foot ring around the apostates.

While the family slept, Alejandro allowed the Rabbi to put his mouth to the center of his heart, so he could recite prayers that would navigate through his blood and purify his entire body.

When the ship entered the dock, the four children ran to the handrail, slipping through the chattering Yiddish crowd that recoiled from them in disgust. With great dignity, Teresa took Alejandro by the arm and caught up with her excited heirs to look contemptuously at the port. Clustered around the gangway, people were selling bananas, grapes, cherries, and many other fruit with strange names—*chirimoyas, nísperos, avocados,* and *caquis*. Others were waving bouquets of herbs and flowers. Their clothes were tattered and they had no shoes. But at the same time they had no feathers, no bows, and no arrows. A bit further off, groups of elegant people under multicolor parasols were awaiting first and second-class passengers. There were ships loading and unloading Italians, Englishmen,

Germans, Swedes, Frenchmen. Painted-up women were pulling on the arms of the sailors, dragging them toward the bars. In their luxurious construction, the buildings on the narrow, flat area beyond the dock, unlike the poor houses covering the hillsides, resembled the mansions of Paris.

The city—civilized, flourishing in a clear, caressing breeze, deliciously perfumed, between the glitter of the rocky mountain range and the murmur of the sea—made Teresa smile, even if her strenuous effort not to show it made her face look like a sun-dried apple. And as an orchestra, which included guitars and a harp, played a kind of polka to a clapping, shouting, dancing, handkerchief-waving audience, Alejandro and the children hugged Teresa because they were carried away by an irrepressible joy.

The disembarking passengers were received with hugs and kisses. A well-dressed group, in the style of the goyim, received the immigrants waving pennants emblazoned with six-pointed stars. To each newcomer they gave a package of food and clothing. They kissed the strangers as brothers, wept, sang hymns in Yiddish, and moved off into the port. Teresa's smile inverted into a bitter frown. She shook off her husband and children as if they were dust and no longer mute, said: "Don't start in with this idiocy! Remember, we're not Jews anymore! We've reached Hell, and not a single devil is waiting for us!"

Picking up a suitcase, she walked haughtily down the gangplank to go through with the customs formalities. Her family followed, trying to emulate her pained dignity. No one checked their baggage. Some dark men with black moustaches stamped their passports and, laughing among themselves, pointed towards the exit.

It was 9:00 a.m. They were in the middle of the street in Valparaíso, the farthest corner of the world, unable to speak a word of Spanish, with no money and no friends. What should they do? Just as she had in Paris, Teresa sat down on the ground, closed her eyes, and said, "Fix things up the best you can. I'm not here."

Fanny, Lola, Benjamín, and Jaime looked at their father. He responded: "Well, I think she's asking me to summon the Rabbi again so he can save our skin."

On this occasion, the Rabbi was unsure. This world was unknown to him. He doubted. "If a wise man is one who knows that he doesn't know, then at this moment I'm a wise man. Let's see. Everything revolves around money and death. Look in your pockets, Alejandro; one golden key opens a thousand doors. Perhaps you've got one last banknote."

My grandfather carefully searched his deep pockets. In the fold at the bottom of his leather coat, he found a tiny coin. Half a kopek: worthless.

Alejandro shut his eyes and dropped down to the ground to sit next to Teresa. A jubilant shout from the Rabbi made him jump to his feet. "Mazel tov! Half a kopek, marvelous! Adonai is calling us. Remember Exodus, Chapter 30:

> The Lord said to Moses, "When you take the census of the people of Israel, then each shall give a ransom for his life to the Lord when you number them, that there be no plague among them when you number them. Each one who is numbered in the census shall give this: half a shekel according to the shekel of the sanctuary (the shekel is twenty gerahs), half a shekel as an offering to the Lord. Everyone who is numbered in the census, from twenty years old and upward, shall give the Lord's offering. The rich shall not give more, and the poor shall not give less, than the half shekel, when you give the Lord's offering to make atonement for your lives. You shall take the atonement money from the people of Israel and shall give it for the service of the tent of meeting, that it may bring the people of Israel to remembrance before the Lord, so as to make atonement for your lives."

"Do you understand, Alejandro? A silver coin, half a shekel, half a kopek, the same symbol, rich and poor giving a half, the mortal half, while receiving the sum of eternal life. You thought you'd lost everything, but Adonai left in the darkest corner of your clothing what you really needed, the half shekel of the offering so you can enter the Sanctuary and establish the union that will liberate you from mortality. Courage! God is waiting for us! You, I, your family, we are seven, the golden candelabra, the menorah! Let us arrange ourselves in proper order and climb up to the top of that peak. Do you see the Temple? There we will deposit your obolus and receive from the Eternal One the impulse toward the new life."

Alejandro squinted, trying to see what the Rabbi was talking about, at the top of that peak covered with clusters of houses. He could make out a gray, rectangular house of some size with a chimney that billowed out white smoke. "The sacrificial fire." As usual, my grandfather completely believed whatever the Rabbi said. He knelt and, spreading his arms, made his way to Teresa, who stubbornly kept her eyes shut.

A chorus of crystalline voices accompanied their short, uncomfortable walk. A pack of dark, ragged children, among whom there were two or three blonds and skeletal dogs, surrounded them, begging for money at the top of their lungs: "A penny! A nickel! A loaf of bread!"

Suddenly a rotten peach exploded against Benjamín's bald head. Everyone laughed and went on tossing garbage.

"Teresa, you know by now that the Rabbi always saves us. If you wish, just go on pretending he doesn't exist, but do what I'm asking you to do with your eyes closed. Line up in the order he tells us and we will go to the top of that peak. There, God will give us the help we need."

Teresa, tense, implacable, breathing only slightly, intent on being a statue of salt, neither moved nor answered. Alejandro knew that his wife's will was intransigent, as did the twins. But when the black pulp of an old banana smashed against her stubborn face, my grandmother opened her ferocious eyes, roared, leapt like a wild beast, smacked one of the dogs in the head with her suitcase. She caught the biggest boy and pulled down his pants. Turning him over her knee, she slapped his buttocks until they were red. She let him loose when she thought the punishment was enough, so he could catch up to his pals who were fleeing at top speed.

With that terrible face that could stop an army, Teresa stared at her husband, sank Fanny and Lola between her breasts and said, trying to give her words the hardness of stone, "A-le-jan-dro-Jo-do-row-sky, it's your fault we are where we are. That insanity about the Rabbi has led us to misery. Here, the advice of your ghost means nothing. And I don't want us to go on living as parasites on the Jewish community. The past is done and gone! New world, new life! This is the last time I'll ever accept help from that freak. I'll line up as you ask, and we'll march up to the top of the peak. Let's see if the Most High Scoundrel gives us the help we need in exchange for half a kopek. But I swear on my life that if nothing happens, I'll leave Jaime and Benjamín with you, take the girls with me, and we'll go to a bar in the port and be whores forever!"

Alejandro swallowed hard, tried to kiss Teresa's hand as she pulled it back in fury, and arranged the family in a line. Next to Teresa, Fanny, and next to Fanny, Lola on the far left. Next to him, Benjamín, and next to Benjamín, Jaime on the far right. The Rabbi stood in the center. "Now we have formed the golden candelabra. Our souls are the seven flames. Now, holding hands, we shall climb up to deposit the half kopek in the Temple."

"First ask your Rabbi if he's going to be the one who carries the bags."

Fanny and Jaime laughed. The Rabbi immediately whispered to Alejandro, "The wise Hillel said: 'If you wish to possess everything, you must not posses something that is nothing.' Leave what you have behind!"

"Teresa, sweetheart, as a wise man said, in order to possess everything you must possess nothing. We have to abandon our baggage."

"Is that what your Rabbi advises? Let people rob the little you have left? Let them throw salt in your eyes, pepper in your nose, and stones at your heart! Let them pull your guts out of your belly, wrap them around your neck, and then hang you from a tree! I hope you turn into a bird and he turns into a cat so he can eat you alive, choke, and you both die together!"

"Enough, Teresa! You promised to obey him one last time!"

"It's pretty certain we're going to prostitute ourselves. You will ruin your life and the lives of your daughters. You will die of shame."

"I believe in him. Let's go!"

The street snaked upward among small, one- or two-story houses with window boxes filled with geraniums or ferns. Compared with the other hills, where mansions, gardens, and churches were clearly visible, this one had to be the most modest in Valparaíso. The Chileans were not aggressive. From their rooms, they watched the family march up the middle of the street holding hands as if they were part of a parade that had lost its body with only the head remaining. They smiled, held out glasses of water or wine or slices of melon. Teresa, huffing and puffing, forced the twins to accept nothing despite the fact that, under this sun that was stronger than anything she had felt before, she too was parched, her lips cracking.

The gray, rectangular building, with a tin chimney spouting white smoke, turned out not to be a temple but a military barracks, with two soldiers standing guard at its metal doors. Barely hiding his despair, Alejandro looked more carefully and realized that the chimney did not belong to the barracks but was attached to a run-down wooden house with a clay oven and a tavern with chairs. A bald old man showing his last three teeth was offering his merchandise, pointing to two baskets covered with empty flour sacks.

"Have faith," said the Rabbi. "Nothing is given to us, we have to earn it. God hides so we will search for Him. By learning to see Him in everything, we are born. The temple is a military barracks because obeying the law of God is the only freedom. And this modest shack that has summoned us with the smoke of its purifying oven is a holy place, the altar of sacrifice. Give me the half kopek of ransom so that, in the name of the Jodorowsky family, I can deposit it in consecrated hands."

When Teresa saw Alejandro fall into a trance, assuming the refined gestures, the high-pitched voice, and the burning gaze of the Rabbi, she began to tear out her hair. "Once upon a time I would have said *My God*, but now what can I say? I'll kill myself! It's better to be a dead lioness than a mangy, living dog."

The Rabbi, with the smile of one blessed, responded, "If God gave us thirst, he will give us water. If He gave us teeth, he will give us bread. Come to the altar."

Teresa, overcome with fatigue, followed her husband. The old toothless man took a triangular patty out of each basket and said, "Cheese, meat."

The Rabbi had no knowledge of empanadas, a Chilean dish made of baked dough stuffed with chopped meat or cheese, but he shouted in astonishment, "Praised be He!" God was speaking to him in symbols. The most sacred sign, the Shield of David, was there before them! He sniffed the meat empanada: "This is the Eternal One manifest in matter." He sniffed the cheese empanada: "And this is the Eternal One manifest in spirit." From the hands of the old man he took the two triangles, and placed one on top of the other to form a six-pointed star. The Magen David, the union of heaven and earth, fire and water, body and soul. "God is the food we will never lack. And he asked each member of the family to take a bite at each of the six points. Then he let them eat until the symbol disappeared.

The old priest began to recite a psalm of gratitude in Spanish, incomprehensible to the others: "Who's going to pay for the two empanadas?"

The Rabbi asked the family to repeat, in a chorus, the holy words. Their mouths, fragrant with cheese, onion, and meat, sang thankfully.

"Who's going to pay for the two empanadas?"

The old man stretched out his open hand, shaking it impatiently. The Rabbi began to leave. "I've completed my mission. Give him the obolus, and the Eternal One will manifest Himself." The Rabbi disappeared. Alejandro, smiling happily, deposited the half-kopek in the old man's dried out fingers. The old man stared at the tiny coin. His face turned into an ocean of wrinkles, his mouth transformed into a grimace like a fallen half moon. But before he could open his mouth to hurl an insult, the ground began to shake.

The shack's lantern, hanging on a dark wire covered with fly shit, bounced around furiously. A shower of dry leaves fell; the dogs barked so loudly they seemed to cough up their guts; monsters of dust out of the ground emerged. Then came a gigantic howl, accompanied by much more intense aftershocks. A few houses collapsed. The screaming began, a mixture of horror and pain. The entire port began to waltz. Immense waves threw the ships against the sea walls. No one could keep his footing. The peaks split open like ripe fruit, showing dark red cracks. Horses fell down the hillsides.

Thousands of citizens were running from one place to another, darkening the streets, keeping clear of the falling walls. Gas tanks split open. Explosions and huge flames magnified the hysteria. The shaking began again, even more ferocious this time. The entire harbor leaned starboard and port like a ship in a storm. No building was left undamaged. The military structure collapsed. The two soldiers stood at attention until a piece of flying sheet metal cut off their heads.

Alejandro herded the children toward an iron bench, bolted into the ground. There, piled on top of one another, they waited for the earthquake to pass. My grandfather began to recite some words dictated to him by the Rabbi. The disembodied one knew a treatise on magic that could calm the furious tremors: KADAKAT, ARAKADA, DARENAK, AKESERA, KAMERAD, ADAKARA, TAKADAK. All of them spun around and trembling with terror, repeated the formula.

Teresa went mad with rage. She stood up on the bench and held her balance with the skill of a sailor. It didn't matter to her that trees, chunks of cement, windows, pieces of glass, and pieces of pipe as sharp as swords were falling all around her. She raised her fists toward the sky, bellowing, "May all the curses Your murderous mouth has poured out since You created this world fall on You! Look at how much You're destroying just to get me to submit! But You will never make me give in! Make the entire planet explode if you like, it doesn't matter to me! What can You do to a woman with a withered heart? Kill me once and for all, because not even earthquakes can make me open my soul to You!"

She was foaming at the mouth, her face was as white as a sheet, and she was trembling even harder than the ground. Alejandro grabbed her by the calves and pulled her down into his arms. With the strength of a madman he pushed her under the bench, silencing her with a desperate kiss.

A deafening screech announced that the peak was splitting open. The old man, squealing like a hog, was swallowed by a crack. The iron bench went downhill, still bolted to an enormous chunk of the hillside. The Jodorowsky family gave a strange scream: a mix of Alejandro's religious fervor, Teresa's rage, the terror of Lola and Benjamín (both too delicate for these quakes), and the euphoria of Fanny and Jaime. To these two, they were on a toboggan going faster and faster. Their only thought was to get as much fun as possible from the ride down, never considering that awaiting them at the bottom was a collision that would smash them to atoms or sink them in the sea.

They crawled out from between the others' feet and stood up on the iron seat, balancing as if they were on the crest of a wave. Tons of falling stone destroyed street lamps, crushed dogs and people, and demolished houses, leaving a trail of ruins and blood. They were nearly spinning out of control as Teresa, under the bench with Benjamín and Lola, who were sheltered under the roof of her breasts, cursed even louder. Alejandro, making a prodigious effort, got up from the bench, took hold of Fanny, and shielded her with his own body. Jaime would not let himself be caught. He leapt off the bench and ran to the far edge of the sliding peak, shouting triumphantly and dodging large bits of wall, glass, roof beams, and human body parts all being tossed into the air by his vehicle.

They smashed against a shoe factory. The building, a modest structure, made principally of concrete slabs held up by thin columns, yielded to the chunk of mountain on impact and acted as an elastic brake, capturing the mass as if it were held in a cradle. The bench finally stopped, still perfectly horizontal. During the whole slide downhill, it would have been possible to hold a glass of water without spilling a drop.

"A Miracle!" said the Rabbi. "*Tohu va'Bohu*, chaos is an egg from which order is born! The new life begins here!"

Without hearing him, Alejandro remained with his family under the bench. The aftershocks lasted for what felt like an eternity. It might have been seconds, minutes, or hours. He never knew and never tried to find out. His people had known innumerable catastrophes, and an age-old instinct made him give himself over to true time, the time that cannot be measured, where twenty years pass like an hour and a second can last a thousand years. He knew that the pain and pleasure of an entire life didn't last more than an instant, but that each step he took on always-foreign lands took an eternity.

When the ground stopped moving, the silence hurt their eardrums. Above it rose the laughter of Jaime, who invited them to come down from the peak by throwing all kinds of shoes at them. There was a mournful chain of succession, thousands of human voices in protest, all mixed up with the howls of dogs throughout the country, up in the mountains and down in the valleys, and the presence of death, the invisible tarantula covering Valparaíso.

Alejandro checked on each of them, then came out from under the bench and gave Jaime a slap. It was the first and last in his life, but nevertheless, that slap marked a turn, inching towards a final separation. Alejandro dug into the ruins to see if anyone could be saved. He found crushed, deformed, ripped-open bodies. He overcame his intense fascination—something, his animal nature perhaps, impelled him to dig through the detritus and smell the blood, see the mystery of the body, the secret viscera revealing their forms in broad daylight—because he heeded the Superior Will and believed that what God placed within the dark interior of the organism, protected from prying eyes, should be respected.

Seeing what has been revealed is an obligation, but the other thing, which appears in the gloom of catastrophe, should be avoided. We must be prudent with our senses. There are things we cannot observe or hear or smell or touch or eat. A great vigilance is asked of us with respect to our organs of perception, and also with respect to our desire, our need, our feelings, and our ideas. We cannot think without limitations. "Concern yourself with what it is permitted to know and forget mysterious things." Ah, the good Talmud!

A cry led Alejandro through the wreckage, and he found a man with a roof beam buried in his chest. His skin, getting whiter by the second, contrasted with the river of blood flowing out of him. The dying man held on tight to the handle of a leather suitcase. With the wise gaze of those who are entering the kingdom of death, he offered it to Alejandro, whispering words my grandfather couldn't understand but could only feel. The man was giving him the most precious thing in his life, the tools of his work. Why? In the worker's eyes there was a profound yearning and, at the same time, the great pleasure of making an offering of his conscience to death, like a wildflower, a sacrifice pure and simple, eternal disappearance, a debt repaid, serpent on the rock, bird in the sky, ship at sea, without leaving a trace, nothing to hang on to, only a small legacy, to everyone, to someone, his instruments, more valuable than existence, his true being. Knowing that hands as dutiful as his own would continue to work with those little angels of wood and metal—wise, useful, holy—would allow him to sink into the abyss with peace.

Alejandro opened the suitcase, took out the tools, kissed them and pressed them with respect to his heart, while the dying shoemaker, with only a tiny thread of voice left, gave him their names and uses in a Spanish so full of love that Alejandro understood it as if it were Russian. Hammer to flatten the leather, pincers to place the model over the last, small pliers for working the backstitch, curved awl to form the instep, spatula to spread the wax in the heels, chisel to cut the sole, stitching awl to perforate the leather, round pliers, gouge, a box of shoe polish, a small packet of pitch, and a bobbin of linen. Seeing my grandfather putting the tools back into the suitcase and taking possession of them, the man gave a long sigh and gave up his spirit with a smile.

The Rabbi said, "Do you see, Alejandro? God has given you a profession. You are a shoemaker." My grandfather clasped the suitcase to his chest and burst into convulsive weeping.

Teresa and the children called him back at the top of their lungs. They were both curious and afraid. Alejandro, scrambling over beams as sharp as knives, reached the peak and climbed up to the iron bench. His family, sitting there as if in a theater, pointed to an approaching figure that was jumping along and shaking its backside wagging a hairy tail that hung from a clown costume. It spoke like a human being, but its face, with its narrow, prominent forehead, its sunken little eyes, its flat nose, its big mouth, and its pricked ears, was like a monkey's. "Hurry up, come with me! There could be another tremor!" it was shouting in Spanish. Teresa shook her head and signaled that she did not understand. The simian repeated himself in Italian, French, German, English, Dutch,

Portuguese, Polish, and finally in Russian. "Hurry up, come with me! There could be another tremor!"

They all ran toward this strange polyglot. He had them board a covered wagon decorated with trees made of sheet metal, resembling a tropical forest where a monkey-like clown seemed to fly over the green treetops. He translated the large red letters over the rear door: "Monkey Face. One-Man Circus." Then he sighed with relief.

"Whew! How lucky we were! On this street they all died. But my wagon and the horses were left unharmed. But we've got to get out of here right away. After the first quake, there always comes another. Without a first, there can't be a second, as the flea said. You two sit next to me and put the four kids on the sacks of straw—excellent food for horses. Now, hooves: do your duty! Giddy up, Whitey! Giddy up, Blacky."

The horse named Whitey was black, and Blacky was white. The beasts moved their bones as quickly as they could, a weary trot thanks to the negligible energy they got from that "excellent food," and they left Valparaíso huffing and puffing. As they reached a valley of dark, almost red, earth, where the trees had hard leaves that glittered like kitchen knives, the second tremor erupted. There was a terrifying roar from the belly of the earth, dense clouds of dust, cracks that opened into long mordant grins. They heard the wails of the victims being crushed in the port.

"That's how the damned must howl in hell," said the simian. And since both his hands were busy keeping the wagon from turning over, he crossed himself with his right foot. He was so flexible that his big toe could reach his forehead. Finally the tremors ceased. The crickets and birds sang. Whitey and Blacky, busy with indigestion, went trotting along.

"I'm not very happy. What with this earthquake, the business is failing. Between Valparaíso and Santiago there are many villages where I put on my show. But now the peasants are probably making for the port to loot the houses and bodies before the army moves in. But in the end, when the going gets tough . . . "

He laughed and suddenly changed the subject: "So then, the fact is that none of you speaks a word of Spanish, right? But do you have friends in Chile, relatives, some society, someone to take you in?"

"No, sir."

"Got any money left?"

"Not even a half kopek."

"Clothes to sell?"

"Just what we're wearing."

"Any jewels, some valuable object?"

"These shoemaker's tools."

"Indeed not, my dear sir. With those tools, you can earn your living in Santiago. And what about you, madam?"

Seraphim—that's what Monkey Face said his name was—looked toward the deep crevice between Teresa's breasts, where a nickel-plated steel chain hung. My grandmother, to my grandfather's surprise—he'd never seen her do it before—blushed. Since everything in her was exaggerated, the flow of blood, erasing her pallor, made her face look like a mask of red clay. The children burst into giggles. Seraphim stopped Whitey and Blacky with a whistle, and with his hands together as if praying he leaned over Teresa, muttering, "The Holy Virgin of dawn," and a deep moan, like the howl of a wounded animal, seemed to escape from inside her.

My grandmother broke that strange moment with a tremendous belch: "I've gone crazy, too! This damned earthquake has made me forget my children. They haven't eaten in ages."

Monkey Face opened a cardboard box, took out four bananas, and gave them to the children. To Teresa and Alejandro he passed two apples. When they'd all finished eating, my grandmother extracted the old watch from the abyss of her bosom. Inside were the seven trained fleas:

Baroco, Barono, Naprepeshev, Sedila, Casque, Barila, and Semudalalá. Semudalalá was the funny one. Before she bit, she executed a series of twenty-six somersaults.

Under the curious eyes of the family but especially of Monkey Face, she placed her right wrist close to the open watch case and called: "Baroco!" A flea jumped out to bite her in the spot where the pulse is taken. She then put out her left wrist and called out "Barono!" Another flea jumped out to begin its dinner. She modestly raised her skirt and placed the watchcase in the concave space behind her right knee.

Seeing the skin gleam like white marble, Seraphim bowed again, praying: "The Virgin of the Snows!"

"Your dinner, Naprepeshev!" And the third flea jumped. The other leg was offered to Sedila, who also obeyed the call. Then my grandmother opened her blouse and allowed her two mother-of-pearl watermelons out. Monkey Face swooned and fell on his back among the sacks of straw. Alejandro instantly took off his jacket and covered his wife. "Casque, Barila!" And the fifth and sixth fleas each took possession of a nipple. Teresa pushed her husband aside, pulled up her skirt, pulled her drawers down a bit to reveal her deep navel, and with a childlike grin whispered, "Semudalalá." The last flea executed its somersaults and burrowed into the delicious hole.

The children applauded. Alejandro perspired. Seraphim began to tremble like a man possessed by a fever of 104. Once their meal was finished, the seven fleas, having received no further orders, hopped toward their refuge. Teresa closed the watchcase and sank it once again between her bosoms, then straightened her clothes. The simian was panting. Alejandro, soaked from head to foot, lost his head. His eyes became bloodshot. His crotch swelled. It seemed as if the monkey man had infected him with his fever. Teresa put on the rest of her clothing. Her husband took her by the hand with an authority that would have tamed a typhoon, made her jump down from the wagon, and dragged her toward a small hill covered with cactus. They disappeared from sight behind the spiny plants.

The monkey man let go the reins and again fell backward onto the sacks of straw, as if in ecstasy. The children got off the wagon to follow their parents' footprints, at a respectable distance. It would have been impossible for them to pass through the cactus tunnel without being pierced by thorns; conversely, the intensity of Alejandro's passion enabled him to clear a path with impunity, leaving in his wake a trail dripping thick, green slime. The children followed it, carefully marking each step so they wouldn't slip and have their eyes pierced by cactus spines.

The wind changed direction and, along with the viscous creaking of the torn cactus plants, it carried the voice of their father, a furious, painful, sexually aroused, lulling, insulting, begging voice: "You're mine, only for me, do you understand? Something weird happened to you with that monkey. You showed him your teats and your navel. How could you? No one should see you, not even a monster. You are for my eyes, for my touch, for my mouth. I don't want any surprises. Wrap your willpower around your waist; don't let madness take control of your sex—no confusion, no strange temptations. Give everything to me!"

In his jealous tone, there were black clouds, lightning bolts, wild gusts of wind. As he spoke, he shouted, sang, undressed his wife, tossing aside her clothes as if they were the sweaty skin of a sugary fruit. The children, picking up each item of clothing, reached the top of the hill and saw their parents rolling, intensely coupled, over the sea of spines. When the steely points touched their skin, they burned, and the thick, hostile plants burst open to become slippery, fragrant cushions. Alejandro was moving his hips so hard he made the mountain shake.

"Take me in! Everything! Farther in! Farther still! Down to your bottomless depth! Try to swallow my skeleton!"

It was his desperate desire for Teresa's skin to split open and cover him like a wing, dissolving him in her blood. Then he could make his way through her absolutely, then nothing of her would be denied to him. He wasn't seeking pleasure. What he sought was the explosion of his wife into thousands of burning crevices, to give pleasure that would spatter her soul.

He moved furiously, more like a madman than an animal. With each lurch of his hips he seemed to want to give life. Enormous prickly husks fell onto his tensed back, with a sound like the cracking of a whip, but it didn't matter to him. Teresa responded by slapping his ribs with her swollen bosoms, ravaging his waist between her mare-like thighs, grinding her voracious hips. But Alejandro's despair would not subside; the more he gave, the more was asked of him. He knew his wife kept a secret, unconquerable citadel. Now his thrusts sounded like gunshots. It seemed my grandmother's pelvic bones were cracking one by one. Attracted by the sugary juice of the smashed cactuses, hundreds, thousands of lizards began to gather, a green and shiny blot around the couple like a living halo. All those tiny tongues savoring the sap made the glassy sound of a stream. My grandfather could go no further. He threw his head back, arching his spine as if he wanted his hoarse whine to pierce the center of heaven, and sank himself totally into his wife's stomach. She gave such a lurch that it tossed him on his back six feet way, with his sex exploding in a white bush.

"Don't make me pregnant again! One more life is one more death! I don't want to manufacture corpses for the Murderer!"

The semen fell onto the vegetal magma in thick, heavy drops that sank in and created small, ephemeral green crowns. From each was born a white butterfly. The tangle of white wings tried to seek out the light, but the lizards skillfully leaped up and carried all of them off, dying in their moist jaws.

Alejandro regained consciousness. He sank his head between Teresa's bosoms and began to laugh shamefully. She calmed him, as if he were a child: "It's nothing, silly boy. It's the earthquake. It's this new land, another sky, another sun. Soon we'll get used to things and be just as we were. Come on, get dressed."

The children cautiously approached their parents to hand them their clothing. Teresa checked to see if the seven fleas were in their place and, satisfied, she covered herself. Her husband did as well. They took the children by the hands and went back to the wagon, strolling slowly as if they were parading through the florid gardens on the banks of the Dnieper in a year without pogroms.

Monkey Face, having recovered from his fainting spell, waited for them to climb aboard and set the horses into motion again. "Get up, Whitey! Get up, Blacky!" Then, his tiny eyes filled with humility and sadness, he begged the couple: "Please, Doña Teresa and Don Alejandro, don't misunderstand me. Don't mistake my animal nature. I've never known a woman. Besides, what woman would want to be with me, with this face of mine? I'm chaste, and despite being thirty I have no more experience than a child. Madam, allow me to explain my reactions. There is nothing lustful in them. According to what I've been told, my mother tossed me into a garbage can because I was ugly. Was she poor? Rich? Sick? A victim of rape or incest? I'll never know. A beggar found me and dropped me off at the Red Cross. I caused a stir. I was two days old but I was covered with hair. They did all sorts of tests on me to figure out if I was a superior kind of monkey or a degenerate human. They settled on the second hypothesis. I regret it to this day.

"If they had declared me a highly evolved animal, I would have had a better life: luxury cages, first-class education, fame, worldwide respect. I was declared human, but the National Orphanage received me grudgingly and did very little to keep me alive. I grew up in a room smaller than a cage in the zoo. The guards only spoke to me to mock me, and the orphans only to teased me. And how could it be otherwise, when even the dogs barked and the cats hissed with their hair standing on end when they saw me? The only friends I had were a spider, a mouse, and a pigeon with a broken wing. When there were official parades, national holidays, Labor Day, the anniversary of the naval battle of Iquique, they left me locked up in the orphanage and absolutely forbade me to appear.

"There, in the lonely solitude of the vast building, where the dark corners hid foul hazards and the shadows were as accusatory as judges, I had no other refuge but the Chapel of the Three Marys. It was a long gymnasium converted into a temple. On the altar reigned three virgins. Since the guards were men, and in the orphanage the boys lived in one building and the girls in another, those statues were the only women I'd ever seen in my short life. One was white, made of marble, the Virgin of the Snows. The next was red porcelain, the Virgin of the Dawn. And the third was black, carved out of ebony, the Virgin of the Night. All beautiful, with the sweetest smiles. With no one to stop me, I climbed up on the altar to embrace them with my small arms and to cover their mouths with kisses, imagining my mother's lips. The marble, porcelain, and ebony was not warm like flesh, but to me their coldness seemed much warmer than the contempt of the guards and the orphans.

"Once I managed to steal a bottle of sleeping pills from the infirmary. Late that night, I slipped through the corridors, entered the chapel, and, kneeling before the three Marys, I decided to end my insignificant life. Just as I was about to throw a handful of pills into my mouth, a gush of milk bathed my face. At first, I saw nothing, blinded by the surge of warm liquid in my eyes. Then I realized that the milk was pouring from one of the breasts of the Black Virgin.

"When that miracle stopped, another began: the White Virgin began to weep. Two streams of water ran from her eye sockets. I leapt to kiss those tears, trembling with fever. When I licked the last drops, I saw that rubies were sprouting from the forehead of the Red Virgin. I thrust my chest forward to be stained with that precious blood.

"In their own ways, my three mothers had spoken to me: 'Place your physical pain and your spiritual suffering in us, and we will nourish you with our love. You are not alone in the world. You exist for us. For that reason, then, live for us.' And I did just that. I cast aside the poison and decided to live. That miracle for me, for me alone, would be the secret that would allow me to face society. God the Father had abandoned me, but the Holy Maternal Trinity, in its infinite pity, adopted me. I thought: I'll have a better chance if, instead of trying to go higher, I race downhill. Instead of fighting for my legitimate human place, I should exaggerate my animal behavior, make myself more monkey than human, pass over their jokes, abase myself much more than they could abase me. If I sacrifice my dignity, make myself all the more the grotesque, they will find me charming. Even if my isolation is complete, I will be surrounded by laughter.

"At dinner, after an anemic soup or a thin stew, all the orphans had the right to dessert—guava jam or quince syrup with cheese or macaroons or, in winter, fritters in hot syrup—everyone except me. I was always served, accompanied by malicious giggles, a banana. They made a spectacle of my atrocious face. It was as if every afternoon, I was trying to hide my simian side—with sophisticated gestures and expressions that were all too delicate—and they were unmasking me. As the saying goes, 'You can dress a monkey in silk, but he's still a monkey.'

"There I was, hunched over, my eyes fixed on the banana. And I didn't eat it. I was going to sleep without a dessert I badly wanted. This time, when they placed the humiliating fruit before me, I surrendered myself to the Three Marys and let a stream of spittle pour out. I beat my chest, I garishly sniffed the banana, I made befuddled faces, I rubbed it all over my body as if it were soap, I tried to eat it unpeeled, and I made wild squeals of disgust. Finally, I peeled it and studied the yellowish flesh, spellbound as if I were seeing God Himself. I stuck my tongue out as far as it would go. I licked my lips, I bit, and chewing with the greatest pleasure, I fell back on the tabletop, scratching my rear.

"The entire orphanage roared with laughter and applause. I'd won my first battle. From that moment on, I would be more monkey than any monkey. After many, many hours of practice, I learned to use my feet in the same way as people who've lost their hands. One day, I could eat the banana using only my lower extremities. What a triumph! To see me repeat the trick, the boys gave me their desserts. I could enjoy myself to the fullest and eat as many as I wanted, the only price being occasional indigestion.

"Soon I had to expand my repertoire—every day I had to eat the banana a different way. With rage: I bit ferociously, interrupting myself to chew with a big grin. This mixture of hate and pleasure won over the audience. With anguish: after hiding the banana, apparently without realizing it, under my napkin, I howled as I looked everywhere for it, even between my legs. My wails broke their hearts, and when I finally lifted the napkin and squealed with joy, everyone applauded. But the most popular number, which I had to repeat innumerable times, accepting desserts but also marbles, tops, cup-and-ball games, and picture cards, was the poisoned banana act. I'd gobble it down like a starving man, overwhelmed to have something sweet into my mouth, a nip to catch a teeny-tiny chunk between my teeth (laughter) and then chew it for a long time as if it were huge (more laughter), swallow it to the tune of a satisfied belch and, a second later, to clutch my stomach as if attacked by an atrocious pain, then twisting up, screaming my lungs out. Overcoming my suffering, I'd drool again, smile, and take another bite. So from piece to piece, from belch to belch, from cramp to cramp, I increased the intensity of the attacks until I died. A highly celebrated death because, in the greatest pain, with my muscles tense, with my eyes rolled back, and with a horrible expression on my face, I would take one final bite of the murderous banana before bashing it majestically against my forehead. So, my popularity grew right along with my estrangement. All human gestures were prohibited. Everyone thought that, by giving me little bags of peanuts, they were making me happy.

"One afternoon, the director of the orphanage had dinner with us, an obligation detailed in some paragraph in the rules and regulations. He saw me perform. The number he caught was 'The Bitter Banana.' In this one, I—the poor, naïve monkey, hungry, deluded—thought I'd found the sweetest banana of all. I peeled it eagerly and raised it to my lips. Yuck! What a letdown! It tasted like bile! Then I walked around the tables, picking up as many sugar bowls as I could carry. I went back to my seat and began to pour sugar on the banana, a little, a lot, a ton, rivers of it, but no matter how much I sweetened its surface, it was still bitter inside. I ended up, helpless, howling not like a monkey but like a whipped dog. Thanks to a little slice of onion I kept hidden in the palm of my hand, I could cry real tears whenever I rubbed my eyes.

"Amid the guffaws and whistles that celebrated my misfortune, there was someone else weeping: the director. My act had touched a nerve. He got up from the table, called me over, and led me by the hand in a friendly way to his office, a mysterious, terrible, sacred place where no orphan ever set foot. The room, painted dark green, was Spartan: a filing cabinet, some diplomas on a wall, a picture of the president of the Republic, a metal desk, a vase with white roses, three leather armchairs, and, on a small side table, the photograph of a young woman wearing a wedding dress. Her skin was translucent, almost luminous, and her blonde curls peeked out from beneath her white veil.

"The director asked me: 'What's your name, my boy?'

"'Seraphim, sir.'

"'Why? That name doesn't fit you well.'

"'I was given that name so that in my ugliness there would be at least one beautiful thing.'

"'I understand. Seraphim, I hope you know you have a great talent. You are a real artist. What you did in the dining room has a deep meaning.

It is, no more or less than the very picture of life as it is lived by all of us poor mortals. We try to sweeten it, but the agreeable part stays on the outside because life is always bitter within. Look at that photograph. She was my wife. I loved her as only a man thirty years older than his wife knows how to love. I was forty-seven, and she seventeen. To say I idolized her is to say nothing. She agreed to marry me; the great number of years that separated us mattered not a bit to her. She made me young again, I assure you. Every caress took years off me. Everything was sweet until reality revealed its bitter core. Three days after our wedding, Rocío, in a fit of joy, started to dance. She tripped and fell out the window. We were living in an apartment on the tenth floor. A foolish tale, a small slip, and an ocean of impudence. I've spent years trying to get over it, trying to have fun, to love again. Impossible. Like you, I have nothing left but to rage at the fruit that can never satisfy me.'

"'I'm very sorry for you. The lady was very pretty. Given my situation, I envy you, Mr. Director. Those three days will be eternal in your memory. I'll never live anything like that, not even three minutes.'

"'There's another lesson you've taught me, Seraphim: things can always get worse. I like you and I'm going to do something for you. I think you have a profession. You're a good clown. You can make a living from your jokes. I'm going to give you a wagon and two horses so you can wander the roads. By making faces, you'll earn money. Tell me how you'd like to decorate the wagon and what name you'd like to have painted on it. I'll have the workshop people do the job.' He pulled a bottle of pisco out of one of the desk drawers. 'Get out of here, Seraphim, I'm going to get drunk.'

"And that's exactly what happened. He gave me this wagon. I never saw him again, but I found out he'd committed suicide by jumping out of the same window. I've been traveling the roads for many years now, just as he wanted. People are poor. When I pass the hat around I pick up, along with a few pennies, a carrot, a fresh egg, a couple of pears. And that's how I've been living. Once the show was over, no one ever came over to talk to me. Why would they? I had to content myself with exchanging whinnies with my faithful Whitey and Blacky. I really suffered when they died of old age, but the love I had for them didn't keep me from slicing up their meat and drying it in the sun to make jerky. My stomach was their grave.

"Luckily, I'd saved some money and replaced them with another pair of horses of the same colors. Putting on shows in Valparaíso, I realized that in the red-light zone there were sailors of all nationalities walking around not knowing a word of Spanish. They stood there, mute, getting drunk with the prostitutes. Sometimes they showed snapshots of women, children, dogs, and they'd wave them around, letting out boozy hiccups. That's where I found another opportunity to get a bit of human warmth: I became an interpreter. I prayed to the Three Marys to help me find an instructor who could teach me lots of languages. The miracle happened: I found the Anarchist, a wise and generous man who taught me quickly and for nothing.

"I then divided my work in two parts. During the summer and the spring, I was a clown. During the fall and the winter, a translator, a mascot for the whores, sailors, and smugglers. It's true that no one bothered to get to know my heart; all they were interested in was for me to transpose what they were feeling from one language to another, that's all. Another escorted solitude, but closer and closer. I could feel on my untouched skin the heat of their breath soaked in tobacco and alcohol. A minimal contact for normal beings, but enormous for me. Do you understand me now? Thanks to the earthquake, for the first time, someone has boarded my smelly wagon.

"When you're all alone, you don't take care of yourself, and I confess I don't wipe myself or wash very often. When you, madam, blushed, I saw the Virgin of Dawn. When you fed your fleas and revealed your white flesh, I mistook you for the Virgin of the Snows. I know that someday you'll turn black—I can't imagine how—and through you the Virgin of the Night will speak. My three saints have sent you. Our meeting was fated. Tell me, please, what do your fleas know how to do besides answering to their names?"

"They know how to jump through burning hoops, play tambourines, play ball, and tell the future."

"Fabulous! You are just what the doctor ordered! The one-man circus is going to expand. If we join together and Madame Teresa presents her little animals, we'll be a hit in Santiago and the other big cities. Monkey Face and Madame Ochichornia with Her Magic Fleas! We'll earn a lot of pesos, which we'll split equally. And that way you two can feed your family."

Alejandro listened to all that not knowing how to react, but the children were fascinated. Teresa, uncharacteristically nervous and indecisive, felt a tingle. To turn herself into a fortuneteller was an idea that—she had no idea why—filled her with joy. Seeing that his proposition wasn't refused out of hand, Monkey Face sighed with relief.

"Without a no, there is still the possibility of a yes. Wonderful! I'm going to suggest something good for you. In Santiago, I have an empty room where you can stay and a few neighbors who can be useful to you, among them the Anarchist. Don Alejandro will look for a corner where he can set up his shoe shop, and I'll introduce you to a dwarf lady who can take care of the children while you, Madame Ochichornia, go on tour with me and return every week with a good amount of money and food. We're partners! Giddy up, Whitey! Giddy up, Blacky! We have to be there tomorrow afternoon!"

Lola seemed to hear the flies on that road singing, in tiny female voices, a celestial melody.

Seraphim lived in a tenement in the Independencia neighborhood. At the entrance there was a sign that read SOCIETY OF FREE BROTHERS AND SISTERS. WE ARE NOT THE STATE. When the Spanish word for tenement, *conventillo*, was translated into Russian for them as "little convent," Alejandro and Teresa did not understand the name. The place was filthy and miserable. Its architecture seemed more inspired by a prison than by a temple, with a long central passageway and rooms arranged like jail cells along it. The families lived packed into those spaces without windows, spaces that were at once living room, bedroom, kitchen, and latrine.

"The Anarchist will explain the situation better than I can. Chile is not Europe. Here there are two separate realities. A few people live in paradise, and all the rest live in the greatest misery. Only the rich can become even richer; all we poor folk can expect is to become even poorer."

"The Anarchist?"

"First, settle into this room, then I'll introduce you. I'll bring in some bags of straw you can use as beds. Other furniture you'll have to make out of some empty boxes I've picked out of the market garbage. Here is a hammer and some nails. And also some onions, goat cheese, carrots, and a little pea soup. Try to use the charcoal stove as little as possible. It's bad for your lungs. Organize the space, and I'll come back to pick you up so you can meet your neighbors. Oh yes, I'd forgotten! In this hole in the corner, you can take care of your needs. It's not very appetizing to mix the smells of the food on its way in with the smells of the food on its way out, but that's how the owners did it to save money on plumbing and make a few more rooms. Money calls the tune. Anyway, you'll see that you'll get used to it more quickly than you think."

My grandparents were happy. No matter how horrible, better a roof over your head than no roof. They had a few morsels of food, an interpreter, nice neighbors, perhaps, and new professions. What more did they need to restart their lives in this unknown land? Teresa, in a short time, used the boxes to make a table, chairs, and dressers. Meanwhile, Alejandro prepared, with great dedication, his shoemaker's bench. When Monkey

Face returned with the bags of straw, he also brought some pieces of fabric, thread, and needles, so my grandmother could sew them together and make quilts, tablecloths, and curtains. He also gave them a collection of empty jars they could use as pots and dishes. He immediately brought them to visit their neighbors. They began with the Anarchist. Monkey Face explained:

"People say that this gentleman is a member of one of the richest families in Chile, but he got disgusted with money obtained by exploiting the poor. The fact is that he came to live in our tenement because he was attracted by the name of the neighborhood: Independencia. And instead of earning abominable pesos, he invents new professions so we can earn a living. In exchange for that, we pay his rent and give him food. You'll see: he's a great man. He was one of the few—I can count them with the toes of one foot—to recognize my human intelligence. A wise man who knows more than thirty languages, he taught me just what was absolutely necessary of several and made me into an interpreter. Money, love, food, vice: what more is there to know? We, his disciples, have formed the Committee of Brothers and Sisters, which does not consider freedom "rebellion," but rather the retention of an imagination without limits under the restrictions imposed by power. Well, he'll explain things better. Step inside, there's no problem here."

He opened the door of Room 9, where it was written, NO NAME. ANARCHIST. INVENTOR OF PROFESSIONS. They were received by a short man of undetermined age, bald, with thick glasses under long black eyebrows. He was biting his fine lips and shaking his pale, almost blue fingers, stained with nicotine. Piles of books that went from the floor to the ceiling hid the walls of the room. Instead of chairs, there were encyclopedia volumes. The tables were also made from mountains of books, as was the object that should have been a bed.

"Greetings, brother Russians. Your homeland, once profound, now mobilizes the new, worldwide error: truth gagged by a centripetal power dictating relationships of vertical obedience. Luckily, you, pariahs of history, have fallen into the best company and belong, from now on, to our anarchist fraternity. But let us understand one another well."

Alejandro and Teresa, their hair half standing on end, their feet frigid, lost in a miserable neighborhood of Santiago de Chile, the farthest corner of the world, listened to that exuberant individual perorate in the most refined Russian they'd ever heard. About politics, they knew nothing. When they heard the "let us understand one another well" part, they tried to hide their donkey faces by opening their eyes wide and cocking, with an index finger, the lobe of their ears.

"We are not the sort of anarchists who rebel against God, Science, or the State. None of that. That struggle only brings upon the poor a rain of beatings and bullets. The State, and through the State, Capital, whatever form it takes, has for two or three centuries won that war. Nothing will change the course of the Industrial Era. The worms have begun to eat the cheese, and no one can stop them. Production will not cease until the planet has completely deteriorated. Few will survive. In a near future, the poor will perhaps have better clothing, housing, and food, but they will still be poor. Which is to say, more and more in debt to power, if not paying with our blood and our lungs, then giving away something as precious as their laughter and their intelligence. The poor man will become a comfortable, serious fool. The obvious conclusion? The main thing is to survive! So that the total collapse of society doesn't destroy us. But sit down, and let me explain."

As stools, he passed them two histories of philosophy, one in French, the other in German. Monkey Face gave the children a bag of marbles and sent them out to the street to play. Alejandro and Teresa still understood very little.

"We, labor, instead of continuing to be exploited by the rich, should figure out some way to exploit them. Not robbing them, of course. None of that. We have to act where they can't, where they don't know how.

This is not a solution for the majority, only for a few fleas with talent. The hog must eat garbage to make blood. The fleas, without getting dirty, suck the blood of the hog. So, when they roast the animal, they also burn the parasites, because the parasites are stupid. They could have jumped off in time and passed to the heads of the butchers. But let's get to the point. Power is not creative, and rich people get bored. They have everything, but they do not have themselves. And it's logical. To find oneself, it's necessary to let go of everything. They, on the other hand, are appropriating everything. See?"

"Yessir! We see!"

"Any man with a known profession—shoemaker, baker, miner, carpenter, painter, watchmaker, doctor, engineer, etcetera—is easy prey for the State, which will exploit him until it sucks out his very marrow. Having a normal profession means losing your freedom. We have to have unknown professions that do not intervene in material life but produce states of consciousness. We have to create new needs for the rich. To do that, we need no other raw material than our imagination. The pig is dexterous but stupid. We can live off his stupidity until the self-destruction happens. Please visit my foster brothers. I've given them new activities that will enable them to survive any collapse of the world economy. Those so-called crises really only affect the poor and the lesser capitalists. The big ones, the few and supreme, do not lose power, which is to say, they lose nothing. The hog passes through the change in fine style. My disciples, in those obscure moments, will hang on to their sows even more tightly."

The Russians were about to leave, guided by Monkey Face, who had listened to the peroration, applauding from time to time with hands and feet, when the Anarchist stopped them.

"Brother Alejandro, allow me to ask you something: your companion says you want to be a shoemaker. Is that so?"

"That's the truth, sir."

"It isn't worthwhile. It's a known profession. The State will end up exploiting you. When you finish making your visits, come back. I'll create a new profession for you. 'Sweetener of Voids' or 'Corrector of Shadows,' something."

"Thank you sir, it won't be necessary. I think that, by the way I go about it, shoemaker will become a new profession."

Monkey Face led Teresa and Alejandro through the tenement, introducing them to the members of the Society of Free Brothers and Sisters. They met the "Disinfector of Mirrors," the "Professor of Invisibility," the "Fantastic Biologist-Body Inventor," the "Funeral Clown," and many others who were unable to explain what their activities were because Monkey Face, accepting a drink at every door, staggeringly drunk, forgot not only Russian but also all the other languages and translated their words into a strange tongue composed of belches, hiccups, and drooling. At the beginning, they at least managed to find out what the "Freckle Trainer" did.

He was a pudgy, dark-skinned man who gave off a strong smell of wine, as did all the other goys they'd see in the tenement. A woman with few teeth accompanied him along with eight children who ran around the single room unconcernedly. The trainer beat a small drum and, opening his eyes with strange flashes of light, ordered the beauty mark to move. In effect, many ladies wanted to have their beauty mark next to the spot where their lips met or on a cheek or between their bosoms or even in more secret places. The naïve client would be told that, over the course of time, the blemish would move bit by bit until it reached the desired spot.

Naturally, the drum, the flashing eyes, and the trainer's hypnotic orders were not enough. The client also had to pray faithfully. After a few sessions, the client would be told in no uncertain terms that the beauty mark had indeed moved several fractions of an inch. If the lady became bored with the many required sessions or if she complained about their slow progress, the trainer would shrug his shoulders as if offended and answer that the fault did not lie with him but with insincere prayers. And off he'd go in search of another victim. There was no shortage of silly ladies to help feed his numerous offspring. Sometimes, very rarely, the beauty marks did move.

After visiting his comrades, Seraphim, thirstier and thirstier, led them to a room at the end of the corridor, just like all the others but with a large sign: HAPPY HEART BAR. About fifty goys—men and women, shoeless, their tattered clothes stitched together, packed into a sweaty and foul mass—were buying, for a few coins, glasses of wine that a short, potbellied Andalucian drew from a brightly painted red barrel, which was in the center of the room. With the skill of a sailor, the quasi-monkey threaded his way through that wave of flesh and returned, hopping on his right foot, holding three glasses—two in his hands and the third in the toes of his left foot. He drank from the one in his left extremity and held out the glasses in his upper extremities to the Russians. Alejandro immediately made a sign of refusal. Certain religious principles prohibited him from drinking in a bar. The fifty goys made hurt faces, and one insisted, "Don't insult us, comrade."

Sensing a storm brewing, Teresa raised her glass and emptied it down to the last drop. The throng of bodies approved with a jolly grunt.

The Rabbi advised my grandfather, "Look here, Alejandro, Hillel the Wise said: 'When you're among people wearing clothes, wear clothes; when you're among the naked, go naked.' Wine for these people is a kind of communion. I don't think you can say no. They might kill you. Drink and apply the proverb: 'As long as you're going to sin, you might as well enjoy yourself.'"

Then Alejandro took the glass and swallowed the wine with pleasure. He shivered five times, and a stubborn burning followed from his throat to his stomach. He began to cough. General laughter. Applause. Monkey Face returned with three more glasses. And the toasts of "Let's drink to happiness" went on for hours. My grandparents, trashed, crumpled, joined of the human block, humming Chilean tunes amid fits of laughter and vomiting. The party was over when the barrel was empty. They awoke the next day stretched out on the cement floor of their tiny room, with thick tongues and tremendous headaches. The new life had begun. The children were hungry.

Five years went by. Alejandro was a shoemaker, and Teresa a fortune-teller. Madame Ochichornia went out on tours that lasted three or seven days, at times two weeks, and always returned with a wide smile and a basket filled with eggs, chickens, loaves of bread, fruit, greens, candy, and other foodstuffs along with a good number of pesos. Thanks to the adoring attention of Monkey Face, who never stopped idolizing her, she learned Spanish quite well, but of course retained her Russian accent, the better to impress the audience. The fleas told the future with incredible accuracy, and whenever they reached a town, their fame preceding them; the poor lined up to ask the same things nearly every time: Does so-and-so really love me? Did I make a mistake marrying this woman? Will my lost love return? Will I get over this illness? Will I find a better job? What good does life hold for me?

Benjamín, Jaime, Fanny, and Lola would hear her coming because of the Whitey and Blacky's jingling bells. They would run up the street, shouting with joy, to meet her. They, too, spoke Spanish now, because they went to the public school, as was required by law. Along with lessons, they were also given a free breakfast. Alejandro, on the other hand, had only been able to learn one word of our language: "Wednesday." Whenever a customer asked him when his shoes would be ready, he would answer, "Wednesday." When they asked how much the repairs would cost, he'd say, "Wednesday." If someone said the weather was fine, he'd say, "Wednesday." But if he had no talent for languages, he had exceptional skills as a shoemaker.

He rejected the Anarchist's proposition and did not sweeten voids or correct shadows, but he proposed, on the other hand, to cultivate his shoemaker's vocation in an extraordinary way, that is, by making shoes to measure not only for feet but for the soul as well. And also with no fixed price: "Let each customer pay what he wishes or can. That will oblige him to take a moral position, to chose between paying the minimum, the proper price, or the maximum. This will help him know himself." The Anarchist liked those ideas and granted my grandfather the title "Professor of Shoeology."

Alejandro went to the city dump and picked up every piece of leather and thick fabric he could find. Also, the skins of rats, cats, and dogs. And pieces of wood and boards. All of that would be material for creating new models or making repairs. Back in his wretched room, he would stretch out to meditate and allow the boots and army shoes he'd shined while in the army for those five years to march through his mind. He saw how they were made and analyzed their parts:

"First and foremost a sole, a portable platform, protective support that should be invisible so that it feels like a second skin—safe, reliable, sensitive, and above all full of love. Maternal soles, giving birth to each step with an iron will, giving full hope of arriving where desired; constant producers of the road, soles that were nations. And the heel? It should support with strength, inspire absolute confidence, be a barrier that cuts away from the past and sets the step on the right course of reality, the resplendent present, allowing the proud foot to conquer, to penetrate, to take full possession, to become the center of the joyous explosion of life. But it should not, at the same time, be hard or cutting, but as delicate as it was powerful, not only pushing the foot forward to the future but also absorbing the oceanic impact of the past. And the tips? They should be fine without damaging the precious toes, so those toes might penetrate with the greatest ease into the future, which awaits us up ahead, which is always a prize, because the end of all roads is God and not death, which is itself only a transformation. May each step a person takes in my shoes carry them to happiness, blessed be they."

His first customers were poor devils who came to have their shoes repaired. Alejandro accepted all jobs, no matter how humble, and from those jumbled patches he made luxurious slippers. Slowly but surely middle-class customers came, and finally, aristocratic ladies and gentlemen appeared, seeking adventure. Alejandro had to recruit helpers. He chose them from the tenement, so they worked without having to leave their rooms. Anyone who had no job could participate in the making of entirely handmade shoes, sewn and glued, no nails used, and made from simple but noble materials. My grandfather swore he would never use one of those impersonal machines. Each pair of shoes had to be a task carried out with love and completely different from the others. A man has fingerprints that are exclusively his, unique in the Universe, and that's the way his shoes should be, for him and for no one else. The money received—"How much do they cost?" "Whatever your good will determines."—was divided equally among himself and his workers. He earned no more than the lowliest of his helpers, the one who prepared the molds in cardboard, despite working an astonishing number of hours each day creating new styles. Ultimately he came to have more than a hundred partner-workers, laboring with faces smiling.

Teresa, returning from each tour wearing more and more baroque turbans, more rings, bracelets, and necklaces, more mascara on her eyes, and with long, violet nails, would become furious: "This is stupid! There is something in your head that doesn't work properly. That damned Rabbi must be to blame. How is it possible that you have an ever-growing number of clients and a hundred employees, and yet you always earn the same amount, a pittance? Five years have gone by, and you still aren't getting any richer. The rich people exploit you. It amuses them to pay you less than they would a beggar. They don't see you as a saint but as a fool. It isn't right! I have to wear out my fleas, making them look into the hopeless future, for thousands of indigents so that we can live in a style barely above misery. You still try to go on earning merit in the pitiless eyes of the Grand Villain. By wanting to be a just man you don't enjoy life. You've sunk all of us in your mystical tomb. God only loves the dead! You have to return to reality!"

My grandfather would smile, kiss his wife on the forehead, and go back to his waking dream about how to improve his product. Now he was looking for the blueprint for shoes that would pray as people walked!

Suddenly Shorty Fremberg appeared, the first Jew my grandfather had seen in all those years. He was really repulsive, with an enormous head, short legs, a long torso, no neck, a potbelly, hairy, with one eye coffee-colored and the other green. He would shake his wrist to show off a gold watch that looked like an alarm clock, thinking that it made him attractive to women. He strutted around in front of the female workers as if, at a snap of his fingers, they would drop the soles to dive toward his fly. He turned up out of curiosity—some friends had told him about the madman who worked for whatever people gave him—to order a pair of low boots. When he got them, he offered ten times less than what they were worth. Alejandro stared at him with his eyes burning and only said, pointing toward the rooms where his helpers worked: "Thank you, for their sake." Fremberg, surprised, ashamed, gave a few more pesos and muttered, "For the tip," and then exclaimed in Yiddish:

"But, please, Don Alejandro! My friends told me you were crazy, and they were right. What does this mean? When you divide up what you earn, everyone, even the snot nose kid who cleans the holes you call toilets here, gets the same amount as you! Do you call that conduct worthy of a Jew? Because you are as Russian as I am Polish. Forget the masks! It seems to me you've confused the goys with Hasidim and confused decay with saintliness! A real manufacturer fixes prices high and salaries low. We're living in the Industrial Age, my friend! There are great opportunities for the middle class. In this land of the lazy, we foreigners can make a fortune. Labor costs are practically nothing. These illiterates have no unions and no social guarantees. The military protects us. If the workers go on strike, just beating them up is enough. You saw what happened in María Elena. They wanted to riot and they were crushed like dirt. Besides, you could set up a store next to the factory and pay them with coupons, that way they'd have to spend whatever they made in our store, at the prices we set. The situation is ideal. Take advantage of it, Don Alejandro! With the artistic talent you have and with my business skills, we can become millionaires. If we become partners, we won't need God to help us."

Alejandro smiled, saying neither yes nor no but still working. And suddenly he whispered sweetly, moved to be speaking Yiddish again, "We'll talk this over some Wednesday, Mr. Fremberg. I have to think it over."

Shorty shrugged his shoulders. It was clear my grandfather, absorbed as he was in innovating a different style for each client, was never going to think it over. Nevertheless, once a week, Fremberg resumed his attack.

Everything seemed to have fallen into an unchanging, eternal rhythm when the letter arrived. A homeless child delivered it. He'd been given a hardboiled egg to hand the letter directly to Alejandro. Although the Professor of Shoeology was illiterate, he recognized Teresa's handwriting—Monkey Face had taught her to write. It was long, important, confidential; if not, why would his wife have gone to so much trouble? He felt a painful foreboding in his chest. Dropping his tools, he ran to the Anarchist to have him read it. The professor ran his eyes over the pages in a couple of seconds—he read at a dizzying speed—shook his bald head with sorrow, had the bell rung that called everyone to a meeting, and dragged Alejandro to the bar. In the Happy Heart, the Free Brothers and Sisters were waiting, forming a wedge around the wine barrel.

"Comrades," said the Anarchist, "this is a delicate moment in a man's life. We shall see the collapse of what he thinks is his natural identity, and we shall see another appear that is hidden under his skin, the man of heart who only awakens if he is mortally wounded. You won't understand what I'm going to read because I'm going to translate it into Russian—his wife knows Spanish. Females learn languages through a kind of osmosis, while we poor males have nothing but our awkward intellects for such tasks. But when you see the facial reactions of this friend, with whom we must sympathize deeply—the wounds caused by a woman are more painful and deep than the slash of a saber—you'll realize what it's all about." And he went on in Russian:

Dear Don Alejandro:

"Don't drink wine, but drink instead this bottle of pisco. Empty it. To withstand the letter, you will have to be very drunk. Yes, I know, your beliefs prohibit your drinking here. Today, make an exception or you may die on us. Come on, have a drink! To your health! Now I begin my translation:

Husband, I know you. You were surprised to receive a letter from me. Of course, when in person we never speak more than three or four sentences about money, the children, or your shoes, what can I tell you in writing? You've thought it must be something terrible, and you've run to the Anarchist. Now you are listening to his translation. After a few moments, you will be asking for my pity. I won't be able to give it to you. I have to tell you all at once, even if you don't believe it and you ask to have this sentence repeated several times: Seraphim and I have fallen in love, and I am his lover. It is such an intense feeling that I cannot go on living with you or the children. You and they represent my past, a time I now see submerged in darkness. I thought I loved you, but it was only an animal need, the desire for a male member, the desire to have children, instincts similar to those of cows. We joined together, but we never saw each other. I was getting fatter, growing frustrated, struggling in each one of our couplings to reach an explosive cataclysm, ferociously, inelegantly. Neither you nor I knew how to touch, to be tender, to fuse the one into the other. You were involved in your world, the Rabbi, God, the shoe factory; I was involved in mine, bread, the house, excrement, hatred for Creation; we were separated. You never knew who I was, what I had within me. You saw a brooding saint in a home that was a tomb instead of a temple. You let me get bored; my dreams meant nothing to you. We behaved like primitives, simple single-stringed instruments. We lost the spice of life, tender pleasure. I was drying up. The happiness I was missing was bloating my body. At times, I would look at other men as if they were marvelous but forbidden fruit. Guilty, hypnotized, I was drowning in you, in your void, your brutality, an unaware illiterate with no doubts about the sacrifice of the best years of my youth. I sought your eyes with mine so that we could live another life, a union outside of this world; but no, you only knew how to possess me with the fury and overwhelming power God taught you. All you could think to give me was a cruel orgasm, and there you were, thrusting your hips, great for breaking stones but not for loving a woman. You were cold and clumsy. I didn't realize it because I had neither experience nor any basis for comparison. Sunken in misery, which your righteous delusions brought upon us, what hope was left for me? But the miracle, not divine but human, exists. Love is a miracle that you couldn't see because you were only self-involved. You put me at your service, just as your father did with his wife and your father's father, obeying the Great Villain who denies above all things the magical pleasure of the flesh. It's true that in my animal state I thought I loved you, but I fell in love with Seraphim as a human being. This is something grand you don't know how to understand. Don't think I wasn't sincere, that I played you for a fool. How I would have wanted to be faithful to you until death so you wouldn't suffer, as I know you are suffering at this moment. But it is not possible to fight nature. It happened suddenly, *without premeditation, a catastrophe as great as the earthquake. When Seraphim picked us up in Valparaíso, remember, he looked at my breasts and I blushed. Without realizing it, I saw in his burning eyes my own repressed desires. His gaze reached my ovaries and filled my sex with water. I did not wish in any way for this to happen to me, especially with a creature that ugly. With a great effort, I dried myself and rejected that strange woman who was taking over my vagina. But a moment later, when I was feeding my fleas, I was overcome by an intense desire to show myself naked to him. I felt him tremble as each inch of my skin appeared, and his uncontainable lust made my cells vibrate, my blood boil. You, in some obscure way, realized that I was in heat, and you possessed me with the power of despair because, without knowing it, you already sensed I was lost forever. And you stole from me a climax that should have belonged to him, not you. That pleasure hurt me as if you'd pulled out one of my teeth. I thought I was insane, I convinced myself that the earthquake had affected my nerves and said nothing because anything to do with Seraphim seemed absurd, shameful. I went back to being what I'd always been, a mother submerged in the dull reality of the family. I went on getting to shield myself from the despair burning within. Without love, my eyes were vacant, my ears withered, my touch was harsh. Air felt poisonous, and each new day I had to cross a black bridge mounted on a blind mare. The tours with Seraphim calmed me a bit, but we did not want to recognize the mutual attraction that was wounding us. He, feeling unworthy of love, placed himself at my service, humble, vulnerable, sad, with the delicate attitude of a monster. I was convinced that he was the ugliest man I'd ever seen in my life. A week ago we performed in the Lota coal mine. The miners wanted us to go down into the deep tunnels so laughter and wisdom might reside there for once in that somber world. Seraphim performed as never before, even making magic: he was a new King Midas, except that everything he touched* turned into a banana. I felt he was saying: 'Everything is food, even pain.' Then I read only favorable predictions, giving to each of those moles the promise of air and light. They loved us a great deal, and as a sign of friendship they put their metal hats on our heads and marked our faces with soot. Back in the wagon, Seraphim looked at me, fell into convulsions, and went down on his knees before me, whispering: 'The Virgin of the Night.' I caressed his hairy nape. He crawled like a child and squirmed between my breasts. Sobbing, he asked me: 'Make the miracle, give me your holy milk.' And moved by the infinite sweetness of his voice, incredible as it sounds, my breasts began to flow, bathing his body with the white juice. Then I wept. Licking away my tears, he murmured: 'The Virgin of the Snows.' Then from my forehead blood burst out, as if a crown of thorns were being pressed into my skin. He said in a trance: 'The Virgin of Dawn.' The full moon made us silvery. 'You are mine, look at me for the first time,' he begged, and I, drunk, with my heart practically leaping out of my mouth, set my eyes on him. And instantly my prejudices vanished; I truly saw him and became aware of his sublime beauty. If Seraphim is compared with other men, and if the old standards of beauty are used, he is a monster. But if you abstract him from this setting, see him in isolation, without references, in himself, he is a perfect being. His deep eyes possess an angelic goodness, his well-delineated features move the soul, his muscular flesh and his silky fur are infinitely agreeable to the touch, his breath is sweet and very perfumed when he awakens, his movements have the grace of dance, each word he says enters my brain with the splendor of a jewel. Actually he never speaks because his voice sings. When he felt the heat of my gaze, he took off his clown suit and showed me his entire body, a living sculpture. During the ecstasy that nakedness produced in me, I held out my hands and let his sex rest on my moist palms. I was used to a voluminous, hard, insensitive member with its arrogant, naked head. Seraphim's phallus is pale, *thin, smooth, and, above all, complete. Its tender foreskin gave it a sensual secret, a modesty linked to a powerful attraction, in sum, the tranquil, animal normalcy without the knife slash of religion, with no debt to God. Whenever you penetrated me, God accompanied you. He had ordered that a piece of you be cut off so he could appropriate your pleasures. I kissed that skin with delight, and I fervently offered him all the openings of my body. Not only did my sex long for him but also my mouth, my anus, my ears, my navel, my pores, and my soul. I led him to me the way a mother leads her child, slowly. He, who'd never known a woman, gave me his celestial purity. No brutality, no haste, tenderness, sensuality, respect. When he was within me, he became the only interest in my life. Seraphim stopped moving, stopped seeking the pleasurable friction, the final discharge, and staring me fixedly in the eye, making me drunk with his breath, began to speak. His voice, the most delicate I'd ever heard in my life, revealed the feelings he'd hidden from the instant when I blushed for the first time. Listening to him that way, fulfilled, I loved him so much that I could stand, even accept, that our love united us to God. Yes, even though it may be hard for you to believe, thanks to Seraphim, to the magical pleasure he was giving me, I forgave the Great Villain because He'd allowed the existence of love. Seraphim told me, and I'll never forget his words: 'There are no limits between you and me. Our chiaroscuro origins mix together, dance in the eternal ocean. We are two screams musically in tune with each other who arise like a jewel from this death, which is nothing more than another mask of God. You and I are the joy of the Divinity made manifest in matter. Between us there exists confidence, the attainment of the sacred, the advent of hope, and the blooming of faith. We are the left and right hands of the great work that is the unification of the world and the offering of forgiveness. Through our pleasure, God is pleased to manifest His love. We are the road transformed into light. We are two solitudes that move forward perfectly intertwined. Our pleasure is a sanctuary.' And he kissed me, and his mouth was sweet. I began a chain of orgasms that grew greater and greater, like waves running through me from the beginning until the end of time. I exploded one hundred times, without guilt, without remorse, oblivious to everything except him. We giggled like mad, we wailed, we shouted, we wept with joy. From then on we haven't stopped coupling at any time of day, in any place, an uncountable number of times, all different. When his member is not submerged in my sex, I feel incomplete. We are like two bonfires that will shine for years. We want to travel, to know the Americas, Argentina, Peru, who knows what. We need little to live, and the miracle keeps going. Now I love the earth, the sky, sunrise in his arms, the taste of air, the planets, and even other human beings. I want to go to parties, enjoy myself, smoke a cigarette, be present. I lose a pound every day. Seraphim wants me agile and thin; I'm going to satisfy him. Good-bye forever, poor Alejandro. I regret the fact that you never knew how to love. Don't search for me, because the Teresa you knew no longer exists. Consider me dead. The children don't need me. I hope that they grow, that they discover.*

—Teresa Seraphim

During the reading of the letter, which the Anarchist translated in a compassionate voice, three of my grandfather's ribs, seized by pain, snapped. They sounded like rifle shots. Bloody saliva mixed with his silent tears. The bar, filled with comrades jammed around the Russian to hold him up when his knees went weak, seemed silent despite the heavy breathing, like that of a wounded bull, of my grandfather and of the soft murmur of the wise man's voice. Those poor folk understood pain and, with pitying deference, witnessed the demolition of his heart. Wine ran down their throats, gurgling like a spring. The Freckle Trainer, to sweeten the mood, began to whistle like a canary. They gave the

Professor of Shoeology large glasses of pisco to help him withstand these huge revelations. The floor began to spin, the walls let in the noise of the world, the laughter of children, the gossip of women, the clatter of broken-down vehicles, the cries of hucksters. Inside, a husband was dying; outside, the city continued on its indifferent march. Someone began to sing; another began to drum on the wine barrel; the entire block began to dance; the party exploded. From embrace to embrace, the victim, brutalized by drink, was passed around, kissing men as if they were his relatives, kissing hands that shoved him so he wouldn't dissolve in a bitter river that would empty into death. He poured out vomit, blood, and pisco, and he finally fell down in a faint. They opened his mouth with a spoon and emptied half a bottle more down his throat. He was drunk for seven days. He visited, one by one, all the rooms in the tenement and embraced every single family—the old, the young, men, women, cats. Smiling, they allowed him in because a lovesick drunk was sacred there. He destroyed his clothes and, naked, raged at the moon. He ran around on all fours with the stray dogs. He threw all his shoes into a ditch and wept, wept, wept.

When he finally recovered, he found himself in his room, with all the furniture Teresa had built reduced to a pile of broken boards. His mouth was bitter, not from alcohol but from sadness. A sadness that fastened itself to the inside of his chest like a somber crab. The images from the letter haunted him, buzzed around in his brain: his wife's moist sex receiving the phallus of a goy; her shrieking with joy, swallowing semen; her legs spread, offering herself, shaking her hips, forgetting all about him in the pleasure of being penetrated deeply by another man, younger, handsomer, more intelligent, more skillful. She, Teresa, so good, capable of giving a pure and honest caress, giving her life to a monster, giving to the monster what she never gave to him. Oh, what a stab! What a savage blow! He judged her guilty, then innocent, then he pounded his head: "It's my fault; I didn't even know how to kiss her, giving myself to the liquor of her lips; not giving her my entire soul, choosing to grant it instead to God; not caressing her; not offering her the place of a total queen; never fastening my mouth to her sex as if I were dying of thirst; making her revolve around me; drowning her in obligations; boring her; giving her an iceberg for a home; possessing her with the thrusts of a billy goat; spitting my sperm into her belly; never trembling with excitement while staring at the landscape; never sacrificing sleep so we could spend the night together just talking nonsense, smelling each other's skin, staring into each other's eyes. I've lost her. And now that she's not here, I finally know how much I loved her. I'll feel her absence for the rest of my life. I love the empty space she's left, where she is not is now my place. The light is gone."

He lost his appetite. Every day, he ate only a piece of cheese and some lettuce. His shoulders slumped, he began to swim in his clothes. He tried to hate her, but he couldn't. Then he tried to hate Monkey Face. He couldn't do that either. That innocent orphan was not guilty. In burning love, no one is guilty: it is a gift of God. He tried to be happy, thinking about Teresa's good fortune, copulating every day with a being she found so beautiful, finally enjoying her life. But the somber crab crushed his chest in its claws. He fell down amid the wreckage of the room, intent on to lie there until he died. The anarchists pounded at his door. They shouted. "Nothing!" He refused to open the door. The shoe workers came. "Nothing!" His four children came. "Nothing!" That sorrow, that humiliation—because humiliation is what it was, so great that his penis hurt, as if he'd cut it with a knife—would never diminish. Nothing tied him to life. "Nothing!"

The only person who managed to break into that room, now turned into a fortress, was the Rabbi. He took up a position inside Alejandro's mind, and no matter how much the man twisted around, spit insults, he would not move, waiting for Alejandro to wear himself out so he could be heard.

"Friend, I know your body. This disaster has withered your heart, and soon you shall die, which is what you desire. But first you must straighten matters out with God. Your pain offends Him because He, Blessed be He, knows what He is doing, and his ways are mysterious to us. You have forgotten you are a Jew. Before you die, you must return to the bosom of the community, which rejected you because of your wife. You became a goy, and just look at what's happened. As penitence, you must leave your name inscribed among the benefactors of our race. While you were drunk, I went to take a look at the synagogue. Just imagine: in this city, they pray without an authentic Torah, on parchment, copied by hand, enclosed in a luxurious ark. What a tragedy, a Jewish colony without its Holy Book! Forget your pain. Go to Argentina and bring back a true Bible. Later you can die if you wish. Your life will have served a useful purpose."

Argentina? He would have to cross the enormous mountains of the Andes on a mule, to and fro, carrying the Torah. He stood up. His entire body, his being, was looking for an excuse to go on living, to fill the universal void left by Teresa. The Rabbi was right. He would show everyone he did serve a useful purpose. By carrying out this huge task, he would regain his dignity. Perhaps Teresa would learn of his heroic act and admire him, just a little.

"No! Enough! I must not give myself hope, because it simply worsens my pain. I have to return to reality, accept the break, and carry out this act, only for myself and for God."

He left the room, sat down at his shoemaker's bench, and ignoring the joy of his workers, began to work. He would make a pair of boots lined in sheepskin for cold nights. He would never sleep again. The sadness of being abandoned, the sorrow of imagining his wife in someone else's arms, eliminated that ability. Sleep disappeared forever, and being perpetually awake made him fuzzy, as if he were living asleep. When he finished the boots, after thirty hours of ceaseless work, he had purple shadows under his sunken, veiled eyes, both present and absent, locked in themselves by the pain of existing; the merest glimpse of Teresa pierced his pupils, walking jail cells which burned like wounds.

He called Shorty Fremberg and signed a contract with him in Spanish, not one word of which he understood. Shorty assured him that everything was proper. Jews could be trusted by one another. He would take charge of the organization, of charging fees and distributing the money, as usual. Alejandro would leave him a collection of shoe models, along with the addresses of his clients. About the children, he didn't have to concern himself. A friend of his would care for them.

My grandfather asked an empanada maker to give him the dog skins he'd been hiding. He used them to make a long overcoat. With only a walking stick and without a penny to his name—his meager savings had been entrusted to Fremberg for the twins in case of a fatal accident—he started out for Viña del Mar with the intention of moving on to Quillota, Llay-Llay, Río Blanco, Portillo, Paso del Bermejo, crossing the Andes, and continuing on along the vast Argentine valley to Mendoza. From there he would make his way to Buenos Aires. Would that be about twelve hundred miles on foot? He didn't know and it didn't matter to him. How long would it take? He no longer had time; it had escaped him. He lived outside of time.

He covered long distances, eating the blackberries that grew alongside the road. He also found pomegranates, figs, and apples. Some carts carried him over short stretches, but his bizarre figure inspired fear, and the peasants preferred to avoid contact. Children hounded him, pelting him with stones, while others gave him water and fresh eggs. He walked by day, he walked by night, hearing his heart beat with ever-greater clarity. How it pained him! He tried not to think about her, but like a cruel wasp she pursued him with unbearable images and sting him. Another man's saliva in her mouth. *God help me!* White sperm, thick with passion, flowing over her vulva. *God help me!* Comparing the perfection of the other man's teeth with his, which were yellow and chipped. *God help me!* She sleeping, extenuated, satisfied, with her lover's testicles in her hand. *God help me!* She, giving herself completely over to him running behind him like a lamb following its mother. *God help me!* Walk, walk. Try to forget.

Filthy, bearded, covered with dust, he was becoming a ghost. So the authorities wouldn't arrest him, he walked in shadows, hunched over, febrile. Finally, he took the road to the mountain range. Unable to find wild fruit to sate his hunger pangs, he ate butterflies, flies, ants, worms, scarabs, and spiders. The sky covered over with clouds, and the night grew darker. Seeing practically nothing, he felt his way along, looking for the paths upward. When the moon was full, he found himself surrounded by snowcapped peaks. The insidious wind blew. Stones and more stones. Nothing seemed to live there, aside from the cold. His lined boots and the dog skin coat were not enough to keep him alive. He might have frozen to death, but jealous fire in his gut saved him. Even though it was impossible for him to hate her—she was right—there was fury and sorrow in his heart, a surge of pain that became a fever. He kept moving forward, against the frost, the wind, the snow, the frozen downpours, against the intense pain in his legs, which, in any case, was less than the pain in his soul. He got lost. Days later, his stomach empty and his throat dry, he fell between some rocks, dying of exhaustion. He summoned the Rabbi.

"You got me into this. I want to finish what I started, so make a miracle."

"There is only one miracle, Alejandro. The miracle of faith! Don't give in. Believe until the very last. As long as you have even a thread of life, there is hope. Keep at it. If you are breathing, it is because God is helping you."

Alejandro smiled bitterly. "Of course, God is helping me." Then he heard the footfalls of animals and barking. Three enormous wild dogs lunged toward him, leaping over the rocks, their fangs bared, ready to destroy him. The Rabbi let out a nervous, embarrassed laugh. But he repeated, "Have faith!" and fled to the Interworld. My grandfather was furious. The attack was the last straw. He was being persecuted too much: he'd had everything taken away from him, he'd been rejected, emasculated, sunk into the grave, and now, to finish things off, the dogs were going to eat him. Well, why not? Did he deserve a dignified death? A contemptible nothing, he couldn't even make the mother of his own children love him? He wasn't worth any more than a dog, so he would act like a dog.

By now the wild beasts, snapping at him, were getting close. He suddenly went down on all fours, showed his teeth, and, shaking himself, bellowed out deafening howls with such rage that the echoes caused a far-off avalanche. Surprised, the three dogs stopped, their fur standing on end, and stared at him, growling. The crazed shoemaker barked again and charged toward them, thirsty for blood. He wanted to rip open their bellies with his teeth and pull out guts—not theirs, but through them, God's. The three dogs retreated. He called them, sobbing, chased them for a mile, wanted to die taking their lives, wanted to show the Supreme Being what His cruelty had made of him.

The dogs scattered, jumping over the ridges, and my grandfather sat down on the stony path and buried his bearded face in his hands, ashamed of his hatred for the Maker. When his breathing returned to normal and the silence of the mountains showed him the bitterness of his infinite solitude, something rubbed against his legs. It was the dogs, returning to accept him as their master. They wagged their tails, they licked him, they frolicked around him, humbly awaiting a pet.

"A miracle!" shouted the jubilant Rabbi. "We'll call them Kether, Chokhmah, and Binah, like the three first *sephirot* of the Tree of Life!"

Alejandro growled. The Rabbi, hanging his head, returned to his astral hideaway. "I'll call them Joy, Sadness, and Indifference," said my grandfather. Worn out, he could barely pat their backs. He slept deeply, as he hadn't slept for weeks. When he awoke, there were the dogs, looking as if they were smiling. And at his feet, a huge, dead hare. With a sharp knife, he skinned it, divided it into four parts, and shared it with his new friends. After they devoured even the bones, they went to lick snow from a peak.

Alejandro continued his march. Joy, Sadness, and Indifference took charge of feeding him, and after a great deal of whining, they forced him to rest, protecting him with the heat of their bodies while he remained awake and they slept. To banish the images of Teresa—who he saw more and more in love with Monkey Face, sniffing his armpits, swallowing liters of his semen, allowing herself to be sodomized, staring at the reflection of the stars in his eyes—he began to pray, using the rhythm of his heartbeats. "I-am-yours-Have mer-cy-u-pon-me." From that moment on, he never stopped repeating these words twenty-four hours a day. The pain remained, curled up behind his ribs, but now it didn't bother him as much.

One night he met a group of men mounted on mules. They had machetes hanging at their waists and rifles hanging from their saddles. One got down to touch him. He wanted to take Alejandro's coat and boots, but their smell made him grimace.

The man asked the one who seemed to be the chief, "Should I cut his throat?"

The robber answered, "Better leave him alone. He's a madman. Jesus protects madmen because he was mad, too. Ask him to bless us."

"Hear that, you holy bastard? Bless us!"

Alejandro, who did not understand what they were saying, spread his arms with his hands held out to show he understood nothing. The thieves took his gesture as a sacred sign, crossed themselves, and went their way. Alejandro realized he would rather they had murdered him. He was no longer the man he was. He'd lost himself. The wound was eating him up. He tried to see himself and found instead a complete stranger.

Bit by bit, he forgot Russian and Yiddish. Actually, he simply stripped himself of those languages as if they were dead skin. He no longer thought, only prayed with the beat of his heart. He barked. A dog among dogs, he scavenged for eagle eggs, ate lizards and snakes, drank in muddy puddles. Finally, he reached the end of the mountains and the beginning of the Argentine pampa. Joy, Sadness, and Indifference stood on the last rock, raised their muzzles to the sky, and howled as if someone had died. They were mountain animals and could not survive on the flat lands. The peasants would shoot them dead. My grandfather also howled to express his sorrow at saying good-bye. Then he pulled three pieces of skin out of the inside of his overcoat, from the sweatiest parts, and tossed them to his comrades. Each one caught his in the air, and carrying it in his teeth, went back to the mountains.

Once again, Alejandro was alone. He prayed with more intensity, adding "I-put-my-faith-in-you" to his cardiac rhythm. From there to Mendoza and from Mendoza to Buenos Aires he did not feel the road. He traversed it sleeping awake. He passed through cornfields, vineyards, apple orchards, rivers, creeks. Some peasants, seeing him pass by making the bubbling sounds of a mute or a moron, gave him pieces of bread, dry meat, and yerba maté. People regarded him with superstitious deference. They let him pass, crossed themselves, and from time to time a rider would gallop to catch up to him and toss a bottle of milk or wine. He reached Buenos Aires not knowing if he'd been walking for days, weeks, or months. A cloud of flies, like a black mist, surrounded him, endlessly biting him. Tired of brushing them off, he let them settle on his face, so his eyelids were covered with them. That way, asking from a distance because the people held their noses, he reached the Israelite Club, site of the synagogue.

At first, confusing him for one of the many vagrants who came from the hinterlands to beg in the capital, they tried to throw him out, drenching him with a garden hose. But when, with the help of the Rabbi, he began to recite from memory, word for word, the first tome of the Talmud, they understood he was a compatriot. That caused a stir. The Jewish colony, concerned about showing the Argentines a good face, was ashamed of this pariah. They bought him clothing and offered him towels, soap, scissors for his hair, and free access to the baths. He rejected all of it. He remained at the door of the synagogue, reciting now the second tome of the Talmud.

A young rabbi opened a window and asked him directly, "What's your name? Where do you come from? What do you want?"

My grandfather could not answer the first two questions, because he'd forgotten his name and his past. The third glowed like an ember of fire in his consciousness: "I want one of the two Torahs you possess for the synagogue in Santiago de Chile."

The young rabbi laughed. "Is that all? It is true we have two. I suppose you want to buy it. It's expensive. Very old. It was brought here from Poland."

"I'll pay with my labor."

"You could work twelve hours a day for the rest of your life, and you still wouldn't make enough."

"I'll work twenty-four hours a day."

"No more jokes. I can do nothing. The Rebbe is locked away studying the commentaries of Rashi to the Holy Book and won't appear in public for two months."

"I'll wait here."

The decision was final. How would the dignified members of the Club react to seeing a lunatic like this one stretched out on the synagogue stairs? Expelling him by force was impossible: he was a Jew, and a wise Jew, because he was now reciting the third book of the Talmud. He consulted with two other young rabbis. They offered him a room and three meals a day. He didn't accept, but, making a titanic effort, spoke to them in Yiddish: "Do you have guard dogs?"

"Of course."

"Then I want to sleep and eat with those animals. Whatever you give them will be fine for me."

No one could change his mind. He responded to every argument by continuing his recitation of the Talmud. When they heard him reach the fourth book, they gave in and let him move into the kennel. The dogs, perhaps because of his coat, received him as a brother.

There, for two months, praying with his heartbeats, he remained, curled up without closing his eyes, gnawing on bones, scraps, and lefto-ver food. Sometimes, when Teresa reappeared before him, naked, with a hot, ecstatic face, he would explode in desperate howls that knocked him out. The young rabbis, thinking he was howling from hunger, tossed him pieces of raw meat, which he swallowed without chewing, as dogs do, perhaps hoping to choke to death.

The Rebbe finished his annual reading of Rashi's commentaries and visited the synagogue, his face luminous, wearing beautiful clothes, doused in cologne. The inspection satisfied him: his helpers kept the place orderly, without a speck of dust in the corners. He decided to check the patio, where the kennels were, to see if they'd received the same treatment. The young men began to tremble. They hadn't dared to tell him about the smelly madman in a cloud of flies who was now reciting the fourteenth book of the Talmud.

When the Rebbe entered, Alejandro stood up tall and straight and, eyes burning, stretched his hands out so far it seemed he wanted to pull his arms from their sockets.

"I want one of the two Torahs for the synagogue in Santiago de Chile."

The old man turned pale and burst into tears. Not thinking about the grime or the flies, he embraced the scarecrow, to the complete surprise of the other rabbis. "Winding and strange are the roads of God. Last night, I fell asleep next to the Scriptures, blessed be they, and I dreamed that a being, half-man and half-dog, emerged from the scrolls. A voice ordered me: 'Do not disdain my emissary, because he is the crown of my heart! Give him what he asks! Through the mouths of the mad I speak!'"

Alejandro left Buenos Aires mounted on a mule, carrying the Holy Book wrapped in fine blankets inside a luxurious box. By order of the Rebbe, he was given two more mules loaded with sausages and all sorts of kosher food of long duration. He retraced the same road he'd used to reach Buenos Aires, only stopping to rest his mules. Very often he shared his food with tramps that were walking over the pampa, going nowhere in particular. Bored, they abandoned their work and began to travel the world with empty pockets. There was something in them—perhaps the humble peace of forlorn hearts—that gave Alejandro a bit of calm.

It was night when he reached the foot of the Andes, his food sacks almost empty. The two extra mules were now a useless burden. He saw a farmhouse where a candle flickered. He approached the house to give away the mules. No one came out to receive him. He pushed the door open and entered. On a miserable cot lay a whining woman. Alejandro touched her forehead: it was burning. He summoned the Rabbi. "You know medicine. Help me cure her. This woman represents Teresa. Perhaps she, somewhere in the world, is also suffering."

The Rabbi examined the woman. "It's very serious. Contagious. You could catch the illness."

"No. It's a human sickness, and I'm a dog."

They spent a week with the woman, reducing her fever by placing cold, wet rags on her abdomen. They gave her liters of juice made from herbs the Rabbi picked on the rocky terrain. When her temperature fell too low and she began to tremble, Alejandro took her in his arms and slept with her. He gave her the tenderness he never knew how to give his wife. On the eighth day, the woman regained consciousness. She was a widow, without children, who had just buried her husband.

Without waiting for any thanks, my grandfather pointed to the two mules, made a gift-giving gesture and then another of farewell, and went off on foot, leading the mule carrying the Torah. After a few minutes, he heard the footsteps of the woman. She was running toward him, barefoot, carrying something wrapped in a blanket. When she reached him, she unwrapped the package and offered him a lacquered-wood cross with a Christ. While Alejandro did not want to take it, she tied it to the ropes holding the Torah and ran off.

My grandfather wanted to get rid of that sacrilegious doll, but he noticed that at its bleeding feet was an inscription in Hebrew. He asked the Rabbi to translate it.

The Rabbi read in Russian, "Father, why have you abandoned me?" Then he corrected himself: "My God, why have you forsaken me?" Alejandro stifled a heartrending wail and continued on his way, keeping the crucifix but wrapping it in the blanket the woman had left behind. Leaping among the snow-covered rock came Joy, Sadness, and Indifference. For the dogs, it was a moment of almost unbearable happiness. They trembled, stuck out their tongues, rubbed against Alejandro's boots, whipped him with their wagging tails, put their paws on his chest, covered his face with saliva. Suddenly they ran toward a cave and, after looking around inside, returned at top speed, each one with his piece of Alejandro's coat in his jaws. Their master kept them as gifts, and they went on together along the steep trail. They brought him what they'd hunted, and he divided it into four equal parts.

They were passing through a narrow gorge, when a rain and windstorm broke out. In a single downpour, entire lakes fell. Torrents of muddy water like giant spider feet leapt over the rocks. To protect the Holy Book, Alejandro, guided by his dogs, took refuge in a crevice and unloaded the mule. The cave was immense, and the light of a candle was shining in its black depths.

There were the robbers, waiting for the storm to pass. They approached my grandfather with mocking smiles on their faces: "The old lunatic again. It seems he likes the pure mountain air. He should be more careful. After all, he's already lost his head, and he just might lose his guts. There are beasts that get pleasure from tearing people up. Ha, ha!"

They patted the mule. They looked over the bundle next to it.

"Well, well, old boy, it looks as if you got rich. What's in this big package and in this little one? Presents for us?"

They unwrapped the Torah. They opened the box, which was encrusted with gold, their brutal faces shining with greed. The Hebrew letters made them step back. Their illiterate instincts recognized the power of those letters.

"I think this is witchcraft," one of them muttered. They opened the small package. By the light of the candle, the Christ revealed his pain. The lacquered finish resisted the water that penetrated the blanket, but the red paint, perhaps of a different quality, was dissolving. Like drops of blood, it ran from of the wounds on Jesus's forehead and side, from his hands and feet. The thieves fell to their knees. The chief whispered, "I told you this madman was a saint. Now I think he's also a wizard. He's got the wounds of our Lord."

The cold had split open the skin on Alejandro's forehead and the palms of his hands. He opened his arms like the crucified Jesus and gave himself over to the murderers. Ever since God had forsaken him, he felt pierced by lances, nails, and thorns. Without Teresa, his soul was bleeding like Christ's body. The two of them, the figurine and the man, were one. The same disappointment bound them. If they wanted to gut him, they should do it now. After all, his mission was a failure. These men without faith would use the crucifix and the Holy Book to make a fire to keep warm.

"The storm is calming down. Let's get out of here before Heaven gives us the punishment we deserve."

The thieves left six apples at Alejandro's feet, along with a bottle of wine and a piece of dried beef. They disappeared in the mountain shadows. My grandfather hugged the Christ against his chest and fell asleep with it in his arms, covered himself by Joy, Sadness, and Indifference. He woke up three days later. The sky was clear and a splendiferous sun transformed the wild flowers into jewels. Everywhere the yellow was bursting into bloom, and the buzzing of bees, multiplied by the echo, transformed the morning into a festival. On the ground were three dead hares, and his friends, wagging their tails, were waiting for their portion.

Alejandro, perhaps because he was rested, felt a bit better. The pain was gone from his guts, but despite even the drunken triumph of nature, a heavy sorrow overtook him, as if his lungs were full of oil. He gave each dog a dead hare, and he contented himself by sucking on a round stone. He realized he would never again be able to eat red meat. Not understanding why, he thought it felt like devouring Teresa. With great tenderness, he carried the Jesus to the highest peak and positioned it facing the immense landscape.

"My friend, I bless the Earth just as you blessed it. And also like you, I bless humanity. Someday our sacrifice will be useful. You are made of wood. I know that soon you will set down roots and then branches, leaves, flowers, and fruits. I'm leaving, but I'll still be here with you."

My grandfather scrambled down from the peak, jumping from rock to rock like a wild dog, and then went on his way. He again ate insects and nettles. His skin took on a greenish cast. Catching his reflection in a puddle, he discovered his mane of hair and beard had turned white. As he descended the mountains toward the Chilean side, the three dogs barked, demanding their pieces of overcoat. He handed them over, covering the dogs with kisses. Then he closed his eyes so he would not see them head off towards the peaks. Carried forward only by gravity, he walked blindly. When he opened his eyes, it was already getting dark. Since the mule needed rest, he camped under a fig tree, fighting with all his strength to keep the scent of the ripe fruit from restoring his taste for life.

At dawn he moved on. He fell into a kind of trance. Neither asleep nor awake, he advanced as effortlessly as the wind. At dawn one day, he reached Santiago, crossed half the city, and knocked at the door of the synagogue. A fat watchman in a nightshirt and bowler hat opened the door, thinking that at this hour it could only be a telegram bearing bad news. In Yiddish, with enormous effort because his tongue felt like wood, my grandfather stuttered, "Adonai sends this holy present to the Chilean Jewish community. Wake up the Rebbe and inform him that the Torah he lacked has arrived."

"But who are you?"

"No one. It's the wind speaking. I am a dream of God."

And Alejandro went off, making leaps and waving his arms, relieved to have fulfilled his mission. The watchman, his eyes shrouded by rheum, watched him fly. The dog fur of the overcoat looked like feathers to him. He ran to get the Rebbe out of bed, to tell him that an angel had brought them the precious scroll from Heaven. Later the religious folk whispered that it was Moses himself who came to bring them the Divine Book.

Alejandro had no need for recognition. All he wanted was to get back to the tenement and submerge himself forever in the making of his shoes. He did not find the sign that read SOCIETY OF FREE BROTHERS AND SISTERS. WE ARE NOT THE STATE. In its place was another: GRAND FACTORY OF WARSAW FOOTWEAR.

The day was growing brighter. In his room, the four children were sleeping naked, in the company of a dozen cats. Alejandro watched them with tears in his eyes. Asleep like that, they looked healthy, bigger. The girls already had brilliant bosoms blossoming. On Fanny's pubis tiny red hairs were growing. He saw the leftovers from dinner: beans, cheese, pork chops. He felt like throwing up. He sat in the doorway to wait for day to finally come.

No sooner had the first rays of sunlight shone like gold through his white beard than a chauffeur-driven car deposited Shorty Fremberg outside the tenement. Shorty checked the three gold watches on his wrist, hastily opened a box set in the wall, and pulled a whistle. The doors of the rooms shook like filthy tongues, and two hundred women wearing blue uniforms emerged to greet the boss. Then they went back into their cells and the dry rumble of machines resumed. Alejandro grabbed Fremberg by his lapels and shook him. He had to bend over to do it, because he was tall and the Pole nearly a dwarf.

"Machines? Whistles? Uniforms? Where is the Anarchist? The Free Brothers and Sisters? What happened to the Happy Heart Bar?"

"Let go of me, Alejandro. This is legal, and there's nothing you can do about it. It's very clearly stated in the contract you signed that I am the one who decides everything. You earn the same salary as a regular employee— without doing anything, if that's what you'd like. Wake up to reality, artist! We're living in 1912, the Industrial Era! People no longer want handmade products. Machines are the present and the future. Open your eyes! You're not in some village! You're living in a great capital city! Around here no one wants to be a saint, and the only God is money! Anarchist dreams are over. The police came and kicked your friends out. I think the most fanatical were shipped to Easter Island. I've rented the entire tenement. In each room there are sewing machines or electric saws to cut leather, make heels. It's a marvel. The orders just keep pouring in. We make hundreds of pairs of shoes every day. And the women we have working follow orders! For three pesos they work a ten and a half hour day with no right to any social benefits. If an agitator turns up, I have him arrested. What do you think? Lose that cemetery face and be happy. Your children are well, though I almost never see them. They only turn up to eat and sleep, but they look healthy and happy. What more do you want? You can work or not, but you get a salary either way. And that's not all you should thank me for: I kept your room just as it was. I could have put a machine in it."

From then on, Alejandro said nothing. He sat at his bench, surrounded by the mechanical screeching, and made shoes by hand and to order for the few clients he still had. Few not because his work wasn't of interest but because he was so stubbornly insistent on making perfect shoes that it could take him a year to make one pair. He would put them together, make corrections, take them apart, start all over again, incessantly, never satisfied. The buyers, fed up with coming back to try them on so many times, ended up not coming back at all. The perfect pairs of shoes, covered with dust, were stacked in a corner of the room.

Shorty Fremberg was moved. He could not stand to see his partner sunken into such solitude. Now he had six gold watches, two cars, a chalet on the outskirts of the city, and four lovers, drawn from among the workers, who went along with his caprices for a pittance.

"Come on, Alejandro. You're wasting your time. Perfection is not of this world. Accept that reality has changed. Come along and take a look with me. You'll see just how beautiful our machines are. And sometimes the girls who run them, too. You're still young. Not even fifty yet. Make an effort."

And the Pole pulled my grandfather along by the hand toward the end of the corridor, to the room where the bar had been. He wanted to proudly show him the machine that cut patterns into the leather. It was run by Fresia, the youngest of Shorty's lovers, thirteen years old, freckled, and with big eyes.

"Why don't you try to work it, Alejandro? You'll see how easy and gratifying it is. You push a couple of buttons and the pattern engraves itself. Try it, please. Let's see now, Fresia, let this gentleman take your place!"

Fresia showed my grandfather how to produce the finished pattern and left him sitting at the machine while she followed Shorty behind a

curtain to give him the oral satisfaction he'd demanded with an imperious gesture with his pudgy fingers. Just as he was ejaculating a flood of
warm magma into the young lady's throat, he heard a howl. The machine
coughed as if clogged up. Fresia and Shorty quickly ran over. They found
Alejandro faint, his right hand caught in the machinery. To get it out
they had to take much of the machine apart. My grandfather woke up
in the hospital in intense pain. The doctors requested authorization to
amputate his hand, but Alejandro refused.

He went back to the tenement with his hand hanging at his side, dead.
He sat in his doorway and stayed there, mute, not even communicating
with his children. Fremberg continued to send Bertita, one of his lovers,
a woman of forty with whiskers and the backside of a mare, to cook for
the children. They would arrive like famished shadows, eat, and then
go back out into the streets. Alejandro, in another world, gave nothing,
asked for nothing. When it began to grow dark, he would light a candle
and, with a nimble movement of his left hand, catch moths in order to
devour them. One morning, they found the doorway empty. No one in
the tenement could imagine where he'd gone. He returned after midday
and sat down again, but something had changed in his eyes. An intense
fire was burning in his pupils. On the back of his paralyzed hand, he'd
had the machine tattoo a heart and inside it the name TERESA.

The first people to realize that Alejandro could work miracles were
the homeless children. One fell at his feet, twisted in pain after eating
garbage. Alejandro put his dead hand on the child's stomach, and the pain
disappeared. A few days later, a boy with mange on his legs appeared.
The dead hand cured him too. The rumor began to spread. A little girl
brought her cat, crushed by an automobile. The cat recovered. A boy
showed him his face covered with pimples dripping pus. After five minutes of the cold contact, he walked off with clear skin.

Adults began coming. They submitted to his paralyzed hand tumors,
fevers, impotence, all kinds of physical disorders. With a sweet smile,

always mute, Alejandro would slowly raise his right hand, kiss the tattooed heart, and place it with a profound, humble delicacy on the sick parts, which always healed. A fetus, condemned to be born breech, he made turn around and emerge headfirst.

He accepted no payment, no money, objects, flowers, or food. Hearing the words "thank you" made him close his eyes and blanch. His love for Teresa had overflown the dikes and spread now toward all of humanity. Because he understood better than anyone what pain was, he was able to ease depression, jealousy, rage, and hatred. A mere touch of his hand to an ailing chest and that person left with new hope. Alejandro stayed for two years in that miserable doorway, curing without interruption every sick person who asked for help.

The Rabbi had nothing to do with those miracles. His journey had brought him to sainthood. Out of discretion, the Rabbi left him alone during that time, but he now had sad news to deliver: "Dear Alejandro, the final moment has come. Your heart has deteriorated completely. You are going to die."

"I'm ready. I've lived all I had to live because God taught me to love. For great evils we need great remedies. I was a man of stone; He made me feel pain. I am infinitely grateful."

After breaking his silence, he asked that the machine be removed, that his bed be brought into what had been the Happy Heart Bar, and that they place a big barrel of wine next to him. He went to bed and entered into a placid decay. The worker girls and their companions began to arrive and drink in a huddle, as in the old days. The Anarchist, who had been in hiding, suddenly appeared wearing dark glasses to hide his missing eye. He said nothing, but on his knees alongside Alejandro's cot, he kissed the dead hand.

The bar began to fill up with wildflowers. They forced their way through tiny cracks in the cement and covered the grayness with a multicolored blanket. Benjamín, Lola, Fanny, and Jaime, accompanied by Fremberg and his four girlfriends, entered, nicely combed, clean, and sad. Alejandro smiled. The Rabbi told him, "At the end everything returns." Alejandro smiled again. The crowd parted slowly in order not to trample the flowers. A slim silhouette hesitated at the door. The children shouted "Mama!" and ran to clutch her in their avid arms. Teresa's head was shaved, she was skin and bones, dressed as a man, and wearing no makeup. She did not cry, but tears ran ceaselessly down her torpid face, a face you'd say was paralyzed.

Alejandro extended his right hand, and his inert hand came to life. The white fingers recovered the color of living flesh and, losing their cold, moved slowly to call Teresa. The woman approached without separating herself from the children and, on her knees, placed her face in the revived hand. Alejandro touched her devotedly, trying to give the hollow of his hand the sweetness of a cradle. He whispered:

"I'm not going to forgive you, because there is no evil to forgive. You obeyed life. Everything natural is good. Your soul is pure light. I thank you for existing. Don't tell me why you've returned. There's no more time. You've come, and that's enough. I am going to die for you, not because of you. You became my teacher. The only thing I did well in this world was to learn to love you. I depart satisfied. Don't put my name on my grave. I want a simple stone with a six-pointed star. In the center of the two interlaced triangles have inscribed: I AM MY BELOVED'S AND MY BELOVED IS MINE."

Teresa kissed his forehead. My grandfather smiled again and let go of his soul. The Rabbi, nervous, shouted to him, "Wait! Hold out a little longer! You want to go, but I want to stay here. The eternal nothingness is not for me. Pass me on!"

"Pass you on?"

"That's right! I am your best inheritance: Tradition. Give me to one of your children."

"To which one?"

"The way things are going, your twin girls will never be mothers, and Benjamín will die chaste. The only one who will be able to pass me on to one of his children is Jaime."

Alejandro signed to Jaime that he should come close. Jaime was not moved. A dull resentment kept him from suffering. He'd often tried to approach his father, always crashing against a barrier of incomprehension. They were different, and that was that. Jaime had the right to not want to be a just man. In a society of thieves and exploiters, egoism was not only allowed but it was also the only intelligent thing a person could do. Nevertheless, once, to please his father, Jaime took on the task of making a pair of boots. For three months, in secret, he dedicated himself to that painful work. The result was not unworthy of Alejandro himself. Proud of himself, he showed his father his work and expected that after the congratulations he would keep the boots in a dresser as a souvenir. That did not happen. The next day, his father sold them to a poor client for an absurdly low price.

"Good shoes should be on feet and not in a dresser. We don't make them to exalt ourselves but to serve. Remember, son, serving is the greatest human value."

Jaime never forgave him. He felt that Alejandro held his work in contempt; that he refused to give him the recognition he deserved. He swore he'd never again make a shoe, never again serve anyone.

"Come here, my son."

He's going to give me a farewell kiss, but what good is it to me now when he never did it before. I would have preferred kisses that began something, not kisses that end things. "I'm coming, father."

He pressed his lips together and brought his face close to that of the dying man. Alejandro, with his resuscitated hand, took hold of Jaime's nape and immobilized his head. Following the Rabbi's instructions, he fastened his mouth around Jaime's nose and breathed, a final, long, interminable breath. The Rabbi entered through Jaime's nostrils into his spirit. Alejandro died. Jaime fell to the floor, writhing in rage and screaming: "I don't want your madness! No! I don't want it! Get out of me, you shitty ghost!"

A pale old woman, waving a newspaper, came to announce that war had broken out in Europe.

Teresa no longer wanted to think about her children. Never again did she bathe or leave the small apartment Shorty Fremberg had given her in exchange for the percentage of Warsaw that belonged to her husband. She spent her time staring out the window into nothingness. If she spoke, it was only to curse, keeping secret the name of the person she was cursing. Fanny, Lola, and Jaime, tired of her incessant bad humor, looked, each on his or her own, for some way to earn a living. Soon they stopped visiting. Benjamín could put up with being mistreated and worked as a salesman in a bookstore so he could feed his mother. They began to sleep together in the same bed.

Lola began to study guitar with the blind woman in Room 28. The old woman knew many songs and went from bar to bar offering her broken-down voice. The drunken patrons, overwhelmed with sorrows of the heart, requested melodies that would remind them of the women who betrayed them, and she always knew the songs. An astonishing memory. Lola, late at night, turned into a guide dog, and accompanied the old woman from bar to bar and singing duets.

Jaime became violent, rejecting the appearances of the Rabbi with epileptic fits. González the Horse, mentally retarded, with a long face, thick lips, and enormous teeth, formerly a champion boxer, accepted him as a student. The boy's aggressive energy enabled him to win good money in that sport. He took part in clandestine bouts: before dog fights, the organizers would present two or three fights between boys, because they were popular with homosexual bettors.

The Horse had very personal training methods. He would go with Jaime to the potter's field at the Public Cemetery to steal skulls. Then, in

Room 35, completely painted white, with posters and trophies covering the walls, which was now transformed into a gym, he would have his student demolish skulls with his fists. "Remember: your punches must pass through flesh, which is illusion, to break the real bones." Every feint or duck provoked musings that, despite the alcohol-soaked voice and cross-eyed diction, taught Jaime how to fight against that fierce enemy, life.

Fanny accepted that Ruby of the Street, the tenement prostitute, should educate her. The sensual dwarf informed her: "With that red hair, that body, and that face, your future is secure. You've got long legs, full lips, a curly pubis, firm breasts, and a round ass, which is to say, you've got everything! All you need is to learn to know men. By knowing them you'll be able to dominate them. Understanding what they're made of, you become their mother. You'll appear docile, and they'll think that they're the boss, but in fact they'll obey orders. And the best way to drag them around by the nose is to give them sexual pleasure. I'm going to teach you all the techniques. You're just a girl, but you'll memorize everything I tell you, and later it will be precious to you, pure gold. Each penis is different and has a special way of getting satisfaction. You will become pliable, malleable, supple. You won't be just one woman but thousands, and your muscles and orifices will be proficient in giving the maximum pleasure. And you won't disdain the use of certain objects. From this moment on, I'll hide you in my armoire, and looking through a little hole you'll see what I do with my clients. If you clean off the soot, every man is a diamond."

Fanny was so interested in this apprenticeship that she decided to become the best whore in Chile.

Teresa never told why she came back until, many years later, Benjamín punched her in the face, fed up with her bad behavior and absurd rage.

Then he tied her to the bed, and using a pail he forced her to swallow half a liter of vodka. The alcohol finally loosened her tongue.

"After sending your father that letter in which I announced our break, I forgot, I must confess, the whole family. I felt as if a dead skin had fallen off my body, allowing me to be born again. For forty days, I stopped having sexual relations with my lover, and I stretched out in the darkness of the wagon to wait for a new hymen to grow within me. I got up free, perfectly sealed. At that moment, we were passing through a tiny village called Las Ventanas. From the street came the smells of bread and wine. Everything in me then was virginal, even my sense of smell. Those perfumes of wheat and grape, transformed by baking and fermentation into sacred food and elixir, moved me profoundly. I wanted with the totality of my being to receive Seraphim's sperm to make a perfect son, the fruit of love, not like you and Benjamín, the fruit of obligation.

"Seraphim did not behave as I saw him—an angel sent by God, who had to cross the entire Universe to reach the stable where I awaited him naked, offering him my thirsty chalice; who slipped through the drone of galaxies being born, galloped over careening comets, and fell into the dense matter of the Earth, engrossed by a core more brilliant than the sun, my interior light. Instead, he insisted on being a monkey, hanging by his feet from a tree, his head hanging down, and he squealed with rage: 'You're mocking me, Teresa. No woman can desire to have a child with me, ever. Another monster would be born.'

"'I do want to have your child! To shine, I have abolished pain. Now, in this place, I am what I am, nameless, without care, a flower open in the present, saturated with love down to the last particle of flesh, which is meaningless by itself. Have faith in my open sex: enter it totally to give content to my empty form.'

"'That love of yours, immense as it is, is not enough to convince me that deformity is beauty.'

"'Who will you believe: those who despise you, or me? If you let yourself be guided by what they think, you are your own worst enemy. Stop hating yourself and accept the miracle! We are two candles on the altar. Our son will be a god. I want him to look like you.'

"I took a branch and broke it from the tree like a ripe fruit. He fell on me, biting, scratching, expelling his insides, the black ocean heaving in my ovaries swallowing up his his passionate liquor with a squeal of pain-pleasure, collapsing exhausted next to my bosom to sleep for nine months. I wanted to conceive with such intensity that I felt clearly the moment when his sperm fertilized me. In the depth of my womb, a point of immense energy vibrated. It opened like a door to another dimension, letting in a river formed of millions of universes. All my flesh, in the presence of that potent flash, felt the drowning of death, the anguish of having lived in the shadows, separated. That new energy flooded my bones, my guts, my blood, purifying and fortifying each cell, eliminated the impurities and pain. My movements became delicate, careful: I was the coffer that held within itself a diamond. I believed I saw a cluster of bright rays emerge from my womb to illuminate the sordid wagon. I was overwhelmed by an epochal peace. Like a bird that begins its migration, my spirit emerged from the rot.

"Soon that divine being would nourish itself from my flesh: I had to reach total extinction before I could offer it a substance produced in the light of forgiveness. To forgive, I had to understand, and understanding meant recognizing essential love. I rediscovered God as never before and stopped seeing him as a murderer. Being Everything, He cannot end. And if we give up our solitude to submerge ourselves in Him, we shall not die. I separated from José, my poor drowned son. For many years I had not let him go, turning him into my accomplice in my hatred of the Father.

"I let him dissolve in the Divine Beginning and I felt him become part of the new being. With indomitable faith, absolute confidence, supreme calm, I opened myself to listen fully. That child was not the confirmation of my existence. He was himself and for himself. He directed, he knew. In complete ignorance, I was there only to obey. My vagina—my uterus, my tubes, my ovaries, full of God—were bearing the savior of the world. Meanwhile, Seraphim went on sleeping. In his dreams, he told me later, some kind of wise carpenter appeared, kind and noble, making a cradle out of wood from trees that flew in from the four corners of the Earth.

"As my belly grew, I felt the child's spirit more and more. He communicated with me, and my pelvic bones responded by separating to prepare a perfect exit. An immense joy invaded my body. My lungs took in polluted air and exhaled pure oxygen: through them, my son was cleansing the planet. As he was becoming incarnate, the heart of the world was forming.

"The seven trained fleas made me enough money to survive. During those nine months, Seraphim neither drank nor ate, sleeping next to me, wrapped up like another fetus. I gave myself over to that marvelous symphony of sensations that is gestation; I did not feel the passage of time. It began to rain fiercely. The huge drops crashing against the clay made the sticky noise of exploding frogs. The sun came out. A white crow brought me a branch of cinnamon.

"The moment of birth had arrived. 'These are the last moments when you are within me. We shall have to separate. Bless me.' Yes, I asked the fetus to bless me because, since he was infinitely superior to me, it did not fall to me to do it. Grabbing a rope that hung from the ceiling, I hunkered down to deliver. I said to him, 'From now on, you are you, and I am me. Let's work together. Between the two of us we're going to carry out a perfect birthing.'

"'Make that three!' exclaimed Seraphim, who woke up at that moment. He got down right in front of my spread thighs and held out his hands to keep the child from falling to the floor. Trembling, he tried not to close his eyes, not to retreat again into sleep, heroically facing his fear of seeing a monster emerge.

"The baby shrewdly adapted itself to my bent body and began a slow rotation, which became a spiral. My vagina caressed every inch of his body with infinite love.

"At the moment when the cranium appeared within the oval of the vulva, forming an eye, Seraphim stepped back a bit. He whispered with veneration: 'I'm receiving you from the side so that you see the world, because you belong to it and not me.' The baby revolved, got out its left arm first, then the right, and finished the rotation, offering himself like someone crucified. Seraphim delicately pulled him by the nape and extracted him from my lips, which kissed his heels with adoration.

"Breathing with difficulty, so proud was he, he held the baby up like a trophy. The boy—he was in fact male, as we had always supposed—was a great beauty. His skin was dark, almost green; his eyes were yellow like sunflowers; his features were fine, Oriental. His elongated skull and his serene expression made him seem like a pre-Colombian sculpture. Shedding tears, Seraphim and I both pronounced the name that suddenly occurred to us without our thinking about it: Almo.

"I received Almo on my bosom, and there he stayed, so calm that his heartbeat slowed mine, and when we awoke in the same beatific rhythm, I cut the umbilical cord with my teeth, because I never, out of respect, would have dared to terminate our sacred union with a knife.

"Seraphim, on his knees, prayed to him: 'Son, you are my master. Teach me to be, teach me to live, teach me to create, open my soul so that I can love even more.' Just then, Almo spread his legs. Below his testicles and before his anus, he had a perfect female sex.

"'A hermaphrodite!' Seraphim shouted in dismay. 'I knew it. Before, you gave birth to normal children. I'm the one with poisoned semen. What could come from me but an aberration? We have to kill it!' He was so desperate and I so worn out that I couldn't convince him that his son-daughter was more beautiful than any normal human, than an androgyne achieved the ultimate dream: to possess both sexes at the same time, like God. I gave myself over to Fate. Without protesting, I lifted the child and offered him to the murderous fury of his father. Seraphim took him, intent on throwing him to the floor and kicking in his skull. But Almo fixed his eyes on his father, and instantly Seraphim's face changed, passing from bestial hatred to a balmy peace, because those tiny golden pupils reached his essence and transported him to a spiritual level he'd never known before.

"Death disappeared forever. His soul recognized itself as invincible, and suffering dissolved into a sweet ocean, which was endless. Time offering its eternal present, Life. Seraphim believed he could guess the thoughts of the newborn and repeated them aloud: 'With this gaze, I seal my alliance with you. I accept you as my father. I give you all the rights because you deserve my confidence, so that you educate the child who is I.'

"Smiling, Seraphim placed Almo next to my left breast and saw him suckle for the first time. A cloud of melancholy darkened his happiness. I offered my right breast. Seraphim sat down whining and accepted the nipple to receive, finally, the milk he'd been denied as a baby.

"We decided for the moment to forget our child was a hermaphrodite: we would figure out how to deal with the problem later. Perhaps Almo himself, our Master, would guide us. We began to travel north, fleeing the rains and liveliness of the south. We needed a dry climate. We were so full of spirit that we could only stand a desert. We performed all along the coast, passing through Coquimbo, La Serena, Copiapó, Taltal, Antofagasta, and Tocopilla, until finally we reached Huantojaya, a silver-mining town near Iquique. There they let us use the great gymnasium of the Coeducational School No. 28. That was the school used by the children of workers from the region's mines: The Discoverer,

The Saint John, The Laura, The Saint Peter, The Disdained—names of prostitutes or saints, as if digging a mine shaft were for them was profane and sacred at the same time. Seraphim, exploring the area, noted that the miners were not our usual audience. The dust, the sun, the hostility of the excavation, the dynamite blasts, the exhausting workdays had hardened them, giving their faces the texture of stones.

"On Saturdays, they would go into the bordellos to play cards; lose the money they'd earned during the week; drink a minimum of two dozen beers, lining up the empty bottles to show how much they could drink; and fall asleep next to the urinals without saying a word. Making them laugh seemed impossible. Seraphim begged me to participate in his act this time. He had to put on a good show, bawdy, one that would yank laughs out of them by brute force, like pulling teeth.

"I was supposed to be the lazy guard of a bunch of bananas. I would ask a monkey to help me move the fruit from one place to another on the improvised stage. While he worked, I would have a nice siesta. The monkey would take advantage of the siesta to steal a banana and try to hide it without finding a place on the empty stage. He would try to hide it in his clothes but would realize he had no pockets. Finally, in a panic, he would drop his trousers and put it in his anus. (Seraphim had invented, using a rubber tube, a special holder hidden under his false tail that would allow him, with great realism, to imitate that penetration.) When he was finished with his chore, I would check him over to see if he was hiding a stolen banana. Satisfied with my employee's honesty, I would shake hands and send him on his way, paying him a tiny coin. The monkey, alone now, with a triumphal air, would try to eject the banana, but it would refuse to leave. After huge efforts, pushes, shrieks, he would manage to excrete it with tremendous pain. Jumping for joy, despite his broken anus, he would peel the banana and try to eat it. But with expressions of disgust, he would throw it far away because now it would have an unbearable stench of excrement.

"The night of the performance, the five hundred school chairs were occupied by a silent crowd of men, women, and children. Sitting there, serious, motionless, they looked like stones in the middle of a desert. When I entered carrying the bananas, transformed into the sleepy guard (thanks to some woolen whiskers and a uniform made of sacks dyed blue and metal buttons made from beer caps, the families applauded. Their hard, dried-out hands sounded like bone castanets. Nervous because it was my debut, I felt like a dove taking shots from five hundred rifles.

"Seraphim made his entrance. He was applauded as I was, but no one laughed. He exaggerated his grimaces. Nothing. He chased his tail, trying to bite it. Dismal silence. Then, with barefaced immodesty, he began to scratch his testicles. An attack of laughter. He scratched himself furiously. More laughter. The more he dug around in his balls, the more the audience giggled. But since he couldn't go on doing that all night, we began, in a once-again silent room, the program we'd rehearsed.

"The weight of those granite spectators pressed down on us. We made the first movements mechanically, burdened by failure. We weren't even sure if they were really looking at us with their expressionless eyes. But when the monkey stole the banana and tried unsuccessfully to hide it, the audience, interested, made a strange murmur. Then, when the animal introduced the fruit into his anus, some growled protests I couldn't quite understand. When the monkey painfully tried to excrete his larceny, they began to stamp their feet and whistle. And when he tried to eat the smelly fruit, groups of furious miners leapt toward the stage with the clear intention of thrashing us with their fists. Seraphim and I didn't understand. Most of those workers had no religious convictions and spent most of their free time submerged in alcohol, coca leaves, gambling, and prostitutes. What could have offended them? They were just beginning to knock us around when a thick voice shouted: 'Halt, comrades! These good clowns weren't trying to make fun of you! Sit down and listen because what I'm going to say is important!' The miners knew and respected that voice because they released us and went back to their seats.

"An average-sized man with black hair and a moustache, penetrating eyes, a sulking brow, and an ungainly manner stepped onto the stage. He wore wide trousers, and the pockets of his jacket seemed stuffed with papers. He shook hands with us out of sincere respect, and, as if he had a thousand years ahead of him, took his place before the audience, looking at everyone there, one by one.

"When he finished that profound and silent contact, he said in a severe voice: 'Good evening, comrades.'

"Most answered, 'Good evening, Recabarren!'

"Out of his pockets, he pulled several small newspapers. 'Here I have for you the first issue of the worker's paper *Workers Awaken*! It only costs twenty centavos, less than a beer. Practice reading, comrades, and stop sleeping. The Chilean worker has no defense against industrialists, neither unions nor social legislation. And even though you know you should fight against the bosses because they exploit you pitilessly, you fight as individuals instead of organizing into cooperatives. The only revolt you practice is theft. Which is why these clowns annoyed you so much. You saw yourselves, as if in a mirror. Don't put on innocent faces. Let me refresh your memory: you mold the grains of silver until you give them the form and size of a cigar. Then you wrap them in a rag you cover with suet and you slip them in, just as this monkey did with his banana. Then you stroll by the mine guards, who have no idea a theft took place. No, don't interrupt me, because I'm not finished yet: once you're outside the mine you expel the cigar with a lot of pain, but sometimes it can't come out and you have to go to doctors in Iquique, who demand most of the silver to carry out the operation. The money you get that way cheapens you, because to get it you sacrifice your manhood. It isn't right to punish a clown because he reminds you that you're screwed over. You should really be thanking him. Stolen money stinks of shit, comrades! We'll have to secure the welfare we deserve the honest way, by forming unions, creating a workers' party, by refusing to sell our votes, and by organizing ourselves to win elections! Circulate *Workers Awaken!* and forma cooperative, starting right now. Together you'll get what you could never get on your own. And applaud these two humble clowns, because they are your brothers, children of the same hunger.'

"The miners did applaud. The man named Recabarren stepped down from the stage to hand out newspapers. Almo began to cry, needing to be fed. We had him covered up in a corner of the stage. While Seraphim passed the hat, I changed Almo's diaper and gave him milk. The workers left, arguing with the leader. Seraphim came back happy, waving a ten-peso note.

"'Recabarren gave it to me in the name of the miners, to evade my gratitude. That man is extraordinary. He wants nothing for himself that isn't also for the others, and he fights so justice will triumph in this unjust world. If I had to choose a father, it would be Recabarren. Let's follow him wherever he goes.'

"Suddenly, out of the shadows emerged a thin, beardless, one-eyed Indian with long hair in a braid. He was wearing a white cotton robe, a straw hat, and a poncho made of vicuña wool.

"'Please excuse this interruption. Let me introduce myself: Rosauro, medicine man for many and witch doctor for some. I can cure all ills with herbs, even internal tumors. I can also set fractures, give massages, remove the evil eye. I can make lost lovers return. I know the legends.' After introducing himself that way, the Indian stood there in silence, staring at us with strange intensity, retaining an emotion that made his one eye moist. The two of us stared at him, disconcerted and frozen, not knowing how to react.

"Seraphim broke the silence with a short introduction: 'Teresa, Seraphim. Glad to meet you, sir.'

"The shaman took off his hat, fell on his knees before Almo, and whispered with great effort: 'Yeco, you have finally come,' and then, curling up his body until he looked like a ball, he burst into convulsive sobs. Concerned, Seraphim brought him a glass of water. The Indian took a sip, went face down on the floor, took my feet, and covered them with kisses. 'You are the mother of God!'

"Thoroughly confused, Seraphim brought him to his feet. 'What did you say, my friend?'

"'The truth! I was going to stay here tonight in a corner of the stage, so I wouldn't have to pay for a hotel room—I'm following Recabarren—when I saw Madam Teresa change the baby's diapers. I was able to realize that he was the hermaphrodite proclaimed by the Tradition. Here in the Great North we believe in a prophecy that comes from the colonial era: before the year 2000, there will appear in the desert an olive green child with yellow eyes and double sex. He will be God incarnate once again, a new Christ who will overcome those who oppress the people: the Yeco, crow of salt and fresh water. Black feathers that become light in flight. As a river bird, he is Energy; as an ocean bird, he is Equilibrium. The salt water Yeco wants to dissolve in the fresh water Yeco, who awakens and begins to fly. As he flaps his wings, he creates things, but when he stops, he destroys everything. And again he goes to sleep so the other will awaken him. And on and on. When he tires of annihilating, he dissolves in himself. There aren't two different crows. There is only one, the ocean crow. The lake crow comes and fuses with him. One bird is male, the other female. After all, Yeco has both sexes. It is a legend, but very real. This divine child will unite the miners and with them initiate the Proletarian Revolution. There will be no more poverty; we shall be partners, not employees; a garden will arise from the arid desert! You, Don Seraphim, do not have to follow Recabarren. He's a magnificent agitator, but he does not possess the allure of a god. On his own, he will not be able to unite men consumed by work and vice. Recabarren will take them one step forward, but later they will take two back. To rid them of alcohol, prostitutes, gambling, and theft we will need something more than a human being. Yeco will do it! The mass of workers will organize around him, and he will achieve victory.'

"'But, sir,' Seraphim answered him, so moved that his forehead, nose, and cheeks—the little bare skin there was on his face—was white, 'we don't know you, and though we would like, with all our hearts, to believe you and accept that Almo has come to fulfill a prophecy, we can't stop thinking that for some strange reason you are mocking us, poor comedians that we are.'

"I nodded, holding the baby against my chest. Nevertheless, despite those natural misgivings, I was overcome by a great feeling of wellbeing, since I'd always believed in Almo's superior Destiny. The Indian's words were the confirmation of my dreams.

"'Friends, in this evil society there is no truth other than money. Let's let it speak,' he said. He took off his hat and extracted from it a thick wad of banknotes.

"Seraphim whistled in shock. 'I've never seen so much money in one place before!'

"'It really isn't much, sir, but enough for what we want. Let me explain: a few of us shamans live here in the north, in the mining region. We are the guardians of the Tradition. Without us, the heritage of our race would be lost. Foreigners have invaded our land with their capital. Now potassium nitrate, copper, iron, silver, and gold all belong to the English and North Americans, who are linked to the government, which belongs to the rich. We shamans have saved up most of the money we've earned in anticipation of Yeco's arrival, so we can offer it to him in his war against the oligarchy. But time doesn't pass in vain. So much misery and social injustice made us lose patience and set aside our beautiful legend to take action against this ugly reality. I was sent here to give our savings to Recabarren and help him create the Socialist Workers Party. Luckily,

God wanted me to take refuge on the stage and see your naked baby. This money is for you. Accept it. It will allow you to rent a comfortable room in Iquique, eat well, and dress decently for four months—the time we'll need to travel around the region announcing the good news and to prepare a triumphal reception for you. The only thing I'll ask of you is that you bring the child to a certain photographer by the port, a friend of mine, so he can take a picture showing the child's two sexes. We'll make copies and distribute them to all our offices. The workers will finally understand that the miracle exists, that God has come down to Earth and is here among us.'

"That roll of bills, coming from a humble man, convinced us. A new life was beginning. A life with a great purpose. And we did go, as he suggested, to Iquique. He went with us. On the way there he didn't speak a word, and when he stopped, he'd hunker down for hours and hours, never taking his eyes off Almo. They let us board Blacky and Whitey in a small hotel at the port and rented us a room with a kitchen, bath, and windows overlooking the sea.

"Rosauro brought us to his friend, who specialized in identity card photographs, and got a picture of Almo with his little legs spread, showing his penis and his vagina. He made a date with us: 'On December 25, I'll be waiting for you in the province of Alto San Antonio, one of the most prosperous in the nitrate region. Look for the San Lorenzo mine. Be punctual. That date is important. Yeco must bring us the light that will begin the retreat of darkness.' He made his farewells, sharing a bottle of pisco, and headed for the desert.

"The four months passed quickly, but a marked change took place in Seraphim. He finally felt himself accepted by society. His child was not a monster but a god. All the injustices he'd suffered in life he now attributed to a dictatorship disguised as a democracy that he was going to help destroy. His abominable poverty and isolation were reaching their last days. Now a free workers' paradise awaited him. All this thanks to the marvelous Almo. Seraphim stopped dressing like a clown. He bought himself two gray suits, shirts, ties, a felt hat, and a razor. He shaved off the hair on his face and used adhesive tape to pull his ears closer to his skull. Though I didn't like the change, I understood. Now he could walk unnoticed through the streets. He was, to his soul's delight, just one more person. After making the most of our vacation, eating delicious seafood, basking in the sun at the beach, and loving each other better than ever, we packed up our wagon to go to San Lorenzo, planning our arrival on the assigned date.

"In those lonely highlands, night came on suddenly. It seemed to rise up out of the ocean and flow toward the mountains like a black wave. We could see each other's faces but not our feet. The dense fog, given off by the extremely dry land, fought to reach the sky, but it was so dense it could not rise. It was a cloud with roots. The mist became so thick that it ate up the road and horses.

"'Let's stop. It's too dangerous to keep moving, and we might fall into a gorge. Think of the child,' I said to Seraphim.

"'The fact is,' he answered, 'that with Almo here nothing can happen. God is protecting us. We now have to show our confidence in him.' And cracking his whip, he made Whitey and Blacky gallop. At first I was terrified. Then, as the wagon seemed to shake without moving forward—our lantern couldn't penetrate the dense mist and the moonless blackness, so we could not see how the landscape slipped away from us—I gave myself over calmly to the swaying, as if I were in a huge cradle. I think Seraphim fell asleep as well.

"We woke at the edge of a white stone precipice, an immense excavation where they mined saltpeter that looked like a stadium. A group of miners surrounded us carrying torches. Rosauro was with them. 'Yeco is making miracles. Even though you can see practically nothing, you arrived exactly on time to the place where we were waiting for you. Follow us.' They guided us to the encampment. 'Come down from the wagon, please. Our comrades will take care of the horses. Pass through here.'

"We entered a bar called Coquimbo Girls. Waiting for us there, all packed in, were about a hundred miners, waited on by three charming young ladies, daughters of the old couple who owned the place. It seemed incredible that the husband and wife, whose faces were so wrinkled they looked a hundred years old, could have such young daughters. But seeing them move made us realize that their wrinkles came from the salt, not from age.

"Rosauro was very excited. He took Almo out of our hands, undressed him, spread his legs, and showed his double sex. The workers fell to their knees whispering: 'it's true. He is the Yeco. Blessed be God.'

"Rosauro turned to us. 'You can rely on these comrades. They come from all the different mines in the region. They've heard Recabarren's speeches and want to fight for workers' rights. But they haven't been able to come together. Now, above them, in Yeco, all our ideals converge. Now, thanks to the presence of this child, they can act as one. Tomorrow we are going to declare a strike in San Lorenzo. Then we're going to spread it to the other centers. Here are the Ruiz brothers, who represent the workers. Yesterday they delivered a request for a wage increase to the mine administrator, Mr. Turner, an Englishman who wouldn't respond without speaking to management in Iquique. The brothers argued on, explaining to Mr. Turner that the miners are paid four pesos for a criminally long workday. The price of a loaf of bread is a peso—that is, one quarter of a day's pay. At that rate, it is impossible to live. Today, bright and early, the gringo told us that the company refused the increase. Which was what we wanted! Our goal is not to earn a few pesos more but to initiate the Total Revolution that will bring down the exploiters and take control of the Chilean government. Now we have a justification to begin the process. With Yeco, the sacred flame, we shall make the grand inferno explode. Thousands of us will abandon our jobs. We shall march down to Iquique like a sea of ants. The authorities will simply have to hear us out. That's how we'll win the first battle. We shall go back to the mines, but we will also demand the right to form unions. Which will not be granted. Then we'll initiate a general strike throughout the nation. The soldiers, who are also of the people, will disobey their chiefs and help us bring down the president and his court of thieves. Tomorrow we shall begin the revolt, and we shall not stop until the final victory!'

"We were able to sleep for four hours before daybreak. At sunrise, the whistle blew to wake up the workers. Instead of the usual three short blasts, there was a howl that went on for five interminable minutes. It was the official announcement of the strike. The group leaders we'd met in Coquimbo Girls were waving Chilean flags and signs, and they marched toward the Santa Lucía mine, which, five miles away, was working. Seraphim and I, holding Almo up like a beacon, led the parade.

"The presence of the child-god convinced all the workers to take part in the strike. Like a gathering flood, we rolled across the pampa for three days, from mine to mine. The workers followed us, bringing their wives and children along with them. That multitude, which grew larger hour by hour, had to spend the cold nights out on the pampa by campfires. Since the fire wasn't enough to keep them warm, the couples began to have sex among their sleeping children. The ground trembled from that forest of febrile lovers, bringing life to that barren and salty place. Seraphim, too, had me lie down on the pulsating wasteland. As he possessed me, I saw the desert become a garden: thousands of ovaries, like my own, were the flowers of that region, which would never be sterile again. The nocturnal dew turned the countless naked bodies into mirrors that reflected the flames of the campfires, flesh burning without being consumed, increased the pleasure for each couple. For hours, massive orgasmic waves rolled across that stormy human sea.

"On the fourth day of the strike, the rumor spread that the chief administrator of the province would come up to Alto San Antonio to speak with the workers. It was false information that Rosauro, working with the other leaders, had circulated. Tomás Eastman, the administrator, was in Santiago, replaced by a secretary with no authority who would never dare engage in dialogue with the strikers.

"The unity of the workers, thanks to Yeco, was beginning to coalesce, but it was still green. What was needed to make it mature was rage. For the moment, the strike looked like a pagan festival. Seeing the great numbers, everyone was certain the crisis would be resolved in a few hours. The industry could not allow a stoppage of this magnitude. They would go en masse to Alto de San Antonio. The place would boil over with the vigor of the workers. Orators would speak extemporaneously from the music kiosk. Raising the miserable salary would most certainly happen.

"Everything happened exactly as Rosauro predicted. The horde of miners invaded the town in a festive mood. The Coquimbo girls, who knew how to sing and play the guitar, organized a collective dance. Four local bars were requisitioned by the Revolutionary commission, so the wine was free. The dancing and the drunkenness lasted until dawn. Then the Indian came running out of the telegraph office waving a phony message that he had allegedly received from one of the Ruiz brothers.

"'The administrator will not deign to come here! He has only contempt for us! He thinks the strike is trivial! Comrades, we cannot allow ourselves to be humiliated! If this son of a gringo won't come to us, we'll go to him!'

"A furious shout of rose from many throats, and the multitude, like a single man, began the march to Iquique. The way was long hot as an oven during the day and frozen at night. Pointy rocks cut feet, and thick clouds of flies gathered overhead, barely letting the sunlight through. In their anger, the strikers had left without bothering to carry food. To get to the port, they would have to fast for two days. No one cared. From living so long among the rocks, they'd become as hard as rocks. Their dried-out bodies were used to enduring hunger. Forty-eight hours without food were nothing. And it would be easy to slake their thirst at night by licking the stones moistened by the mist.

"Rosauro called an emergency meeting of the leaders.

"'We have to spread the word that no one is to go down there carrying a weapon. There's a lot of dynamite in the region, and it's possible that some fanatic will try to use it. Let me remind you that this first phase of the Revolution should seem inoffensive. We'll show the bosses—peacefully—that without us the industry won't function. Seeing us united like this, they will certainly raise our salary. Then we'll go back to the mines and, little by little, arm ourselves for the final phase. Also, to avoid catastrophes, we have to give our march an intelligent head. As we go through the streets of Iquique, the Yeco will go first, along with his holy parents, then us leaders. After us, a group of comrades whom you will choose because they fully understand the political situation, thanks to the teachings of the anarchists or Recabarren. No more than two thousand. And finally, the enormous mass of workers whose only guide is misery, a mass we will have to learn to control.'

"The marching order was adopted unanimously. The shaman had the talent to be a general.

"On the fifth day of the strike, a Sunday, we appeared in the hills above the port, surrounding it like a pack of ants. We made our way down the slopes without a single sound, darkening the brownish earth. The people of Iquique filled the streets expectantly. When we entered the town and organized ourselves according to plan, a slow and mute parade, not even our footsteps echoed on the asphalt—almost all of us were barefoot because the sharp rocks had destroyed our shoes. The people of Iquique ran to offer us baskets filled with food, proclaiming the heroism of our long and self-sacrificing march from the highlands for the sake of justice.

"The authorities, on the other hand, treated us with a cold disdain, as if we were a small group of crazy pilgrims. But among those stiff bureaucrats trembled Guzmán García, Tomás Eastman's secretary, denouncing this unheard-of arrogance. The Ruiz brothers approached him, demanding an immediate verdict. His clothing soaked through with sweat, the secretary muttered: 'I can say nothing. But the chief administrator has left Santiago and will arrive here tomorrow. He bears precise instructions on how to deal with the problem.'

"The forty thousand strikers assumed the battle had been won. They began to hug one another in an eruption of joy. The strike leaders ran from one group to another but could do nothing to stop bottles of wine from being uncorked and the food baskets from being emptied. Many workers, convinced that triumph was imminent, tried to return to the pampa. For a few minutes, chaos ensued. It ended with the arrival of a legion of cavalry and infantry following a noisy military band. By the time they surrounded us and the music stopped, the people's delight had chilled.

"Guzmán García, shouting nervously despite the deathly silence through which you could hear the buzz of the desert flies, proposed to house the strike leaders in the Santa María school and the rest of the workers in the Sporting Club hippodrome. The town would lend us camp stoves, supply us with wine, fish, and beans. We applauded, and in perfect order, marched, guarded on both sides by the soldiers, in a column that filled the street. We first went to the school, whose students, it seemed, were on vacation. The two thousand worker-leaders filled the classrooms and immediately stretched out on the benches for a siesta to rest after the march. Once the other workers got to the hippodrome and found themselves out of the watchful eye of their severe comrades, they scattered over the extensive property and recommenced the party, welcoming with pleasure the arrival of a multicolored flock of prostitutes on their day off. The Coquimbo sisters agreed to sing, and the snapping heels of the *cueca* dancers made the track tremble, as if herds of demented horses were running around it.

"Two hours later, in the school building, Rosauro woke everyone up and, with help from the Ruiz brothers, organized work groups to work out a proposal to end the conflict. In addition to the raise, they would ask for greater security on the job—there were many accidents, and many miners, a few children among them, had been blown to bits by dynamite—and better hygienic conditions: the saltpeter powder affected the workers' lungs, and they received no medical assistance. Their miserable living quarters were infested with fleas and lice.

"But while the head was deliberating, the body was giving itself over to drunkenness. So that the workers wouldn't forget what the goal of the struggle was during the heat of the party, Rosauro suggested that Seraphim, Almo, and I visit the Sporting Club. But we were to do so covertly: to keep the reprisals of the bosses from falling on the child, his messianic nature had been kept secret. When the multitude marched down the hills in exemplary obedience, it repressed any shout that might have revealed the marvelous secret. The Yeco united them with a silence more powerful than ten thousand inflammatory speeches. Even though the streets were filled with police, they didn't stop us. For a second, their faces would turn toward us with interest and immediately turn away indifferently, as if they'd only seen three skeletal street dogs walk by.

"At the hippodrome, the drunken party was in full swing. The bodies were shaking, drawing unsuspected energy from the depth of exhaustion. The Coquimbo sisters, with booming voices that seemed unimaginable from their delicate throats, were singing verses stronger than cavalry charges. In corners, people were vomiting and fornicating. Seraphim, seeing the multitude completely out of control, began to stutter: 'Wait a bit, Teresa. What are we going to do here? These drunks will never take any notice of us. Besides, we've already carried out our mission. The strike is victorious. Let's leave right away!'

"And overcome by reticence, he took hold of me as if to protect me and tried to walk out. But a couple interrupted their hip-shaking and ran toward us murmuring, 'The Holy Family. Blessed be you.' They kissed the blanket wrapped around the baby, and immediately, with sincere respect, invited us to begin a walk around the racetrack. Other workers surrounded us with such fervor that we couldn't say no. As we passed, the couples would stop dancing; join hands as if they were praying; and whisper, obeying the rule of keeping the secret: 'Thanks, Little God.'

"But no sooner had we passed than they went back to dancing frenetically. We felt like we were carrying an island of peace through a stormy sea. It took us much more than an hour to walk the entire course. The unexpected reverence of those thousands of poor Chileans filled us with a limitless optimism, satisfying our deepest needs for security, love, integration, and social recognition. For once, 'we' was much more important than 'I.' I felt that roots were sprouting from the soles of my feet. This land had become mine.

"Seraphim said, 'After this, it doesn't matter to me if I die. These people love and respect me; what more can I ask of life? I never dreamed I would attain so much. I owe it all to you.'

"I answered by giving him a long kiss, and we returned to the school, where we realized that it wasn't called Santa María by accident. Rosauro and the comrades thanked us for our sacrifice, and since we were worn out by the long march, they gave us the director's office so we could sleep in his comfortable armchairs.

"The enormous orgy lasted all night. Just at dawn, silence once again reigned. All Iquique slept until two o'clock on Monday. The people's deep sleep was interrupted by a long, rasping blast from a foghorn. It was the warship carrying the chief administrator. We ran as a mob to the dock and lined the seawall. The army followed us like a gray shadow. Three hundred sailors armed with polished rifles disembarked from the ship to form a double column through which Tomás Eastman soon made his way.

"He was a thin, dried-out old man dressed in black. Taking small steps, he walked toward the administration without raising his eyes from the sepia puttees adorning his honor guard. We crowded together under the main balcony with a knot in our throats, anxious about the cannon pointed at us from the ship. Eastman came out onto the balcony and spoke only one sentence before going back in: 'I carry official instructions from the government to resolve the conflict. Go back to the pampa.' A jubilant din drowned out the sound of the waves. The workers considered their contribution to the strike over, and now it was up to the leaders to negotiate the best conditions. Accordingly, they headed for an esplanade where the train tracks passed.

"We then heard train whistles, and two locomotives arrived pulling a long line of flat cars. The miners and their families crowded onto them. They looked like herds of animals. After this train pulled out, many more pulled in. The mining company had organized an efficient but undignified transportation system. The group of two thousand workers possessed of social awareness ran to the hill called La Cruz, which overlooked the esplanade, and from there, waving flags, they shouted, 'We aren't sheep! Don't leave, comrades! Nothing has been decided yet!' But no one paid them any attention.

"No sooner had the last train pulled out, than the army, declaring a state of siege, herded the rest of the revolutionaries toward the Santa María school. Rosauro told everyone to obey, that nothing had been lost, and we shouldn't give the authorities any reason to justify the use of force. As soon as we entered the school, the military surrounded the building. The combined force of soldiers, sailors, and police was about eight hundred men. Not content with simply pointing their rifles and machine guns at us, they brought in a cannon and placed it opposite the main door.

"'Victory, brothers!' shouted the Indian. 'If they're waving around so many weapons, it's because they're afraid of us. And what do they fear since they know we are unarmed? They fear our spirit! Perhaps some spy told them about the Yeco. That makes me happy because now the auspicious moment has arrived. The prophecy, which until now has been accurate at every stage, says that at the feet of the Sent One all armies will fall to their knees. If we send Don Seraphim and Doña Teresa to show the child to the troops, the Yeco will shine like a sun, appearing in all his majesty. Seeing him, a colonel mounted on his white horse will fall as if struck by lightning. And the regular soldiers, realizing we are brothers, will turn their weapons against the exploiters.'

"At that very moment, a trumpet sounded. We went to the windows and saw a colonel arriving on a white horse. With a castrato's voice he shouted to us: 'This is Colonel Roberto Silva Bernard speaking. I order you here and now to evacuate this school to be transferred to the hippodrome. There you will be sentenced for insurrection. You have five minutes to leave. If you disobey, I will order my men to fire.'

"Seeing that the arrival of this Napoleon coincided with the legend, the miners smiled in relief. Everything was happening as if in a marvelous dream. The Indian suggested we open a few bottles to make a toast in our honor, the Holy Family. We drank a glass of wine. Then the workers hugged us with great emotion and walked us to the main door. When they began to open it, I felt my legs weaken. I lost strength and had to ask Seraphim to carry Almo. I felt unbearable shame. I had never been a coward and didn't understand why now, when I needed the most courage to be an example, I was feeling dizzy. I took the arm Rosauro offered me and mumbled to him: 'Friend, for the sake of what you venerate most, keep me from falling. I don't want the comrades to realize my weakness and think I'm having doubts. I, more than anyone else, have faith in the power of my son.'

"'Don't worry, Teresa,' he whispered into my ear. 'I'll escort you, holding you up until the spell passes. Be brave.'

"And, with an explanation to the strikers I didn't hear because I was holding back vomit, he walked out into the street with us. We were four human beings against an army armed to the teeth. Under my perspiring feet, the ground moved like the deck of a ship on the high seas. My dry tongue had turned into a piece of wood. Seraphim held up the child and spread his legs to show his two sexes. I took a deep breath and concentrated my will, trying not to faint. Almo smiled. I waited for him to shine like a sun so the colonel would fall as if struck by lightning. Suddenly Rosauro took me by the back of my neck and brutally forced me to run toward the soldiers. I was so weak I couldn't resist. When the soldiers, smiling, opened a path for us, Silva Bernard howled: 'Open fire, Goddammit!' And a cannon shell blew my lover and my son to pieces. It had to be a nightmare. The Indian was laughing. There on the street, the flesh of my two beloved ones was falling in shreds like a slow rain.

"The machine guns began to bark. The soldiers tossed hand grenades and tear gas. They put on masks. They fixed bayonets. The cannon thundered again. The school door became a splintered sun. I forgot my name, forgot where I was. An overpowering need to sleep made my eyelids heavy. I knew my heart was tearing apart, but I felt that pain as if it were distant, above; my body transformed into a black well where my consciousness was submerged. Soldiers and sailors dashed into the school. Everything became mixed up. Shouts of rage and agony. Packs of dogs coming to lick up the blood. Men, women, and children shot to pieces on the upper terraces. Miners running through the street with their guts in their hands. Brutish soldiers finishing off the wounded with knives. Masked men in gray dragging corpses by the hair. I begin to faint.

"The Indian carried me like a package, entered the administration building, went upstairs to an office, and locked the door. He threw me into an armchair, lifted my skirts, tore my panties off, mauled my breasts, and possessed me three times in a row. I vomited in his face. He laughed and dragged me by the foot to the bathroom. He took off his clothes, finished undressing me, and turned on the shower. Under the cold water, he raped me again. Whistling a popular song, 'We Who Love Each Other So,' he brought me back to the armchair.

"I fell into a deep sleep. When Rosauro woke me up, it was already nightfall. I barely recognized him. He was no longer an Indian or even one-eyed, his skin was much lighter, his hair was short, he was wearing a suit of an English cut, a striped shirt, and a green tie with a clip in the form of the Chilean seal. Seeing my surprise, he twirled like a fashion model. Guffawing, he took me by the waist, and forced me to look out the window. While the soldiers, with innocent faces, piled corpses onto garbage trucks, he, standing behind me, assaulted me sexually like a wild animal.

"Hatred mixed with suffering—but pleasure, a pleasure only located in my sex—increased and I could do nothing to stop it. It was like a soft crab that grew in my guts, stretching out its sickening legs further and further. My body betrayed me. I exploded, wanted to die, punish myself. I tried to jump out the window. He punched my breasts and tossed me, splayed out, onto the armchair. He penetrated me again and, with no restraint whatsoever, roared and drooled until he ejaculated.

"I screamed, insulting him. Then he tied my feet together and put handcuffs on my wrists. He pulled over a chair, opposite me, and lit a cigarette: 'You won't get anywhere screaming, Teresa. No one will come. I suppose they expect me to kill you. There's still some room in the last garbage truck. You must want to die as well. But I'm going to disappoint you. I've decided to keep you for a while. The moment I saw you breastfeeding the baby in that miserable scene, I decided to take control over you. A Russian like you, with huge tits, a big ass, and skin whiter than your own milk—that's not something you find every day in this country.

"'I asked for you as a prize if I carried out my task. The government has wanted to cut off that damned Recabarren for a long time. With his poisonous newspapers, preying on the eternal discontent of the poor slobs, he was churning up political agitation that was very dangerous for the mining companies. Even though it would have been easy, it wasn't convenient to assassinate him. Transformed into a martyr, he would end up unifying the workers around his myth. Better to defame him. The secret police sent me disguised as an Indian so I could catch him in something bad. I followed him for months, shadowed his every footstep, but it was useless. The bastard is straighter than my dick. He even looks like a saint. He doesn't smoke and doesn't drink, so he won't assist bourgeois business. If you offer him cocaine, he rejects it in a fury. He's faithful to his girlfriend and has no children we would have liked to lead into degradation. He never goes to parties and only likes to read. This shitty traitor is an enlightened nut. I was about to throw in the towel when I saw you clean your kid's ass. At first his double sex disgusted me. Then I was happy, because a nice plan came to me, a plan that would win me a promotion, money, vacation, and your ass. I made up a legend in the asshole style of the Mapuche Indians, and you and your husband, like all parents who just drool over their kids, swallowed the hook.

"'I sent you to Iquique for four months to have time to spread the story among the superstitious miners and convince them, showing them the photo of the monster, that he was God incarnate. I communicated with my chiefs, we coordinated the action with the mine administrator, the city, and the army, and the plan was set. We managed to eliminate all the strike leaders. The dragon lost its two thousand heads. The mass of workers, who only think about fornicating and getting drunk, will be happy with a pay increase of a few pesos. Recabarren will need many years to recruit new disciples. And what you thought was cowardice was the effect of a sleeping drug I put in your wine during the last toast. I'm talking to you, but I don't want you to answer. What you think or feel doesn't matter a bit to me. So I can make good use of your body, I want you to keep your mouth shut. And if you do say something, I'll knock your teeth down your throat. We're going to spend two months by the sea, far away from the world, in a chalet they've lent me, located between Iquique and Tocopilla. I'm going to have you at least six times a day. When I get tired of you, I'll sell you so you can work as a whore in Peru or Argentina. If you do everything I want, you can grow old in those slimy bars, but if you make trouble, I'll blow your brains out.'

"I gave in. Something in my brain had broken. I stopped thinking or feeling. I assumed the role of his faithful bitch—to the point that when my executioner went to buy provisions, leaving me locked up, I whined by the door until he came back. I had to follow him wherever he went. When he cleaned his pistol, I stretched out at his feet, naked, waiting to be raped. I actually licked his boots clean and smiled when he peed on my face.

"One day, after he drank a dozen beers, he fell asleep in my arms. Suddenly I recovered my identity along with my anger and fury, and with one snap of my teeth, I severed his jugular vein. He got up and ran along the beach with a red line trailing behind him. He fell in the sand, transformed into a white rock. Even though I knew he was dead, I fired his pistol into his head. His skull split open, and a gray mass flowed out, which the crabs immediately devoured. I let them eat until they had enough. Then I dragged his remains to the hills, dug a deep grave, and buried him. When I'd tossed on the last shovel of dirt, I realized I had no idea what his real name was.

"I cleaned up the blood, and among his clothes, I found a suit, a shirt, shoes, and a hat. I put the rest of his things in two suitcases and buried them, too. This way his bosses would think he'd left with me for some other country. I cut off my hair and, disguised as a man, with the little money I found, I bought a train ticket for Santiago. No one bothered me on the trip, because I pretended to sleep with an empty bottle in my hand—just another drunk. If I'd had anywhere else to go, I wouldn't have come back to the tenement, to a past that was no longer mine. I got here when Alejandro was dying, the last person I might have been able to confide in. It didn't matter to me that the World War had broken out. Maybe it even made me happy, since I could take it as a kind of revenge.

I knew I would be isolated, desolate, useless forever. Life? To be born for no reason, to suffer constantly, to die ignorant. God? Present but unreachable. Blind, deaf, and mute for His creatures. Human society? A prison filled with lunatics, thieves, and drunks. Everything and everyone deserve only my curses.

"So now you see, Benjamín. You wanted to know the Truth; here you have it, with its rotten smell. Stop groaning, untie me, bring more vodka, and let's drink together. The best thing in this world is not to have been born."

My uncle untied Teresa, brought another bottle, and they began to empty it. He'd felt himself described in my grandmother's final words. He understood that, much more than hating other people, he hated himself. He was a transparent angel fallen into a filthy sewer, his body. Before starting to snore with his nose stuck into his mother's navel, he muttered:

> *The night comes with its she-wolf fury*
> *Promising the birth of a sun in love*
> *But shade can only give birth to shades*
> *Nothing is born, nothing dies*
> *And creation is oblivion*

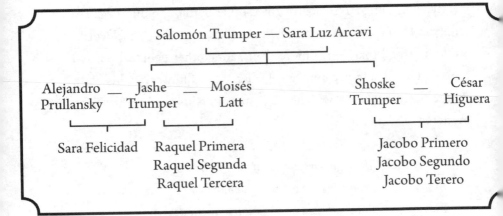

Salomón Trumper — Sara Luz Arcavi

Alejandro   Jashe — Moisés   Shoske — César
Prullansky   Trumper   Latt   Trumper   Higuera

Sara Felicidad   Raquel Primera   Jacobo Primero
                  Raquel Segunda   Jacobo Segundo
                  Raquel Tercera   Jacobo Terero

FOUR

THE PROMISED PAMPA

T HE THIRTY-FIVE days of the voyage passed quickly. The powerful *Weser* cut the waves with the ease of the waiters in first class
who cut slices from their collection of French cheeses. Whenever
meals were served, those mixed odors of milk and dung descended like
oily waves along the metal ladders and reached steerage, making the
1,200 dried-out mouths of the Jewish emigrants water. But Alejandro
Prullansky, without envying the luxury surrounding his ex-colleagues
from the Imperial Ballet, eagerly went on with his daily exercises.

Poised on a rope strung between two enormous packing cases, he
repeated hour after hour his entrechats, leaps, and cross-steps, following the rhythm Icho Melnik generously supplied with his harmonica.
In his memory, the pimp retained countless melodies by Chopin,
Liszt, Mozart, and others. When his lips began to hurt from blowing
so much through his small instrument, he would begin to recite lines
from Seneca rhythmically, revealing a level of culture that seemed
absurd in a man of his profession, all so his friend could continue
training: "Work is not a good in itself. Then what is a good in itself?
Contempt for work." Icho would laugh but immediately continue:
"On the other hand, those who make an effort to obtain virtue without allowing themselves to become dejected deserve applause." And
when he pronounced the word "virtue," he used his fingers to mimic
the act of counting money.

Jashe joyfully observed her husband's perfect body. The splendid functioning of those wise muscles, making gestures of superhuman delicacy, aroused in her a pleasure that made her forget the corruption of the flesh, evil, and hunger. She did not fear the future and, knowing she was pregnant, gave herself over sweetly to the new life. Her Alejandro was a living temple, and his dancing would change the world. The six prostitutes lavished tender care on her, making the voyage as comfortable as possible because she read the Tarot for them, giving profound answers to their silly questions: "Will business improve if I dye my pubic hair red? Will I find an old man who will give me jewels and furs? Will I know love?" She predicted that two of them would marry military men; Marla, the tallest and most powerfully built, she saw paired up with an important politician; she lied to the other three, nervously covering up her sorrow with laughter, promising them long lives, health, and riches. They believed her because the gigolo began to make them work during the crossing. At night, he sent them to the cabins of the ship officers or to the service staff. They would come back at dawn carrying fruit, cigarettes, caviar, champagne, and chocolates. They shared everything. Icho, his belly swollen and with a smile from ear to ear, would quote before falling deeply asleep: "Life is a play. What matters is not that it lasts a long time but that it be well acted."

The coast of Argentina came into sight, and the ship made for the Río de la Plata. It was then that Simón Radovitzky, a tall, long-nosed boy with protruding ears, as skinny as a string bean, appeared before the prostitutes. He was followed by a small band of matrons frantically trying to help his mother, who was tearing her hair out. Because of Simón's black, bulging, and fanatical eyes, the rest of his body was practically invisible after a few minutes. When he spoke, the words seemed to come from his pupils: "Gentlemen, your good wives shave you every morning. Please allow them to cut off my beard. I want to get this superstitious tradition off my back. The past is a cage."

While his mother twisted her fingers and howled "oy" piteously, her huge tears soaking the wool shawl covering the heads of her fellow gossips, the young prostitutes, happily chirping, lathered up Simón's head and face. His mother tried to stop him for the last time by reciting a few proverbs in Yiddish: "A man's stupidity complicates his path. With a lie, you go far, but you can't come back. If you give the devil a hair, he'll soon want your whole beard." But the girls, after taking off his black overcoat, his fringed vest, and his leather cap, began to shave him.

When his payot, his side curls, fell, his mother muttered: "You are lost!" and bent over, clutching her abdomen as if she were having a miscarriage. Her women still held her up so she wouldn't fall to the floor. Making a supreme effort, she recovered; "It's annoying to carry a hunched back, but painful to separate yourself from it. This man is no longer my son. He's a drunk, a *shikker*. May your mother be one of these six *kurvehs*! May your brain dry up, may the worms start eating you while you're still alive, may you walk on your hands as many years as you've walked on your feet, and for the rest may you drag yourself along on your backside!"

The Jewish matrons left steerage without looking back, reciting magic verses to purify themselves from the sacrilegious air they'd breathed.

Simón Radovitzky was happy to see his bare face and bald head in the hand mirror with the floral frame that Marla handed him. He exclaimed:

"Being a Jew is much more than a disguise and a mop of hair! You can't spend your life believing in fairy tales and vengeful gods! We're living in the twentieth century! We're arriving at a young continent. We have to stop separating ourselves, stop living in an imaginary universe. Race, nationality, religion, customs—they're all unlucky limitations. We belong to the world, and the world is ours, in the same way that all human beings belong to us. Let's open our eyes, because the awakening of Awareness depends on Justice."

Wearing white trousers and a yellow shirt with blue polka dots that Icho Melnik gave him, the new Simón Radovitzky, followed at a distance by my grandparents and the whores, ran to the deck to show himself off to the religious Jews, offering himself as an example. They all fled without looking at him before he approached. He spread his arms, shouting at the top of his lungs, "Brothers, I'm not a wolf, and this is not a henhouse! Listen to me, I beg you! I too have tried to be a saint, but there is no virtue to be gained by separating ourselves. With your noses buried in the Torah, you can only see yourselves, cut off from the world as you are by that 'sacred' text. For not wanting to give anything, for continuously washing your hands so as not to participate in sin, you have ceased to be useful to society. But since the universal law is that everything has a purpose, society uses you to make you into victims. You have constructed for yourselves a Destiny, to be clowns who take knocks from others. Enough! I will unite myself with the horrors of life. Whatever happens to others, happens to me. I shall denounce in all possible media—letters, newspapers, shouting in the street, if it comes to that—the economic injustice that allows a few egoists to live in idleness, exploiting the labor of the workers. I shall ceaselessly demand the abolition of that authoritarian monster which is the State. I shall vomit on the lie of matrimony, a mercantile contract that legitimizes unions without love; I shall vomit on the patriotic lie that exaggerates natural affection for one's native land to turn it into fanatical stupidity that keeps the proletariat from understanding that the social problem is cosmopolitan. And I'll vomit on the religious lie that foments in the masses a servile attitude and enough resignation that they can bear the iniquities of earthly bandits with the hope of a celestial glory. I shall always denounce political necrophagy in favor of dynamic anarchy."

The bearded religious Jews whispered to one another, touching their temples with their index finger: Meshugganah! Then they erased him from their memory. Simón spit toward them and went back to the whores' corner to brandish a knife he'd stolen from the kitchen. He swore, "From now on my life ceases to be at the service of death. Instead, I put death at the service of life. Tyrants become vulnerable when a resolute individual appears."

For my grandfather, those words shouted by the young fanatic were a revelation. Locked away from the age of five in the elegant prison of the Imperial Ballet, with no horizon other than dance, he was unaware of the pain in the world. Life seemed to him a constant party. All he had to do was move to experience the pleasure of art. He saw everything as a dance where stars, landscapes, animals, multitudes and machines mixed together in a harmonious union. But Simón's inflammatory speech brought him out of his naïve radiance and submerged him in the fog of madness.

The *Weser* began to skim along the banks of the river, entering the outskirts of the immense city of Buenos Aires, a hive of proletarian dwellings and unhealthy factories, a human worm nest. From those dark places poured garbage, chemical liquids, rotten hides, greasy cans, excrement, making the water into a pitch-colored magma. On the banks of pestilential streams, garbage and rats splashed around on the ground that flooding had turned into mud. The mists from the leather factories, the smoke, and the soot from chimneys darkened the sky. Arrows of swarming green flies slashed open that dense, gray air, buzzing with murderous hunger.

The giant dancer, covering his ears on the bosom of the small woman, fell to his knees. Immobile and white, he looked like a cadaver drained of blood. It was not the flock of men, women, and children working in the tremendous labyrinth of sordid factories that affected him, but the mooing of the steers they were sacrificing in the chilled meat plants to freeze and send it abroad. There were thousands and thousands of sheep in mile-long lines, being led to their death. Their anguished moans, their squeals of terror, their dying cries, the rivers of dark blood, the mountains of guts and skulls, the filthy piles of hides, the fetid stench all came together in my grandfather's mind with the ghosts of even more millions of four-legged animals that had already been butchered, day after day, for years. Pyramids of knives worn right down to the handle, torrents of yellow teeth, smashed eyes floating in lakes of pus, planets of meat dissolving into worms.

"Why this total lack of awareness? They suffer, they are beings, part of myself. There they are before me, skinned animals, legs spread in a cross, an ocean of Christs with bleeding anuses, saints dismembered with mathematical slices. I know the pain of sheep; I've been raping them since I was in the sperm of Alejandro I, my demented grandfather, writing for help with the guts of his victims. And then in the vital liquor of my degenerate father, murdering women and children like the owners of those factories. Forgiveness was already granted; my mother devoured the cadaver of my progenitor and purified it by immersing herself in white. White! White! I love you! My God, forgive the Argentines for they know not what they eat, because they do not realize that their country lives on the production of frozen cadavers!"

Suddenly my grandfather saw, galloping toward him over the waters of the Río de la Plata, numberless sheep metamorphosed into furious dogs. As they bit him him until they'd devoured his body and there was nothing left but a voice rising from the void, he began to howl:

Because I walk in the valley of the shadow of death
I fear all evils if you are not with me!
Free my life from the power of the dog!
My God, hasten to help me!

Jashe, seeing her husband sink into madness, desperately put one of her breasts in his mouth so he could suck as if he were her child. Then she put the red shoes on him. No sooner than he felt those ancient shoes on his feet, my grandfather gave a satisfied smile and began to snore. The swarm of flies scattered, shocked by the sirens in the port. The *Weser* was entering the capital of Argentina. The ships were all packed together like a nest of giant ants, dead ants drying out next to deserted sea walls. Not a soul walked among the mountains of merchandise piled up on the docks.

Under a murderous sun, five thousand freight cars loaded with agricultural products were waiting to be unloaded at the warehouses. A huge banner made of cloth fluttered weakly, caressed by the tiniest breeze: WORKERS YES! SLAVES NO!

When the *Weser* dropped anchor, it emitted a long blast of the fog-horn, and without lowering the gangways, it seemed to pull back into itself like a sleeping turtle. The hours went by. Night fell. Dawn came. Marla, the captain's favorite, carrying a Swiss cheese and some Italian nougat, brought the news: the Federation of Stevedores had begun a work stoppage supported by coachmen and other groups that had degenerated into a general strike.

The conflict erupted because the stevedores, whose workday lasted fourteen hours, were forced to carry sacks that weighed more than two hundred pounds. The rationale behind this was that the importers from South Africa, who had black laborers stronger than camels, expected large sacks. The federation demanded a limit of one hundred and fifty pounds and workdays of ten hours, energetically demanding for its members the right to be considered human beings and not beasts of burden. The bosses were outraged and obdurate, calling the strikers malicious foreigners. Accordingly, they proposed a bill of expulsion to the government. Now the Congress was locked away in a special session to approve the law, declare a state of siege, obtain the right to raid citizens' homes, dissolve riots and belligerent meetings, use troops for an armed defense of "the dearest thing the nation has: its grand harvest," and above all, censor most of the newspapers.

Smiling, Icho Melnik shrugged his shoulders and quoted a thought of Maecenas: "Cripple me, make me lame, slap a hump on my back, loosen my teeth, crucify me . . . if you leave me alive, I'll feel fine."

Simón Radovitzky turned red with rage: "This period in Argentina will be tossed into the garbage can of history. In the future, no citizen will want to recall such infamy. Only a few scholars, while reading in some dusty library documents containing these miserable petitions to Congress, will shut their eyes in shame, afraid of infection. How can one human being force another human being to carry two hundred pound sacks fourteen hours a day for a salary he can't live on? These millionaire parasites have gone insane: they think they are the soul of the nation, when in reality they are devouring the nation!"

At midday, the asphalt began to tremble and a metallic, heavy noise brought thousands of stevedores out of the shadows. In a few minutes, a sea of human bodies filled the docks, roasting in the merciless summer. Fatigue and anguish had transformed the workers into a tamed flock. Five cars appeared, filled with soldiers and police, who quickly pointed rifles at the brutalized crowd.

"What insolence!" Simón exclaimed.

From a motorcycle, protected by an armored car and a group of thugs, came the chief of police, Colonel Roberto Falcón. Some twenty or so men ran toward him to hand him papers. "Disgusting informers!" muttered Simón. "Look at them handing their vile blacklists!"

Roberto Falcón jumped on top of a barrel and, with ferocious contempt, stared at the strikers. His impeccable suit without a wrinkle; his black hair plastered down with hair tonic, shining like a helmet; his patent leather boots; his striped tie with pearl clasp; his white silk scarf; everything about him contrasted sneeringly with the filth and poverty of the silent workers. Suddenly the colonel began to shout like an animal trainer, as if he were talking to dogs:

"The jig is up, faggots! You lost the battle! The Congress unanimously voted to give us legal powers to launch the largest repressive campaign our country, Argentina, has seen to date! The general strike is liquidated! We're going to cleanse the nation of anarchists, active militants in trades unions, leaders of workers, the editorial staff of critical press, seats of labor, and the rest! Hear what I said, you jackass gringos? Get back to work immediately, if you want to save your scummy hides, and let us get on with the arrest of the malevolent agitators whose names we have on these lists our wise informers have given us!"

The soldiers penetrated the crowd, guided by the snitches that shouted out the names of the guilty at the top of their lungs. The accused, with their eyes down and without trying to run, turned themselves in to the men in uniform, who beat them first with nightsticks and then locked them away in black riot trucks. The other stevedores headed for the mountains of sacks and began to carry them. The rays of sunlight made those packages shine and gave them the appearance of shells, transforming the distraught workers into slow-moving reptiles. The ships, shaking off their lethargy, filled with sailors. The cranes screeched, the gangways stretched out their eager arms, and the port gave out a dismal whine like the tremors of a woman giving birth. A dense circle of flies, flashing green in the sunlight, paused over the colonel's head. He extracted a thin stiletto from his walking stick and plunged it into the buzzing planetoid. The flies separated and fled toward the carloads of rotten vegetables.

"Fucking bugs. Only force can separate them. The only call they heed is the whistle of weapons. Remember my name, you living ragdolls. In the name Falcón, there is a falcon. Anyone who doesn't obey will fall into my clutches and get the pecking he deserves. If you can't listen, I'll reward you with a knuckle sandwich. You are the scum of your nations. If you want to live in this country, don't act like uppity parasites. Gringos have no rights here. No say, no vote. Be thankful we've let you live. Anyone who stops working today, even if it's to pee, will be shot to pieces. Tough laws only apply to some people, which is the way it should be. Get the hell out of my sight!"

Haughtily, the colonel grabbed a young man with the profile of a Greek statue by the shoulders of and rode off on his motorcycle, heading for the center of the capital. The strong blast from the exhaust pipe gave Radovitzky chills. He waved a kitchen knife around, muttering, "You get the hell out of my sight and may you rot in hell, Roberto Falcón! I know we shouldn't hate the dog but the dog's owner, but you carry out your disgusting task with too much pleasure. You add torture to the legal punishment, only to blow up the stinking balloon of your powerful persona. One day a knife will burst that balloon and return you to what you've always been: a dead man."

"Calm down, boy, and hide that knife," said Icho. "What you say about the colonel is true for all living beings. What is life if not a slow death?"

My grandfather woke up well rested, but it took him another ten minutes to recover his senses. Meanwhile Jashe combed her blonde hair and made a braid down to her nape. Then she examined that piece of work intensely. Seeing the dancer's transparent beauty, his blue eyes like a constant dawn, pouring an ancient love onto the world, that smile of a newborn, that powerful chest breathing with such delicacy that the foul air left his mouth transformed into a balm, my grandmother wept with ecstasy and thanked heaven Alejandro hadn't seen the atrocious beating. She wanted to be a magician, to cleanse the world of ugliness, and to offer this divine man a life equal to his purity.

The first-class passengers began to disembark. The Imperial Ballet was received by an elegant committee that filled the arms of the ballerinas with roses of all different colors. Marina Leopoldovna, making her way down the gangplank, cast a darting look toward the emigrants crowded together on the deck. When she saw the blond giant shining like a lotus flower in the pool of pitch formed by the Israelites' black overcoats, she muttered spitefully, "Your career is over. You will never dance again. My father will have your legs cut off." They all got into a dozen taxis and left the port for the colonnaded Colón Theatre.

As the procession passed, the workers took off their caps and saluted the ballerinas as if they were magical abstractions; butterflies of human flesh, emissaries from a paradise yet to come. Seeing the tremendous impression they made, Vladimir Monomaque thought to satisfy the crowd by tossing out handfuls of coins, which for dignity's sake no one picked up. Marina Leopoldovna, refusing to flash her famous smile, preferred to sink into the seat of the car and, under the guise of a sneezing fit, hid her face in her shawl.

When the Ballet and the committee disappeared, eight immigration inspectors entered the ship to receive the Jewish farmers. Seeing those bizarre costumes, those long beards, those interminable sideburns, they were astounded. Then they burst into profanities: "We asked for farmers, not a bunch of lunatics! These skinny worms couldn't even lift a shovel!"

The immigrants waved their pale hands to show the calluses they'd acquired on the voyage from rubbing their hands with ropes.

The chief inspector howled, "Captain, send barbers! No one gets off this ship wearing a beard, sideburns, and long hair! And to salute our flag, they all have to take off those ridiculous little hats!"

When some of the stewards appeared waving razors and scissors, the women went down on their knees howling dogged lamentations. The men gathered behind them, ready to die before they let anyone cut off a single hair. Not knowing what to do, the immigration authorities went up to the bridge to communicate with their superiors by telegraph.

Icho Melnik said, "Our compatriots worry a lot about something that matters little. After all, how important can it be to avoid for, a little more or less time, the inevitable? They'll end up shaven!" He spread his arms to receive his brother Yumo, who came to Buenos Aires three years earlier. It was he who sent the tickets. He ran a bordello for the wealthy in the center of town. All the girls were foreigners, preferably Jews, because they were the most sought after.

The fat pimp spoke with his brother in hushed tones, and then said to his new friends, "Alejandro, Jashe, Simón, as my master teaches, the place where we stop matters little, as long as we can arrange a good exit.

For the moment, you have no place to stay. It would be better if you came to our bordello. There, no one will bother you and, in exchange for some small services, you can stay as long as you need. There are lots of empty rooms. While Jashe helps in the kitchen and Simón makes the beds and brings fresh towels to the rooms, Alejandro can give dance classes to our protégées to fatten their asses. Agreed? Well? Then come along with us. The authorities, with regard to whores and money discretely paid, will provide all we need to disembark.

In the car that carried them to the center of the city, away from miserable neighborhoods and toward the baroque buildings where many styles and luxurious materials all mixed together, Alejandro was discovering an infinite field of new possibilities within his spirit. Unable to contain himself, he poured into the ears of my terrified grandmother words so optimistic that in this world, sinister for being so unfamiliar, they glittered like demented jewels.

"Do you know, Jashe, until now I never thought? I lived like an animal, only feeling. But that young anarchist's speech caused a moral earthquake in my soul. You said my body was a temple, and you were right because God has appeared within me. He speaks to me ceaselessly. Listen to what he says:

My son, you are what you are in the present. Leave the past behind; don't carry remorse. Eliminate all anxiety about the future. Prepare to work for your progression until the last moment of your life. Let no one be your judge; be your own judge. If you want to triumph, learn to fail. Never define yourself by what you possess. Never speak about yourself without allowing yourself the possibility to change. Consider that you do not exist independently, that what you do does itself. Only by accepting that nothing is yours will you be the owner of all. Become a total offering. Give, but oblige no one to receive. Make no one feel guilty; you are an accomplice to whatever

happens. Stop asking for things and start thanking. Acquire in
order to give away.

With tears in her eyes, Jashe kissed her giant, even though he was
unable to cut off his monologue. Their four lips stayed together, and
he deposited in her throat his unremitting string of axioms:

"Discover the universal laws and obey them. Don't eliminate; trans-
mute. Teach others to learn from themselves. With the little you have,
do the most you can. Give a hungry man something to eat, but don't
keep him at your table. Don't ask yourself where you are going; just
move ahead taking the proper steps. Leaping is as beautiful as crawling:
don't compare yourself to others, develop your own values. Change
your world or change worlds."

Alejandro said so much that Jashe could only remember a tiny
bit, to her profound regret. They reached the bordello. A sumptuous
house surrounded by rose bushes, quite proper looking, but with a
red light at the door. Twelve girls dressed in bright costumes, wearing
exaggerated makeup, which, even at that time of day, could not hide
their cracked faces, received them. They passed through a salon covered with golden drapes, furnished with red velvet upholstery. They
marched up four flights. There they were given an attic decorated in
bohemian style with lots of cushions and a grand but low bed opposite a huge mirror. Alejandro, still in a trance, was aware of nothing.
Like a boundless river, he spoke without eating or sleeping for three
solid days:

"What is necessary is possible. If you want to end the vices of others,
purify yourself. What you see is what you are. Sickness is your teacher.
Do not touch another's body to get pleasure or to humiliate him; touch
him to accompany him. Don't boast of your weaknesses. Act for the
pleasure of acting and not for the favorable results it may produce.
Forgive your parents."

Then he slept for three days. My grandmother had already learned the words necessary to survive in this country, while still on the ship—from the lips of Marla, who spoke Ladino. With unflagging energy, she had flyers printed up extoling the ex-first dancer of the Imperial Ballet and distributed them among the people who formed immense lines outside the ticket office of the Colón Theatre. In the neighborhood of the bordello, she found a large study, rented it, and received the enthusiastic girls and effeminate young men who wanted the opportunity to learn classical dance with a high-ranking professor.

On the fourth day, she woke her husband, bringing him breakfast in bed, fresh fruit. Waiting for him in the gymnasium were 150 students. Alejandro ate an entire pineapple, threw on his clothes, and noted with surprise that one of his red shoes, the right, had turned blue.

"The grand change is beginning. From intervention I'm passing on to reception. I will not teach classical techniques, because they correspond to the limitations society imposes. To the contrary, I shall liberate their bodies so they once again find their natural expression. Animals are in a continuous dance. So is man. God creates the gestures, which is why every sincere movement is a revelation."

The Argentine students, the children of the rich, knew little about the history of dance and did not intend to dedicate their lives to art. What they were looking for was some cultural varnish to justify their idle lives. And for that, the classes given by the Russian were perfect. Alejandro, without realizing how frivolous his students were, dedicated his entire being to the exercise. He felt a constant communication between his body and the Cosmos, coming to believe that the slightest movement of his fingers could influence the Destiny of the galaxies. One night he embraced Jashe excitedly and declared, "I'm going to recount a miracle. Today I made a chain of dance steps so beautiful that up in heaven two suns were born."

The months passed. Alejandro, never weakening, like a shepherd of wild goats, buried himself in his academy, making his fickle students rehearse a ballet titled *Life* about a thousand times. He only returned to the bordello to kiss his wife—who was showing a belly that was more and more prominent—spread her legs, visit the secret temple, rapidly deposit his offering, and then sleep like a stone. From time to time, Icho Melnik and his brother Yumo would visit the attic Jashe had transformed into an enchanted palace with paper flowers and bottle fragments. There they would drink boiling, heavily sugared tea with lemon and complain about the cruel manias of their clients and consult the Tarot.

The good life was making Icho fatter by the day. In the kitchen he had a personal refrigerator full of prize beef, two hundred pounds, and at every meal he would eat six steaks along with the other dishes on the menu. He justified his gluttony by quoting Seneca: "If you do not take control of time, time will run away from you."

Yumo preferred moderation. Despite his hair, which was red but closer to a carrot in color, his face marked with freckles, and his muscular torso resting on thin legs, he tried to dress with elegance. For him, prostitution was a respectable business, and he had visiting cards printed up with his name and below that "Supplier of Feminine Beauty. Imported." He was not ashamed to visit the synagogue, even though the congregation refused to great him, thinking he was a *teme'im*, an impure person.

He argued, "I do not understand your disdain. My girls are as sacred as the Torah. We Jews are a chosen people, and our mission is to lead the goys to holiness. God is hidden in the depths of the Hebrew female sex. Every vagina is a sacred place. When the member enters there, it receives its baptism of fire about which so many speak without knowing what it's all about. In a certain sense, the clients die when they possess my hetaeras. And when they withdraw, they are in reality born. A new life awaits them. To ejaculate into Jewish whores is, dear friends, doing it in the open emptiness of God."

No one bothered to listen.

Simón Radovitzky also came to visit Jashe, but only on the odd after-noon. Always busy, he did his work with the same fanaticism with which he defended anarchism. Every bed he made was a work of art: well-beaten mattresses, geometric folds, total absence of wrinkles. He would hand his clients perfumed towels and then stand before them with impeccable dignity, making himself invisible, only allowing his ardent eyes to float about. When they gave him his tip, he thanked them with an elegant nod of his head. That elegance was actually comic, because the shame of being reduced to a beggar made his protruding ears bright red. During his tiny bit of free time, especially during the early hours—the whores slept from seven until three in the afternoon—he dedicated himself, not earning a cent, to writing for clandestine anarchist publications and then selling them, risking his life in the process. Aside from attacking the tyranny of the government and its "barbarous thugs with sabers and whistles," the mass arrests and the expulsion of "pernicious foreigners," which were all grist for his mill, he attacked the socialists, those "traitors and cowards who took advantage of the persecution to accuse the anarchists of being violent and take over the leadership of the trade unions."

One May, there was a strike by restaurant waiters protesting a munici-pal ordinance that forced them to shave off their moustaches. Simón, even though he no longer wore that virile ornament, because he'd decided not only to live outside of religious customs but also outside of seduction (*Never adorn. The free man does not sell himself, does not per-form tricks, does not solicit; he creates bonds because severing them produce archipelagos of island-beasts makes no sense. The free man's encounter with a woman should be magic, instantaneous, without calculation, definitive, and total. Why seek her when all the powers of the Universe have her reserved for you anyway?*), accepted the idea that the strikers considered the new rule a grievance and opposed the cutting of that bit of hair with energetic resistance: the oligarchy needed eunuchs to serve them, and in this instance testicles and moustaches had the same meaning.

Writing in the pages of *The Sun*—the only workers newspaper which hadn't been closed, as its editor was a well-known native Argentine poet—Simón, who wrote his articles in Russian and saw them translated not only into Spanish but also into Italian, German, English, and French for the immigrant workers, ripped into the authorities:

> *The climate of cowardice engenders tyrannies. If everyone says 'let's give in,' they become accomplices in the raising of the machete, in thought control. This infamous attempt to castrate the workers originates in the upper classes who, in order to erase the spiritual power of the individual, make all uniform. Everything uniform—be it religious, military, or unionized—is an assault on the always-different nature of each being. Protest, brothers! Protest out of self-defense, out of pure self-interest, because tomorrow all will be measured by the same yardstick, because the abuse committed against any member of a collective, even the most insignificant, becomes the shame of those who tolerate it.*

Radovitzky's words affected his readers like a lit match dropped into a lake of alcohol. The coachmen's boys joined the strike along with the leather cutters from the shoe factories. Then the port workers, sailors, stokers, and stevedores. They all asked for human dignity and a ten-percent salary increase. With the good wishes of the police, the intransigent companies began to employ strikebreakers. To stop the unloading of ships, the strikers attacked the traitors. The fracas extended along the docks. Simón Radovitzky, part of the tumult, took out a revolver and fired. Other workers carrying weapons followed his lead. But the timidity of the workers, accustomed to bowing, caused the bullets to fly over the heads of the police and land in the mountains of rotten melons waiting to be loaded. The soldiers' ferocious cruelty, their lack of imagination, and their strict intelligence caused all their bullets to land in the heart of Paolo Zapoletti, an Italian emigrant, who fell backward with his chest turned into a sieve. An enormous red stain surrounded the body until it became a halo like those that surround the Virgin.

The fighting stopped. That single casualty grew in the minds of the spectators until it became a giant. Many hands lifted the fallen man. They put him on a cot to carry him on a slow, silent march, interrupted from time to time by hoarse he-man voices singing revolutionary songs with such heartrending force they struck like darts. In that way, they marched for hours through the poor neighborhoods. More than ten thousand new strikers joined the funeral march. Simón began to shout, "An eye for an eye, death for death!" The crowd followed him, repeating his slogan louder and louder. The police, afraid that the public outcry would surge and that the workers would attack the police stations, used a detachment of cavalry to stop the procession, disperse it with sabers, and take away the body. Once the fright passed, a wave of anger surged among the workers. Even though they outnumbered their enemies, they panicked at the presence of a small group of horses and a few whistles.

Simón howled, "Comrades, to break bones you've got to sacrifice some meat! Let a few of us die willingly to exterminate all of them! Let's be daring! Let's continue the strike until we finish off the State!"

More modest souls requested that the meeting be dissolved to allow time for the various associations to meet and publish statement of protest, supported by the organs of the worker bloc: Socialist Party, Federation of Dependents, unions, anarchist groups, etcetera. The workers of Buenos Aires, setting aside their ideological differences, would march united, as a colossal body, denouncing the abuses of the stinking cops so the exploiting classes would understand that social unrest could not be solved with prisons, persecutions, or deportations.

Two days later, with government authorization, the demonstration began. Having received an order from Roberto Falcón, the workers did not wave red flags. They agreed to suppress the vehement criticism against the measures adopted by the police during the state of siege, all in order to avoid bloody reprisals. More than forty thousand workers marched with stern composure from Constitution Plaza to Plaza Lavalle. Police were standing guard all along the route of the march, and many agents on horseback followed the demonstrators closely. When they reached Plaza Lavalle, the speakers took their places on an improvised stage.

Simón Radovitzky pulled out a red flag he'd hidden under his leather overcoat and waved it in the face of a thug on horseback. The soldier charged toward Simón, intending to crush his skull under the horse's hooves. Several demonstrators interjected themselves, trying to prevent the confrontation. The man with the big ears would not let up. He waved his rag as if he were facing a bull and shouted to him in precarious Spanish, "If you strike me, you strike yourself, you savage on a horse! Let your murderous blows fall on me, cover my skin with red spots where you'll be able to read your Destiny!"

Those words were incomprehensible to the uniformed worker. He took them as insults, so he unsheathed his saber and, making threats, swung it around wildly. Simón, shrieking euphorically, fired five shots into the air. Roberto Falcón, on his motorcycle, sitting behind his helper with the Greek silhouette, whispered into his ear. The driver honked his horn three times. Instantly the police opened fire on the workers. A single fusillade was all it took to cut down many victims. Amid an enormous confusion, a general retreat began, but the situation worsened when companies of firemen arrived and used their powerful hoses to demolish the demonstrators. The motorcycle honked its horn again. Silence. Colonel Falcón smiled in satisfaction.

Scores of wounded and dead were leaking blood that seemed to write out a melody on the five parallel lines painted on the asphalt. The only person who could see it was Radovitzky, who watched the massacre hidden in a cart loaded with artichokes. He copied out the musical phrase in his notebook and watched the police chief pass by on his ridiculous motorcycle, probably on his way to a press conference where he'd communicate the official version of events to calm public opinion. Then he slipped off the cart, and staying close to the shadowy walls, lightly made his way toward the bordello, satisfied.

By provoking this loss of blood, he'd created martyrs, who in turn would create hatred and the desire for revenge. For him, the most powerful weapons in a revolt were innocent victims: "The lives of many are won with the death of a few." He did not feel guilty, because he himself was ready to sacrifice himself at any time. He'd donated his existence to humanity a long time ago.

As soon as he reached the mansion with the red light, he asked Icho Melnik to play (never mentioning its source) the musical phrase created by the workers' blood on his harmonica. Out came a proud lament which, in tango rhythm and arranged for accordion and a string trio, became the house anthem and made the sensual orgies of the clients more enjoyable.

Jashe, on the eve of giving birth, all dressed in white, wrapped her arms around her enormous belly and danced that pulsing tango, which came from the floor below, with her unborn daughter for a partner.

In the absence of Alejandro, who would come home after midnight, give her a kiss on the forehead, and collapse into bed to (for the first time since they met) snore like a locomotive, she conversed with the fetus, communicating her hopes. For her, there was neither past nor present, only future. Nothing existed here and now, not there and not before. Everything was nowhere and later . . . Yes, someday things would come to be. The money they'd saved would be enough to buy a property with mansion, gardens, and private cemetery. The cypresses would grow around that house, and their children and grandchildren, playing trombones, tubas, and cornets, would put their bodies inside a grandfather clock to throw them, limbs interlaced, into the well-mausoleum, which would reach the enormous heart of fresh water that was the center of the planet.

The indefatigable giant dancer, with his blond beard and mane of golden hair that caressed his waist, persevered in trying to stage his ballet,

Life. It was like trying to trace a star on the surface of a lake with one finger. His undedicated students did not like rehearsals or philosophical messages, but they did spend whole hours before the mirror admiring themselves in their tights, tutus, wool stockings, wide belts, and slippers with steel toes. Alejandro would pull them out of their self-amazement by striking the floor with his long walking stick to make them repeat, once, a thousand times, the four parts of the choreography.

First, "The Great Yes" would express the struggle against doubt through the unconditional acceptance of existence. Second, "The Unlimited Gratefulness" would show the end of yearning and the ecstasy of constant gratitude. Third, "The Rapid Farewell" would describe the abandonment of all possessions and the tranquil acceptance of death, making it the most beautiful moment of life. Finally, "The Instantaneous Return" would show the rapid reincarnation of souls, not as punishment but as a means of progress. But the Argentine dancers thought that dance was a circus and were only interested in competing to raise a leg higher or complete more spins on the tip of a toe.

Alejandro, with his minimal Spanish, tried to open their minds and reveal to them that God inhabited them and to convince them to yield their bodies to mystery so they could carry out movements that were unimaginable to human reason. Useless! Locked within their proud mediocrity, they could not allow their legs, arms, torsos, or hips to live their own lives as autonomous organisms fed by the wisdom of the stars. My grandfather, at times right in the middle of this inept group, would fall to his knees sobbing desperately. His female students fought to dry his tears with delicate licks; panting so hotly that shame would burn their cheeks. He would get up in a rage, his body shuddering and shaking off those sexual advances as if they were fleas.

Jashe gave birth with help from the bordello midwife, an old German woman, Bettina the Turtle. She'd acquired that nickname because a jealous Argentine had clipped her ears and nose. My mother, Sara

Felicidad, was born, a baby as white as marble with two huge lapis lazuli eyes and four nipples, which would later become, I think, four large breasts where I could suck, unless it's a false memory, a double portion of milk. Alejandro didn't realize he'd become a father. He was so stubbornly intent on his work that, besides the dance, the world vanished. He no longer saw people but misty shapes. He marched through the world without belonging to it, listening to the interminable river of phrases God dictated to him: "I am the summa of your calls. Present is the complete perception of yourself. Don't try to be another, allow the other to exist in you. Never express more than what you feel. To give is to know how to receive."

A tranquil Jashe fed her unseen daughter, preparing monumental fruit salads that Alejandro, now a vegetarian, devoured directly from the plate, on all fours like a ruminant. The woman had to buck up her courage because my grandfather, trying to express his animal nature freely, took it upon himself to defecate in corners or on an armchair, sometimes under the table. Jashe, in these moments, saw them as past and cleaned up those eccentricities with good will, thinking about the future of sanity and happiness that awaited them.

On her own, she devoted herself to educating Sara Felicidad. On the wall next to the cradle, she tacked the seventy-eight Tarot cards so her daughter would learn to count early by pointing to the cups, coins, clubs, and swords. At six months, the child said her first word, "*MAT*," and by one she already knew how to speak some Russian and a lot of Spanish. Instead of saying "papa," she loved to say "paradise" and instead of "mama" she would say "marvel." At eighteen months, she began to sing, first imitating Marla's nightingale, then the violin from the tango quartet, later the she-cats in heat, and finally Bettina the Turtle, who during the Catholic festivals of the month of May intoned "Come, and let us all go with flowers to Mary" so the Virgin would grant her the miracle of allowing her to grow another nose and two new ears.

The high, crystalline voice of the baby made the dust fall off the mirrors and, for a few seconds, calmed the drunken clients. As soon as they started flashing their knives, Jashe would come down with Sara Felicidad so she could sing "Canción Mixteca," transforming rage into nostalgia and then into beatitude. The bestial masks would fall off, and the little boy faces would appear.

Meanwhile, Alejandro, who remained blind and deaf to the existence of his daughter, was beginning to lose hope in the realization of his dance. Whenever a girl managed to learn the intricate steps, she would fall in love, get married, become pregnant, and abandon art forever. If it were a young man, he would get his law or architecture degree, or kill himself, or run off with some low-class lover and his mother's jewels. Alejandro would get furious over nothing, a slice of apple with a seed in it, a distracted look when he was speaking about his problems with the dancers. He would threaten to beat his wife to a pulp. Then he would fall to his knees to kiss her feet, begging forgiveness. One day, at three in the afternoon, his breakfast time, Yumo Melnik burst into the dining room, waving a blue telegram:

"Girls, eat quickly and run to fix yourselves up and slip into your sexiest clothes! Two hours from now, the chief of police, Roberto Falcón, will honor us with a visit! He's coming to throw a party for his twenty bodyguards. Every year, as a bonus, the chief grants them a wish. This year they asked to screw Jewish whores. Dear hearts, you are model professionals. It's extremely important for the future of our business that you not reject any whim. They are murderers, yes, of course, but they see sex like boys. If you don't contradict them and submit smilingly to their peculiarities, they will be as tame as little lambs. And swallow these pills, which will keep you awake until the stiffest pricks collapse!"

Simón Radovitzky, his face solemn, took the opportunity to approach Marla, who was drinking her coffee in the shadow because daylight irritated her eyes.

"Marla, I know you're going to be very busy with those killers. Even so, and with the greatest respect, I'm going to ask a favor. My life won't be long. Maybe it will be over before the sun comes up tomorrow. Don't interrupt me, please! What I'm telling you is serious, because I'm talking to you as if I were sentenced to death. Look: in this jacket I have all the money I've been able to save. I'm giving it to you. It's more than you earn in a month of work. Initiate me, Marla! I'm a virgin. Make me a man. I want to learn, in the two hours we have before the police come, the depth of pleasure, to pour out the semen of entire life, to fornicate in different positions and through all doors, to give you my heart like an animal on the sacrificial altar. I want my spirit to bury itself in yours and die there so that later they shoot what is only an empty body. Oh, Marla, forgive me. I think I love you."

The prostitute said nothing. She slowly put the money into her black satin bag, finished her coffee, took Simón by the hand, led him to the third floor. They entered the room decorated like an underwater grotto. She stripped him, bathed him in the big marble conch, dried him with a towel cut in the shape of a sardine, got into bed with him under silk sheets printed with breaking waves, and gave herself to him in body and soul.

After those two hours, a different Simón Radovitzky walked down the stairs. The adolescent had become a mature man. His footsteps were heavy, intense, decisive, but his eyes were veiled, like those of a dead man. He sat down next to the armoire filled with clean sheets and waited with the patient calm of a dog sleeping in the shade on a summer day. Roberto Falcón offered his followers a party without limits. They devoured three roast pigs and emptied uncountable bottles of brandy. While they danced the house tango, they let themselves tear the dresses and underpants of their partners, to carry them again and again to the private rooms. Finally, staggering, they possessed them right there in front of everybody, on the salon carpet or on the bar chairs. Falcón drank, accompanied by his driver, without touching the girls. When he saw them all going awkwardly through the motions like swings, then fall, vomit, and snore in surfeit, their testicles empty down to the last drop, he made a sign to the boy with the Greek profile, and the two of them, with the discretion of shadows, locked themselves away in the preferential suite on the second floor.

Marla, squashed under an orangutan who'd wet his pants, saw Simón, barefoot, make his way up the stairs and enter the luxurious apartment. She felt her heart was breaking, forever, like a crystal vase, and she bit her lips trying not to sob. A red drop slipped down her chin until it fell into the open mouth of the hairy client who, without waking up, savored it smiling. The next day, she would have her left breast tattooed with the letters S.R.

Simón committed the first murder in ten seconds. Falcón was on his knees, with his head buried in a pillow, while his assistant penetrated him with rapid and violent thrusts of his hips. The shrieks of pleasure-pain silenced the steps of the anarchist, who, with his animal acumen, cut the lover's jugular vein with one slice of a kitchen knife. He did it so decisively that he almost separated the head from the body, and without stopping, as if it were the same graceful movement, drove the knife between the two bodies and cut off the driver's member, which remained stuck in the chief's anus. While the body fell, spurting bright red, Simón put the knife in his other hand, took out his revolver, and pointed it at Falcón: "Don't scream or I'll blow your brains out! Stand up and face me, because I'm your death, faggot!"

The colonel, whiter than the corpse of his lover, stood up next to the bed. The piece of phallus slid out of his anus and, with a wet noise, fell between his feet like a mollusk without a shell. He vomited.

"Lick up your garbage!"

Falcón went down on his knees and passed his tongue over his puke.

"Swine! I should give you a shameful end, stick this knife into that stinking hole and open you up right to your guts, pull out your tripes, and tie you to your boyfriend, then break your skull, empty out your brain and shit in it, as if it were a toilet bowl! Give thanks to anarchism, you moral dwarf. I don't want to dishonor my comrades by exterminating you with the same viciousness you used to torture and murder so many innocent workers just to satisfy your vanity. I'll give you a clean ending."

"Have mercy. A sack of diamonds for my life."

"You're mistaken, colonel. I've always wanted to live in noble poverty," Simón answered with a sweet smile and killed him with a perfect shot right between the eyes. Then he sat down opposite the two dead men, put a finger in the pool of blood, and drew the A of Anarchy on his forehead. The bodyguards, roused by the shot, quickly kicked open the door. Radovitzky was beaten to a pulp—broken nose, three broken ribs, and six broken teeth. They dragged him down to the bar and tortured him in front of the prostitutes. Even though they slowly but surely ripped off all his skin, he died without betraying any member of his group. The police arrested all the witnesses, cursing them the whole time.

The crime stirred public opinion. The authorities blamed the Jewish community, especially the Russian immigrants: "The government is firmly resolved to take energetic measures to avoid the entry into this country of dangerous people and to eliminate those found here," the new chief of police declared. Resuming the state of siege, he began a search for anarchist leaders among the non-naturalized Jews. Under the Residence Law, several hundred were expelled from the country. Among them were the Melnik brothers and their whores, who, without a cent (the police had confiscated their savings as the price they'd have to pay for the "favor" of not sending them back to Russia), were put on a train that took them directly to Uruguay.

When they got out in Montevideo, Icho rubbed his enormous belly and said good-naturedly, "If the wise man thinks above all about poverty, even if he is surrounded by wealth, we, amid poverty, will think above all about wisdom. Courage, girls! Every man is a possible client. Don't ask God to give, but that he put you where they are."

The Turtle, who had been set free because she was a pure German and an Argentine citizen, came to the study, passed through the rows of students, and with her strange, nasal voice urged Alejandro to run to the jail to get his wife and daughter before they were both shipped to Europe. The news of his friend's death had shaken my grandfather and brought him down from the clouds. He suddenly felt alone and realized that he had a daughter and a wife who felt a great love for him, and it was thanks to their love he went on living. To lose Jashe and Sarita would mean becoming a tree without roots, floating aimlessly in a river of turbid water. He reached the prison waving press photographs, programs from the Imperial Ballet where his name appeared in big letters, his Russian passport, and his marriage license. In the room where he spoke to the police, he demonstrated by giving the three highest leaps of his entire career, along with the most sublime suite of steps. His blond mane brightened the somber building. The guards admired him openmouthed and released his small family.

Out on the street, Alejandro fell to his knees and kissed the feet of his wife and daughter, begging their forgiveness. The shoe that was still red turned blue. Jashe, her breath short from emotion, raised him up to offer him her mouth. He kissed it as never before, trying to press his lips to hers forever. Sara Felicidad began to sing the tango Simón Radovitzky had brought to the bordello. The melody began tragically, only to fill with triumphal tones. Alejandro felt his heart full of light. "You are my soul," he said to the child and, putting her on his shoulders, began to leap along the street, trying to fly. After twenty blocks, he fell exhausted next to a garbage can. Sarita went on singing. The passersby gave them coins. They piled up before them. When Jashe reached them, she silenced her daughter and picked up the coins, her face burning with shame.

Alejandro took her by the waist, looked at her with infinite tenderness, and said, "You gave me a daughter, you brought me out of madness. A great change has just taken place in my spirit."

"Simón's marvelous sacrifice and this charity have made me understand that as an artist I've been a parasite. My dancing is only entertainment for rich people who applaud as long as you don't show them anything real. I mean, human misery and the industrial devastation of the planet. I've been training my entire life for an audience that requires beauty without truth. I've submerged myself in myself, becoming an island of form without mind, in an exhibition of naïve vanity. The Imperial Ballet separated me from the people, and Vladimir Monomaque separated me from human feelings. I grew up like someone maimed, with no relationship to others, drunk on my own limitations. Dancing is a trap that makes us complicit with exploiters and murderers. The money they gave me and the money I've earned giving classes to frivolous students is stained with blood. We should give it away. If I want to be a real artist, I have to know poverty, share life with my brother workers. I know, Jashe, that I'm asking a great sacrifice of both of you; that you and Sara Felicidad put up with misery, for how long I don't know. For that reason you have to decide right now: either you leave with the child and you make a new alliance with a sleeping man who will give you comforts attained by robbing the well-being of others, or you come with me to the poor neighborhoods to redeem the injustice of this world with the sacrifice of your life, as Simón Radovitzky sacrificed his."

Without hesitating, Jashe answered, "To whom do we give the money?"

"If we divide it, each recipient will get little. It would be better for a single person to get all. God tells me it should be poor Bettina. Our gift will console her for her injuries."

The workers in the meatpacking plants didn't last more than five years. They would die or catch chronic illnesses. For that reason, getting work there was easy for Alejandro. He left Jashe and Sara Felicidad living in a room that was seven feet wide and nine deep, with a chamber pot for a bathroom and an electric grill for a kitchen, and went to carry out his penitence.

The frozen meat industry, controlled by foreign capital, was "untouchable" by the national authorities. Because there was no union, the working conditions could not be worse. Alejandro began in slaughtering. In the open areas where the animals were killed, he was permanently exposed—in winter to rain and cold, in summer to gaseous emanations and sickening smells. After the initial cut, the blood poured out onto men and tools and then ran, in part, through the floor, forming dark red layers. Amid excrement and urine, he had to skin animals and then toss them onto tables, divide them up, and carve them.

The saws whined, tossing into the air the sawdust of bones. The mill, the carts, the pulleys, the chains, the grunts of the dying animals kept him from talking with his fellow workers, those sad, bloody, and fetid men who wore all amulets around their necks to keep the animals from infecting them with skin tumors, mouth ulcers, trichinosis. In those early days, Alejandro had some very difficult moments. Not only was the work horrifying because of the huge number of murdered animals but also because of a hallucination that incessantly repeated itself: the ghosts of sheep transformed into furious bitches sank their teeth into him. Restraining his anguish, he let his body be devoured, never ceasing to cut, select, and put into separate piles the intestines, the livers, the kidneys, the hearts. He imagined that the thousands of snipped-off tongues were his own, and he made them recite in chorus, "Now I live in a reality that is as terrible as madness, but at least I can share it with the needy. I can no longer allow myself private nightmares. I am no longer an individual. Work is the madness of the poor."

Making titanic efforts, he managed to free himself from the demented images and, with the help of his inner God, went on with his disgusting labors. When he brought the pieces of meat to the cold room, everything instantly froze. Often he saw workers who entered there daubed with blood with frozen faces or with their hands stuck to their knives. To avoid that, Alejandro, like the others, wrapped his head and his extremities in rags and newspapers and put on old wool vests, one on top of the other. If his clothing was soaked with blood, it froze immediately. When he couldn't take the cold any longer, he would go outside and warm himself by placing his legs, hands, and face inside the bodies of the steaming animals that had just been cut open.

In the divisions where saltpeter was used in the preparation and conservation of meat, the chemicals ate away shoes and boots. In a short time, the workers' feet developed open wounds that never healed. My grandfather passed through all that. His powerful physical constitution allowed him to survive longer than the others, but his arms turned red, his joints swelled, and a mass began to grow under his chin. Fearlessly, he asked to work in the phosphate fertilizer section, the worst part of the industrial chain, the "human slaughterhouse." Those who fought in that hell for two years either went to the hospital or the cemetery. It was there the remains were dried and the bones ground to extract the albumin.

All the workers had to cover their mouths and noses with huge handkerchiefs to avoid the stench, but the ammoniac composition of the fumes made the smell impossible to neutralize. A smoke with the taste of acid penetrated and bit the throat. Coughing and gagging, the workers, to fight the cold, tried never to stand still and would run from one place to another, as if they were insane. Alejandro, forgetting his pains, gave himself to that crazy tumult with profound devotion, but at the same time taking aesthetic pleasure in what he saw as a beautiful dance. He understood that real art appears only in a secret place between life and death. As his blue shoes began turning white, the voice of God repeated to him: "There is a precise instant when the world is marvelous: now."

Meanwhile, in the seven-by-nine-foot room, Jashe painted the walls white. She built a folding bed and invented, using boards and hinges, a table that could be hung on the wall after dinner and a box containing five more boxes, one inside the other, that could be used as chairs. Thus she began her struggle to dominate space: every single thing she allowed to enter that room was essential and had a precise shape so it would fit in with the others. Objects took on the existence of domestic animals. (My grandmother never forgot her tender blanket made from stray dog fur. She would call the dogs over, give them leftover food, and then shave them. Nor did she forget her humble wooden cup that each morning opened its mouth like an enchanted frog.) And that way, like someone who comes home and can't find their cat and anxiously searches for it in all the neighborhood streets, if suddenly she did not have her electric stove, a solid and simple apparatus in which she cooked (using bones and vegetables picked out of the market garbage) the most complex stews, she would have suffered.

Because the tenderness she had for her small helpers was reciprocated, and they, she was sure, were worried about completing a task that would be impossible outside of an environment like that one, Jashe wrote one afternoon to her sister Shoske:

"A plant the doorman gave me because I begged him not to throw it in the garbage had apparently died. With its dead stems and all, I put it next to the window and stopped worrying about it for a long time. But every day I watered it, distractedly, thinking about other things. Suddenly, just yesterday, I don't know through what miracle, it produced a leaf. It surprised me so much I began to cry. I understood that love is a grand thank you to the other for existing."

Two months before Sara Felicidad turned four, Alejandro arrived with a bouquet of daisies and his minimal weekly pay:

"Jashe, this morning God said to me: My son, today you must stop working. You've grown thin, you're losing your hair, your teeth are beginning to rot, your cartilage is inflamed, you have a tumor, your lungs have become weak, and you can no longer move with your former grace. But your soul has been forged in suffering and shines like a great firefly. Go back to dancing: those physical limitations are your honor and make you a man instead of a machine. Show the world what Art is. Yes, Jashe, I wasted my time teaching the children of the rich. Now I will dance by myself, but only once. Sincere works should not be repeated; they have to be unique. The performance will be short, ten minutes, but it will have such intensity that anyone who sees it will never forget it. I don't want to present myself in a theater but out in the open, at night in the kiosk of a poor plaza.

"I won't need spotlights, because I will be light. Even if there is no moon or stars, everyone will see me. And I don't need an orchestra: the voice of my daughter is enough. Don't worry about costumes; God tells me that only a naked body can reach the sacred. The press will take an interest. It will be an historic event. After my performance, dance will change. I want rich and poor to come, to mix around me. The wealthy, at the end of the act, will toss banknotes, which will be distributed to the poor. I was first dancer at the Imperial Russian Ballet; Argentina has to respect me. While I'm visiting newspaper offices, you, Jashe, will have to work."

My grandmother was hired as a worker in a felt-hat factory. The site was soggy and humid. The fumes from the mercury used in the preparation of the hair formed a thick mist that poisoned the place. With her hair and clothes always wet, breathing in that vapor, Jashe began to tremble, a tremor that spread to her lips, her tongue, her head, until it took over her whole body. She put up with those symptoms with a smile, and then rheumatic pains soon followed. Because visibility was so poor, several of her fellow workers lost fingers, and one child laborer, nine years of age, dropped dead, poisoned.

Not many articles about the show appeared in the newspapers. The journalists saw a filthy giant limping toward them wearing a tattered suit, his eyes opened far too wide, speaking an incomprehensible Spanish, and took him for a drug addict. The few lines that did appear were written with contempt and mockery. My grandfather did not lose courage:

"Only a few spectators will come, but if they are high-quality spectators, they will be enough. Only twelve witnesses saw Christ, and all humanity learned of Him. My dance will be engraved in the collective memory."

The great day came. That morning they celebrated Sara Felicidad's birthday. They gave her a can of peaches in syrup and a ballerina doll made of rags with hair made of yellow wool. That afternoon, Alejandro gave her the final instructions:

"You will sing without stopping, no matter what happens, until I stop dancing. You will forget all the songs you know to allow your voice to take the paths it wishes. Make yourself into a channel open to the course of two rivers: the dark and the celestial. What your will tries to do is of no interest to you, only what you receive will be good."

When night came, Alejandro stood in the center of the kiosk of a rundown plaza, and his daughter began to sing. The only spectator was Jashe. No one, poor or rich, came. No reporters either. Some dogs tried to howl, but the girl's voice enchanted them, and soon they listened to her in silence, wagging their tails. Rising from the half-light like long crystal knives, my mother's voice reached every window. Strange sounds uninterrupted by silence, due to the fact that her vocal chords vibrated both when she breathed in and when she breathed out. Those superhuman notes woke exhausted families of workers and little by little the plaza filled with men, women, and children who came up to the kiosk with the same respect with which they entered church every Sunday.

Alejandro Prullansky, very slowly, as if he had a thousand years to do it, took off his clothes. It took him half an hour to remove his trousers and his shirt, the only clothes he was wearing. He kept his white shoes on. With the same slowness, he crouched to open the cardboard suitcase and remove from it an apple. With a serious, rhythmic voice, imbued with an immense goodness he said, "The artist defines the world and transforms it into his work. If a poet eats this apple, that act is a poem. If a musician does it, it's a symphony. And a sculptor, on eating it, will be making a sculpture. I dance."

And, slowing his movements even more, he bit the fruit. Sara Felicidad and he looked like two black statues in the darkness of that cloudy night. Despite the intensity of the singing, which was so fine it cut the leaves of the few trees like a scalpel, dropping a dark green rain on the heads of the workers, the noise of the chewing arose intact and gave the steely tones of the girl a watery bed. No one blinked. Aside from the sound, nothing was happening, but the shadows of the kiosk promised that something important was going to take place.

Alejandro opened his spirit in two wings of great length and absorbed the taste of the apple. From the center of his brain came an iridescent ray that pierced the sky. The clouds were swept away by his breath, and stars appeared, which began to spin around the seeds he kept in a triangle on his outdrawn tongue. There he placed his attention and showed it to the public as if it were a sacred host. Following the silvery roads directed by his daughter's voice, bathed in the light of the stars, he launched the crown of his thoughts into space. The sacrificial animal appeared, a man of pure flesh, headless, pouring out his restorative blood to quench the thirst of so many people in misery. That was the mission of Art. Now he had to overcome his swollen joints, give strength to his wasted lungs, recover the elegance of his footwork, and gesture toward the point where limits dissolve.

He removed six bottles from his suitcase; removed the corks; emptied the gasoline they contained over his entire body; lit a match; set fire to himself; and, transformed into a bonfire, showed humankind what true dance was: a body making sublime movements in full ecstasy as it was consumed.

Jashe shouted of horror, then she covered her mouth with her hands, ashamed of herself, of her egoism. Her beloved was giving himself to the world, dying for it, and for that very reason, causing an immortal Art to be born. By including Death in the creation of beauty, he ended death.

Sara Felicidad, obeying her father's order—"You will sing without stopping no matter what happens"—saw him run, leap, laugh, and combine marvelous steps, all with his flesh spurting flames like a sun. That image engraved itself in her mind, and she transmitted it to me, her son, every night during my childhood. So that as I would fall asleep, she would sing me a lullaby in which her father, transformed into a star, crossed the firmament, granting men a Destiny:

"Making tracks in the sky is like opening their soul. That torch Alejandro lit, you, who bear the same name, must in turn transmit it so his sacrifice won't be in vain. Someday, thanks to you, humanity will become aware of this ephemeral spectacle, eternal monument to the art of dancing, and millions of hand will applaud your grandfather with thanks."

Prullansky, the giant, without realizing he was dying, almost burned to a crisp, made an enormous leap and, like a bird with long red and yellow feathers, fell in the center of the plaza. The people who had witnessed the act, respectful, motionless, fascinated, were suddenly panicked. The beauty seemed to them terrible, and they ran screaming to their houses to close doors and windows, afraid the monster would enter in order to burn up the little they owned. Jashe interpreted the noise of shutters and wooden frames slamming on sills as the announcement of future applause. Her husband gave up his soul dancing and, in full flight, fell to the pavement as a pile of smoking bones.

The child stopped singing. Her mother removed the Tarot from her bosom and, card by card, burned it in the glowing coals, where the remains of the red shoes glowed like two red rubies. In the fire, they had recovered their original red.

"There will never be another like him, Sara Felicidad. His memory will accompany us forever. I'll live alone only so that you can grow up well, but in reality what you see is a body moved by the tiniest part of my soul. The rest went with him. The woman who will marry again, have more children, get old, and die will be a different woman."

Sara Felicidad witnessed the change to her mother's face. Her skin, with its mother-of-pearl sheen, darkened; her nostrils became smaller, allowing only two needle-fine breaths of air to pass; fine wrinkles snaked along from the edge of her lips toward her chin; and her eyes were covered by an invisible curtain that separated her from life. The Jashe of today was possessed by the Jashe of the future—a long-suffering, indifferent lady, her senses asleep, passing through the days like a ship with no navigator. Before plunging her daughter into that gray existence, she said, "I'm going to ask that as long as you are with me that you never sing again."

At that moment, my mother was four years old. Tall, like her father, she looked ten. The same golden hair reached down to her waist, and her eyes were dark blue, translucent at the edges, each one as big as her mouth, shining with epochal depth. Alejandro's immolation did not upset her. On the contrary, it was a model of strength, enrichment of soul, treasure of beauty, fountain of joy. But Jashe's request struck her like a fatal bolt of lightning, a threat that was not only moral but also biological. Her body fell into agony. To take away her singing was also to rip out her tongue, fill her heart with sand, burn up her life's fate in one jolt. She had to defend herself. She had to mature in just a few minutes, form the armor of adulthood around her innocence. Down her legs ran a hot, thick, sticky liquid. Blood. At the age of four, she had her first menstruation. She ceased to be a child and became the protector of the near-empty shell that was once her mother. Since she was forbidden to sing, she also stopped talking. But as the absolute mistress of her interior world, she filled it with music. She constantly repeated songs she knew and immediately invented others. She created for herself a symphony orchestra and composed her accompaniments. And that way, developing her mute voice more and more, she became an opera singer who dominated all registers. For years she was a performer as well as her own audience. That unending interior singing gave her the happiness that sustained her in the sad world that would swallow a large part of her youth.

Jashe put the calcified bones of her husband into a cracker box, which she tossed into the Río de la Plata. She tied the box to a rubber ball so it would float until it became lost in the ocean. Then she worked one final week in the hat factory, and one Monday morning she went to ask help from the Jewish Colonization Association.

Aboard the *Weser*, Marla had told her that the Jewish immigrants, who had separate kitchen equipment and livestock so they could eat kosher food, were going to Argentina at the invitation of the Jewish Colonization Association, which had at its disposal more than five hundred thousand acres of land and maintained close ties with the highest circles of both the provincial and the federal government. The purpose of this society was not to extract earnings from its enormous investments but to establish in the new country an ample and solid stratum of Jewish peasants who would, each of them, work their own land and derive from it a convenient living. Therefore, the JCA could easily give her a farm on the pampa. After all, she was still as Jewish as the others, and, despite the tremors that shook her, she was capable of farming a piece of land that would feed herself and her daughter.

To save the trolley fare, she walked with her daughter from the industrial outskirts to the center of Buenos Aires, twelve miles. They were exhausted when they reached a five-story building with a façade of white marble and no windows but with two enormous, light-blue columns on both sides of its entry gate, where a six-pointed star was shining. The haughty luxury of this palace stooped Jashe's shoulders and made her aware of the hunger biting her stomach. If something could get them out of misery, it was this institution. She nervously looked over at Sara Felicidad. She looked more Russian than anything else. She sighed in resignation. In any case, her husband's name was written in the passports, and she could do nothing to hide the fact that she was the widow of a goy. She shook her stitched-up overcoat and did the same with her daughter's, naively trying with a few pats to turn their rags into proper clothing.

She timidly pushed the metal doors, whose hinges were so well greased that they opened wide. Not finding a living soul, mother and daughter wandered the gleaming stone corridor in this labyrinth decorated with pictures representing the life of Moses. Finally they entered a gigantic hall filled with silent men modestly dressed in peasant clothes, pale women with sad backs, and astonishingly thin children. Their fetid breath told Jashe that they, like her, had empty stomachs. They were all staring toward a barred little window, at which an elegant functionary with slicked-down hair, rings, and a gold bracelet arrived to observe them. He was as severe and immobile as a wax mannequin.

One of the immigrants, a creature who seemed to be thirty years old in his body and seventy in his face (because he was toothless), approached him to say in the hushed tones of despair: "Please allow me, Mr. Representative of our worthy association, to introduce myself: Moisés Latt, elected by chance to speak for the colony of Clara. Our penury is so great that we have come to ask you to communicate to Baroness Clara de Hirsch, widow of our benefactor, who has left us orphans with his premature passing, this letter that I will now read to you:

> Madam: With all our hearts we long to become a nation of farmers, as your husband dreamed. But help us to persist, so our children do not die of hunger and need before reaching that goal."

The functionary opened the barred window; stuck out his pudgy hand; accepted the letter; and without saying a word, closed the window again and disappeared into the palace's interior. After half an hour, a natty gentleman, looking rather like a banker, appeared at a high balcony and whispered, perhaps because raising his voice was unsuitable for his position, "The JCA has learned of your problems and will communicate this missive to the Baroness. For now, we can do nothing more. Return to your hearths, and if the Council decides to give you help once again, we will inform you. Now, please leave the hall quickly, because we have to wax it for Shabbat. Thank you."

And making a slight bow of farewell, he stepped back until he disappeared. The settlers remained still, thinking over with difficulty a situation hard for them to digest.

The toothless man smiled bitterly: "We've done all we can. We propose, and now may God dispose. It may be that this time He decides to stop punishing us for some old sin of which we have no memory."

Dragging their feet, they began to make for the exit to the street. Seeing that the place was emptying out, Jashe ran to Moisés Latt and tugged at his sleeve. (Why did she choose him and not another of the hundred or so men who filled the hall? It was certainly not because he was handsome. That mouth, with its black, hard gums, like a crack in dry dirt; that head, shaved as if by knife slashes, which tossed left and right two huge ears with fleshy lobes covered with hair; that skin of a brown tending toward watery chocolate; none of this made for a very attractive combination. Nevertheless, she wanted to join with him for the rest of her life. He was the insignificant companion that answered the need of her worn-out heart.)

Moisés Latt was thankful, in the deep pit of his solitude, for that tug at his sleeve. He was the human version of an stray dog: an orphan, ugly, poor, toothless, a pariah. When he was ten, during a pogrom, a Cossack forced him to drink a bottle of poison. He was dying from spring until fall. Along with the autumn leaves fell his thirty-two teeth. He had to learn to speak all over again because his tongue, deprived of the barrier of incisors and canines, tended to fly out of his mouth along with a rain of saliva. His gums hardened until he was able to chew the small ration of hard meat allotted him by the community of Grodno, the place where he was born by means of a long cut to his dying mother's belly. By clacking one gum against the other, he could imitate the sound of Spanish castanets. Thanks to that noise, highly celebrated by the cooks, he managed to double his meager ration of meat (and shrivel his dignity a bit more). He was delighted that this lady had a daughter. He never aspired to have a wife but a mother—distant, absent, as dead in life as that small woman, young but aged, scum of an ruthless society. He and she, remains of different shipwrecks, stuck on the same shore.

"I need your help, Moisés. My name is Jashe Trumper, widow of a goy. This is my daughter, Sara Felicidad. I am from Lodetz, Lithuania."

"Jashe Trumper? Trumper? Oh, yes! On the ship that brought us there was a Shoske Trumper, married to a crippled Sephardi, César Higuera."

"Oh! That's my sister! Shoske in Argentina and married!"

"Married and lucky. The Jewish Association gave them good land in Entre Ríos."

They looked at each other, openly, without trying to hide their intentions. Sara Felicidad tactfully moved a few steps back.

"Let's go and work with them, Moisés. We'll get married. I'll give you children, God willing, and we'll finally live quiet lives. My sister will get us out of this misery."

"Yes, Jashe. Thank you. Come with me to Clara, so I can liquidate the little I have, and then I'll go with you to your brother-in-law and his wife."

They left the other settlers sitting in the street next to the iron gate, where they embarked on a hunger strike to demand return tickets to their countries of origin, and went to the waiting room at Retiro Station to sleep. At 5:00 a.m. they squeezed onto a train carrying Italian immigrants to work on the plantations in Tucumán. The cars were packed with miserable people. Each one had received from the Immigration

Committee a half-pound of bread and a pound of dried meat for a trip that would last two nights and two and a half days. Digging around in his underpants, Moisés found a wrinkled banknote that allowed him to buy two rolls and a small goat cheese from a blind woman carrying a basket.

It was very cold, and an icy wind blew. Crowded together on wooden benches in rows, they were being ground to pieces by the bouncing train. They were kept awake by a continuous coughing, along with the wet sound of the workers' mouths as they spent hours chewing the bread and the bland meat without swallowing it, so the tiny amount of food would seem to ease their hunger. With a weak smile taking up half his face, Moisés Latt divided the cheese in half, one piece for Jashe and the other for Sara Felicidad, and he gave them the rolls. "Eat and don't worry about me. I'm never hungry, perhaps for lack of teeth."

Secretly swallowing his saliva, he made the two women eat. When they'd devoured even the tiniest crumbs, he covered them with his huge cape and, shivering, watched them sleep. In his chest, despite the cold, he felt an pleasant tingle. He would never again be alone in the world: finally he had a family. Seeing the girl's bluish toes poking through her worn-out shoes, he took off his socks, shook out the dirt, and dutifully put them on her. He then picked up the wrinkled bread wrappers and covered up his own feet before putting his boots back on. He lit a cigarette butt he kept with another three in a little tin box and, taking a short puff, let time pass.

A fly landed on his hand. He didn't shoo it away. He let it walk around and suck as much as it wanted. Then he slowly opened the window, stuck out his arm, and waited for the wind to blow it off. He was very fond of those animals, because they were his only playthings when he was a boy. He would open his pockets wide and put a few grains of sugar inside so they'd fill up with flies. He moved and walked with extreme care so he wouldn't hurt the insects. When he thought about the sweets that children with parents ate, he would skillfully pat his trousers to scare his little friends, who would fly out of his pockets like a buzzing black cloud, making him smile again. He smoked half of his fourth butt and finally fell asleep.

In Tucumán, a squad of police woke everyone by banging their nightsticks on the sides of the cars. Not wanting to hear explanations, they forced Moisés, Jashe, and Sara Felicidad to get out along with the workers. From a carriage pulled by two horses, a government employee, loudmouthed and despotic, ordered them to follow him. They all pitched their belongings onto their shoulders and were forced to walk almost two miles to the Immigrants' Hotel. The Tucumán natives frowned as they walked by, and the children sneeringly shouted, "Gringo bastards!"

At the "hotel," actually an empty barn, they could throw themselves on the ground to rest. No one was allowed to go outside. They were prisoners. Moisés opened his tin can and offered a guard the half butt he still had left, as he tried to explain that he and the women hadn't been contracted by any company and that they were traveling on the train on their own toward Clara. The soldier spit into the can, ruining the butt, and slapped Moisés so hard he fell among the workers having their siesta on the dusty floorboards.

No one brought them food or water. In the afternoon, they opened the door and began to load the workers onto some flat open carriages. There were thirty passengers standing on each platform, shoved against one another in a dreadful fashion. It was raining, a fine drizzle. They passed a loaf of bread to each one and drove them off, soaking wet, to a distant farm. Dying of thirst, the travelers stuck out their tongues to drink the water falling from the sky.

Moisés, holding the child in his arms so the others wouldn't trample her, pelvis to pelvis with Jashe, apologized with a discreet smile for the erection he couldn't hold back. Jashe realized that Destiny had put Moisés in this tight spot to make him overcome his timidity. For years he'd thought his penis was dead, but now, thanks to that long and direct contact, it was erect, alive, hard, almost burning his stomach.

They traveled that way until late at night, happy, establishing their friendship, pressed together among those wretched souls trembling with fever, tied to contracts that would have them work without rest for some stew and a handful of corn. Three German foremen with pistols on their belts received them along with a detachment of drunken soldiers. Under the celestial dome with its thousands of stars, they had to rest stretched out on the moist soil. It had been seventy-two hours since anyone had eaten a hot meal. Then a cart appeared loaded with raw meat. They gave a bloody piece to each person, three hundred grams carefully weighed on a portable scale, and they made a fire so the immigrants could cook their meat as best they could. The penetrating drizzle did not cease all night. They awoke in a puddle.

The foremen, beating iron pipes, hustled them onward so they would run to work. Moisés, making a thousand bows, approached a German with the intention of showing him his papers to make him understand the mistake. Barely had he said "Good day, sir," when four soldiers grabbed him, hit him with their rifle butts, tore off his cape, and kicked him in the back, smashing his forehead into the ground. Then they aimed their rifles at him, and one barked that they would shoot him if he spoke another word. Jashe, in desperation, took off the handkerchief covering Sara Felicidad's head, lifted her up, and shook her so her golden hair would wave like a flag. The beauty of those long, luminous tresses fascinated the foreman and his guards. My grandmother took advantage of the calm, opened their passports before their eyes, and made them understand the injustice they were committing. Moisés got up to calmly dry the blood running over his face. They let them go, giving them seven pounds of wormy corn as an apology.

An orange seller, who couldn't keep his hands off Sara Felicidad, took them away on his cart, pulled by a nervous burro, all the way to Clara.

Numerous Jewish families lived packed into small rooms, huts made of mud and straw, freight cars abandoned on the tracks, or in tin shacks, exposed to wind and rain and suffering hunger and cold, surrounded by the cries of sick children. Outside every door there was a huge pile of dry manure they used instead of wood to warm themselves and cook.

"This is how things are, Jashe. Not even in the worst Russian villages were living conditions this precarious. And what's worse is that the Jews already established here, the owners of these shacks, charge us rent as high as a third of the monthly salary we earn during the winter season. That is, if we manage to work. There is such a supply of labor and the harvest time is so short that our compatriots prefer to employ peons who aren't Jews, people they aren't ashamed to exploit. We had bad luck.

"We came here because we were told this was the new Eldorado. Many of us, naïve, brought leather valises we were going to fill with the gold and silver we'd earn. When we got to Buenos Aires, Rafael Hernández, the owner of the lands where we were supposed to settle, backed out of the contract signed in his name. During the seven months since he authorized his representative on the old continent to sell us land at a certain price, its value on the market went up considerably. According to the original contract, the Argentine government lent us the money for our passage so we would pay for it—and the land—here with the earnings from our labor.

"Hernández's betrayal left us poor and in debt up to our eyeteeth, with nowhere even to drop dead. The callous, uncaring authorities piled us onto a train so we could beg work from the Jews already established in the Clara colony, named to honor the wife of Baron de Hirsch. It was the end of August, on the eve of Shabbat. Since we were forced to travel, breaking the ritual resting period during Elul, our sacred month of penitence that precedes the New Year festival, we felt cursed. With our spirits at their lowest, we found out that our tribulations were only beginning.

"You, Jashe, are seeing what kind of lodging we had. Penury cost us our character, and an atmosphere of suspicion, accusation, and fights tore us apart. Couples stopped living together, children fell ill and died in scores, girls fell into the nets of the impure and became prostitutes. Others, begging help for years, managed to return to their native cities. Those of us who remained have had to go from door to door hungry and desperate in search of work and bread. But your sister Shoske has been lucky. Those who came invited by the Jewish Colonization Association were given comfortable farms and, apparently, good land in Entre Ríos. Maybe there we three will find a place. We are members of the same family. We'll help them make the land fruitful and live without despotic and capricious foremen."

Moisés showed them the tiny cabin made of rotten wood, covered with burlap sacks, where he'd slept for so many years with his legs bent for lack of space. Jashe gave him an inquisitive look: why had they made this atrocious trip when there was nothing of value here? Just a few rat skins Moisés used to make belts or wallets, perhaps to go out as a peddler in the workers' communities. Moisés pulled up one of the floorboards, dug into the earth below, and pulled out a rusty can. He opened it. Inside there were fifty gold coins, three rings, a gold watch, and a green scarab.

He put the scarab back into the can and said, blushing, "Well, this little bug is worthless, but it does bring good luck. The rest is a treasure left to me by my mother. It was given to me when I was seven, and I've always kept it. Now I'm giving it to you. It may get us out of a serious bind. Although, I have to say that until now, for three or four generations, despite expulsions and pogroms, no one in my family has found himself in a serious bind. You will be the one who decides how to use it. In giving you my gold, I give you my life."

When Jashe kissed Moisés on the mouth, she did not feel love because that sentiment had been pulled out of her by the roots. But she did feel a profound respect, an intense thankfulness, and a sincere friendship.

Feeling no disgust, she licked his hard gums, and then, possessed by a strange spirit, she said, without understanding her own words, "When you broke the old mirror, you made me yours. And when you made me yours, you were mine. I am the door of dreams, the infinite oyster, the devourer full of death-life, of light mounted on darkness. But you can walk my labyrinth without getting lost, because you have become the pearl of answers. Cross my arid world, follow my river of lost souls dissolving in the acid of illusory times, walk down my somber circles, find the swamp of ebony and become its star. Then rise up, trace the rings of glory and, higher than the peak, take your place like a magnetized moon to receive the song of love from all the beings that live within me. Now I am the perfect mirror of your infinite feelings. Come, unite yourself with me!"

Moisés Latt stopped his mind and murmured, "Thy will be done." Then he submerged in the non-being of both. Jashe took the gold rings, placed one on Moisés' left ring finger, another on her own, and the third on Sara Felicidad's right thumb. With that ceremony, the marriage contract was signed. Now they were a family, united until death did them part.

Moisés suddenly shouted, "Dolores!" And an old black mule came out of a corral and galloped limpingly toward them, chased by clouds of flies that took delight in the stench of her backside. "My poor and faithful friend, you are going to make your last journey. You will take us to Entre Ríos. Once we're there, you will die of fatigue. Console yourself with the thought that with your end our sorrows will end."

The three of them mounted the animal, and under a huge umbrella covered with indecisive patches of colors, they began the slow, four-week journey that would get them to Shoske and César's farm. During that time, they slept outdoors and ate, because Moisés managed to get small jobs like splitting logs, fixing shoes, rooting out nettles, cleaning lavatories, cutting hair, delousing children using a fine comb, and sharpening knives on his rat skin belt.

Meanwhile, Sara Felicidad hid her joy. She saw no misery anywhere. Traveling like that was a gift. Sleeping at the roadside, protected by the sky loaded with stars; breathing in the fragrances of the earth; saturating herself in the blessed smell of the mule; eating delicious dry bread accompanied by a tender, wrinkled apple; sharing landscapes with sparrows and ants; passing beneath trees, feeling the different caress of each shadow on her skin; all of it gave her the sensation of having no limitations. Within her spirit, a chorus made up of all human voices, those of now, of the future, of the past, began to resound in her spirit, a grateful sun arising from an infinite ocean of souls above which flew, illuminating it all, her father, transformed into a comet.

Yes, she had to hide, aside from the song, her delight. Jashe and Moisés, to subsist without love, fed on sadness. Submitting themselves to what they thought was Destiny boosted their mutual respect, giving them the pride of struggle. The ability to withstand anything united them more than any passion. If they realized they were living in abundance, they would cease to be essential to one another. It was better to let them get along on the black mule, under the patched umbrella, placing their hopes in a future that would never exist, putting up with the present as if it were a curse.

They reached Entre Ríos. The fertile, dark, moist lands became milky, arid, hostile. A frozen wind carried along balls of burned grass and huge tongues of dust. In those solitary places, amid a wheat field so dry that the ears of grain sounded like bones rattling in the wind, languished Jashe's sister's farm. Before they entered the property, Dolores fell, shattered. Having no shovel, they covered her with chunks of dirt as hard as rock and reached the door on foot.

"Jashe!"

"Shoske!"

Their sobbing embrace lasted for a quarter of an hour. A dark skinned man with curly hair and round eyes, of medium height but with large hands, watched the new arrivals with a timid smile. Hiding behind his robust right leg was his left, crippled by some childhood illness. Moisés offered him a game bag made of rat skin and a bouquet of wild flowers he'd cut on the road. César Higuera accepted the gift and embraced in his muscular, short arms the dry body of the man without teeth. The two sisters dried their tears and went into the modest house made of whitewashed adobes. Despite the year's difference in their age and the fact that their bodies were different, they seemed like twins. Even though Shoske was much smaller, with narrow hips and very small breasts, now—because Jashe had abandoned magic—their two spirits had become identical, and the same sadness made them victims for all eternity. Shoske, without consulting her husband—not out of dominance but because of their absolute agreement—said to them, "We are one family. Just as one part of my heart belongs to you, half of these lands, from now on, belong to you. We shall divide earnings and losses, our few joys and our many sorrows, and also this small cabin, which consists of nothing more than a dining room, bedroom, kitchen, and bath."

Jashe, also without consulting Moisés, answered by emptying her treasure on the table. She gave her sister twenty-five coins and the watch, because they kept the rings. They drank a glass of brandy and immediately went to work. The wind never stopped blowing all day, constantly bombarding them with tiny stones and carrying off a large part of the wheat they were trying to store in a broken-down barn.

Sara Felicidad waited for them, wandering around the untilled land. She knew that lost place in the interminable plain would be her new home for a long time. Instead of rejecting that soil closed to the hand of man like a curled-up porcupine, populated by aggressive forces in the shape of scorpions, poisonous spiders, and snakes, she stretched out, face down in a crack, kissed the arid land, and, opening her heart, poured into it an infinite river of love. She gave and gave until she fainted. When she regained consciousness, she knew that the land had adopted her by making a carpet of blue flowers to grow around her. The buzz of a beehive, hidden between the wheels of an old cart, called to her, offering honey, and a flock of sparrows perched on the barbed wire fence formed a wall of feathers that offered her a bit of cool shade. Snakes slithered over her legs, giving her long caresses without biting. She had placed love where there was none, and the wild land gave it back to her multiplied, transformed into a marvelous garden. When the sun went down, she went back to the house and waited for her elders, playing with her rag dancer. They returned with their eyes red and swollen, their hands covered with scratches. Shoske heated up some lentil soup containing bits of meat.

"You might as well know it, Jashe, Moisés, and Sarita. The meat is cat. We're overrun with feral cats that eat our hens. Since we have to kill them, we've learned not to waste their meat. I suggest you start eating it right now. This land gives us very little food."

My grandmother and my mother pursed their lips and stared at the plate with badly hidden gloom. Latt emptied his glass in one gulp and raised a piece of cat to his mouth to grind up, making exaggerated sighs of satisfaction. Jashe, with her habitual forbearance, followed her husband's example. The meat had a strange but not disagreeable taste. She took a bit of it and forced it into her daughter's mouth. Sara Felicidad wept away a couple of tears and, aware of her obligation, ate another piece. This communion over the sacrificed feline relaxed the mood.

Shoske interrupted it: "Sister, you have to know: papa and mama are dead."

Moisés and Sara Felicidad gripped Jashe, holding her up in their arms.

"When you left, I felt very alone, like a shadow that had lost its body. Not having anyone to follow, I felt non-existent. A short time later, César arrived looking for work. He came from Russia. He was a schoolteacher, but tired of the jokes his students made about his limp, he decided to change countries. Remember how our parents were: two complicated people fighting all their lives to be simple. They believed in good and evil spirits, in magic, in the powers of every animal, object, or plant, but because of a fear that encompassed the entire Universe, they sank themselves in ignorance. They never read a book or talked to each other. They spoke only to communicate practical things. When they had nothing to do, they were mute, one next to the other, staring at the fire or the clouds in the sky.

"César, because of his brash personality, which perhaps comes from his name, stayed here, taking on the task of filling our heavy idle moments with an incessant chatter, even if his leg makes him a terrible peasant. I learned everything they didn't teach me from him. Reading, for example. Without knowing how it happened, we became engaged and soon after married. About the same time you gave birth to Sara Felicidad, I gave birth to Salvador Luna. He would have been the same age as her, but he died, strangled by the umbilical cord. We were so sad that we decided to live in Russia, in order to forget.

"We were about to leave, when my father said to me, 'Dear Shoske, you are the only relative left to us. You've been a perfect, obedient daughter. Now that you're leaving, we have nothing left to do in this life. We've lost interest. We need you for one final service. Your mother and I, even though we're in good health, have decided to die. No, don't think we're going to commit suicide. In no way. We are going to abandon existence, that's all. You will bury us. To live, you have to love. When you stop loving, life is over.'

"What could I say to them? They had already made their decision, and nothing or no one could have convinced them to change their minds. They had a good meal, bathed, put on their Sabbath clothes, lay down on top of the bed holding hands, looked at each other for the last time, closed their eyes, and after a long wheeze, they died. Don't suffer for their sake, Jashe, because, just as I'm telling you, they passed from one life to the other with complete ease.

"César, back in his village, went back to giving classes in the school. The boys made fun of him again. After a few months, an agent from the Jewish Colonization Association came around and, in the name of Baron Maurice de Hirsch, proposed that we immigrate to Argentina. They would give us passage and fertile land. They assured us that the Russian authorities, happy to get rid of its Jews, would give us passports and exit visas. Finally, we would possess a corner of the planet where we could throw down roots! The moment of the new Exodus had come. We accepted the voyage with pleasure, and here you have us, on the Promised Pampa. At least we're back together. God knows what He's doing."

César Higuera, seeing the consternated faces of Moisés and Jashe, brusquely stood up, opened the window, insulted the wind that barked crossing the plain, closed the window, sat down again, angrily chewed a piece of cat meat, and, taking long swallows from the bottle, launched into a speech:

"The powerful go mad, and we poor pay for the broken dreams. Baron Hirsch, for most of his life, was a Jewish aristocrat, a citizen of the world, equally comfortable in Bavaria, Belgium, France, Austria, and England. Thanks to his privileged connections, he was in no way affected by the bloody persecution we had to endure. He lived on the margin of our disasters until his son Lucien, thirty years old, was cut down by death.

"That the Cossacks massacred our children by the thousands had not the slightest importance. But that such a thing should happen to him, the possessor of one of the greatest fortunes in Europe, that he should lose a son—and not from a shot or a beating but from a sickness so that he died in his bed—was a disaster that all Jews, present and future, should remember! Shit! What does he know about life, real life, the one you have to earn with the sweat of your brow? What does he know about the poor multitudes of the world when he inherited from his banker father and grandfathers an immense fortune made even larger by the dowry of his wife, also the daughter of bankers?

"A man like that, absorbed in international business, dealing with powerful governments, intoxicated by the heights, manages to forget the fifty-six years his compatriots have been stoned, insulted, stripped of rights. Only when he loses Lucien does the torrential pain that over-runs him open his eyes: 'Good heavens, others suffer as well!' But vanity closes them again: 'To honor my deceased son, I will mobilize millions of dollars in order to become the new Moses. I will be the father of another immense migration. And even if Jews have not had their own land for centuries and have instead cultivated their mental faculties, this does not mean that they can't be magnificent peasants. Their pale hands, their shriveled bodies, and their brains that navigate in the meanders of the Kabbalah are ideal for covering the soil of Argentina with vineyards and fig trees. Those lands are for sale precisely because no native dares to farm bottomless swamps, sandy sweeps, and steppes invaded by scrub, where torrential rains are followed by droughts, plagues, and windstorms. I will give them a new home there as free farmers on their own land, ignorant, long-suffering, giving their lives to the land, that is, buried alive. Without creating political problems that hurt my prestige, they can become useful citizens for the nation that tolerates them. I am good, I am grandiose, I am a great benefactor; my name will shine in all Jewish encyclopedias, and my son Lucien will be applauded for centuries for his inspiring death.'

"Nonsense! Even if this place is, as its name suggests, between two rivers, like the ancient Holy Land, this pampa will not be ours or anyone else's. It can't be farmed. Given his influence among the Turks (it was he, after all, who built for our eternal enemies a railroad line through the Balkans to Constantinople, with immense financial benefit), it would have been better if the Baron had sent us to Palestine. That money he invested here, trying to become a prophet, could have opened the doors of Eretz Yisrael."

Shoske corked the almost empty bottle and interrupted him: "Shut up, César! You're drunk again. Stop insulting the dead. At least Baron Maurice tried—mistakenly it's true—to help us, in his way. There are others who wouldn't give a hair off their ass for their compatriots in dire need. Enough anger. We're not going to stay here forever. We'll figure out a way to save, and our children, because we shall have them, will become educated—they'll get to be doctors, engineers, architects—and will have the life a human being deserves. Now, let's stop jabbering and go to sleep, because early tomorrow morning begins another rough day."

That first night, Jashe, Sara Felicidad, and Moisés slept on the cement next to the kitchen. At dawn, the crowing of an army of roosters awoke them. It was colder than ever, and a torrential rain mixed with hail as big as eggs bombarded the zinc roof, transforming the house into a drum. Shoske put some wood on the fire.

"The annual hail. At midday, the rain will stop and an invasion of mosquitoes will begin. Take these strips of veil to protect you. Soon you'll get used to it. Sometimes I have my entire face covered by them, but I don't waste time scaring them off. There will be so much mud that we won't be able to work today. Let's drive the cart to town. We'll buy another bed. When night comes, we'll put plugs of wax in our ears so we can carry out our conjugal obligations without hearing one another. But my niece will have to sleep outside. We've been thinking of getting her a wooden barrel, hot when it's cold and cold when it's hot."

Back from the general store, they hung a curtain between the two beds and put the barrel behind the house. Moisés installed a little window in it and a door through which you'd have to crawl. Jashe covered the inside with a floral print cloth and put a straw mattress on the curved floor. Sara Felicidad entered that small space, which looked to her like a palace, and the years began to run by. Years struggling against the annual monsoons, droughts, parasites, floods that would destroy everything growing, windstorms that little by little blew away the topsoil, leaving enormous sand dunes. Years trying to decipher the signs that predicted cold or heat, storms, fires that would burn up dried out brush. Years building low dikes to stop the advance of the sand; installing mills, tanks, reservoirs, sheds;

spending almost everything they earned on maintenance; at the same time carefully rotating crops in order not to exhaust the soil.

And when they thought they'd overcome the attacks of nature and everything seemed to be flourishing, along would come locusts trying to eat it all down to the last green leaf. The hungry hordes would advance in thick rows, five hundred or even a thousand yards wide and twenty or thirty yards deep, covering half a mile a day. They had to channel that voracious army using metal fences vectored toward a long ditch they'd prepared urgently, digging day and night. The leaping creatures would fall in, getting tangled up among themselves because of their long, spurred legs. They killed them by covering them up with dirt, smashing them with sacks of sand, or burning them with kerosene.

The smoke from the burning wings had an aphrodisiac effect. Losing themselves for a moment, the two couples would also fall into the mile-long ditch and thrash about on top of the cushion of dying insects that gave off a deafening buzz announcing the end of the world. The couples would get up ashamed, their bodies covered with dead locusts, figures so strange that all the dogs would start howling. When on the way home they passed by Sara Felicidad, who could not help but see the epileptic tumbling and celebrated it with jubilant laughter, Jashe slapped her and ordered her into her barrel with nothing to eat until the following day.

Time passed, and their four faces were becoming wrinkled, their shoulders hunched, and their spirits embittered. César and Moisés, after serious conversations, reached the conclusion that it was useless to cultivate vegetables, wheat, corn, grape vines, or fruit trees. If they wanted to rise out of poverty, they had to become cattlemen. Even though it was an almost sacred tradition to not spend it, they convinced Jashe and Shoske that they should invest the rest of the inheritance in the purchase of sheep, which were the white gold of the pampa.

Once again, they plowed the land and simultaneously planted alfalfa and rye. The rye would sprout first and protect the alfalfa until spring.

The weaker alfalfa would be planted between the furrows of rye. Then the fragile but perennial plant would last for about five years, while the strong but short-lived plant would die that year. Jashe and Shoske understood the language of rye and alfalfa: they would one day be widows. That thought united them more than ever.

When the crops were growing well, the two men made a trip. They visited Río Negro, Viedma, Patagones, anywhere they might buy sheep or cattle at a decent price. By preference they went to zones where there was a drought or the grass was thin. The fifty gold coins, the three rings, and the watch enabled them to buy 1,500 thin sheep and some Lincoln rams for breeding. When they got back, they set about fattening the animals and then sold them to refrigerated meat companies for four times what they'd paid. They also retained lots of lambs. They picked up a hundred cows, almost skin and bone, and a pair of bulls, to which they quickly added sheep, lambs, capons, and young rams. They learned to work the land to fight erosion, choosing crops more and more suitable for fattening cattle. And the business grew.

The two sisters announced they were pregnant, and eight months later they gave birth on the same day: Shoske to a boy and Jashe to a girl. Two dark-skinned children, Jacobo the First and Raquel the First. A year and a half later, again on the same day, they gave birth again, Shoske to a boy and Jashe to a girl. Another two dark-skinned children, Jacobo the Second and Raquel the Second.

During that good period, they had to employ Russian peons, perhaps the same Cossacks who'd killed Jews during the pogroms. Now they were thankful, people who worked ten-hour days for a few pesos and a piece of roast meat. When the sun came up, Jashe, carrying her daughters, each one sucking on a bosom, followed by Shoske, also feeding her boys, came to Sara Felicidad's barrel. Jashe, disgusted, observed Sara Felicidad asleep with her nose stuck in the yellow wool wig of the dancer doll.

"Wake up, woman. Yes, even though you're young, you've turned into a woman because of your menstruation. The Russian peons never stop their sly looks at you. One of these days you might be raped, and to make sure there are no witnesses they'll kill all of us. That mane of blonde hair, those blue eyes, and your white skin is too attractive. Put this infusion of walnut on your hair, start wearing these dark glasses, and stop bathing so the dirt makes you as dark as us. Also, bend over when you walk, because you're too tall, a giant like your dead father."

My mother smiled, sang a ballad in her heart, dyed her hair, put on the glasses, bent over, stopped bathing, and only came out of her barrel at night to go to the kitchen to eat leftovers. She knew she just didn't fit in with the family and tried to pass unnoticed. When everyone slept, she would use some private singing to attract frogs by the thousands. They would come out of the swamps to croak around her, following her silent melody. They opened their jaws wide, hoping that the fireflies would fall into their throats. In the darkness, those mouths filled with light looked like the stars in the firmament. The Earth disappeared for Sara Felicidad, and she felt herself floating in a space without beginning or end. Like one more star.

One morning during the month of April, as usual, the women got up half an hour before the men to prepare breakfast. They felt some irritation in their eyes, but what caught their attention most was the darkness that persisted at that hour when the most beautiful light should be sweetening the hostile landscape. They tried to go outside to see if the sky was covered with black clouds, but they found the door locked. They had to wake up their husbands, and all four of them had to push to open it. A thick layer of ash covered everything.

The peons brought the news: the Descabezado Grande volcano, located in Mendoza, had thrown into the sky an immense eruption of ashes that the trade winds and counter-trade winds had scattered over hundreds of miles. Swallowing curses, they plowed the land again and again, trying to mix in the ash. Impossible. The hungry animals cut open their gums chewing the grass covered with mineral dust. An anthrax epidemic broke out, and all the animals died. They would have to start all over again! They dug the rubber bag in which they'd hidden their earnings out of the excrements in the black pit, and Moisés and César went out to buy livestock. They came home with an enormous herd of pigs.

Shoske and Jashe, terrified, ran to hide themselves in a bed, pulling the sheet over their heads: "Forbidden food! God will punish us! How could you buy those disgusting animals that adore garbage? They are the Devil!"

César and Moisés, delicately folding back the sheet little by little, finally got the women to show their faces. Since they didn't want to stop complaining, Moisés rattled his gums, producing a deafening clickity-clack. Impressed, the two women fell silent. César gave them each a glass of brandy, serving himself a large glass as well. Then, drying his mouth with his sleeve, he said, severely, "Ladies, times change. We have to adapt or we'll die of hunger. The volcano ruined our land. Years will go by before the ash is washed away by rain or gets mixed in with the mud. We'll never equal our production from before the disaster. If you want our children to have, some day, the economic means to study and get to be respectable citizens, we must progress. Forbidden or not, these pigs are right for us. They eat everything, and they are tough. They're not even exported. Instead of fattening them and selling them off to the frozen meat industry, we will install a factory right here to produce hams, sausages, bacon, lard, and many other products. We'll make lots of money."

"But what will the other Jewish settlers say?"

"When there's no more meat, it's time to gnaw the bones. If what you want in this world doesn't exist, you have to want what there is. Our compatriots can say whatever they like because we'll stop seeing them. We don't need them for anything. If they hold us in contempt, we'll marry our children among ourselves, even if they are cousins. The Law

239

does not forbid it. Do you want to get out of this hell someday? Then let God take care of tomorrow, and let the pigs take care of us today. Decide! Moisés and I are going to roast a piglet. Eat with us. All roads, even the smoothest, have stones in them. Harden your feet!"

One hour later, Jashe and Shoske came over to the fire and sat next to their husbands who cut big, juicy slices off the piglet and offered them. With sighs of resignation and their eyes raised to heaven, they chewed, slowly at first, overcoming their revulsion, only to devour pork later with an irrepressible appetite. When the banquet was over, the two women announced they were pregnant. Eight months later, they gave birth, as usual on the same day, one boy, Jacobo the Third, and one girl, Raquel the Third.

Time galloped on. The emblem of the Flying Hog ham factory, a pig with swan wings flying over a landscape painted in the colors of the Argentine flag, became famous all over the nation. When World War I broke out, they had to bring in workers from Buenos Aires, all goys apparently, to keep up with the numerous orders that came from abroad, especially from England. The exploitation of flesh forbidden by the Prophet allowed them to get through the crisis, amassing a huge fortune.

Since they did not want to live the rest of their lives isolated out on the pampa in the nauseating stink of their thousands of pigs, they decided to move to Chile. Iquique was a port visited by ships of all nationalities; with schools appropriate for the children, all kinds of businesses, enormous hotels, theaters, libraries; and boulevards where tourists, mine administrators, sailors, and workers who came down from the mines to spend the money they'd made over months could provide an inexhaustible source of income. They would open a huge store where there would be everything: food, clothing, furniture, kitchenware, toys for children, clocks, watches, jewels, and—why not?—a booth for buying and selling gold and silver.

While all that was being discussed, my mother turned thirteen without her family realizing it. Still faithfully dyeing her hair, wearing dark glasses, never bathing—her skin was covered with a dark, greasy coating that stank like the pigs—and walking bent over, she had made it so no one wanted to be anywhere near her, not even the workers who butchered the animals. If she accidentally wandered near the house during the day, her half-brothers and half-cousins would howl with terror and she would run off.

But Sara Felicidad did not suffer. For her, this shabby side of things belonged to the world of forms. Beneath that was the world of essences, which only she could perceive. There she could sing as loud as she wished and show herself with her white skin, golden hair, blue eyes, and her six-foot-three height. There, the Earth was an amorous presence granting long caresses lasting millions of years, where atmospheric changes were the jovial games of a God at play, and where human beings were angels riding on pigs that really did have wings.

Late on nights when there was a full moon, Sara Felicidad would climb the ombu tree and watch as second, transparent bodies emerged from the sleeping men and animals, allowing them to travel throughout the Universe, without their being able to remember it when awake, until sinking into the final abyss. There they would find the consciousness that was the origin of life, and then emerge covered with luminous scales, larger than the planet Jupiter, and spin and dance with the spirits of the dead, who are always happy, making the music of a whirling top.

For Jashe, Shoske, Moisés Latt, and César Higuera, bringing Sara Felicidad along was a problem. Secretly, they all wanted to leave her with the pigs. No one would dare suggest it, so when the time came to leave, they gave her a third-class ticket while they and the six children traveled in first class. They hoped the wind of the train would carry off her fetid stench. When they got to Iquique, they would replace the barrel with an annual allowance and a room in a boarding house, as far away as possible, so they could once again forget about her existence.

241

Jaime Jodorowsky — Sara Felicidad Prullansky

Alejandro + Raquel Lea

FIVE

JAIME AND SARA FELICIDAD

IT WAS EXTREMELY difficult for me to bring Jaime and Sara Felicidad together. When it became necessary to incarnate myself again in this world, the man I chose to be my father was in a circus, way down in southern Chile, being hung by the hair. And the woman who was supposed to be my mother was locked away in a desert sanctuary way up north. Separated by more than two thousand miles, they never would have found each other if I hadn't decided in 1919 to take those two people so different in character—which is essentially to say they were opposites—to be the founding elements of my future body.

I don't know if my memories of the time before my birth correspond to reality or if they are mere dreams. That doesn't matter. In any case, reality is the gradual transformation of dreams; there is no world but the world of dreams. I am convinced that I chose and united the sperm and the ovaries that allowed me to be born again for the . . . who knows how many times I was born? Thanks to my iron will, when the chosen moment came in the proper place—an oasis in the middle of the pampa—I intensified the magnetic suffering that forced the paternal penis to penetrate the maternal vagina so that, each cell overwhelmed with cataclysmic joy, it would let fly the radiant arrow that buried itself in the eager depth of her magic blackness.

I slid through that crack opened in space and time, intent on preserving my memory because I would need it to carry out the plan I'd been developing from life to life. But as almost always happens, the trauma to the delicate body as it penetrated the dense planes of this existence caused me to lose a large number of memories. Little remains of that continual development of a spirit knowing itself. It's a fragmented magma of shadowy sensations, colossal spaces, eternal times, births and collapses of universes, savage rivers of swept-away souls crossing infinite splendors in dizzying orbits.

During some periods, there was total silence, as if God had never created ears, and after, the racket of galactic cars, carnival trucks showing off the spangles of their suns, advancing with no goal, pushed along by the goodness of an inexhaustible emanation, a unique principle that feeds myriad beings who only receive. With no fear of the ridiculous, I accept the fact that I was a metallic crag wandering through dark immensities with a passionate thirst for light. Within my extreme density lived but one desire: to create language, song, the Word itself, which had drawn me out of the nothingness. That ideal must have inflamed me. Perhaps I exploded into stars and planets and became crystal, amoeba, plant, animal, and then lost myself in an continuous line of men and women being born and dying in murderous religions, labyrinths of legends and symbols until I learned to open the eyes of my senses and learn to see that pure light that arises from the original fountain with my soul, without intermediaries.

Then the language of thought echoes, the silent voice that speaks to Being, repeating itself itself through time in order to create the true Tradition, "That which is received." It seems that I was an initiate born in Germany in 1378. It's clear that the year—composed of 13 and of 78, which is 13 x 6—carries a message. Those who have received a Masonic education will understand what that mans. In that miserable life, my parents abandoned me at the doors of a convent. The monks—who, in the absence of a sexual life, develop their intellect until it becomes a tumor—taught me to speak and read Greek and Latin before I was six.

When I was almost an adolescent, I accompanied the abbot on a journey to Jerusalem. He died there, granting me a freedom that by then had become essential for me. I sought the Truth among old Kabbalists, but when my organs of knowing developed, I understood that, unable to be universal, it presented itself as a violent belief. Then I sought a technique that would release me allow me to disconnect from that archaic desire. Truth would only be the world without my desire for it, and the technique would be to learn to disappear as a separated individual. To accomplish that, I had to confront inspired thought in other masters.

Egypt showed me its secrets in a numerical system: 1, 2, 3, 5, 8, 13, 21, 34, 55, etcetera. Ascetic Turks showed me how to fall into a trance: I could open my abdomen with a knife, empty my guts out onto a plate, and dance, spinning dizzily, and finally put them back in their place and seal the wound without leaving a scar. In Fez, I studied alchemy, how to spiritualize matter, and magic, how to materialize spirit. Finally, the Knights of Heliopolis, those who consider physical death a sickness and who have the incredible patience to live more than fifteen thousand years, visited me in a dream.

Those ancients treated me like a person they'd been waiting for a long time, and each one (there were seventy-eight) gave me a summary of his knowledge on a rectangular sheet. When I was able to order those drawings into a hexagonal mandala that resembled a snowflake, I thought I understood the constitution of the Cosmos and the mystery of life. Considering—as did my masters—it useless to go on remaining in one single body, I decided to live 151 years and to continue, in another life, my work, which was to lead all beings to Awareness, progressively eliminating God by absorbing Him in existence so that we would all become an exclusively human Universe. All of that was achieved with the consent of the Father, who, out of absolute love, creates us to be his tomb. From the putrefaction of the divine, our eternity will be born.

I returned to Germany, where I adopted an orphan girl. I instructed her for some years until she became my wife. With the immense fortune I accrued transforming base metals into gold, I had a temple constructed in the Alps, carved from the rock of the mountains themselves. I led the workers there blindfolded and returned them home without their knowing the site's location. There, with my young lover and four friends chosen from among the most highly developed spirits of the era, we locked ourselves away in our secret fortress to decipher the miraculous language of geometry. Almost a century went by. I saw my disciples die placidly. I had met them too late, after society had already implanted in their minds the programing of death and the triumph of old age. Since they believed in those two concepts, they achieved them.

Federica, my companion, educated by me, grew up without those prejudices and accompanied me until I was 151 years old. Young, only 110, she wanted to die with me, but I forbade it; she had to go on living for several centuries, if necessary—until, in another incarnation, I would recall her and seek her out to achieve our final union, the sacred androgyne.

The two of us constructed a seven-sided crypt. In the center of the roof, we hung three lamps filled with oil we'd managed to extract from gold, which, thanks to a wick made from chameleon spittle, could burn for a millennium. At the center of the heptagonal floor, we erected a round enclosed altar with a copper plaque on which I engraved *Hoc universi compendium unius mihi sepulchrum feci* and other important things that, unfortunately, I've forgotten. Finally, in a glass coffin, I lay down with my seventy-eight cards hovering from one hand to the other like a rainbow.

Under the serene gaze of my faithful Federica, I began to give up my body. I separated first from my feet, in which I felt the fervent faith of the always-growing toenails, the strength of the instep, the solidity of the soles giving roots to intelligence, and the clarity of the heels, round fertilizers of the planet. I loved them the way you love during farewells: more than ever. Then I withdrew from my skin, flesh, bones, viscera, until, separated from my matter and my needs, I began to do the same with my desires, which was relatively easy. Only one difficulty arose: the profound attraction I felt for my companion.

A sperm as brilliant as a jewel had been waiting for many years to inseminate her. I'd had to sacrifice that natural desire for reasons related to my initiation, which I do not understand. Then came the farewells from all the humans who gave me wisdom, from all the plants, animals, minerals, an army of beings with which I had established tender links and which I also thanked and quickly abandoned. Finally, from my spirit I eliminated my unfinished works, anxieties of being, doing, and living. With an immense contentment, I gave myself to the change and emerged in the limbos of the Interworld. I wandered in the Interworld, where space and time are absorbed by the extraordinary creator, Eye.

In that splendor, slowing the collapse of my awareness, I waited for the manifested Universe to perish and be reborn, in order to reincarnate in an advanced era where man has overcome his animal inertia. But I made a mistake and let myself be trapped by a certain orange-tinged light that cast me into an avid ovary during a primary era that corresponded in no way with the dates of my death. Trapped in the past, I was born in Lisbon in 1415, in the body of the Jew Isaac Abravanel.

I had the good luck to be part of a family of notable and eminent Talmud scholars, among whom I learned numerous languages. I distinguished myself in the study of Law and developed the powers of my spirit, finally being named Minister of Finance by Ferdinand of Spain. In that country, I met Salvador Levi, a lion tamer. Staring into the eyes of his beasts, hunters of souls, I managed to turn one corner of the veil and remember the seventy-eight arcana that had been revealed to me previously by the Knights of Heliopolis. The rest of that life you already know. Do you remember? Thanks to the expulsion of the Jews in 1492, I ended up in Italy, where, after many adventures, I decided to die like the clowns, by balancing on my head with my red shoes toward heaven.

By introducing the Tarot into the Levi genealogical tree, even if my material form hadn't dissolved in their genetic codes, I made it mine. From the Interworld, with an astral vibration that might be likened, if I may take the liberty, to human satisfaction, I watched the development, from generation to generation, of Cosmic Consciousness, which, no frivolous wordplay intended, is enormously comic. He who understands philosophy understands laughter. That mysterious Word at the beginning, mentioned in the Bible, is a divine guffaw.

All the ancestors of the woman who would be my mother were receiving, little by little, the infinite joy that emanates from the Creator. They shone like golden fruit among the branches that spread higher and higher. But none glittered like Sara Felicidad. Her intense glow went beyond our solar system until, liberating itself from the magnetism of the galaxy, reached the limits of the Universe and penetrated into the Supraworld, perhaps even farther than that. So much purity in love was irresistibly attractive to me.

I chose that woman as a crucible and, entering into her ovaries, I populated them with an imperious call. The task I took was a hard one, commensurate with my enormous life-will: to make Jaime, whom I chose for his colossal energy, transport his sperm from the distant forests of the south to the desert where my mother awaited him. That journey would take ten years. For mortals, an infinite waiting period, but for me, used to the time of the Eternal One, less than a tenth of a second.

Sara Felicidad's illumination began after a long journey through abandonment. Ever since she reached Iquique, relegated to a room in an obscure boarding house on the outskirts of town, the gaze of the family and of others broke her down instead of helping her to integrate herself. No one could be a positive mirror to reflect her values. No. All they showed her was disgust, indifference, or irritation. Who would want to be friends with a strangely curved girl who smelled bad, was greasy, hidden behind thick black glasses, her hair gathered into a filthy beret, and who, although not exactly mute, never spoke except for a few catlike whispers? No one bothered to teach her to read, but she didn't need reading. Ignorant, she was capable of conversing with the earth, the sky, the sea, and with all kinds of fire. She understood the language of the birds and of many other animals. Even rocks spoke to her. No element refused to sing with her, whether they were barbed plants or the clouds of red sand that rolled down the mountainsides like gigantic caterpillars. Human beings behaved in a different way toward her. In the boarding house, The Schoolboy, a building of boards and cement with small windows that faced a bald mountain, Sara Felicidad ate lunch and dinner in the family dining room, where no one bothered to say hello to her.

One hot day in July, a cart stopped outside the boarding house, teeming with people in costume, men and women of all ages. The dust, the burning sun, and the blinding glare brought them to a halt. After swallowing a few bottles of water, gathering strength from a mysterious faith, they played drums, trombones, triangles, and horns and started dancing on the patio, where instead of plants there was only cat and dog excrement. One group, separated from the others, played flutes that, as it seemed to Sara Felicidad, imitated the cries of birds announcing rain. She tried to understand the costume of the dancers. What were they dressed as? Birds? Each wore a coffee-colored costume composed of a light helmet, a shiny shirt, trousers with lace hems, a belt covered with little mirrors, and a leather skirt, open in front, that reached to the heels. Also, a small white cape covered their shoulders. Multicolored flowers were embroidered on the chest and leg area of their costumes. One of them, in the ecstasy of his ritual dance, shouted, "Long live the Chinamen of the Virgin of the Carmen!"

My mother, from the fervent intonation, instantly understood that the word "Chinaman" meant "servant" for these people. The cap could be a crest, the skirt a tail, the white cape a pair of wings, the belt with mirrors reflecting the faces of the others, a desire for union, love of one's neighbor. And the coffee color corresponded to the earth. The Earth transformed into an ornate celestial bird carrying its offering, a collective consciousness, to the Universal Mother through the Cosmos. Birds that dance, calling the rain to this inhospitable desert, fertilizing the sleeping dust with their dance steps, pouring out hope. Musical instruments making the mountains echo to herald the birth of a planet with a heart. To serve, to give oneself, to dissolve in the shared uniform, to be a furrow open to all seeds, obeying the orders of the Lady Owner. Birds who believed that by celebrating the rain in drought, they were creating it.

It began to drizzle, though the sun was shining brightly. Fine, almost imperceptible drops fell, forming a dome above the costumed people, an ephemeral temple. Sara Felicidad, who had dance in her blood— Alejandro Prullansky's movements had engraved themselves on her memory, crumbling into thousands of perfect sculptures—did not disparage the footwork of these poor folk. The beauty of art was not within them, but there was sincerity like that of the water in a fountain. Each jump, each crossing of legs, each spin was at the same time a giving of thanks and a gesture of adoration.

Sara Felicidad felt transported and, joining the group, she too began to dance. Intoxicated by the drumbeats, she forgot to bend over, and her erect body reached its six-foot-three height. She shook her head, her beret fell off, and her splendid blonde hair, which she'd kept hidden, spread like a luminous spider. The drizzle concentrated on her, washing away the grime accumulated over so many years. Her white skin became whiter still among those dark-skinned people, the dancers stopped their practice in wonder.

That giant girl could symbolize the purity that frightens away demons! Excited, they invited her with them to worship the Virgin in the La Tirana sanctuary, forty miles across the desert. They gave her a white gown, some cardboard wings covered with silver spangles, and a magic wand. No one asked what her name was. They adopted her with the simplicity of their people, where the group counts more than the individual.

They packed themselves joyfully onto the wagon and, still singing, went up toward the Tamarugal Pampa. They traveled that whole day and the entire night. At dawn, they caught up to other pilgrims walking in endless lines. Each group wore a different uniform but all in bright colors. There were Indians, gypsies, shepherds, blue princes, bears, tigers, and caliphs. All chanted hymns to the Holy Virgin:

> We march along in search of her
> We wait and wait and wait
> We've traveled every land
> Along crooked roads and straight

Those multitudes in festive mood—who, in their search for communion, allowed faith to enter the world through their humble hearts—rewarded my mother for the gray years she'd been forced to live hunched over. She tossed away the final item from that dark time, the black glasses, and no longer felt ashamed of her blue eyes.

The wagon, followed by a tail of dust, reached La Tirana. Spangles, feathers, mirrors, ribbons, embroidery, lace, fringes, golden buttons, handbags covered with coins, necklaces, pennants, capes, masks, turbans, handkerchiefs, helmets, musical instruments, dances, prayers. Sara Felicidad, right in the middle of the febrile multitude shaking outside the church made of stuccoed wood, gave herself over to carnival. The military marches, the African rhythms, the play of flutes, put wings on her heels and made her want to speak aloud for the first time since her father died.

She wanted to say, "I love you all!" but instead of spoken words out came a song, so clear and powerful that it did not seem human. The multitude stopped its shaking, and the bands gradually stopped playing. The angel spread her arms and opened her hands to bless them all. They fell to their knees. The wind brought a flock of brown clouds that dissolved in a thunderstorm. The rain proclaimed by the birds had arrived. The alliance of sky and earth was confirmed. Again the bass drums resounded, then the flutes, trumpets. The pilgrims, with more energy than ever, began dancing again. A priest, whose cassock was trimmed with red, white, and blue wool came after her: "Child, stop singing and come into the sanctuary with me! Don't change the festival on me! It isn't you but the Holy Virgin of the Carmen who should be revered!"

And to hide her, he locked my mother up in a confessional. At night the religious brotherhoods lit bonfires, trying to protect themselves from the intense cold that replaced the intense heat. After celebrating the explosion of some firecrackers, with astonished laughter and shouting, they began to enter the church. Without pushing or fighting for space, quite calmly, the bodies pressed together, yielding to the slow current that pushed them toward the altar.

Some inched forward on their knees, leaving behind bloody tracks that were erased by the innumerable feet of the human caterpillar. Finally, there it was, before them, the sculpture carved in a single rock, the miraculous Virgin with her child God in her left arm and a woodcutter on his knees, adoring her amid lots of burning candles. The beseeching posture of that man of stone was identical to that of the throng, all asking for something, for themselves, for others, directing their problems toward the only solution.

Sara Felicidad, who barely fit into the narrow confessional, waited for hours for the homages to cease. When the supplicants left to eat and sleep around the bonfires, walking backward, accompanied by the priest who set an example by braving the glacial wind right along with them, she left her hiding place. She went to check that the doors were locked, approached the altar, climbed up right next to the Virgin, and, with extreme care, removed her crown, her mantle, and her gown. Sara Felicidad spoke to the Virgin in silence, knowing she would hear her:

"They all never stop asking you for things. So it's necessary for someone to give you something. I'm not asking for anything. Your infinite goodness moves me. You've spent so many years here offering your grace that you must be tired. You're smiling, but your shoulders support the weight of our suffering humanity. Allow me, please, to take care of you. I am going to massage your stone to remove the invisible coating formed by the pain of others."

And Sara Felicidad began to massage the Virgin's cold back, her chest, her stomach, her arms, her legs, and her head. Little by little, the stone warmed and after a few hours reached the temperature of human flesh. My mother continued her effort until she thought she could hear, beneath the Virgin's small breasts, the beating of a heart. She redressed the now-living statue and received her thankful gaze. The Virgin of the Carmen accepted her services and made Sara Felicidad her personal maid. Drunk with joy, she ran to hide in the confessional again. The sun had come up, and the multitude was impatiently pushing on the doors. No sooner did the parish priest open them than the leaders entered, placed themselves at the service of the Virgin, and then announced the order of the guilds. These in turn entered one at a time on their knees to offer burning candles, not troubled that the hot wax was burning their hands.

After dancing for five minutes, they left, always walking backward, to allow the next group to enter. There were so many, and the air was so steamy that Sara Felicidad, worn out from the massage (she'd put her soul into every caress), fell fast asleep. No one and nothing could awaken her—not the canticles, not the processions, not the drum rolls, not even more fireworks.

She opened her eyes the next morning. A great sadness came over the plaza. All of the pilgrims, with wild eyes, piled onto the vehicles that had brought them and head back to their places of origin. The priest locked the doors of the sanctuary with two huge locks and left with them. A soft wind brought a cloud of dust, and my mother, still wearing her angel costume, was left alone, without food, water, or a place to sleep.

Three months passed. The priest, accompanied by Doña Pancha, a spirited devotee dressed in all black, arrived from Iquique in a small station wagon filled with brooms, feather dusters, scrub brushes, pails, rags, soap, and a barrel of water to begin the seasonal cleaning. Almost a mile away from the sanctuary, they began to hear the buzzing of bees. There seemed to be thousands. They counted about a hundred honeycombs hanging from the branches of the few trees in the area. The bustle of the insects was unremitting. They entered and left through the church towers.

In the semidarkness of dawn, the priest and his pale assistant saw a glow rising from the windows. The house of God seemed full of light. Doña Pancha clutched her rosary and began to exhale a long prayer. They could clearly see that the two huge locks were intact. Through the cracks, coming from within the church, came the pungent aroma of violets. When they opened the two carved-wood doors, they were hit by a powerful wave of perfume, and for a moment, their pleasure took their breath away.

It was hard for the priest to believe his eyes. Doña Pancha wept like a baby. The candles were lit! Those tons of candles offered to the Virgin three months earlier were still burning with their brilliant tongues of flame without being consumed. The myriad bunches of carnations looked so fresh they seemed to have been placed before the altar that very morning. Next to the Virgin of the Carmen, a girl, blonde and naked, was deeply asleep. The priest remembered the angel that sang with the voice of a celestial trumpet. He looked around. The church was clean, the floor shone, and the bees came to feed at the flowers that were now perennial.

"A miracle," muttered Doña Pancha.

The priest, rapping his knuckle on her head, said, also in a low voice, "Quiet, woman, this may be the Devil's work. Run to the station wagon and bring me my spare cassock."

Sara Felicidad awoke, smiling.

While the disciple dressed her, the priest, asked with his back turned, "Tell me, my girl, who are you? How did you get into the church when the doors were locked? The windows don't open, and the little holes through which pass the ropes for ringing the bells only let the bees in. How long have these candles been burning? Why don't they melt? What did you do to keep the carnations from wilting? And there is neither food nor water here, so how did you live?"

My mother, who by now measured six feet seven inches in height (she would subsequently grow another three inches), bent over toward the priest and placed her hands below his nose. The man jumped back in horror. From those smooth palms, almost devoid of lines, arose the intense fragrance that permeated the temple. When she tried uselessly to speak, musical notes came from her mouth, which smelled like honey, instead of words. The priest thought quickly. The beauty he was witnessing was too great to be demonic. A shame, because it was easier to expel a devil than an angel, but there's a remedy for everything, even miracles, so better to roll up the sleeves and take the saint by the halo. He picked up the old lady, who had fallen to her knees and was striking her chest, and said in a severe tone, "Listen here, Pancha, let's talk things over man to woman. For fifteen years, you've been at my heels. You bring me my chocolate in the morning, and you put out my lamp at night when I fall asleep reading. You are more than my housekeeper, and if it weren't for the chastity imposed on us, you would have been my wife long ago. And it would have done you a world of good, because as a headstrong spinster you've begun to sprout whiskers. Face the facts, woman: what brings you close to the altar isn't God but hormones. You're in love with me. Easy now! Don't faint! I'm speaking to you in this brazen fashion because the situation is serious, and you'll have to make a choice. I'll make it clear: you have to choose between God and me. I recognize that the Virgin has produced a miracle, and that this mute, feeble-minded girl may be a saint, but political interests sometimes have to take precedence over religious interests.

"The festivals at La Tirana instill faith and spread our religion among the people. Any instruction given in the name of the Holy Virgin of the Carmen is obeyed under any circumstance. We've found a way to absorb the ancient indigenous superstitions, and the annual carnival channels the miserable workers' despair, which is so great, toward hope. The calm and perseverance our Lady gives them are essential elements for the proper development of Chilean society. For that reason, everything must go on in the same way. This young woman, so beautiful, blonde, white, tall, pure, and witness to a miracle in the eyes of the miners, could become the Virgin incarnate, a new Messiah, a catalyst for the masses. They won't settle any longer for coming here to dance and march past the idol. No, they will take the angel away from this place to transform her into the leader of who knows what kind of revolutionary army. Peace in this country, which is as tranquil as a paradise, will end, and chaos will ensue. Do you understand, Pancha? Either you run off to tell about the miracle to all the faithful or you shut your trap and stay at my side, promising me you will never reveal our secret. Well then, make up your mind: God or me?"

Doña Pancha, red as a tomato, replied in a hushed voice, "You, Lolo." And since there was nothing to clean as there was not a speck of dust in the sanctuary, she left to wait in the station wagon.

"Look here, girl, you don't know how to talk, but I'm sure that you can hear and that you'll understand what I'm saying. I realize that out of love for Our Lady you have become her servant. That sentiment credits you, and all I can do is accept you since She herself has done so. But there are certain important conditions: you cannot live on miracles, perhaps by drinking dew and eating only honey. I will bring you fruit, vegetables, and jam. And bottles of water, too. You will go on dressed in discreet fashion, in my cassock. You will extinguish the candles and allow me to remove all these flowers. And the honeycombs. I'll come back later with the proper tools, and we'll knock them out of the trees. During the three days of carnival, you will blend in with the crowd, and you'll wear rubber gloves so the scent of your hands won't arouse suspicion. Only then will you be left in charge, seeing how well you've done these past three months cleaning the church. Deal?"

Since the death of her father, Sara Felicidad was accustomed to living hidden away. It was easy to nod her agreement. In any case, my spirit had already entered her ovaries, pointing her inexorably toward the meeting that would lead to my birth. Nothing would be better than absolute solitude in which to wait ten years for the man who would inseminate her. Satisfied, the priest handed her the keys to the two locks, and, taking the carnations that began to rot immediately, he drove off in the station wagon, defending himself from the "Lolos" and caresses that Doña Pancha felt she now had the right to shower on him.

In Santiago, the divided Jodorowsky family reached the year 1919. They thought it catastrophic, but you just never know. Some painful cuts today can tomorrow bring lushness to a tree that was drying out. In any case, they felt like doves kicked by a mule. And they weren't alone. Every Chilean felt a monsoon falling on his straw roof. In an instant, with the end of World War I, the export of nitrates, raw material for explosives, collapsed. Even though the market recovered in the following years, the workers, who could not see the future clearly, bottled up as they were in mines and factories, felt they were on the edge of unemployment. A malaise spread among the poorer classes in the country.

The rich also suffered their kidney punch: the Red Octopus, not content with spreading chaos in its own territories, dared to found a Third Communist International in order to stretch its tentacles around the entire world, intent on fomenting workers' revolutions. Of course, the military had the bottom dogs under control, but in any case it was inconvenient to dance the Charleston with stones in your patent leather shoes. Could it be that because of this uneasy atmosphere, the devils were loose in an island country that had never concerned itself with what was going on beyond its borders? Who can guess? If every event, the sum of all causation, is a byproduct of the whole Universe, why ask questions?

The first to take a beating by Destiny was Lola. My aunt had become so thin that the drunks at the bars where she went with the blind lady from Room 28 called her "The Knife that Sings." She had big deeply set eyes, an expression of constant terror, and the only thing that could have made her attractive was her thick mane of straight black hair. But she insisted on braiding it and wearing it rolled up on her head like a large cone. Her thick lips, like those of a black woman, also tried to assert their femininity, but she silenced them with a layer of flesh-colored lipstick. To disguise her womanhood even further, she flattened her bosoms and used round glasses to feign nearsightedness. Doña Pair—that was the name the blind woman gave herself, "because des-pair comes from hoping too much"—got used to Lola's company. She took pleasure in teaching her to play the guitar, and they shared her tiny room and the tips the customers gave them. Perhaps out of nostalgia for the songs or because they were the least sensual couple in the world, they always respected both women and never tried to make them drink.

"Tell me Doña Pair, please, how many songs do you know? I'm copying down the lyrics and melodies in this notebook. I count more than two thousand!"

"You've done a very bad thing, Lola, in writing down those songs. They're free. That way you make them into prisoners."

"But if something were to happen to you, God forbid, you'd take a treasure to the grave."

"I'd be taking nothing, child. I have no memory. My head is empty. There are no melodies inside it. The songs are like invisible birds; they go all over the place, flying. You call one, and it comes to perch on your tongue. If you fix it in a notebook, you kill it. When our Father made the world, along with the animals and flowers, He created songs. Once upon a time, all human beings could receive them, but their ears have been closing up. I think mine opened when I went blind. Aside from music I have nothing. I'm like a hollow reed. The songs can come to me because nothing disturbs them. Perhaps one day you too will receive them. There aren't thousands or millions—there is no limit. Do you think I'm lying to you or mouthing idiocies like a senile old lady? You're wrong. Even though I'm ninety-two, I'm still young inside. My teacher, who blessed this guitar, is one hundred and eleven. I always divide the money in three parts, two for us and one for Carmelita, whom I visit every Sunday."

"Oh, Doña Pair, how I'd like to meet your teacher! Wouldn't you introduce me? I could also write down what she knows. Maybe we could make a book some day."

"But what a stubborn fool you are, Lola! Whatever I tell you goes in one ear and comes out the other. Songs are born, they die, and if they want to come back, they come back. It's they who decide, not you. And that way, without forcing things, everything works well. Things are perfect when they are left as they are. There's no reason to interfere. Look at that puddle. You think it's filthy, but it's tranquil. If you put your hand in it, the germs that live there go mad and may bite your fingers. Don't break the equilibrium, because you can bring us bad luck. Have faith. The world is like a record: everything is being documented. To recover something all you need is the right needle. Give me the notebook. I'm going to tear it up. All right? Good. That's how it is. You've understood. Tomorrow I'll take you to Carmelita's."

Near Mapocho Station, they took a tram that went along San Pablo to Matucana Avenue. There they got off and continued walking until they turned left onto Andes. Beyond was Manzana de Altos. A square block of two-story houses (they could have been taller, but structures had to be built smaller because of the earthquakes), all linked together. There was a legend that the police didn't go there because the few who dared enter never came out. Their bodies disappeared. Well, 98 percent of their bodies disappeared, to be precise. The remaining two percent, the testicles, were tossed from a window onto the street in a tin can.

The block was a refuge for cardsharps; worn-out whores; pickpockets; drunks with rotten peaches for noses; crazy children; unemployed workers; and blurry, perpetually pregnant women. At the center of the block was a patio with an opening like a pit, where everyone threw their garbage and emptied their chamber pots. Right below ran the powerful San Carlos canal. More than one child had fallen in. The current never asked questions and just carried everything away.

Lola, behind Doña Pair, made her way through the labyrinth of passageways, dodging a rat from time to time. The stench of wine came from every room, along with wit the smells of frying, rancid sweat, and excrement. If a ray of sunshine came in, it filled with dust, and its golden tinge on the heavy ground would be appropriated by a mangy cat. No one bothered them. Carmelita lived in a room that opened onto the central patio. Her white door was framed by flowerpots filled with lilies and carnations. She'd glued a blazing heart of Jesus onto her windowpane. From within came an agreeable chirping of canaries mixed with the aroma of toasted flour.

Doña Pair opened the door, which was not locked, and without announcing herself, had Lola enter behind her. There, in that clean cubicle, with only a bed, a table, and a gas burner where a pot was warming, was a tiny old lady, almost a dwarf, wearing a chocolate-colored bathrobe and some high men's boots. She had one incisor in her mouth, her eyes had lost almost all color and were a faded gray, on her head a net of fine white hairs did not hide her freckled baldness, and her hands looked like two small oceans of wrinkles.

With the voice of a child, the old lady said, "Come on in, girls. I've got hot milk and corn porridge. Would you like some?"

She got off the bed where she'd been sitting and, caressing her guitar as if it were a spoiled cat, walked slowly toward the table, whistling like three canaries, and prepared two little plates of the sugary corn porridge. Meanwhile, the blind woman pulled out a roll of banknotes tied up with a pink thread and put it into a plaster figurine of a squatting little man, who seemed to be defecating a peach pit.

"Thanks, Pair, for feeding my shitass there. God will give it back tripled. Oh, I see your little friend also brought her guitar! Let's sing. After all, that's why we came into this world."

Lola began to play along with the old ladies, but after a few chords, she felt alone. Doña Pair and Carmelita strummed with such delicacy that almost imperceptible musical phrases appeared from their instruments. She made a huge effort and managed to distinguish the beauty of the melody, a lullaby so tender, so saturated with maternal love that her eyelids became heavy, and she was about to fall asleep like a baby full of milk. She was distracted by something like a cool breeze making its way through the sunbaked grass of summer.

The old women were singing without moving their lips, their eyes fixed on the same infinite point. When Lola got used to that almost total absence of volume, she could listen to the words, verses as perfect as a pearl necklace, intense, revealing a sacred respect for life. Like clouds driven by the wind, the words sometimes changed rhythm and the song would acquire such force that its phrases seemed like rays of light. Then the immense calm would return, along with the oceanic sway of the rhymes. Lola began to suffer; those two ancients, luminous worms in the heart of a rotten apple, were creating an art that would not be transmitted because there weren't enough witnesses. She did not deserve to be the only public for this marvel. That music was a national patrimony. All Chileans should know it. What a crime to allow such a heritage to be lost! Trying not to be noticed, she took a slip of paper out of her purse and tried to write down the music and the words that floated like a gold thread above the daily noise. Carmelita instantly stopped playing, as did the blind woman.

"That scratching of pencil over paper is so ugly! You're offending the angels, my girl. If you wanted to write all they sing, there wouldn't be enough forests to produce enough paper. You want to give others the songs you yourself don't know how to receive. That's negligence. You interrupted a holy rhythm. It may be that without wanting to you've provoked something terrible. Let's pray that the Holy Spirit forgives the wound your pencil made in Him."

The two old women made my aunt kneel and began to pray for her. Loud knocks shook the door.

"Open up, granny, your throat cutters are here."

Six men, neither old nor young, in shirtsleeves, wearing muddy white sneakers and jeans, each one's right-hand pocket inflated by a knife, entered. They were smiling drunken smiles, and each one carried four bottles of pisco. Since there were no chairs, some sat on the edge of the bed and others on the table, their legs dangling.

"We were lucky, Doña Carmelita. We mugged a rich guy, and we're celebrating. You'll have to forgive us. We still have some pisco left, and we want to down it with a musical accompaniment. So, play. You know that nobody denies a poor man a song. And your friends can accompany you. To your health!"

The blind woman, used to dealing with drunken oafs, adapted calmly to the situation and, strumming her guitar, cackled out a jolly tune. The old lady accompanied her and invited Lola to shake off her stupor, whispering in her ear, "Don't even think of resiting, girl. Sing without stopping until the wolves turn into groundhogs."

Following the galloping rhythm of the three women, each bandit emptied a bottle of pisco with one swallow. The effect was instantaneous. Their gestures became soft. They sweated, and babbled incoherent phrases with swollen lips as they made the floor shake with their heels. The wriggling went on for more than an hour. They demanded song after song, their favorite Chilean cuecas. Then, worn out, they drank half of the second bottle to get back to form. Then they demanded sailor songs, which they joined in with their harsh voices. They went on drinking.

When they finished the other half, they started to get gloomy. The trio interpreted *tonadas,* songs from southern Chile, that talked about rain hanging from the sky like rags; about forests without owners, dying of sadness during the month of August; about swallows with clay masks. The third liter went down their throats like a funeral procession. Each swallow was a flaming coffin, and suddenly their sorrow burned off, and with their hearts becoming wounds, they began to laugh so hard it seemed they were vomiting. They rolled around on the floor, covering the tiles with spit and tears.

The most powerful took out his knife and sliced the air. They stopped laughing. Suddenly they found themselves there, crouching down, not knowing who they were or in what world they were sitting. Everything lost meaning. It was strange to be "that," a body with head, trunk, arms, and legs. An infinitely empty instant. Ugly women playing at being scarabs and singing, far away, incomprehensible. Horrified at themselves, to be a man or a spider is equally odd. Someone made a sound in a voice that didn't belong to him, to mumble words he half understood: "Stop playing, ladies."

The singers instantly obeyed. The satisfied killer farted. Then he smiled, squeezing his lip and stretching his mouth in a grimace that seemed to split his face in two: "My fellow muggers, I think this ruin, Carmelita, has lived enough. God's going to kill her soon, don't you think?"

"We do!"

"Well then, why should we let that asshole have all the fun. Let's kill her ourselves! Agreed?"

"Agreed!"

"And you, Grandma, do you agree too?"

The old lady, with her usual calm, answered, "If God decides that you are the one to finish me off, I agree."

"Forget all that resignation, Grandma. Before I kill you, I'm going to rape you. What do you think of that?"

"I'd say I was sorry for you. I'm so ugly you're going to suffer."

"That's just what I want: to add more pain to the pain of being alive. Destroying the good is what counts. In this shitty world, goodness is the worst violence."

And with a sudden roar, he leapt on top of the old woman, pulled off her underwear, spread her legs and pushed them back over her head. He penetrated her brutally, kissing that sagging, wrinkled mouth with his entire soul. Barking euphorically, another two jumped onto Doña Pair, splitting her black glasses and sticking their tongues into her eye sockets to lick her cataract-covered pupils. Then with two sweeps of the knife that opened two red furrows in her flesh, they ripped off her skirt and penetrated her sex and her anus simultaneously. The three remaining raped Lola. The one who got her mouth shouted, "Do a good job sucking. If you bite me, I'll slit your throat!"

The two old ladies, with that peace you see in gazelles hanging from the jaws of a lion, allowed themselves to be tortured without moving or screaming. The chief murderer buried his dagger in Carmelita's neck. A spurt of blood left her, pushed by a long, intense wheeze that became fainter and fainter, but never finished, as if it were a serpent of air with an infinite tail. The men began shouting, because at the sight of the red blood, all six ejaculated at the same time. Following the example of the leader, they took out their knives and sank them into the body of the oldest woman. Amid slurs, grunts, and coughs, they dismembered her, emptied out her guts, and decapitated her. Only when they shoved the plaster shitass in her vulva did the blind woman start screaming, as if she were seeing it. They threw themselves on top of her and cut her, too, to pieces.

Pale, huffing and puffing, soaked with blood, they opened their last bottles and emptied them in the pot of corn porridge. To make it look like a bowl of punch, they threw in the four ears they'd cut off and a bunch of fingers. They forced themselves to swallow more than their throats could take. Then belching and belching, they stared, with wide smiles, like little boys asking someone to compliment them for something clever, at Lola, who sobbed, hugging Carmelita's guitar. The glut of alcohol began to drown them. They piled up the body parts in the only sheet on the bed, made a package, and stepped out onto the patio. The chief walked over to the pit that led to the San Carlos canal, staggered, and threw the remains into the current below.

"Bye-bye, little friends. See you later."

He smiled, thought for a second, looked toward the square piece of sky that crowned the rectangular chimney full of windows, where neighbors looked out with the apathy of nocturnal animals, and said, "Let's not leave for later what we can do today! Anyone with guts should follow me!"

Jumping like a broken doll, he dove into the pit. One of his comrades shouted, laughing, "A perfect night for a swim!" And he too dove toward his death. Barking with desperate jubilation, the other four followed suit. The inhabitants of Manzana de Altos halfheartedly applauded each dive. Silence came, slipped under the white door, and filled up the bloody room like thick syrup. It seemed that all the calm of the Universe had concentrated there. Lola, without understanding why they'd left her alive, threaded a needle she found in a small sewing basket, mended her ruined clothes, combed her hair, put the old lady's guitar in its case covered with flowered cloth, and, holding it close, limping, made her way through the labyrinth of passages and short stairways, trying to find the exit. No one spoke to her. From time to time, a door would open and an index finger would point the way. After an eternity, she found herself on the street, knowing that in a couple of months she'd have to have an abortion, that her ovaries would become infected, that after an almost mortal fever, they would have to be removed, and that never in her life would she have an orgasm. But none of that seemed terrible, because with the holy guitar she held in her hands, she would be able to capture thousands and thousands of angels in the form of songs.

What happened to Fanny in that damned year was very different. She had no talent for victimhood. Above all things, she admired executioners, considering them champions. When she turned sixteen, she considered herself a professional. The dwarf whore, Ruby of the Street, had nothing left to teach her. For a teacher she had her body. Her red hair hung down to her waist like a gush of blood; her legs, fleshy but long, marched along with the elegance of a giraffe; her thick lips looked like two sleeping piranhas; her fertile pubis produced hairs so hard they passed through whatever she was wearing like tiny flames. Each breast was so full it seemed to contain an infant, and her prominent ass—fat, jolly, aromatic, with its deep crevice—would make any temple envious. Sculpted like that, she felt able to drag along any well-off man by the moustache. The only weakness she had left was her virginity.

Considering it dangerous to give it to a man—it might create sentimental ties—she decided to use a chair as a lover. She flipped it over, greased up one of its legs, and squatting over it, absorbed the wooden column as she finished eating an empanada. Now she was ready.

To move the world she would need a fulcrum. A strange intuition—so strange that though she obeyed it, she herself thought it insane—ordered her to look for that point in the outskirts of the city, along the highway to Valparaíso. She walked for six miles, until she found a dingy gas station with blind hens squabbling about on the cement floor, covered with black grease. The attendant, a wide, undefined man with a tonsure-shaped bald spot and hands full of fingers as large as bananas, fell to his knees, splashed around in the oily gelatin, kissed her feet, and ran to light a candle at the statue of the Virgin Mary, who reigned in a niche protected by green, fly-specked satin curtains. He saw Fanny and heard her say, "Unless you object, sir, I'll be your lover for a short time. The only thing I ask for is a dish of food, a bed, that you bathe before sleeping with me, and that you let me dispense the gasoline. I don't need a salary."

Did Fanny put her trust in the will of Destiny or did she force it to act as she wished? Impossible to explain. If it was absurd to sink into a cloaca to reach the heights of society, perhaps for that reason, because reality is not logical, it worked out for her: after three weeks of patient waiting, the luxurious car of a government minister stopped there. My aunt observed the man, the son of people from Cataluña: in his fifties, a chest like the prow of a ship, teeth like a horse, and the short legs of a thieving conqueror. She saw in his dry skin the melancholy absence of pleasure and in his irritated nostrils cocaine substituted for love. When the driver, a dark-skinned man proud of his uniform with cap and gloves, gave her a tip, she exhaled deeply into his face, a breeze hot enough to make him drunk: "Pick me up tonight, as soon as you're free. I feel like dancing."

He obeyed her order. As soon as night fell, the automobile arrived, flashed its lights, and honked its horn three times. Fanny, wearing her immaculate white dress, her red high heels, her mane of hair exalted by brilliantine, gave a farewell pat to the garage attendant's sex. She sat down next to the chauffeur, plastered her lips to his mouth, and absorbed his entire tongue. The dark-skinned chauffeur, shocked, thought her vigorous sucking would pull the tongue out by the roots, but a fit of manly desire ate at his brain like an acid; he relaxed and, almost choking, conceded his rough appendage. For this woman he would sacrifice even the ability to speak. She released him and told him to get going, and as they approached Santiago, she bent over between the shift lever and his legs and worked so hard that Ceferino went off the road, slamming on the brakes too late, and found himself ejaculating with a dying cow under his wheels.

That's how Fanny began her ascent. She never lied to anyone. She warned each man that she was a short-term gift. From Ceferino she went on to the doorman at the Ministry, from the doorman to the messenger, from him to an assistant to the subsecretary, from there to the secretary, then to the chief bodyguard, then to the principal councilor, and finally she was received by Don Manuel Garrázabal, the minister. All in fewer than fourteen weeks.

The frowning official looked at her above the photo of his wife, a vain dependent, and a pair of children, tyrants growing up to be cynics. He coughed, lit a cigarette, and offered it to Fanny. My aunt uncrossed her legs, pulled her skirt up (she wore no panties), and introduced the cigarette into her small sex with its pink lips. With her thighs spread, she showed that she knew how to smoke through there, exhaling spirals of smoke. Meanwhile, as if her circus act were the most natural thing in the world, she proposed an amorous relationship to the functionary in exchange for a spacious house where she could carry on her business, that is, a luxury bordello.

The man went crazy. With delirious gusto, he fell on his knees between those alabaster legs and kissed her sex so hastily that he swallowed the cigarette. After half a dozen rapid, uneasy assaults, he agreed to everything—but only if she swore absolute fidelity to him. Fanny, who said her name was Princess Rahula and showed, as proof of her blue blood, the black beauty mark she had on her forehead, accepted the murderer imposed on her as a guard dog, so that at night, with his pistol in his belt, he would sleep under her bed.

That sacrifice was worthwhile. She created a decent bordello, which had a sublime success. Her ideas were original. Instead of demanding a mansion in a well-to-do neighborhood, which would end up causing scandals among its sanctimonious neighbors, she asked for all the little houses along a passage off seedy Bulnes Street, always full of atrocious whores. The men who ventured into that territory came out with their lapels destroyed by the eager tugging of the women trying to seduce them, all ugly, drunk, and falling apart. Politicians, important businessmen, famous men, aristocrats. To each one she offered a complete apartment supplied with a salon, bar, bedroom, kitchen, bathroom, and a garage from which they could enter the house. That way, no busybody could see the client get out of his car, and discretion was absolute.

My aunt had her ideas about masculine sexuality: a man who hires a whore is not, deep inside, looking for sex, but tenderness. More than a woman, he wants a confessor. She scoured all of Santiago looking for twenty expert women between the ages of fifty and fifty-five. She chose, if not the most beautiful—after all, so many years of prostitution, alcohol, abortions, and pimps took their toll—then at least the most dignified. She gave them austere outfits, hairdos like ladies, and tasteful makeup. She taught them how to speak delicately and to erase lasciviousness from their faces, to exchange it for the look of tender mothers.

"Sexually speaking, you know everything, but about maternal affection, you know nothing. Learn to touch the clients as if they were your own sons. At the beginning, during first contact, if you arouse their revulsions (they perhaps hold deep anger against the author of their days because of a bad birth or a lack of milk and care or who knows what, some wish left unfulfilled), it doesn't matter. Go to them so they can reject you. Let them love those enemy hands, and let those hands begin the massage. The first thing you must respect are defenses. And as if you were all Virgin Marys, caress them inch by inch, right down to the heart, with extreme delicacy and total attention, dissolving the tiniest spasms, one muscle after the other, giving firm support to each area, so that the client never gets the impression that any part has been overlooked, no matter how small. To massage in that style, you should breathe regularly, with absolute calm; you must revere; be an empty receptacle, with nothing to request, nothing to impose, a simple refuge, not an invader, an infinite and eternal company, discreet, ready to become invisible at the slightest movement of rejection. If you give in with love, it is God who will touch the other through you. If you don't give your hands to God, they can't really touch. If the mother is not divine, she is not a mother."

Instructed this way, those women knew how to use their sweet voices; to bathe the politicians, singing them lullabies; to powder them with talcum; to take them in their arms; to squeeze an ear between their breasts and hold them there for hours, submerged in the rhythm of the heart; at the end, when they were stretched out on their backs in bed, with no defense, to caress their sex in such a vigorous fashion, from scrotum to glans, that they would emerge from their mental stupor transformed into dragons. They possessed those old ladies, who on all fours made obscene squeals, called out with a diabolical lasciviousness, and led the men to an indecent pleasure bordering on madness. Then they would accept the lash that the temptress would pull out from under the pillow when she sensed they were reaching an orgasm. They would spurt the final discharge under a rain of whips.

Afterwards, they would pay considerable amounts of cash. Fanny's success was so great that the clients had to sign up two months ahead of time to get a date. When there was party involving several men, Fanny would offer the rear apartment, which was three times larger than the others, decorated in French style. Gorged with champagne, cocaine, and women, they would demand the famed eccentricity of the house, as a challenge, in order to prove who was more macho. My aunt brought three nandus, Argentine ostriches, to the patio. The gentlemen, standing on top of a hassock, laughing their heads off and making obscene faces, would possess the birds.

Princess Rahula had to live in a setting worthy of her rank. She had her rooms decorated in maharaja style, with shiny curtains, columns being born from thick lotus flowers, immense cushions, Buddhas, Ganeshas, Shivas, offerings of rice pudding, candles instead of electric lights, and incense that stank of patchouli. She would wear a turban; a long, sleeveless vest; baggy trousers; and slippers whose toes pointed up—all of it in velvet, cloth-of-gold, and transparent silk. Besides, the Minister, as payment for her absolute fidelity, covered her with jewels. Fanny was taking discreet steps in order to be introduced to the president of the republic, when suddenly her periods stopped. To give birth at seventeen did not trouble her a great deal. Her protector tripled her salary, because her breasts that promised milk and her protruding belly made her even more attractive.

Fanny discovered she could meditate crossing her legs, just as her Buddhas did it. In that position, one day at dawn, resting after having scrupulously noted the earnings and expenditures of the day, she heard a telepathic message from the fetus: "Remember me? The last time we saw each other was in Russia, and you were a little girl. I introduced myself as a cobra trainer. I told you that in a previous life, where I had been your father, a king, you were named—"

"Rahula! That's true. Now I realize I never forgot you."

"We share a long history. In even more distant lives, you have been my father, my mother, my brother, my sister, my wife, my lover, my teacher. We have passed through almost all the forms of the realization of love. Now we have nothing more to do in this world. In the next transformation, we shall be one entity. Our souls, finally amalgamated, will help in the gestation of a new Universe, more conscious than this one. The only thing I haven't been for you is a stillborn child, present in your spirit all the days you have left of life. It will be the greater love, the love of the frustrated mother whose breasts drip milk without a precious mouth to suck them; with hands like the eye sockets of the blind, holding an absent body; a trunk grown old without seeing the branches grow; a heart weeping for a child with no name, no body, no age, no presence; pure promise; a never-sprouted seed; a mute road where known and beloved footsteps will never echo. That great love will unite us definitively. Later, the joy of transcending the limits of flesh and the ecstasy of transparency. For having been faithful for so many centuries, we deserve to be the architects of new worlds."

From that day forward, at every dawn, the fetus repeated the same words, and she listened to them each time with the same feeling, as if she'd never heard them before. She stopped smoking opium to see if the message was an auditory hallucination produced by the drug. Nothing changed. The spirit spoke to her for nine months. In March of 1919, the wind carried a dry leaf through the window. It settled on her lap. She made an emergency call for an ambulance. The birth was normal, easy. A beautiful child with open, emerald-colored eyes. When it was placed at her bosom, it smiled, fixed its penetrating eyes on hers, took a deep breath, crossed its legs, joined its hands in the manner of prayer, and died.

A black dot, like spilled oil, appeared on its forehead and spread rapidly until it covered the baby's face, head, neck, and, finally, its entire body. The flesh fossilized. Fanny left the hospital, carrying a small ebony Buddha in her arms. Despite the fact that its fate had been revealed to her, an animal grief invaded her cells, pierced her like a red-hot dagger, surrounded her soul with a corset of thorns. It severed her ambition to be Queen of Chile.

She went back to the inconspicuous bordello, placed the idol at the head of her bed, spent her free time praying before it, and gave herself to the Minister, faking torrential orgasms to convince him to build a secret tomb on San Cristóbal Hill. And one morning, in November of the same year, she walked down the marble steps of the newly finished chapel, got into the bronze coffin with her petrified child in her arms, closed the lid, and abandoned this plane of existence forever. Two days later, Don Manuel Garrázabal was murdered by unknown assailants, perhaps killers in the pay of the man who would be his successor. It is possible that accidents, sicknesses, and attacks are hidden forms of suicide. Since the politician had used prisoners that he then ordered killed in jail, no one ever found out about the existence of the subterranean mausoleum. For her mother and siblings, Fanny disappeared without leaving a trace. The prostitutes claimed she'd run off to India to enter a monastery located on an island that had the same shape as the Sanskrit syllable *aum* or that she'd been carried off by a rajah who held her prisoner in the harem of his palace in Mysore, only feeding her French garlic sausages and pink champagne.

For Benjamín, too, those were evil times. He was eighteen and still obeying his childhood desires. Without a single hair on his body—not on his head, face, armpits, or even his pubis—he was as smooth as a tortoiseshell doll. Always disgusted by his animal parts, he would also have preferred to have no teeth or nails and to be translucent like a jellyfish. But he did not get what he wanted. His nails grew hard and long with wide half-moon marks; his teeth were amazingly white, well rooted in pink gums. Even though he never wanted to brush them, they seemed intent on resisting a century of bacterial attacks. His skin was as smooth as a girl's and shone with a flesh color that was so natural it looked artificial. To cover up those talon-like nails, he covered them with polish the same color as the skin on his fingers.

His way of speaking was so complex and his gestures so exquisite that no boy wanted to become his friend. Aside from his mother, with whom he dined every night and slept in the same bed (taking advantage of the fact that the lady slept like a log, he sucked her breasts passionately), he knew no one. He worked like a sleepwalker in the Rubén Darío bookshop, desiring only one thing: to be a poet. How was that vocation born in him? Benjamín explained it enthusiastically to the first person who did him the honor of accepting him as a comrade, Birdie Baquedano (a boy typographer with a wire-shaped body and the black eyes of a Spanish gypsy, which he inherited from his father, an immigrant who never wanted to work a single day and who, abusing his charm as a singer, his heron-like silhouette, and a member more robust than those of ordinary mortals, lived off Birdie's mother, a long-suffering, hard-working laundress).

"Benjamín, explain to me just what it was that made you decide to write poems."

"Oh, it was the void, a dominion where light supplants the forms. It appeared in my heart, which in turn began to imitate an opening in the heavens. Life swelled and blurred the lines; illusion beat regularity. I had to remake reality according to other combinations. What was known was nothing more than a preamble to the imagining of the unknown. My coarse impulses leapt beyond thought, giving voice to Art amid the deformed silence of the world. And my temple was swept away by the emboldened elements."

"Hmm . . . I understand what you mean. What is your goal?"

"With just one more step, I'll be a phantasm of potential forms, discovering another dawn at the end of this night where men-boys wander around not knowing their brothers, in a false absence that gradually corrodes them."

"Quite clear. What do you see?"

"Beyond death, whose simulacrum I feel, I half-see, knocked down by ecstasy, an eternal reality. All that remains in the empty world is the palpitation of our two souls."

Answering that final question as if in a trance, Benjamín emerged from the depths of his abyss and bit his lips, because he realized he was making a declaration of love to his first friend. Birdie Baquedano, subtle thing that he was, instantly caught the insinuation. He smiled mockingly but did not reject it. He was made for solitary types. Even in the cradle he'd been rejected by everybody, even though he was a pretty, charming, and intelligent baby. He was born with only one defect, a big one: stench. He reached our planet with a mysterious glandular disorder, secreting a stink so horrible that not even his own mother wanted to put her nipples in his mouth.

The sour stink was unbearable, bitter, irritating, and sticky as well—it saturated everything his skin touched: clothing, books, food, furniture, family members. After a few minutes, it would pass through the handkerchief of the person who gave him his bottle or changed his diapers, causing retching and vomiting. He grew up isolated, without friends, embraces, or toys. Even those who had to see him didn't dare come closer than three yards.

The only position allowed him was goalkeeper in soccer matches, though he had to wear thick rubber gloves to touch the ball. He never would have found work if it weren't for a socialist who—nauseated but still applying his humanitarian theories—taught him from a distance to use the machine that made letters from lead. He made him a typographer.

On Mondays, his only day off, he would visit bookstores, since women were out of the question. Seeing as the other customers and the staff ran away when they smelled him, he would simply pocket with impunity whichever books he wanted, and if he didn't do that, the owner would run after him to beg him never to come back and that, by the way,

ALEJANDRO JODOROWSKY

he might take with him this "gift of the house" since the paper stank so strongly after his hands touched it.

The first person not to retreat from his presence was Benjamín. The bald man stared at him with his angelic eyes and smiled warmly. He invited him to look over a collection of poets translated from the French and had a long conversation with him, inviting him to lunch the next day on his free time. In reality, my uncle, in his immense desire to eliminate animal traits, only ate rice and dried fruit and lived with a numbed sense of smell. He did not need olfactory perceptions. As he put it, it was a good sense for dogs or cats, but for no one else.

The lunch began badly because the owner of the restaurant, between bows and smiles, covering his nose with a napkin soaked in mentholated alcohol, begged them to leave immediately, hoping they'd have the goodness never to return. Pale Birdie Baquedano walked out to the street, hopped on a streetcar, and tried to get lost in the city. Benjamín, insane, ran after him for about two hundred yards, chasing him on foot between the rails until, exhausted, he fell on his knees, touching his forehead without eyebrows to the unresponsive cobblestones. Four blocks ahead, Birdie was kicked off the tram, which continued its journey with windows wide open despite the cold.

Benjamín bought two apples, some cornstarch pudding, and a bottle of wine. He happily invited the typographer to a picnic in the garbage dump next to the Mapocho River. There, surrounded by a pestilence that for them was non-existent but which scattered passersby, they could cultivate their friendship. My uncle, searching for a language that would be worthy of his friend's beauty, dedicated himself to getting him out of his depression:

"Everything you fought for and seemed a defeat, a mire of dry leaves, opaque emotions, plans that smashed into walls, and, even more, nightmares, desires suffocated by enormous shame, now burst out transformed into fertile land, like a fire of such living green. It comes from below, from the clear root of sex, which feeds on the great hidden coal, and its growth—if you don't fight it; if you learn the language of what is pure, conscious power; and if you give it blindness as a goal—will drag you toward all that you thought you desired, but which after all was the desire for Life seeking itself."

Birdie Baquedano, without realizing it, drunk on those words and the wine, ate the two apples and the cornstarch pudding. Benjamín became lyrical:

"Open doors toward the south, the north, to the right, to the left; that's right, open yourself as if you were a flower, from the center extending your invisible petals. Make yourself a wheel of hands that give, bless, and receive. Transform yourself into a long bridge along which pass extraordinary energies, which are impossible to define but in which you feel that distant enormity that soaks you to the bones. Let the entire Earth come to you so you push it toward the sky. Let spaces without depth come to you so you can submerge them in the earth. Make yourself a point where all roads cross."

A small stray dog clutched Benjamín's calf with his front paws and began to hump him. The poet refused to take any notice of such lowly stuff and, without bothering to scare him away, left him in his rapid hip work, continuing with his fiery speech:

"The angel of flesh, the angel transformed into earth, there, within the dark skull, pure from the beginning of time, accumulating virgin energy, he, with his cosmic trumpet voice, speaks to you, singing from the flower of the instant. His belly, like an oven hotter than a thousand moons, spurts out tongues of cold fire that dissolve the frontiers of our two languages. Your body swimming in its own soul, thanks to that grace, will always have something new to offer me. Open your mouth so the cataclysm may enter!"

At that moment, perhaps hypnotized by the last sentence, Birdie Baquedano kicked the dog aside and kissed my uncle Benjamín on the mouth, a kiss that lasted at least five minutes. When their lips separated, they didn't know what to do. The poet stood there with the muse caught in his throat. They were staring into each other's eyes as if a mountain had fallen on their heads. The first to speak was the typographer:

"Let's not be ashamed. The greater suffering is to be separated. Let's accept the freedom of tying ourselves to those we love. What we give, we shall give it to ourselves. We are recalling the existence of the bridges because everything that seemed severed has been united for all eternity. Let's plunge into each other's dreams, and let's find the infinite road."

My uncle was left agape, in blessed admiration. Birdie too was a poet! They kissed again. Benjamín felt a desire to dance. He tried a few steps in the garbage, but he was chased off by a furious rat. Birdie smashed it with a brick. Feeling protected, Benjamín dreamed aloud:

"Let's imitate the poet Augusto D'Halmar and Tolstoy, Gorky, Zola, and Maupassant by going to live in the virgin territories of southern Chile to plant roses and fruit trees, to teach literature to the peasants.

"Look, Baldy (please let me call you by that pet name), it's my duty to remind you that when D'Halmar, equipped only with a wide-brimmed black hat and a Spanish cape, reached Concepción in his search for Arauco, he couldn't even find anything to eat, he found nowhere to sleep, and he got lost out in the country. He was almost raped by a group of horsemen. He quickly came back to the capital and with three friends founded, just outside the city, an agrarian colony that failed because they planted out of season, their neighbors stole their water, and their oxen ran away."

"Quite right, Birdie, but we can save ourselves from the materialist world living like the 'Group of Ten' in a tower facing the sea."

"I'm sorry, Baldy, but those writers froze in the winter because the tower's windows had no glass in them. Then it filled up with bats. Finally—remember, they wanted to live only from fishing so they wouldn't exploit the people—some sea urchins they pulled off the rocks near the beach (none of them knew how to dive) gave them such bad hives they all ended up in the hospital, covered with rashes and swollen so much they looked Chinese."

"Why is your name 'Birdie' when you put up so many obstacles to taking flight? "Could it be because your last name, Baquedano, ends with a 'no'? Change it to a 'sí!'"

"Baquedasi? I'm Chilean, not Italian." So let's stop beating around the bush. What we want is to sleep together. At the printing house, they've lent me a room (for obvious reasons) out on the upstairs terrace, where no one ever goes. It isn't a tower, but it's just as isolated, and from the window you can see the ocean; it's on the building across the street, which has a seafood restaurant in it, so it's all painted blue. Shall we go?"

Benjamín, with a broken voice, answered in verse:

> *Like transparent vessels*
> *Sailing immortal*
> *Along the river of death.*

Then he lowered his eyes, blushing, only to raise them again immediately, because they fixed on an indiscreet bulge growing in his friend's fly. They walked along the banks of the river, holding hands. Benjamín's mind filled with words, but he didn't dare speak them. (I only want to breathe the air that comes from your mouth; kiss you with ten thousand lips; cover your body with my saliva, that of a revived dead man; run my tongue over your brain with the thirst of an Arab dog; place you on the pedestal of the goddess. I also want you to murder me with kisses, like someone who enters the darkness of a millennial temple seeking the luminous frog in order to cook it nailed to a cross. I want you to pierce me surrounded by a black aura so that nothing else happens and everything becomes eternal.) This mixture of high-pitched lyricism and volcanic desire aroused a strange feeling in him, where happiness galloped along, riding atop anguish. The struggle turned into rabid hunger. When they reached the fire escape ladder, he didn't dare climb it and suggested to his friend that they go into the seafood restaurant.

"What are you talking about? I'm broke. Besides, you're a vegetarian."

"Don't worry. I've got my week's pay on me. I should go to the market to do my mom's shopping, but we have to celebrate finding each other. Let's have a banquet."

"And then what will your mother eat?"

"Parrot food: banana and rice for seven days. It will do her good because she's getting very fat."

"In that case, let's have the banquet!"

Benjamín went in first and asked for an isolated table at the rear of the garden. Birdie Baquedano followed, crossed the main room so he'd leave just a whiff of himself, and sat down, shouting out an order for two bottles of *chicha*, or corn whiskey, and the menu. They chose fried silverside, mussel soup, conger eel with tomato, meat and vegetable stew with algae, stuffed crabs, meat with tomato and onion, and fish stew. For dessert, two more liters of chicha and crullers in syrup. Alternating between mirth and high seriousness, they devoured everything, satisfying at once both their hunger and many years of unhappiness. Before leaving, Benjamín, in the style of an Oriental prince, emptied his pay envelope into the waiter's hand.

"Keep it all. Whatever's left is your tip."

The old waiter, after counting the money, ran after them: they were eighty cents short on the bill. The typographer dug around in his pockets, but found only some type: the word "hope." Benjamín luckily discovered a peso in the hem of his trousers.

"You keep the twenty cents left. They don't mean much in monetary terms, but they do if you accept that the person giving them to you is a future celebrated poet of important historical value."

Laughing their heads off, they reached the "fire escape ladder," which was not a ladder but an ascending row of rusty iron bars stuck into the wall. They would have to climb four stories, clinging like lice to those precarious steps to keep from smashing into the sidewalk. Birdie was used to risking his neck climbing up and down at least once a day, so he suggested that my uncle go first so that he, right behind, could keep him safe, pushing him along on the buttocks. Admitting that he suffered vertigo, he accepted this rather undignified help and began to climb up. That hot hand on his backside produced an uneasiness that was so out of place in his spirit that, with a shake of his head, he immersed his spirit in an interior monologue:

"This matter of having half a soul is a serious thing. You make your way along the river of illusions with a thirst for something enormous, which is nothing more than the other piece of the lyre. And that thirst, understood as solitude, is satiety. Because both parts, no matter how far apart they are, have never stopped being, from the start of History, united. Yes, beloved, it seems we've been walking together forever. But it's one thing desiring it, imagining it, and another finding it. What a cataclysm, what pleasure, what uneasiness, what doubt, and also what a marvelous blooming of enthusiasm! Your paradisiacal gardens sprouting in my earth, which before you seemed a desert. Your painful caresses that fill my . . . my shoulders with happiness. And this shameful desire that you spit into my nine doors. It seems that in the dream I've lived in, you are the first reality. Sometimes I believe it, sometimes I don't. What does it matter! Our love will be as long as God's tongue."

Finally they reached the terrace. In one corner lurked a small, white-washed room with a thin door and a window not even a cat could slip through. Before he entered, Benjamín tensed: he'd glimpsed a bed. He rubbed his chest, trying to calm the unruly beating of his heart.

Baquedano shouted, "If we want to make a necklace, we have to pass the string through the first bead!" and with a push he forced Benjamín to enter. Since the room was dark, the typographer tried to light a candle. Benjamín blew out the match. Transforming the half-light into an accomplice, they fell, embracing, onto the bed. My uncle, on the verge of a heart attack, allowed himself to be undressed by his friend's eager hands.

"You don't have the smallest hair on your body! Your skin is like that of those women who don't want to come near me."

"Friend, let's not think about the flesh but about the spirit. Let's join our voices, allow our words to caress each other until they fill with flames. Let each of us be the perfect mirror of each other . . . "

Birdie Baquedano, deafened, interrupted him by letting all the desires he'd held in for so long loose. He flipped my uncle over and awkwardly— he had no experience—penetrated him with his sex, enlarged and about to explode. That brute contact cut off the poet's breathing, erased his language, and made him gasp like a fish out of water. He had a touch of lyricism left to compare himself to a feathered galaxy and then he yielded to the vigor of his friend, now transformed into a beast. He took him in completely, flew over a golden ocean, crossed forests of petrified trees that creaked noisily and produced green branches, rose toward a space studded with distant stars; he went, he went, he went, and suddenly he fell, vertiginously, through atmospheres that became thicker and thicker, sulphurous, rotten, only to be recreated once again. Animal pleasure, rejected until now, flooded his flesh like a tidal wave, giving life to what seemed sterile: he recovered his sense of smell. The abominable stench of his lover—atrocious, nauseating—assaulted him. Without realizing this change had taken place, Birdie Baquedano galloped with tremendous strength, his saliva, the opposite of perfumed, all over my uncle's neck. The poet held in his gagging, then his stomach ached, and later, with dizzying rapidity, came the grandest of diarrheas.

A spurt of hot, fetid water bathed the typographer's stomach. He jumped back only to receive another, uncontainable blast right in the face. The liters of chicha, plus the soups and seafood, along with other material and fecal juices, stained the bed, the floor, the walls a coffee hue. Even the ceiling was spattered. When that storm ceased, the two lovers, covered with shit from head to toe, stared at each other in alarm.

Birdie Baquedano, assuming the tone of a man of the world, tried to say something, but Benjamín, crying out in pain, ran along the terrace in search of a non-existent latrine. A new attack had begun. He spent several hours squatting over a pail until his guts evacuated along with his heart. He washed himself off as best he could in a tub of disgusting water, got dressed, climbed rapidly down the vertical stairway, and walked toward his apartment followed by a pack of stray dogs who sniffed at him, wagging their tails. He took a shower, soaping himself seven consecutive times, and never saw his friend again. Nor did he want to meet any other men. He abandoned poetry and, aside from taking care of his mother and selling books, began to wait for a blessed illness to get him out of this world. His apathy reached such a point that even the absurd ending of his first and last friendship left him indifferent.

Later, one of the iron bars in the ladder gave way, and Birdie Baquedano fell, striking his head. Since he was unconscious, he was taken to the Red Cross. A male nurse, unaware of Birdie's nature, seeing him on the stretcher, assumed by the smell that he was a cadaver in an advanced state of decomposition and put him in the morgue's refrigerator. There, locked away, the typographer perished, frozen to death.

Jaime too in 1919 suffered a collapse of his plans, to the point that he found himself tossed toward cloudy pathways without knowing exactly why he was walking them. González the Horse had made a good boxer of him, but it wasn't the technique he'd learned nor the strength he'd developed breaking skulls with his fists that gave him wins by knockout in each of the seventy-five bouts he fought: it was rage.

All the Chileans he fought had roots, grandfathers, homeland. In their blood circulated beloved drinks and dishes cooked with wistfulness. They talked about "my" land, "my" mountain range, "my" sea. They felt they were the owners of the air they breathed and were convinced that the very ground loved the caress of their footsteps.

On the other hand, he—"Jaime the Russian," ferocious champion from the steppes, raised by bears and a two-headed eagle, also known as "The Bonebreaker" or "The Ring Murderer" or "The Damned Gringo"—had no one to grant him even an ounce of tenderness. His father? A saint drowned in the glow of goodness. His mother? A crazy renegade with hands so hateful that they burned rather than soothed. His brothers and sisters? Martyred emigrants from the Kingdom of Never Ever, with their souls enclosed in a diver's suit into which no air was ever pumped, islands without bridges, relating to one another by smacks, like billiard balls.

The fury of not belonging made his punches whopping, real "Here I am!" punches that broke ribs. He was eager to enter the country by breaking the bodies of its neighbors, winning recognition by destruction. He loved to challenge the audience. When their favorites fell with broken jaws or with their kidneys or liver smashed, or knocked cold and on the verge of death, he received their jeers holding his testicles with one glove while he made the gestures of a penetrating phallus with the other. That hatred was his food. Money aside, he fought not for the pleasure of winning but to aggravate rejection and to turn that into his homeland. To be an anti-hero was a thousand times better than living anonymously and separately.

The illegal bouts, which always came after dogfights, were bloodier than the animals'. There was no boxing; the fighters simply beat each other without stopping until one fell over. The matches were held in improvised rings in bars, slaughter yards, garages, vacant lots. The high betting made people thirsty, and barrels of wine, beer, and brandy were consumed. Jaime did not win easily. Since no one bothered to make sure the boxers were of equal weight, sometimes he was up against tanks. In those difficult cases, he would use the tricks of the trade the Horse had taught him: elbowing, low blows, head butts to the cheeks, scratches with the inside of the gloves, blows to the neck, suffocating clinches, foot stomping, sarcastic remarks that made the adversary lose composure. No matter what, he always came out with a swollen eye, his ribs bruised, and his nerves wrecked. The aftereffects would last two weeks; he would sleep badly, dreaming about cats eating his penis, and wake up screaming. In June of this dark year, González the Horse came to see him and said in his nasal voice:

"Enough with these illegal bouts. We've been offered a nice contract for the National Championship, in a real ring. You'll have your picture in the newspaper. If you win, they'll pay us very well, and the good life will begin. If you accept—you'd be nuts to play hard to get and turn down the opportunity—I'd have to prepare you using my methods, because there's no time to perfect your technique. You've got more than enough strength, your hooks are like mule kicks, and you've got winning in your heart, but you're missing something. Maybe it's something you've got too much of—rage. You put too much into it, you lose control, waste energy, drop your guard, and have the bad habit of charging with your head unprotected, risking a split eyebrow and being blinded by blood. All that is from a surplus of hatred. I want you to be capable of indifference. In a month, you'll face the Baby, a colossus who weighs 265 pounds. Before turning professional, he killed three in the illegal bouts. If you learn to control yourself, you'll win."

"You want me to change my nature in a month? You're crazy, Horse. It can't be done so quickly, and besides it's impossible."

"If you're a man, we can give it a try."

"You doubt my virility? I'm no fag."

"Maybe a coward."

"Me? Let's see."

"We will see. First, it will be easy. I'll tickle you with a feather, and you'll have to hold in your laughter. When you get past the tickles, I'll move on to the second test, and that's when you might begin to break down. To comfort you, I'll tell you that my secret method has only four steps. Few but decisive."

"Go get your feather. If I decide not to laugh, I won't laugh. With will power you can achieve anything."

Things weren't that easy. The feather was hard, an eagle feather: bearable in the armpits and the back but annoying on the soles of the feet and a torture in the nostrils and the inner ears. It took Jaime a day to dominate those feelings and make himself feel nothing. Only once did Horse catch him off guard and make him jump up—by scratching his anus. Eventually, he could touch the feather to Jaime's open eyes and he wouldn't even blink.

Then the pricking began. He had to let himself be pricked with a needle without reacting. That took a week. His teacher showed no mercy. He sunk the tiny point in everywhere, including the genitals. Jaime put up with the pain, overcame his reflexes, and became as inert as a corpse.

Horse gave him four days of rest while he went north to find an important ingredient for the third test. He returned with a carefully sealed cigar box with tiny holes in the lid.

"What I've got here are a dozen tarantulas. I had to go all the way to the Andes to hunt them down. They're big and very poisonous. Luckily they walk more slowly than turtles. Look."

He opened the box. There were the hairy animals with their long legs and the orange stripe on their bulging bellies. Horse took a twig and flipped one over.

"Take a good look, my Russian friend. Here underneath the thorax they have two black teeth. They will use them to bite and kill you. They aren't aggressive, but they have a very bad disposition. The slightest unexpected movement makes them snivel, trying to inject their venom. And just so you see I'm not lying . . . "

With some tweezers he picked up a tarantula and tossed it on a mangy dog that had wandered into the slum to sniff around the garbage. The dog jumped three times, howled, tossed the spider off, but after a few minutes began to wheeze, fell to the ground shaking, and died. Jaime swallowed hard.

"Go to bed early because tomorrow we'll get up at dawn."

Before sunup, they left with the cigar box and a cask for San Cristóbal Hill. Horse poured the tarantulas into the cask and turned it over next to Jaime, who was lying on the ground, trying to turn himself into stone. They waited a couple of hours until the sun warmed the ground. The spiders lost their torpor and tried to get out of the cask. To do that, they had to walk along Jaime's legs, stomach, sex, chest, and face. He was naked. His body temperature seemed agreeable to them, so they stayed on top of him for half an hour, which to my father seemed like an eternity. But it wasn't disagreeable because, detached from his body, he fell into a beatitude that united him to the entire Universe. He realized that beneath the terror of existence—that life threatened by hunger, catastrophes, illness, human beasts—there extended an infinite peace. A sentence came to his mind and he repeated it again and again while the tarantulas were on top of him: "I without the world, no; the world without me, better." Finally they left. González the Horse, pale, handed him a heavily sugared cup of coffee he poured from a thermos.

"You are an extraordinary boy. You'll be the champ because you're not afraid to die. Now all you have to do is learn to become invisible. You'll move on to the final test, the hardest."

When Horse explained what he wanted him to do, Jaime became furious and called him a madman. Then he was engulfed by the cosmic peace he'd acquired with the tarantulas, and he accepted with indifference.

At six o'clock in the afternoon, when the zoo was closing, they visited, Don Gumercindo, the old watchman, a friend and former admirer of Horse, with four bottles of red wine in hand. He received them with open arms. The business of spending nights alone with the roars, crowing, and erotic whistles had made him thirsty, not only for wine but also for human company. The boxer had him swallow glass after glass until most of the four bottles was in his stomach. He collapsed onto his military cot, snoring so loudly that the three-year-old calendar on the wall went flying.

Horse checked through some drawers and found a ring of keys. They walked to the big cage of the Bengal tigers. There were four adult tigers, one male and three female, along with half a dozen pups, each no larger than a cat. Night was falling. The tigers, emerging from their daytime torpor, suffocated in that space (which, even if it was big, was restricted by bars), pacing back and forth with a consistency that seemed unreasonable.

Jaime's task was to enter the cage, sit down in the center and remain there until dawn without being eaten. My father put the key into the lock, turned it slowly, opened the door inch by inch. He slipped in, shut the door. Oblivious to himself, an empty vessel, he walked to the designated spot, passing among the tigers without their noticing his presence. He sat down with his legs crossed and remained there—blending with the air, the darkness, the cold, with no divisions, without a single word coming to his mind, without a single feeling occupying his heart, without wanting or needing anything, beyond all possession.

The beasts did not see him. Moreover, a female came over to him to sniff, scratched the ground, and peed a hot spurt on his back. When, with the first rays of sunshine, the bars made long black tongues that cut the floor into brilliant rectangles, Jaime, walking with normal steps, not trying to hide, zigzagged among the supine tigers getting ready to sleep and left the cage. Unable to move his mouth to smile, he emptied a little bottle of rum the euphoric Horse handed him. Together, proud, they jogged six miles back to the tenement.

"Now you're ready, my Russian friend. The man who can beat you hasn't been born. Baby Face will leave this bout with an old mug. You will be National Champion."

The fight was widely publicized in the newspapers, and the basketball court where the ring had been constructed was full. Everyone was a fan of the Baby, and they all came to see how he would break my father's neck. Jaime walked toward the ring accompanied by Horse amid hisses and thrown bottles that burst scattering beer or urine. After the customary introduction, the fighters took off their robes, and the audience burst into laughter. Opposite that tall mastodon, wide, heavy, full of muscles, my father looked like a weak dwarf.

One fan shouted out, "I bet Baby knocks him cold in under two minutes!"

No one argued the point; they all applauded. Jaime, little by little, began to disappear. When the bell sounded to call him for the first round, he was invisible. He was a body with no one inside, a demolition machine, nothing more. The giant had no idea where to begin. Every punch landed in the void. His enemy was an agile, icy shadow that ducked and stepped back without ever showing himself. When the rest period came, the Baby, sweating in the heat, his breath short, felt alone. He was fighting against a waft of air that stared at him with the eyes of a dead man.

The bell sounded. Baby again found himself transformed into the center of a comet that spun around him counterclockwise. How the hell was he going to land a punch? Upset, he dropped his guard for a second and felt an explosion in his liver followed by a hook to the jaw that made him stagger. The audience was silenced. The shadow struck again, and the left eyelid of the favorite opened like a ripe pomegranate. Before he could react, he was hit with three more smacks of the glove.

The blood poured out, leaving him only one good eye. Jaime used that advantage to break Baby's nose.

The round ended. The three members of the champion's team closed his cut with Vaseline, stuffed cotton into one nostril, and passed him the pail so he could spit out two broken teeth. They assured him that these contusions were a mere accident, a common mistake, we all get distracted for a second; they predicted that in the next round he would make the poor contender into mortadella.

The bell rang. Jaime, tranquil, observing at a distance of two thousand years, advanced toward his rival with his arms hanging at his sides. Baby lurched forward, transformed into a bull on his judgment day, and began to throw a series of punches that were lost in a space that had become immense. The enemy offered no resistance, and suddenly he clenched with Baby, and boxing became dance. He wasn't a man but a snake. Disconcerted, he stopped in the center of the ring, emptied of aggression, waiting for a response.

Jaime began a kind of dance, jumping forward and backward, cutting at times to one side then the other without throwing a punch. The audience began to protest. They no longer knew which one they were against. The Russian lost that nationality along with his face and silhouette, his person. No one could judge him; he was someone being no one. Baby, tired, perhaps hypnotized, dropped his gloves, and then the lightning bolt struck. He received an incessant beating, in the stomach, the ribs, the chin, the nose, the eyes, the temples. He looked like a house being torn down.

Jaime's punches, implacable, accurate, echoed like shots, penetrating the innumerable holes in the stupefied defense. The colossus, bent on a knee, groaning, almost suffocated. The referee counted to eight. Baby came staggering back into the fight. One of Jaime's punches seemed to break his ribs. Another bloodied his mouth. His swollen lower lip hung like a dead oyster. A jab seemed to burst his eye. The huge man, reaching desperation, terrified, stretched out an arm to ask for help from his trainers, wanting them to throw in the towel. Since it was a useless gesture for the fight, it surprised Jaime, and purely by chance, it caught him right in the forehead. His head shot back, scattering a halo of sweat. The impact wasn't strong enough to knock him out, but because it was such a surprise, it produced a mental short circuit; a space the Rabbi used to introduce himself into his spirit and take control.

For many years, since the death of Alejandro the shoemaker, the Rabbi had not revealed himself. Jaime resisted him with his attacks of epilepsy. But now, with all his accumulated yearnings to exist, he turned Jaime into his mount. Jaime seemed to grow thin, his shoulder hunched, his gestures became delicate, his voice became shrill, and his eyes burned. With infinite pity, he observed the bloodied Baby, who was so beaten up he was completely bewildered. He embraced him, kissed his cheeks, and said, "Brother goy, I can't go on hitting you. Commandment 216: 'We should love our fellow man.' Commandment 251: 'It is forbidden to hurt another with wounding words.' If bad words are forbidden, then the prohibition logically extends to punches. Commandment 300: 'It is forbidden to hit anyone without authorization.' God, blessed be He, has not authorized boxing. Neither you nor I is a criminal to warrant flagellation. Commandment 302: 'It is forbidden to feel hatred for our fellow man or humiliate him in public.' Forgive me, Baby, for what my ignorant guest has done to you. Commandment 319: 'It is forbidden to strike one's parents.' All human beings in one moment of history have been or will be our parents. For having damaged your body, Jaime deserves throttling. Forgive him. From the depth of my being, I implore you, oh Lord!"

Baby, during that monologue, had enough time to recover, and seeing his enemy with his flaccid arms extended toward him, took advantage and hit him with a left hook to the abdomen that finished the speech. An enthusiastic roar arose from the audience: "The kitchen!" The fans were begging the champion to splatter the traitor's stomach. He went on punching. The Rabbi did not defend himself. He even offered his face for punishment:

"If that's the way you want it, come on, brother. Punch until you're tired. I shall convert your hatred into embraces."

Baby smashed his face. The Rabbi asked for more punches. Baby smashed his ribs. Jaime raised his arms as if in the shower, to offer a better target. A molar went flying. The Rabbi smiled, spitting red with a saintly face. He began to look for punches, and he found them. He charged forward, threw himself into the arms of the ferocious monster to be broken, eaten. The murderous crowd asked for more. The Rabbi, miraculously still on his feet under a punishing deluge, began to recite a psalm: "Truly my soul finds rest in God; my salvation comes from Him."

González the Horse threw in the towel and immediately jumped over the ropes to pull Jaime out of Baby's arms. Baby, desperate because he couldn't knock him out, was squeezing his throat to strangle him. Horse dragged Jaime to his corner and emptied a pail of ice water on his head. The sudden chill made Jaime react and frightened the Rabbi away. No sooner had the spirit fled than the pain began. My father fell, writhing, to the floor with four broken ribs. He had to be carried out of the ring on a stretcher. His boxing career ended that night.

Horse got drunk so he could tell him, with great sadness, "My boy, you could have been number one, but you're crazy. We missed the train, and there won't be another. I'm old now. I'm going to Chañaral to the house where I was born. I'm going to plant tomatoes, because they'll remind me of boxing gloves. Goodbye."

It took Jaime three months to recover from the beating. When he left the hospital, he found out that Horse had given up the room in the tenement, so he'd have to find a new one. He went to the apartment of Teresa and Benjamín to see if they'd let him stay there for a while.

It was December 1919. The heat was unbearable, but all the shops were decorated with snow, sleds, and Santa Clauses dressed for a polar cold. In that ridiculous festive setting, imported from the European winter so it could be transplanted into the heart of summer, the wicked surprises continued. Now it was Teresa's turn. Simply put, she went insane.

Where did she get the rifle? No one ever found out. She stepped out onto the balcony and began shooting. Luckily, her rage was tempered by her rejection of death; she only wanted to wound people in the legs, as she screamed amid the firing, to keep her victims from marching in obscene flocks. The hatred that seized her was directed at all uniforms. She would shoot and shout, "Down with equality! Long live difference!"

She maimed one policeman, two soldiers, a café waiter, a lycée student, an ice cream man, three boys wearing soccer uniforms, a government official, a nurse, and a Santa Claus who passed by selling sugared peanuts. When Jaime arrived, the shooting had been going on for half an hour, and the victims were moaning where they fell in the street, trying to staunch the blood pouring out of thighs and calves. The Red Cross was slow in coming. Benjamín and Lola, on their knees amid the wounded, implored their mother to stop firing.

When the neighbors formed a chain to keep passersby from walking into danger, Teresa, with extraordinary marksmanship, began to kill pigeons, howling that those birds from hell were also in uniform. Then she shot at shadows because they were all the same color. When she decided that human bodies were uniforms, because they were all—head, trunk, and extremities—the same, chaos ensued. Benjamín and Lola fled, dodging bullets, and hid under a cart. Finally the police arrived along with an ambulance and a fire truck. They recommended waiting until she ran out of ammunition.

When they heard some clicks from her weapon, the ambulance personnel ran to pick up the wounded, and the firemen stretched out a ladder to block the window and keep the mad woman from diving down to the street. Had she really run out of bullets or was she crouched down with the reloaded rifle, waiting for someone to approach so she could open her vengeful fire again?

Jaime, without asking himself that question and forgetting his own pain, ran up the firemen's ladder, slipped over the steps, and, making a huge leap, landed right in the dining room. On the table, with only her head protruding from the soapy, dark water, Teresa was lying naked in a metal tub. The rifle, empty now, was taking a bath with her. Her eyes were wide open, round, flashing, and the skin on her face was stretched, as if it were too small to hold in so much bitterness. Without recognizing her son, she spoke through him to address someone who was standing behind her back:

"Don't ask yourself who you are, because you are no one. You've never existed. Like me. We are impostors in this world, which is not authentic, where there is nothing true and what is real is a mirage. Uniforms all over the place, copies of copies of copies, each suit, each body, each soul is a disguise. The surface is everywhere and the center nowhere. A piece of rock, a piece of flesh, a flood, a fire, a massacre, the void's same old hypocritical game. We've been dead since the beginning of time. No one has ever been born. Strangle me, get me out of this lie!"

Teresa's disillusionment was so great that Jaime stretched out his hands, wishing to obey her. She got on her knees, revealing her long, wide bosoms, large bananas that reached her navel.

"I've lost my strength. You, a good executioner, change the world. Make it finally be born."

Jaime, with the compassion that was leading him to matricide, ran to open the door. The police came in scrambling like clowns from one place to another, shouting orders, pointing their carbines, shaking clubs, trembling as if the poor woman were a rabid gorilla. Behind them, whiter than a paraffin candle, came Benjamín and Lola. Teresa did not recognize them either. She sank completely into the water, trying to drown herself. The cops could find no other way to save her except tipping the tub over.

The water splashed over the floor, giving off a pestilential stink. Aside from the grease and the soap, it contained leftover food, books dissolving into jelly, pieces of photographs, excrement, and little crystal balls.

They tied her hands, wrapped her in a blanket, and carried her away. As she passed by Jaime, she had a lucid moment: "My son, go see Recabarren. He was the only one who didn't lie to us."

Then she howled like an animal, foaming at the mouth, and began to fight against the uniformed medics. Her screeching could be heard until the ambulance that finally carried her to the insane asylum became a white dot far down Independence Avenue. Lola left, following the police and firemen without a word. Benjamín, holding back his sobs and his nausea, put on one of his mother's aprons and began to wash the floor. He too said nothing. Jaime felt like a stranger. He knew his brother would see to it Teresa was moved to a decent clinic. After all, the old girl belonged to him. She was almost his wife. Offering him help would only arouse his jealousy. It seemed far better to lock oneself in a cheap hotel until this damned year ended.

He spent seven days in Room 13, without turning on the light, without talking to himself, without reading newspapers, stretched out like a corpse. When the sirens announced the New Year, he paid his bill with the last money he had and walked out to hug people in the street. The first person to fall into his arms was a muscular dark-skinned woman, beautiful and virile. Their embrace grew closer and closer, each one advancing without modesty toward the intimacy of the other, charging like two warships, giving each other kisses like cannonades, and there, standing up, they fornicated for hours.

After ejaculating four times, Jaime asked what her name was. It turned out to be Isolda, the Lightning Bolt from Limache, a knife thrower. My father showed her the empty lining of his pockets and proposed that she take him on as her assistant. From her knapsack, the girl removed seven wide knives, placed Jaime next to a wooden entryway door, stepped back a few paces, and with icy severity challenged him: "Will you take the dare?"

Jaime felt his knees grow weak, but his hunger counseled him to risk his skin, despite the alcohol on the woman's breath.

"I won't even blink!"

She threw the knives at him. The first almost caught his ear. The second ominously just missed his ribs. The third brushed his calf. That took care of the left side. Three more tosses balanced out the right.

"Spread your legs a bit. Still going to take the dare?"

Jaime separated his legs and said nothing, not out of bravery but because he'd lost his voice. The seventh knife struck so close to his perineum that if scrotum hadn't contracted like a cotton vest washed in hot water, she would have castrated him. The year 1920 offered him his first opportunity: he would be the target of dark-skinned Isolda in Toni Carrot's circus.

The tent, formerly white but now gray from being handled so often, spotted with patches and stains like purulent wounds, was small. For seating, the spectator was offered a gallery of splintered planks, and the performance space, marked by gasoline cans painted red, white, and blue like the Chilean flag, was covered by a carpet of potato sacks since it lacked good mats. In one truck traveled the baggage and the trained burro and in the other, the entire company, composed exclusively of family members. Toni Carrot, whose real name was Don Hernán Cañas, dressed completely in orange. He said he was a descendant of José Joaquín Cañas Aldunate, the priest of Carahue, who in the high spirits of the days of Independence committed the indiscretion of starting a discreet family. He was the artist's grandfather.

His wife, Emilia Cañas, a.k.a. Toni Lettuce, was completely dressed in green. For her part, she claimed to be the granddaughter of Blas Cañas Calvo, the priest who organized the Congregation of the House of Mary, who, on the day the convent was inaugurated, imbibed too much punch and sinned with a nun. As soon as her belly began to protrude, she was expelled and had to give birth on the watermelon truck giving her a lift to the Talcahuano whorehouses. She managed the business affairs of the group, distributing the pesos and the food with a severity worthy of King Solomon.

The two trapeze artists, jugglers, tightrope walkers, trainers of the donkey who knew how to bray the national anthem, were the parents of Isolda and her three brothers. The three remaining women were the mobile wives of those same brothers. Each night, they drew lots to decide who would sleep with whom. The children, an indeterminate number, called all the women mom and all the men dad.

The most tedious aspect of the performances was the continuous costume changes. Toni Carrot and Toni Lettuce retained their identity, but the others, dressed as musicians, began playing a polka next to the ticket stand, improvised on the bed of the passenger truck to attract the audience. Then they would run to put on the jackets of an usher, sweeper, assembler of trapezes, seller of balloons, chocolates, or lollipops. Then the changes would multiply, because it was the turn of the contortionists and acrobats, those who mounted a bicycle, eight at a time, those who danced a rumba on the tightrope, those who tossed the burro up in the air to catch him on the soles of their feet and make him spin around with two huge wooden balls.

For Jaime, who wasn't born in a circus tent, who hadn't grown up on a truck, and who, for those very reasons, found it difficult to learn all these tricks, they found an easy but spectacular act. Aside from having to risk his life allowing his lover to outline him in knives, he was hung by his hair. Since he hadn't had a haircut since his last match, he had a black mane that was thick and straight. The acrobats coated it with pitch, inserted a wire as an axis, and transformed it into a ponytail that ended in an arc of steel. All he had to do when they hoisted him ten feet from the floor was to show off his muscles, eat the empanada that was his dinner, and then read the sheet of newsprint in which the empanada had been wrapped.

This new life, for all its magic, was a matter of routine. Monday: break down the tent. Tuesday: travel to another town. Wednesday: set up the tent. Thursday: march through the town in a publicity parade. Friday and Saturday: endure two performances. Sunday: add a "children's mati-nee," and then at night, get drunk and make love under the grandstand. Sometimes the circus drew a crowd; most of the time, it was almost empty. Sometimes they performed for three or four people. No one felt sad. They didn't want to get rich but rather to earn a living. In the spirit of those artists, there was no future. They had the mentality of birds. They got up at dawn, penniless, and worked all day to fill their bellies. They were all possessed of a strange happiness that soon spread to Jaime.

To travel that way was a gift—free, with the family, enjoying the pure air of the open road. With no haste, with the calm of migratory birds, they traveled the nation, village by village, always heading south. They knew how to take a simple chicken, season it with herbs they found in the forests, and transform it into a princely banquet. They filled the monotony of travel with songs and jokes. Isolda was a lover with such a wide range of orgasms, from a girlish squeal to a mammoth's roar, that Jaime never felt the weeks go by. Toni Carrot, always arm-in-arm with Toni Lettuce—between them their ages added up to almost 190 years—came over to say to him:

"Little friend, you have made our only granddaughter so happy that we want to give you a gift; we're going to tell you a joke we've invented for you and you alone. Keep it like a jewel and don't tell it to anyone so that when your first granddaughter has a lover who makes her happy, you can give it to him intact. Listen carefully, because we won't repeat it:

"A man sees a frog. The frog says to him, 'Kiss me, please.'

"The man thinks, 'A frog that speaks must be an enchanted princess. I'll kiss her, she'll turn back into what she was, she will marry me, and

I'll be a millionaire.' The man kisses the frog, feels an explosion, and finds he's been turned into a frog.

"The first frog says, 'How wonderful. You were enchanted for ever so long, and, finally, I was able to save you!'"

Jaime never knew what effect the story had on him but instead of laughing, he began to cry.

The two elderly clowns applauded in satisfaction: "We were not wrong. You're a sensitive man. Good jokes, like happiness, should provoke tears."

When they reached Puerto Montt, they were caught by winter, and the rains became torrential. There they remained for three weeks, hoping the deluge would end. Water fell, fell, and fell some more. It was impossible to raise the tent on mud. They killed time playing cards in the truck. The women went out to look for work so they would have something to eat. Jaime offered to accompany them, but the men simply put his cards in his hand and placed before him a loaf of bread, some cheese, and a huge glass of wine, insinuating that in the family, by tradition, the men never worked among the rubes, by which they meant all human beings who did not belong to the circus.

"We are pure and they are false, like slips of paper stacked to look like money."

The grandmother was the only woman who stayed behind, taking advantage of that compulsory rest to try to train a toad. According to what Jaime was told, she'd begun with this one about ten years earlier, managing to make it say "mama," but that wasn't enough for a public show.

"Do toads live that long?"

"Like turtles, they live more than a century. Maybe one day Toni Lettuce will get this one to take a mouthful of gasoline and spit it into a candle to produce huge flames."

Toni Carrot was sure his wife would train the toad: "If she trained me, and I lived as a thief, stealing on the trolley, she can do it. She taught me my first number; dressed as a clown, I would make my way through the passengers; I would steal five wallets, toss them into the air, juggle them, and return them intact to their owners. Then I'd pass the hat around. By saving up those charitable offerings, we bought the canvas to make our circus."

The women always returned with full hands. No sooner did the rain stop than they put on their shows and continued traveling south. When they reached Punta Arenas, they would turn around and travel north, toward Arica. They thought to live their entire lives that way, for countless generations, becoming a magic pendulum that would rise and fall along the narrow, long body of the nation like a never-ending caress.

They pulled Jaime up by the hair so often that he began to have intellectual ambitions. He really began to read the newspaper way up there. The circus folk made fun of him:

"We, luckily, are out of the rube world, which is pure foolishness and lies. Nothing they tell you is true. Reality is not a pile of letters. The only defect you have, Jaime, is that you learned to read. Do you know why the rubes write so much? They transform into words the gestures they don't know how to make with their hands."

All the headlines on the first page celebrated the heights the economy had reached. Jaime became upset: their continuous travel throughout the country allowed him to see the degrading misery in which the peasants and workers lived. How could they celebrate industrial success amid all that hunger? To understand that an even sharper mind would be necessary, one accustomed to having a bird's eye view of events. Not knowing how to analyze what he was reading gave him a feeling that was much like having one eye swollen shut in a fight against a champion who attacked from the blind side. He made a big decision. One stormy night, when the women did not return to sleep ("Don't worry," said his comrades. "They've probably finished their work late and, to avoid getting soaked, they're sleeping in some cheap hotel, as they have on similar occasions."), he hid in the cargo truck where they had the burro sleep to avoid being struck by lightning. After making sure the animal was asleep (he didn't want even an unreliable witness), he summoned the Rabbi.

The Rabbi, surprised by the sign of interest from someone who'd gone as far as epilepsy to banish him to wander, dying of boredom, through the gray deserts of the Interworld, obeyed enthusiastically, like a lost dog that had found his master.

"You shitass ghost! Stop bouncing around like a drunken crow and sit still in front of me, because I have a proposition to make you."

"Well, Chaim."

"My name's not Chaim, not that or any other weird name! Call me Jaime, or I'll expel you from this world!"

"Well, Jaime."

"That's better! I don't know if you really exist or if you're a family hallucination. My father died insane, and my mother is following in his footsteps. I wouldn't be surprised if I were demented too. Be that as it may, you appear when I call you and you say coherent things I hadn't even thought. You may be useful to me. I suppose you want to exist, which is why you're here. But you depend on my will. Now listen: I have to understand what I'm reading in the papers. Chile interests me. The Jews and their tradition have nothing to do with me. I want you to wear different clothing; I can't stand seeing you decked out as a rabbi. Invent a sober suit for yourself, a normal one, not that wild crap in central-European 1800s style. Appear without a beard and with short hair. Study this reality in depth, and never speak to me again about Adonai, the Torah, Kabbalah, or the Talmud. What do you say?"

"Even though you abuse your power, Jaime, I realize that times change and that the truths of one era and one place don't work in other times and other places. My physical aspect, though for an eternity I haven't wanted to admit it, is pure illusion. I'm not made of matter but of memories. I'll let them go straightaway. Look."

And the Rabbi, heroically overcoming his nostalgia, transformed into a clean-shaven, well-combed man dressed in an elegant gray suit, a white poplin shirt, a tie with discreet stripes, and an umbrella. Smiling, he said, "At your service, sir. What do you think?"

"I think the umbrella is superfluous and the smile useless. I'll call you only to discuss the news."

"Something, however small it may be, is much, much more than nothing, sir."

"Stop calling me sir, and speak to me in familiar terms. Now get lost."

The obedient spirit dissolved. From then on, Jaime would see him whenever he excused himself to defecate. A solemn moment that justified the newspaper he carried folded up in one hand and permitted the solitude necessary to engage in conversations that, to the others, seemed like a madman's monologues.

"Jaime, I've finished studying the matter. This period of prosperity the journalists talk about so much is a whited sepulcher. The truth, absent from the editorial pages, can be found in the business section. The country you call yours, I hope you're not making a mistake, is being sold, mine by mine, field by field, to the Yankees. Of course, the dollars seem a blessing for those who live by speculating, but they are paper that will vanish. Foreigners are taking the wealth of the land away. Your Chileans are not getting rich but getting into debt. A dangerous situation. The people's hunger may produce a revolution, but with the presidential elections they're going to try to cover it all up."

"I don't understand."

"Jaime, you are already a circus man. You know that the big-time rubes use lies as a general remedy. Remember the comic numbers: a clown can't make people laugh by himself. He needs a partner to be his straight man and make comments. Toni is exuberant, charming, full of colors and wise cracks; his partner, Augusto, is disagreeable, severe, gray, and says little. They seem like enemies, but between the two of them they create the laughter that makes the circus work.

"At the moment there are two candidates for president: Arturo Alessandri, the Toni, who is emotional, outspoken, popular, and optimistic; and Luis Barros Borgoño, the Augusto, who is academic, cold, aristocratic, authoritarian. The first one talks about a prosperous future, the second about a menacing present. One asks for freedom, the other oppression. Behind them, both have the same supporters. They both want the same thing: to fool the poor, making them believe they participate in the Destiny of the nation. The more disagreeable Borgoño gets, the more Alessandri will shine among the people, who, uniting around an illusion, may elect him president.

"But the capitalist regime, aside from some superficial reforms, will go on exactly as it is. It will go right on selling the country, and hunger will only be pacified with bullets. There is a third candidate that few see, who has no possibility of being elected because he preaches outside the circus, that is, from jail. He's proposing an impossible truth, this Luis Emilio Recabarren. Instead of asking for small victories, like a monkey in the zoo who demands to be well treated by his keepers—a few extra nuts—but doesn't consider destroying the cage, Recabarren wants everything; he wants to abolish borders, to turn the planet into one single nation, declare war on war, expropriate land to distribute it among the peasants, end private property, demolish the capitalist system, give sovereignty to the people, strengthen public education.

"In sum, he wants to repeat the Russian Revolution. This man will suffer a great deal. There are no large fortunes to support him; he works against power, and the immature people prefer to listen to the 'luminous' words of Alessandri, contenting themselves with promises. Even though he's an almost saintly warrior, he does have a defect: like Don Quixote trying to follow in the footsteps of Amadís of Gaul, Recabarren tries to imitate Lenin. The thing is, the Chileans, high and low, have lost their

identity because they've been dominated for so many centuries by foreign conquistadors. It's always the neighbors who tell them what they
should want. No level in this society has its own ambitions. Everything
is done by imitation. The capitalists copy Europe and the United States,
the workers imitate the Bolsheviks. Too many mirages, Jaime. Those
implanted desires will lead them to catastrophe and violence. Recabarren,
because he is incapable of inventing his own path, will some day end up
the victim of his ideals."

These conversations with the Rabbi went on for most of the winter.
But wherever they went they heard nothing but talk about Alessandri.
So great was the fervor for this candidate that on the days when the rain
allowed them to perform, the audience, before the show began, would
stand up and sing, as if it were the national anthem:

> *We'll have victory,*
> *Little Darling,*
> *The radicals,*
> *Little Darling,*
> *So that all Chileans,*
> *Little Darling,*
> *Will be equals.*

Jaime, hanging by his hair, after having exposed himself to the tossed
knives of the Lightning Bolt of Limache, felt that the skin on his cranium,
as it stretched, unfolded to turn his brain into a flying carpet. Teresa's
crazy words—"Change the world. Make it finally be born."—dogged him,
buzzing like wasps. His mother was asking him to become a prophet, him,
the most miserable and rootless of beings, the one who believed in nothing, who wandered about, begging, content in a world without meaning.

It all made him want to keep hanging there, spinning forever, never
coming down until he dried out. Or the opposite, to plunge himself into

the impossible struggle of the workers, to be a scapegoat, to become a martyr, to donate his grain of sand so the Earth could become a paradisiac garden, where good people, without anguish or war, would run about like simple ants, trying to resuscitate God so that His punishments would deliver them from boredom and restore their taste for life. Bah! It was better to slip the cylinder into your woman's hairy tunnel in order to spit your despair, transformed into semen, into her carnivorous flowers.

In Osorno, it rained for nine days, and frozen rocks poured down. The patter didn't let them sleep or play poker. They tried to set up the tent, but the wind shook it so hard that the patches flew off like a flock of dirty pigeons. The men, happy deep down about the incident because it gave them something to do, spent their time secluded in the truck, sewing up tears while the five women worked in the city. That night they did not return, and they stayed away the next night too. On the third day of their absence, Isolda's father asked his sons to go with him and find all the women. Jaime insisted on going with them. They shrugged their shoulders: "If you want to come, come along. You're one of us. You'll understand."

Toni Lettuce gave them a tiny piggy bank where they'd put away some meager savings. Protecting their heads with ponchos, they moved through the storm, soaked to the skin. They went directly to the police station. Of course, there they all were, waiting for the men to pay their fine. They'd been arrested for the illegal practice of prostitution. The business was swift. Clowns and acrobats were accomplices. The piggy bank always contained a few banknotes for such cases. In the towns, everyone knew that when the circus couldn't put on shows, the circus women would put on another kind of performance. From time to time, to satisfy the wife of some mayor, they were fined. It never went further than that. Sleeping with a circus artist was a highly prized pleasure.

Jaime returned without speaking to anyone, staring at the ground. When they reached the truck, the women removed from their sex the money they'd hidden. The men applauded. They ran to buy food, and the party began. Jaime, risking being sliced open, gave Isolda a slap when she tried to kiss him. Toni Carrot grabbed him by the arm, dragged him into a corner, and whispered into his ear:

"If you put a cube of sugar in your tea, it dissolves. If you put in a cube of marble, nothing happens. What matters is the feeling. The other is a mere rubbing of flesh. Fornicating with a rube is just another job, the same as hanging from a trapeze or balancing on a tightrope. No need to be jealous. If she's unfaithful with someone from the profession, another circus man, that's different. You can kill her or scar her face. That's customary, take it or leave it. We have no other way to survive. That's how we've lived until now, that's how we'll go on living."

Jaime's head began to ache. He liked to travel this way, but he couldn't stand his lover being a whore. Hanging by his hair became torture. His temples throbbed as if they were going to explode. Amid the haze of a high fever, he saw forty-foot-high waves coming and began to scream to scare them away. Toni Lettuce made him swallow a liter of hot wine with lemon and cinnamon. He began to pour out sweat and fell asleep.

In those moments of deep depression, I entered his organism. When he awoke, with his pulse normal again, he felt his testicles. They seemed different, more compact and noble. He wasn't alone. He was the root of a tree that would spread its branches throughout eternal time. I was asking to be born, to rise toward the woman I needed to be my mother. That made him consider his relationship with the Lightning Bolt of Limache.

What did he feel for her? Something like what dogs feel for bitches. At the animal level of desire, he or any other would be the same. A warm body, a welcoming hole clinging to his savage thrusts, the explosions of orgasm and the cow-like company, the daily nonsense, sentimental marmalade, moistening the chatter of cracks. Aside from throwing knives and prostituting herself, Isolda had nothing extraordinary to her.

If he stayed with her, he would never progress. His head ached again. One of Isolda's brothers practically carried him on his shoulders to the outskirts of town, where he deposited Jaime in a forest that spread out in the distance and covered the hills.

"Follow this path for one mile. When you find a rock painted black, make three long whistles. A Mapuche Indian named Tralaf will come for you. He will cure you. A lady in the audience told me."

Shaken by chills, Jaime marched through the trees. A frozen wind made the rain fall from the leaves. As he moved forward, he broke through the frost that covered the ground. He reached a clearing of red earth. There, in the center, surrounded by exuberant vegetation, there was a huge black stone. It looked like an eagle rolled up in itself, in the style of an armadillo that rolls itself into a ball whenever it feels threatened. To Jaime it seemed that it was sinking its beak into its chest to drink the blood from its own heart.

Dense clouds began to cover the sky. The light changed, and the eagle slowly vanished so that, without the contrast created by light and shadows, it transformed into a smiling human cranium. My father, nervous, felt his forehead to see if he still had the fever. It was frozen. He shook his head and whistled three times. It began to rain and lightning began to flash. Thunder made the ground shake. The sun came out again. Jaime, soaked to the skin, was about to whistle again, but footsteps interrupted him. They were so soft and agile that Jaime climbed up on the rock, fearing a puma. An old but vigorous Mapuche appeared, carrying a full sack.

He said, mockingly, "Hey there, *huinca*, what are you doing there on top of Amoihuen? It can't be you're afraid of a poor old man like me, can it? Come down, this place is protected. No puma, wildcat, big fox, or peccary, not even llamas or mice dare to pass through here. Say hello to my *huecufe*. Mari, Mari . . . If you've come to see me, it's because you're suffering. Say nothing: I see with my hands."

He knelt before Jaime, and beginning at his feet and working his way up, he examined his body. When he reached Jaime's head, he emitted a knowing cough.

"Here the apparent evil reveals itself. But it's good. With children, their jaw hurts if they get new teeth. Your cranium hurts because your spirit is growing. Many centuries ago, you lost the landscape, and without roots there is no health. You are trying to open the cocoon to start flying. Your hair has been pulled so much that a lot of blood has accumulated beneath it. If you want the pain to go away, you must allow your hair to be cut."

"I can't do that. They hang me by my hair in the circus. It's my job."

"Change jobs. It is not good for any man to live hung by other men. The only one who has the right to pull us up is Amoihuen, the mask of the Supreme Being."

A change happened in Jaime's spirit. He abandoned the circus abruptly, just like that, without thinking it over, like something made over a long time in the darkness that suddenly emerges, complete, toward the light.

"I agree, Tralaf. Cut off my hair."

The Indian rubbed his head with a tree bark that produced foam, and, using a sharpened stone, he shaved him. After that, he pinched the skin of his scalp and gave it two crossed cuts. Jaime shrieked in pain.

"You've got to take it, huinca. There's a lot of daylight left, and the road you're going to follow is long, endless. I have to make eight more crosses."

And around his cranium, like a crown, he made other cuts. The blood ran down his face, his ears, his neck. My father began to tremble.

"Be brave, huinca. Our eagle came from the sun. You are not alone. The soul of an ancestor is with you. He sustains you. Stop whining like the horse that didn't want to walk on a suspension bridge. Give yourself over to the control of the rider. Advance step by step, attentively, awake.

If you get distracted, the abyss will devour you and you'll fall into the river of death. There you will dissolve because you do not carry the flower of awareness. The one who is asleep knows nothing about you. Only awake can you open the door so the Supreme Being can enter."

Tralaf took a bottle of water out of his jacket. It contained nine leeches, and he placed them over the wounds. They immediately began to suck blood. The Mapuche started a fire with branches of a reddish coffee color that gave off a smell like bread and began to sing following the rhythm of a drum. Time passed. Now engorged, the leeches—which had been long and thin—looked fat, enormous. They began to uncouple and fall into a clay platter the shaman placed before my father's knees while making him lower his head. He squeezed the leeches so they would vomit the blood they'd sucked. Then he washed them and put them back in the bottle of water. He dug around in his bag and found some dry twigs covered with very smooth bark, as smooth as human skin. And with a small mallet, he pounded them in a mortar to mix them with the coagulated plasma. He kneaded it into gelatinous, blackish bread. Then, using a carved spatula, he gave it the form of a snake.

"If you've got good aim, the fox won't get away from you. Overcome your disgust, eat the *caicai*: serpent of serpents, enemy of human kind, it brings the flood from the depths, erases everything; you cease to be flesh and are left pure spirit. It won't give you health, because you already have it; it will only dissolve the sickness you create."

Jaime, with his mind clear for the first time in his life, thanks to the blood, discovered the essential trait of his character: curiosity. He loved nothing but wanted to know everything. Whichever way he went, he would find ignorance. Any idea seemed like violence, the description of a feeling never stopped seeming ridiculous, the substance of a concept led to another concept, and so on until infinity. Thinking was merely believing; meanings changed as rapidly as clouds; reality was covered with mental constructs that, in collusion with one another, became a language. And he wanted to push aside the veil, know the meaning of life, the secret of the Universe, the structure of that which people called God.

"We always follow the trail of the good. Don't miss this opportunity. Run and see, huinca!"

As the Mapuche pounded the drum made of wood and horsehide, Jaime, holding back his gagging, devoured the blood.

His entire body began to tremble; his temperature rose; he perspired; he became cold; he lost dimensions; he felt himself a giant, then tiny; his tongue burned; flames shot out of his mouth; his left ear grew until it was five times larger than the other; he understood the forest animals; each roar, meow, trill, buzz, taught him something; even the belches of the toads transmitted profound thoughts. In the face of such wisdom, he felt himself to be a miserable being and giggled at his ignorance. Then his skepticism fought against the drug.

"They're auditory hallucinations. Whatever the animals say I invent. I'll have them sing an Italian song."

And from the forest arose an animal chorus singing the melody of "Torna a Surriento." Tralaf gave him a ferocious kick in the chest. A bloody wound opened. He felt that his heart was pouring out of that wound, but in its place arose a black feline, rolled up like a fetus.

"The cat can't see the mouse without wanting to kill it. No matter what they say, the animals speak to you in any case. They provide the raw material; you make the message. Ditch the cat, let the mouse live."

Jaime split in two. Everything he saw became a mirror. Then he was three and finally four. He realized he could multiply until infinity and be in innumerable places at the same time. Again he laughed. For so many years, an entire lifetime, he'd been one, a prisoner of an imagined body, like concrete, clinging to its exterior form purely out of fear. What cowardice, this being stuck to the Earth! Better to toss the burden overboard. He began to feel himself lighter, floating. Tralaf jumped and fell on his back, transformed into a green puma. He drew his muzzle close to Jaime's left ear and said in a hoarse voice, "Now you've got the gaze of the condor. You are going to fly to Tierra del Fuego to give life to the forgotten gods."

They skimmed through winds and storms, above dismembered coasts lashed by waves, shaped like cathedrals; they crossed archipelagos, fjords, canals, and descended into a volcanic crater, right in front of an extensive field of lava. The cavity was dotted with burned human skeletons. Flames burst out of the green puma:

"Accept the purification of fire. Be able to imagine yourself calcified. Deliver the persona that limits you. Make yourself a receptor without edges."

Jaime allowed his body to burn. From the depth of the cave three painted-up Indians advanced, leaning on one another, like a group of sick men. Beneath the dots and the horizontal and vertical bars that decorated them, their mummified flesh appeared. They complained with every step.

"That's the pain of oblivion. They are the creators of the world. Kosménk, the father; Xalpen, the mother; Keternen, the son. You, who have been able to turn your form into a fire, let Kosménk possess you. Give your awareness over, now!"

And Jaime ceased clinging to himself and became an invisible vulva the size of the sky to allow himself to be possessed by the father, an infinite force that dragged him out of time and space. Kosménk entered absolute negation, falling as if down a black well, where everything that appeared was instantly erased; crossing levels of existence that vanished; rejecting so that at the end, the heart of the infinite No would be the greatest of affirmations. Out of unlimited goodness arose Xalpen, his wife. Jaime was crumbling into a cloud of burning drops, and knowledge came; he circulated in all the currents of the firmament, of the earth, of the ocean, of sap, of blood. He expanded into a network of waves, like a disproportionate spider made of spirals. Life was an empty labyrinth twisted by a torrent of passion, Xalpen, the continuous orgasm. Kosménk, eternally still in the dark night, root of all suns and of all conscious light, father of Xalpen, becomes her lover in order to sink into matter, itself transformed into a song of happiness, and then to be born as her son: Keternen, the golden child, fragile and tender bread that feeds the one who destroys it. Keternen, born from the sacrifice of Kosménk, savior of the human race, creator of the new universe where no one eats anyone else and flesh is transparent, where all beings, transformed into conscious comets, trace a cathedral of fire in the sky. The pleasure of the Mother is so intense that it seems pain, because the explosion is vertiginous and never stops growing. Then it grants its greatest gift, Death, so that everything once again returns to Kosménk.

Jaime awoke naked in the forest clearing. Tralaf, next to the black rock, was playing something that looked like a violin: a bow of bone held by a single string of woven hair that he leaned against his upper incisors to play with another identical bow, coaxing from the instrument a wail that was between human and divine. Jaime had never known that immense feeling. His thoracic cage was beating as if his trunk had become a single heart. He felt he had no head, decapitated. He was viscera with arms and feet, nothing more. All his life he thought that he lacked sensitivity, that he was emotionally dead, but now he realized that he'd been asleep. Now he expanded, continually giving.

His spirit belonged to another world, outside of forms. He perceived everything as presences, energies, entities that had no relation to the size of the bodies in which they manifested themselves. An immense raulí tree mattered less to him than a baby eagle that landed on his shaved head. That was because the ancient tree bent over, transformed into a thin hair of violet light, while the bird gave off golden rays in all directions of space. He began to vomit congealed blood. The Mapuche held his head.

"Like the tiger, you looked, opening your eyes halfway but choosing the fattest llamas. He who decides to live never again breathes the breath of Death. Since the war is over, you shall dance as long as you have heart. Good work, huinca. Cheer up: you have returned from the zone of the ancient gods; you will no longer be the same. You will go on fighting, acquiring, but you will be from far off, because you know that everything is changing, fading, and that any bond is a trick."

The gagging ceased, and Jaime, his stomach empty, without pain in his head, felt rested, tranquil, in peace.

"Thank you, Tralaf. Your drug has cleansed and enriched me. I'll never go back to the circus. Something mysterious is asking me to go north. That there, at the far end of the nation, my realization awaits me."

Obviously, it was I who, taking advantage of that magnificent occasion when my future father delivered himself to lunar reception, impelled him to embark on that pilgrimage so he would again give me the possibility of being incarnate. Jaime dressed, bade a thankful farewell to the Indian, and set out on the road. As he advanced along the narrow path, the virgin forest did not seem dark, dangerous, or strange. For the first time, he felt he owned the earth, with roots as deep as those trees that caressed him with a thousand different vibrations. He was going along like that, enjoying the openness of his senses, when a tremendous roar made him stop short. Right before him stood a puma showing his teeth. Abandoning caution, he turned on his heel to try a vain run. He collided with Tralaf.

"So the huinca thought he was leaving without paying me!"

"I'm sorry my friend, I had no idea. I came without money."

"That I know. When you were out of your head, I checked your pockets. Zero! Nor did I find a bottle or two of pisco, which is the custom. You're the kind that always thinks they deserve everything free. That the knowledge you give them, you get just like that without lifting a finger."

"Forgive me."

"Excuses are worth nothing. I spent a good part of my life suffering horrors to obtain what I have given you. If you get it for nothing, what value will it have for you? Do you know how far I had to walk through the mountains to find that bark you ate? Try to catch just one leech. Find the cavern of the ancient gods. A lifetime wouldn't be enough for you to reach it."

"Calm that puma of yours, please. Let me go. I'll work for a few weeks and come right back to give you whatever I've saved."

"If you know you have to give it, you'll never earn any money. That's how you huincas are. You hate to pay your debts."

"Not me!"

"You're lying. You've been lent a life, and you spend all your time complaining because someday you'll have to give it up. If you don't pay me right now, I'll set the puma on you!"

The puma, as if to confirm the witchdoctor's threat, came forward, growling, toward Jaime. Then it went up on its hind legs and rested its huge front paws on Jaime's shoulders. With the beast's huge maw in front of his face and its three hundred pounds resting on him, my father weakened and sank to his knees.

The Mapuche said, "Tüngn." And the animal stepped back to leap onto the trail, sniffing the maqui bushes. Tralaf pulled a necklace of human teeth out of his jacket.

"I need one molar to make it complete. When I have it, I'll be the owner of my soul. I'll be able to enter and leave the *huenu*, the place of the spirits who know. Give me that tooth! You'll be left with a hole in your gums and that will always remind you of the freedom you obtained."

Jaime said nothing. He opened his mouth wide. The Indian chewed some herbs, spit them out in the form of a paste, coated the base of the molar with that green material, and then, tying it up with a little hair rope, pulled it out with one yank. Jaime, who had his eyes closed, suffered not one bit. When he finally raised his eyelids, neither the puma nor Tralaf was there.

Returning seemed easy; all he had to do was to follow the tracks he himself had made on the muddy path. Unfortunately, it began to rain. In a short while, the ground turned into a long puddle, erasing the path. When the rain stopped, a dense mist darkened the forest. Jaime began to walk without knowing where he was going. He walked for hours. A glacial cold hardened his wet clothes.

Worn-out, he finally found himself on an esplanade where a church stood. He ran to beg refuge. The three doors of the wide portico were locked, as were the windows. On both sides of the wooden building, the roof hung down, providing some protection. He stretched out there to rest on the dry ground. He slept deeply until the cold woke him. It was snowing. He could barely feel his feet. If he stayed there any longer, he would die frozen. With strength drawn from desperation, he kicked open the main panel of the central door and entered the nave.

Judging by the amount of dust that had accumulated, it was clear that no one had visited the place in a long time. Jaime undressed and used a small lace mantle that was spread over the altar to dry himself. Suddenly he felt he was being watched. From a corner, half-hidden by the semidarkness, a priest was watching him. My father, naked as he was, hiding his sex with his hands, walked toward the priest to apologize. He found himself facing a cast-iron Saint Francis, dressed in a wool cassock.

Laughing like a madman, he stripped the statue of its cassock and put it on. The wool heated him a bit, but the temperature went on dropping. He searched the church. In a small armoire, he found candles and matches. He broke up two chairs, piled the pieces on the altar, and made a fire. The heat lulled him. He sat down at the foot of the cross that was on the back wall and went back to sleep, accompanied by the serene gaze of the wooden Christ.

A gust of wind came through the broken door and made the flames fly up. Jaime awoke in the middle of a fire. The ardent flames were devouring the temple. Half of the roof collapsed. Instead of escaping immediately, amid sparks, flames, and tongues of smoke, almost blind, Jaime—who knows why—fought to pull off the wall the cross, which along with its Christ must have weighed more than a hundred pounds. Finally, carrying it on his back, he managed, with a few light burns, to make his way to the esplanade.

The building was a total loss. By daybreak, it had become a large rectangle of ash and blackened beams. As the sun rose, amid a deafening chorus of birds, the heat came. Jaime found himself clean-shaven, dressed as a Franciscan monk, and without a penny. If he didn't want to return to the circus, the only chance he had to get some money was the crucifix. Then the thought came to him:

"In every town there is a church. I'll carry the cross for a few miles, no more than ten for sure, and I'll give it to the first priest I see, explaining to him that I saved it from a fire caused by lightning; that in committing the heroic deed I lost my clothes and ended up naked, attacked by the immodest flames, and that I had to cover myself with Saint Francis's cassock, which miraculously escaped the fire. Yes, Your Eminence, all the money I had in the world was turned to ash, but what does my misery matter if this most holy Christ was saved? Of course, a bit of help from Holy Mother Church, if willingly given, would not be scorned. And if to those abundant coins or banknotes, whichever pleases your good will, could be added trousers and a woven vest, and perhaps also a T-shirt to be worn below it, because wool scratches, and a pair of shoes—socks are unnecessary because I never use them—my thanks would be sincere and my faith solidified."

Hope gave him courage, and he carried the weight of the grand crucifix, assuming with a smile the posture of Jesus marching toward Calvary.

"It is," he thought, "after all, a comfortable position. Resting the base on the ground helps a good deal. If you keep your spine straight, there's no need to get melodramatic."

After an hour and a half, he entered a village. Disillusioned, he noticed it had no church. He calculated, judging by how few houses there were, that no more than four hundred people could have lived there. He swallowed hard and advanced, sweating, step by step along the town's only street. The few inhabitants who were at their windows watched him pass with their mouths hanging open. A few children came running out to follow him. An old lady approached and, after giving him two potatoes stuffed with meat, dried the sweat on his brow.

"Ma'am, where does this road go?"

"It goes up toward Valdivia, holy penitent."

Holy penitent? Now they were confusing him. Better to keep moving in order to find a church as soon as possible. He passed through four more towns. In each, he was given food and wine. As he passed, the men would remove their hats and the women would weep. When night fell, a peasant let him sleep in his stable, preparing a good bed of hay for him near the cows. After kneeling before the cross and praying, with a pail of fresh milk next to him, he gave Jaime a wrinkled banknote he'd been keeping in the lining of his hat: "For when you reach the Sanctuary. Light some candles in my name, Juan Godoy."

He heard himself say, sweetly, "That is what I shall do, brother," before he fell asleep snoring. He left early in the morning, after evacuating the diarrhea caused by so many empanadas, fruits, glasses of wine, and gallons of milk. After four hours of easy walking downhill, he reached the Llollelhue River, which wound its way around a small city, La Unión. In the distance, the steeple of a church stood out, calling the faithful to mass with its bells. As he crossed the bridge, a lady approached dressed in black, carrying a basket filled with cheeses and bottles of chicha.

Jaime did not need to be asked twice. And while the lady struggled and puffed under the weight of the Christ, he swallowed half a liter of the chicha and devoured a cheese.

"I have to make this effort. Because of my bestial nature, I killed my husband. I made him screw me every night until dawn. When his heart exploded, he spit a spurt of blood into my mouth along with his last words: 'Horny bitch!' I was right in the middle of an orgasm, and he cut it off. I've endured ever since with that lack of satisfaction. I can't stand it."

"How long ago was it that your husband died?"

"I buried him yesterday."

Jaime understood. The woman wasn't ugly, and under her mourning costume, the bulge of her buttocks was promising. Without saying anything more, they walked into a wheat field, allowed themselves to be covered by the sheaves, and fornicated until the sun began to set.

"Take this money, holy penitent. When you reach the Sanctuary, light a few candles before the Holy Virgin in my name, Guacolda Verdugo."

That was the second time he was told the same thing. He asked, curious but shrewd and addressing her in familiar terms,

"Are you sure you know what I am and where I'm going, Guacolda?"

"Do you take me for an idiot, Pedrito?"

He had told her his name was Pedro Araucano, just in case this slut became pregnant and tried to find him.

"Dressed as a Franciscan monk and with a cross on your shoulder, you must be a tremendous sinner. Maybe you killed your own father and have vowed to carry that heavy cross on foot to the Sanctuary of the Virgin of Tirana in the grand north. That kind of penance is very popular in our region. Several before you have tried to carry it out, but the heat of the desert killed them. Look here, Pedrito, I have another banknote! If you like, you can give me a farewell."

And the widow kept him prisoner between her powerful thighs for an hour and a half. Jaime did not enter the city. He decided to skirt it. He realized that walking around clean-shaven, dressed in a cassock, and carrying a crucified Christ was good business. He would slowly make his way through the villages being fed by simple, superstitious people, passing himself off as a repentant sinner. Then he'd get to Santiago, plump and with a bankroll.

That night and all the following nights, it was easy for him to find someplace to sleep. All he had to do was knock at a door and beg for a bed with a martyr's face. They would give him a bed, dinner, and, if it was a woman by herself, even naked company. Jaime was surprised to discover that holiness was a powerful attraction for female believers. Before leaving, he was in the habit of saying, "If you wish, I'll light some candles for you when I get to the Sanctuary." They would always slip a carefully folded banknote into his hand.

When he passed by a large estate near Valdivia, he saw a long line of trucks carrying peasants. All of them, even if they lacked Sunday clothes, were well combed and had a clean handkerchief tied around their necks. Before they helped them onto the trucks, some well-dressed strongmen gave them a cardboard box adorned with the face of the presidential candidate Don Luis Barros Borgoño. Jaime bent over as if totally weighed down, put on his tragic face, and advanced as if an invisible centurion were whipping him. The driver, the strongmen, and the peasants all crossed themselves. An elegant fat man ran behind him and, helping him lift off the cross, gave him a cardboard box:

"Pray for us, holy penitent, but do it now, because God will hear you better than anyone else. Today is Election Day, and our candidate has to win!"

Jaime went down on his knees, put his hands together, and, since he knew no prayers, muttered the multiplication tables. He tried to cross himself: he touched his belly, then his head, then his right side, and finally his heart. It didn't occur to him to kiss his fingers.

When he saw they were staring at him in an odd way, he said, "Whatever I say or do does not come from me. God has made me crazy in order to separate me from men of sin and make me His slave. Don't try to understand. The snail is also a rose."

They were dumbfounded. Jaime went his way toward Valdivia. In the box he found half a chicken, half a liter of wine, half a bar of chocolate, half a pack of cigarettes, and a five-peso note. How little a vote was worth! It saddened him to think about those ignorant people trucked like sheep, selling their freedom for a miserable sum. He passed by the entrance to another large farm. Again he saw a line of trucks carrying peasants. Bribery much like the first case: these too were handing out boxes. The only difference was that the candidate's picture had changed. Now it was Don Arturo Alessandri Palma.

My father pretended to stumble, fell on his knees, and with crocodile tears began to mutter multiples of five, the ones he knew best. He waited for everyone to make the sign of the cross, carefully noting the movements so he wouldn't make another mistake. He too made it, and then, trying to improve the business, shouted, "Long live Christ the King!"

They all responded at the top of their lungs: "Long live Christ the King!"

Then he added: "Long live the Lion of Tarapacá, our future president, Alessandri!"

The reaction was less enthusiastic but more professional. Despite his efforts, they gave him a box and nothing more, asking him to pray for their triumph. Then they helped him to put the Christ back on his shoulders. He walked a couple of miles and sat down to rest under a willow tree next to the river. Majestic white clouds were passing through the sky, the wild flowers were offering their nectar to the greedy insects, the birds were singing to celebrate the first warmth of spring, and the murmur of the river tainted the world with its peace.

Jaime opened the box of the stubborn bourgeoisie and also that of the candidate of the Liberal Alliance. Both Barros Borgoño and Alessandri offered the same menu and the same miserable amount of money. It was clear that the food came from the same wholesale caterer. Jaime, in a terrible mood, put together the two halves of the chicken. They fit together perfectly! Astounding coincidence! He'd been given the two halves of the same chicken. In his hands he was holding the long-sought national union.

He tried to join the two halves of the chocolate bar, but that did not work. He felt disillusioned. It would have been fantastic if they, too, had fit together. Then he would have been forced to believe in miracles. Finally he settled for having reunited the body of the chicken. He decided not to eat it but to give it a proper burial. He was on the side of the road, digging a hole, when the trucks belonging to the two parties passed in Indian file, a demented worm infecting the calm with its false enthusiasm:

"Hurrah for Don Luis!"

"Boo! Long live Don Arturo!"

"Boo!"

When peace was restored and the trail of dust behind the trucks had dissolved, Jaime opened the half liters and drank from both bottles at the same time. Then he put both half bars of chocolate in his mouth and, with his cheeks ballooned out, lit the twenty cigarettes in order to smoke them all at the same time. Then he vomited, shit, and wiped his backside with the two five-peso notes. He wanted to sleep and never wake up.

No matter what he did, no matter what he searched for, no matter what he found, he'd always end up without roots, living somewhere between heaven and Earth. Despite the fact that he firmly believed that to have a nationality meant being sick, that patriotism was also caricature, that imposing borders on the Earth was a blasphemy, that speaking a single language was a form of mental retardation, he desperately desired to acquire those limits. Jodorowsky. What a hideous last name he'd been given! Jodo, *joder*, to annoy to a great degree, to fuck, to rob, to walk with bad luck. From then on, he would use only his first name, just Jaime. At least in French and by adding an apostrophe Jaime turned into *J'aime*, I love. Do I love? Did I love? Shall I love? What does that mean? What concept with no basis in reality was being talked about? By naming something, all you create is one thing: a new word, as empty as the old ones, another illusion. He felt like calling the Rabbi. He refrained from doing so. He began to think:

"If I give him a lot of importance, that freak will end up invading my mind the way he did with my father. Why do I want to see him? So he can analyze this political masquerade for me? He won't tell me anything I don't already know. Both the landowning oligarchy and the Liberal Alliance fear the independent development of the proletariat because it could lead to a revolution. Alessandri, a clever demagogue, will take control of the masses, promising the moon and the stars all in order to subordinate them to the economic interests of the bourgeoisie. And the immature poor will sell their rights for a bowl of lentils. Appearances are always deceiving, and words take the place of realities.

"This crucifix, which is supplying me with a delightful life simply because I carry it, is another falsity. Why do they sculpt Him in such pain? A simple fakir can sleep on a bed of nails and pierce his flesh with needles without blinking an eye. Three or four wounds are going to make a God moan? Absurd. It hurts, sure, but it's something anyone can stand. His situation is a joke; he's been sentenced to death, him— he's immortal. Up above, the Father, the Holy Spirit, and the angels are laughing their heads off. After the farce of dying, barely three days later, he will arise again in full majesty.

"Nailing him to a cross cannot reduce His power much, not He who can produce an earthquake with a shout, split the veil of the temple, and paralyze the sun, causing such an uproar that the dead leave their graves to see what's going on. Why don't they show a luminous, triumphant Christ in churches? It would be a bad example to the workers. If I, instead of lugging around these hundred pounds, were shooting light all over the place, I wouldn't get money, food, and sex—rather, I'd get whippings and a sore backside for being a political agitator."

He felt a desire to go to the city to see how the bribers watched over the herd to make it vote correctly. He staggered as he walked. That wine was pure alcohol. He saw an old man sitting on a paving stone.

"Good day, holy penitent. May God forgive you and help you. Want a piece of my sausage?"

"No, my good man. The Eternal One has already given me my daily bread and wine. But, tell me, aren't you going to vote?"

"I wanted to, but the hen got sick, and I took care of her and missed the truck. They'd already left."

"Which trucks?"

"Either group. It's all the same to me. As long as they pay me."

"Does that seem right to you?

"Not exactly right. If it were a ten-peso note and a whole chicken, then that would be perfect."

"So why don't you walk to the voting place?"

"For nothing? Never!"

"Look here my friend. I'll buy your vote."

"I believe you. You can't be making fun of me, because the saints don't lie. How much?"

"Come with me. When we get there, I'll give you a whole chicken and the ten pesos you wanted. Deal?"

"Deal! For whom do I vote?"

"Luis Emilio Recabarren. I want him to have at least one vote. He deserves that."

And they went to Valdivia. Before they entered the city, they crossed paths with the trucks that now carried a flock of drunks. Each one had invested his five pesos in red wine. They no longer cheered the candidates, but they were certainly shouting:

"Long live my buddy Lucho!"

"Hurrah for my bay mare!"

"The Calle-Calle River shall triumph!"

He made sure the old man voted and didn't betray him. He then bought him a liter of wine, a chocolate bar, a pack of cigarettes, and handed him the ten-peso note. The peasant, out of pure pleasure, began to dance a cueca that made him shake so much his false teeth fell out. Jaime, disgusted with himself, walked right down the main avenue, intent on crossing the city, all the time thinking:

"I too act like a jerk. In truth, I walk around disguised as what I am. I've always lived like a martyr, carrying the weight of some mysterious guilt. The only ugly thing is that I can't be myself except by concealing myself. When I take off the mask, I lose my identity. Walking this way, through here, I run the risk of meeting up with a priest. He'll treat me as a thief, a fraud, a profaner, and he'll be right. They'll throw me in jail. Maybe behind bars I'll find my homeland. Name: 34735870. Nationality: prisoner. Country: jail. Sex: unsatisfied. Special markings: mutilated in the faith."

He stopped outside the church. It was locked up. He took off a shoe and threw it against the door with such force that the impact made the bell vibrate. A priest came out, his face red with rage. He stared at him from the portico. Then he hitched up his cassock and picked up Jaime's shoe. He poked his index finger through the holes in the sole. He slowly walked down the steps, staggering like a drunk, and threw himself into Jaime's arms, transformed into a fountain of snot and tears. His weeping was so heartbreaking and his embrace so sincere that Jaime, either out of contagion or shame, also wept. The monk separated himself, went running into the church, and returned with a pot of water, towels, and soap. He began to wash Jaime's feet, murmuring in a heavy German accent, "This is how I should imitate Christ. So many years sacrifice calls me and I continue clinging to my obligations, which give me excuses for not carrying the cross on my shoulder. You redeem us, holy penitent! If we do not imitate Jesus in His martyrdom, how will we know his infinite pity? Carrying this crucifix along the roads, you transform the whole nation into a temple. If now I cannot abandon my flock and go with you, at least give me the opportunity to follow your footsteps."

And the German took off his brand-new boots and put them on Jaime's feet. The fact is that my father had been suffering because of his worn-out soles and the new boots, solid and fine, made with the love of a blessed shoemaker, gave spirit to his brave walking. But instead of rejoicing over this gift, Jaime grew sad. He remembered the bitterness he held for his deceased father. He too had made a pair of boots, plac-ing his tenderness in the work, and Alejandro, instead of keeping them as a souvenir, sold them to some flea-ridden fool for almost nothing.

Now those shoes, which he had considered lost, were restored to him in order for him to forgive his father, a man thirsty for holiness, serving his fellow man out of love for the divine work. Whether or not the Creator existed, what difference did it make? The help was the same! Now it was his turn to discover motiveless love with no other future than the worms of the grave, with no rewards, no harps, no halos, no wings on his shoulders. Even if God were an invention, the greatest devotion to the world was owed Him, in this way, without reason, without moral obligations, without commandments carved in stone.

As Jaime left Valdivia behind, the priest had the bells rung. The faithful came to their windows to watch him pass. Soon a procession of about two hundred people was following him. They sang hymns and tossed flowers at him. When he reached the river and began to cross a bridge for carts with no guardrail, they waved handkerchiefs, giving him a fervent farewell. Since the cross practically immobilized his head, he twisted around as much as he could, holding in the "I'm a fucking cynic" that filled his mouth, and gave them the blessing they expected. He began to shout, "In the name of the Father, of the Son, and—" but he couldn't finish, because the stumble he made against one of the arms of the cross threw him off the bridge. He only fell ten feet, and the water served as a mattress, but the thick wood smacked right into his clavicle, throwing it out. The crown of thorns scratched his forehead, and with his face bathed in blood he began to drown. His lungs filled with water. He lost consciousness.

He awoke late at night with his shoulder bandaged, stretched out on a grave in a cemetery. A gentleman with calloused hands offered him hot coffee in a clay cup.

"I'm the cemetery guard, the gravedigger as well, and in my free hours a bone setter. I fix up twists, breaks, dislocations and give massages for stiff necks. Luckily for you, you got only a dislocation. I fixed it up perfectly. Eleodoro Astudillo, at your service."

"Many thanks, Don Eleodoro. How much do I owe you?"

"Saints don't pay. Pray for me, that will be enough."

"I certainly will. Could you tell me where and with whom you learned your trade?"

"I learned it here, and my teacher's name is Don Pepe. Don Pepe, come over here!"

A gray cat came running through the graves and rubbed itself, purring, against the gravedigger's legs.

"He taught me everything. Consider this: if you touch your joints carefully, without allowing yourself to be distracted by any thought, you'll understand how the animal has been set up by God. A small pressure here, another there, and after a few more, he comes apart. See?"

The gentleman, not causing Don Pepe any pain, disjointed his legs and neck. The feline was left stretched out on the gravel path like a rug, purring even more loudly.

"In the same way, digging graves is nothing for me now. Before, yes, it was hard, and that was even when I was young. But little by little, I set pride aside and let the Earth be my teacher. She showed me her hard spots, her soft spots, her empty places. If you take a good look at where and how you sink in the shovel, the ground opens and in you go like a knife through butter." In a few seconds, he reassembled the cat's neck and legs, and off the animal dashed, chasing a nocturnal butterfly. "Do you understand the language of things? Look carefully at that small refuge."

Jaime realized that Don Eleodoro was enjoying himself immensely talking to him. Perhaps it was the first night in many years he had company like this, drinking coffee under the moonlight. In any case, he turned to look in the direction the knotty finger was pointing. At the end of a branch, a nest glowed.

"What does it say to you?"

"It looks pretty, like a magic fruit."

"It may be true but that is what you create; pretty or ugly comes from you, not from the nest. The truth is that the little house is built at the end of a fragile branch. The bird calculates by instinct the weight of the branches that crisscross and the weight of the little birds that nest there in order to construct his work at the limit of the bearable. One gram extra and the branch breaks or bends, causing the chicks to fall. If it builds its nest on a thick, safe branch, the cats will come to eat everything. As it is, no feline will dare come close. So I understand that sometimes it isn't good to seek security, because it leads to death. Sometimes it's better to live in uncertainty. But you know these things because you're a saint. What work it has cost you to purify you soul. I saw it on your body. You've been beaten, had ribs broken. You've had to fight against many wills. You feel your parents didn't love you as they should. All that weighs more than the Christ on His cross. If you like, I'll lighten you. Memory is like a corset. Your memories stick to your chest, your back, all over your skin, and they form an invisible shell that separates you from the world."

The gravedigger stripped him and began to scrape him with a bone knife, inch by inch, with intense dedication, as if he had to pull off a label glued to each part. He began with the soles of Jaime's feet, using the scraper with such skill that he felt no tickle. Then he went up, along his legs, sex, and anus to his chest and back, not forgetting the arms, neck, and finally Jaime's entire head. When he finished, dawn was coming. Since Don Eleodoro had undone the bandage so no part of his body would be missed, Jaime had a pain in his shoulder that seemed light because of the joy he was getting from the rest of his body.

He felt that he'd taken off many, many years of suffering. His body breathed like a huge lung. Each pore, transformed into a tiny mouth, sang a hymn to freedom. All his fears had been removed: fear of dying, getting sick, being abandoned, being invaded, failing, losing, suffering, being bored, having no meaning, going unnoticed, growing old. For the first time, he enjoyed his matter, and the flesh was no longer an executioner allied with Time taking away his life in little bites with its seconds, but a paradisiacal garden where his spirit danced like a shapeless angel.

"My friend, holy penitent, in this region there are many witchdoctors who call themselves wizards. They're going to offer you plants that grant visions and take you to other levels of reality. In my opinion, seeing things as they are, united, not separated, that's a miracle. Are you sleepy?"

"A bit. We haven't slept all night."

"Make an effort. Come with me. Out in the fields stands a solitary apple tree. If we know how to see it, it will speak to us about this plane, which is as marvelous as one of those hallucinations."

He led Jaime out of the cemetery. At the entrance, was the cross, standing upright in a niche in the high wall. Christ looked so well there it seemed as though He'd been carved for that site, like the figurehead on a ship manned by the dead. They followed a path bordered by lavender bushes that purified the air with their sweet perfume. In the middle of a field of dark, almost black earth grew a leafy tree covered with yellow apples turned into gold by the rays of the rising sun.

"What do you see?"

"A tree with lots of ripe, shiny apples."

"Is that all?"

"I can't say it's beautiful or ugly, because that would come from me."

"Don't look with your eyes but with your spirit."

"My spirit tells me those fruits are very sweet, and my stomach believes it."

"Since you feel half-blind, you don't face the bull and you start playing. It would be better to dance. Here everything is dancing, from the stars to the smallest speck of dust. Realize this: the tree stuck into the planet spins with it around the sun. Each apple, according to its position, receives the sun's rays in a different way. A young light that will go from weakness to strength will bath some, those that hang on the side where the sun rises; others, those who face the sunset, will receive an aged light that will go from strength to weakness. A mature vertical light, short but always intense will feed those that grow at the top of the tree. Each apple is different, because during their growth each receives the sun in a different way. Each has a different taste; some are friends of the morning, others of the afternoon, and a few of midday. But there is one apple, the highest and most central, in intense communication with the zenith, that is the queen."

The gravedigger stretched out his arm and cut off an apple. Then, with astonishing agility, he climbed to the top of the tree to cut another.

"Take a bite of one from below. Now eat a piece from this one, the queen, and compare."

The first fruit, fresh, with hard, sugary flesh, seemed delicious to Jaime. He bit the other, and an intense, vibrant, resilient force overwhelmed him. The tense and juicy flesh, like sweet crystal, crunched melodiously. When it dissolved into juice, beneficent acid, it instantly penetrated Jaime's tongue and went into the stream of his blood, which heated up, giving him a blissful fever. When he finished eating that apple, he felt that his life had been extended.

"I think we are the same as the trees; in each situation, we grow a thousand gestures. We have to prefer the kingly gesture, the one closest to the vital principle. And we should make that one, not the others. But never disparaging them. They are the power behind every realization. Well, I'll let you sleep. Get into this grave. I've put a blanket in it. You'll have to get used to this deep bed because I have no other to offer you."

Jaime dropped into the grave and, lulled by the sweet and sour smell of the earth, fell asleep. He dreamed he was in the arms of a dark-skinned woman. Between their two naked bodies, he noted there was a huge quantity of white jelly.

"What's this?" he asked the woman.

"Don't worry, it's my depilatory cream."

"You like to lose your body hair, but I, a man, feel it to be a catastrophe." He felt anguished for a moment, then he said to her, "Rub my back with it. My shoulder blades are covered with hairs. When they fall out, two wings will be able to grow there."

My father awoke full of energy and came out of the grave like a newborn. The gravedigger was waiting to offer him two fried eggs, bread, and a cup of coffee.

"You won't be able to carry your cross for two weeks, friend. What will you do? You can't stay here; a crowd will come to see you to ask for miracles. In their eagerness they will trample the graves and the plants. Maybe one of those believers will lend you a room. Meanwhile, I'll take care of your Christ. When you're better, you can get back on the road of penitence."

"Don Eleodoro, I have other plans. I'll take the train to visit my brother in Santiago."

"Wearing that cassock and with no cross, you'll look odd. I'll undress a dead man. He's fresh. I buried him yesterday. A traveling salesman with no relatives or friends."

After half an hour he came back with a suit of a brilliant, exaggerated green, plus a shirt and shoes.

"I hope you don't mind the color. The more you use the suit, the less noticeable it will be."

"Never look a gift horse in the mouth. Thanks. The shoes I won't take. I'd rather keep these boots. I thank you as well for all you've taught me."

"It's the all-knowing cemetery that's the teacher, not me. I've got death so close to me that I see life everywhere. When you think you're suffering, look at yourself in a mirror and remember where your suit comes from. That will give you spirit. Good-bye, friend. It was good to speak with a living man."

At the train station, Jaime bought a newspaper; the two principal candidates both claimed victory. He looked for the details of the voting; in Valdivia, Luis Barros Borgoño received 2,500 votes, Arturo Alessandri Palma, also 2,500, and Recabarren 1. Jaime boarded the train proud to be the source of that single vote.

The third-class car was packed with poor people traveling with packages, baskets, dogs, and chickens. The arrival of the gringo wearing the parrot-green suit produced a hum of laughter, but all it took was a defiant clearing of the throat for my father to shut them up. His black beard and short hair gave him a fierce air. Fearful, they offered him a seat next to an old lady, and soon the rumble of the steel wheels put him to sleep:

Looking out the window of a building under construction, he observed the recreation area of a school where a teacher was showing his students how to manipulate invisible objects. He realized that the teacher's technique was imperfect and that he masked his lack of precision with a confusing flurry of gestures. Then the students raised their eyes to him, asking for help. From above—impassive, slow, and precise, with impeccable technique—he manipulated an invisible object to show them how to proceed properly in such cases.

The teacher abandoned his class and entered the building, climbing the precarious ladders that led to the seventh floor. Pursing his red lips, he pointed his index finger to his inside jacket pocket and asked him for a four-word motto he might embroider there.

He answered, "Permanent impermanence, nothing personal."

331

Despite the teacher's admiration, he said to himself, "In any case, I have to teach you the technique for the perfect manipulation of invisible objects."

A screech of brakes woke him up. The train had stopped at a small station surrounded by vineyards. Through the door at one end of the car entered three drunken soldiers, each one with a full bottle under his left arm and an almost empty bottle in the right hand. Their swallows were as long as their guffaws. Through the door at the other end entered a short, hunchbacked man, carrying a white bag. When the train started moving, he sank his hands into the sack and pulled them out full of eggs. In a high voice, he began to shout, "Get your hardboiled eggs! For every rooster's trick you buy, I'll give you a packet of salt!"

The hairless face of the hunchback had something womanish to it, and his voice trembled like the clucking of hens. The soldiers, elbowing each other, pushed their way to him, snatched the white sack and began to eat the eggs so gluttonously that they swallowed them without removing the shell. In a few moments, they devoured three dozen, the man's entire stock. Emptying their second bottle, they went back to the bench they used as bed and urinal. The hunchback followed them, demanding payment. The soldiers grabbed him by one leg and held him upside down shaking him: "Empty the gut you've got on your back. It must be full of eggs!"

Carried away with their game, they began to beat his head against the floor, clearly intending to smash it.

"Stop at once!" shouted Jaime, without even thinking the situation through. His indignation was involuntary, as were the gestures that followed: with a feline leap, he flew over the passengers' heads, landed in the center aisle, leapt again, and found himself facing to the savages. Then, using his good arm, he punched them in the mouths. Teeth flew all over. Then he smacked their chests and sides, knocking them down between the seats. Finally he kicked them in their heads, leaving them unconscious and bloody. When he snapped out of his furor, he found himself carrying the hunchback, who was both sobbing and laughing triumphantly, thanking Jaime a thousand times.

"Listen, sir, you have nothing to thank me for. The fact is I don't like bullying, that's all. I didn't attack them to defend you but to defend an idea."

"Whatever you say, but the truth is you saved my life. You punched all three with only one fist. You can see from a mile away you're a boxer, and a good one. It's a shame God didn't give me your body, that way I could work in peace. If you'll forgive my curiosity, could you tell me where you're going?"

"I'm going to Santiago, but I have to get off in Rancagua. I didn't have enough money to go farther."

"What a coincidence! I live in Rancagua, and if your pockets are empty, I can offer you a job, even though I appear poor."

Going up a steep hill, they took advantage of the train's slowness and jumped off to avoid reprisals from the army. Luckily they were only two day's walk from the city, and the hunchback, whose name was Jesús de la Cruz, made the walk shorter by singing beautiful tunes in his tenor voice.

"Well, as my name says, I'm a victim nailed to the cross of my hunched back. A load like this is very hard to carry. When I pass through the taverns to sell my hardboiled eggs, the drunks always end up beating me. I understand them. They—workers, peasants, miners—are constant victims of the injustice of their bosses. They discharge their accumulated rage on me. I have a German hurdy-gurdy that contains pretty melodies. I can sing as I crank the handle and then sell bananas and eggs. You, strong as you are, disguised as a gorilla—I have a costume I found thrown in the garbage after carnival—could protect me. Many organ grinders are accompanied by little monkeys who collect money in a little can. Mine would be bigger. Admit it: the idea is good, my friend. Wearing the mask, no one will recognize you, and after a short time, we can split the profit between us. You'll save up enough to buy a ticket to Santiago."

Jaime was not surprised that fate would transform him into an ape-man. His mother had fallen in love with one, and perhaps for him it was good to identify himself with a simian form, which, indirectly, would give him the sensation of receiving the maternal love he lacked.

Meanwhile, the two presidential candidates, after each claimed the win, accused each other of fraud. Amid turbulence among the people, along with the threat of military intervention, the election was decided by an honor tribunal that gave the presidency to Alessandri.

My father lived a year submerged in the gorilla suit, visiting bars and restaurants every night of the week. At first he had to bloody a few drunks so that they'd learn to respect the hunchback, but later the job was easy. Everybody wanted to shake his hand or hug him, smiling like children. One night, out of pure boredom, he took a hanky out of the pocket of a customer and began to dance a cueca. A general clapping of hands ensued, and many wanted to accompany the gorilla, pounding their heels intensely. Jesús sold all his merchandise.

During the day, my father did not take off the disguise and, seated in the town's main square, he amused the children. It did him good to live anonymously, within a hairy shell. He needed to lose himself, to discover the zero point. Deep down in the depth of his soul, he believed in nothing. He felt intensely separated. He'd been dropped in a world full of locked doors but given no keys. He looked for meaning to existence, always finding that nothing was worthwhile.

Hidden within the gorilla suit, as if in an alchemical crucible, he was dissolving, transforming into a formless spirit without personality or definition, with no values to affirm, free of models, of ties. He stopped being a gringo. A false monkey was accepted but a Russian immigrant was not. He challenged himself, dressed that way and without taking off his mask, to conquer a woman. Why just one? Many! His weapons of

seduction were his eyes, his bare hands, his voice, and an interior force
that pierced the animal skin and surrounded him with an erotic aura that
married women, his preferred victims, perceived as blue-green waves.

Between three and five in the afternoon, when those ladies were
preparing dinner and their husbands were far away at work, he easily
managed to possess them in any old corner of the kitchen. It was best
for them not to know his name or his face. They yielded to pure pleasure
with no ties, free of all guilt. When the act was over, they slipped him a
banknote or a packet of flowers and food. These impersonal relationships
allowed my father to know the root of pleasure, a brutal enjoyment that
was mysterious, devoid of modesty, where each female showed her basic
heat. He didn't exist, and the mask, granting him the quality of being a
mask, transformed him into the ideal male all women bear within. Each
one of them molded him to make him into an excrescence of their own
flesh and that way they could possess themselves. Jaime knew he was
walking through a space where there was no becoming.

One morning, Jesús de la Cruz, highly excited, woke him: "Jaime,
today you can take off your monkey suit and put your parrot costume
back on. I mean, you can dress like a normal citizen even though the
color is loud. We're going to a workers' demonstration. The city is full
of thugs. Recabarren is coming!"

"What? Recabarren?"

"That's right, Recabarren, your idol! It's the First Congress of the
Communist Party of Chile. They are going to officially declare their
allegiance to the Communist International whose seat is in Moscow.
Being inside that gorilla suit and bouncing all over the place, you haven't
been aware of anything. The leader has come out of jail, been elected a
deputy, and the doors of Congress are open to him. Now it's going to
be difficult to cut him off. Tonight, for certain, there will be no beatings,
even though they've put up posters everywhere that say, With Body and
Soul We'll be Red!"

"But why are they meeting here, in Rancagua?"

"It must be because there are so many peasants and also because lots of workers can come down from the El Teniente copper mine. They're already arriving, peaceful, wearing their Sunday best. They say it's one of the most transcendent events in the history of Chile."

"They say, they say. Who the fuck does so much saying? Pure publicity!"

Jaime, not knowing why, had awakened in a bad mood. There was something that deeply bothered him, a foreboding that arose from the foundations of that city, with its typically Spanish design formed of eight-by-eight blocks with a plaza at its center. The surrounding streets did not start at the corner of the tree-lined rectangle but from the center of each of its sides. It was there that 1,500 patriots, defeated and perhaps betrayed, had died. All that put Jaime in a bad mood. He walked to the church, sat in a pew, and, pretending to pray, summoned the Rabbi, who was not slow in coming. Jaime, treating him coldly but courteously, laid out the situation. He got the answer he feared:

"You're right to be worried. Never disdain symbols. The Plaza of the Heroes is between four streets that form a cross. For a Catholic civilization that signifies martyrdom. In 1814, Bernardo O'Higgins (Christ) occupies the plaza to stop the Spanish army from advancing from the south toward the capital. Juan José Carrera (Judas), two leagues away, remains with a detachment of cavalry in order to support the bulk of the army when his help is requested. This, for reasons no one has been able to explain, he does not do.

"Attacked in four places, the infantry is decimated, without giving up. The hero does not allow himself to be crucified, and in a ferocious attack opens a path to escape the disaster. The motive for the cruel sacrifice: naïve confidence in a bad ally. You, who, like all Chileans, know this battle by heart, are upset seeing Recabarren reproduce the same disastrous configuration without realizing it. By founding the Communist Party in

Rancagua, he is expressing that, deep down, he is preparing for betrayal and defeat. He, a just spirit, a redeemer, a human canal of the Supreme Father, Lenin, will be badly judged, understood by few or none, and will see the people massacred around him. His triumphs will be tactical retreats; he'll have greater sufferings. He will be abandoned and alone in adversity, deserted even by his guide. *Eloi, Eloi, lama sabachthani?*"

"Fine. Now you've told me what I needed to hear: Recabarren should never have founded his party in this city of defeated heroes. Now go away. I've had enough hallucinations for one day!"

And with his bad mood transformed into fury, he returned to the tiny room he shared with the hunchback. He shaved, cut his hair, and put on his green suit. Jesús de la Cruz looked like a boy going to the circus. With an air of complicity, he showed Jaime a package of chocolates and mints. He showed off a T-shirt with a mountain peak embroidered on the back. He had dyed his eggs red.

A great crowd tried to enter the lecture hall of the municipality. Miners and peasants huddled outside, orderly, knowing that the hall was filled to capacity. When they heard a round of applause, they too clapped and shouted support, not knowing for what and why. It took Jaime and the hunchback an hour to cross that serene and dense sea. They managed to get by saying they were carrying food for the congressmen. When they got into the hall, Recabarren was speaking. There was nothing extraordinary in his looks. He was a serene man, clean-shaven, gray around the temples. His gestures were modest and friendly. His voice—devoid of oratorical tremolos—was plain, direct, and common, but it also possessed a conviction so deep that it electrified. His words went straight to the heart of his fellow believers with no need for shouting or gesturing.

"Comrades, without the blood of the thousands of worker martyrs cruelly spilled by the exploiter classes in the ferocious repressions that have taken place since 1900 right until today, 1922, without the anti-imperialist struggle kept up for years by patriotic elements, it would have been next to impossible for the conditions to be created in Chile for our dream to become reality. The Communist Party is born by assimilating the ideology that corresponds to the proletariat: Marxism-Leninism. The Party is born carrying high in the air the red banner, the emblem that synthesizes the most noble ideals, the purest aspirations, the most sublime visions of those who desire to construct a better humanity, a more perfect, more human society that will definitively liberate man from exploitation, that will eliminate need, that will extinguish the anxieties of insecurity, that will tear open all the veils of ignorance and inaugurate the kingdom of happiness."

Despite the pain the purity of that man gave to him by fighting for ideals that manifested his immense love for humanity and which would lead him, when he collided with innate human perversity, to martyrdom, Jaime found himself applauding, galvanized like the rest. Recabarren, fearless, read a declaration of principles, attacking the juridical, political, and economic structure of society, appealing to the class struggle to inaugurate, by means of the proletarian revolution, a Communist government.

As an essential measure of that program, he announced the foundation of a newspaper that would be the organ of the National Executive Committee. Then a brass band, not quite in tune but energetic, played "The International," which was sung by all present under waving red flags. Recabarren, not wanting to be the center of this fervor of the people, disappeared among the Congress members, but many workers began to shout "Recabarren!" so he came back with his arms outstretched (like Jesus, thought Jaime), in order to receive the vibrant ovations.

My father, dissolved in that enthusiastic mass, tried to approach the politician he admired and felt so sorry for, not with the hope of speaking to him—many rings of comrades surrounded him, making incessant commentaries, trying to hear from his lips a phrase that would be a personal memory—but to get the energetic contact of his invisible aura. He managed to get five yards from his goal and felt happy. He could see the chest of the historic man rising and falling. Perhaps he'd have the luck that his eyes, which already belonged to legend, would meet his own for an instant.

Surprised almost to paralysis, he heard the leader say to him, "You there, the young man in the green suit, come over here."

The bodies immediately separated, opening a narrow path. As if submerged in a dream, with the intense palpitation of a heart witnessing a miracle, he walked toward Recabarren, who gave him a hearty handshake and invited him to follow along to a private office where he was going to rest.

Now Jaime began to think: "Could he see that I'm inhabited by a Jewish monster? Did he recognize Teresa's face in mine? It isn't possible that I, among thousands of enthusiasts, could interest him! Maybe I do. He's an extraordinary man; he must perceive things differently, see into our interiors, know the quality of our souls. I've always known that I'm great, that my secret spirit is as pure as a diamond, and that I have the strength to move mountains. If he organizes a workers' army and gives me command of it, I won't lose a single battle. No Rancagua for this boy. I'll even demolish the ruins of this sick capitalism and pitilessly cut all the heads off the dragon!"

Recabarren observed him calmly, offered him some tea in the cup from a thermos, and asked him: "Tell me, young man, where did you buy that suit?"

Jaime tumbled from the heights of grandeur down to the size of a flyspeck. "To tell the truth, I didn't buy it. A gravedigger gave it to me. It belonged to a dead man who had neither friends nor family."

"Family he did have, at least one, me. Vicente was my uncle, a traveling salesman in the clothes business. He made that suit from the fabric on the mattress of his mom's bed. He was always an old bachelor, very discreet. When my grandmother died, he poisoned the thirty cats that lived with them. He was the only son of that recalcitrant widow, and he buried her on a bed of cats. As you see, thanks to your glaring clothes, we're almost members of the same family. Besides, you get an inheritance. Cut open the shoulder pads: Vicente always hides a few pesos there folded up in case of emergency."

"Thanks a lot. I'll do just that, Don Luis Emilio."

"What's your name?"

"Jaime Jodorowsky, at your service."

"An odd name. Is it Polish?"

"It is, but my family is Russian. I'm lying. They're Jews."

"But do you know how to speak Russian?"

"I'm lucky enough not to have forgotten it."

"Want to work with me?"

"Of course!"

"My obligations as a member of Congress require me to live in Santiago. Here on this card is my address. I have a pile of Russian books, all disorganized. You will be very useful to me. Not only to me but also to the entire working class. Your translations can be published in our newspapers. Come to see me as soon as you can. But remember: the trains leave on time and if you're a second late, you'll miss a long trip."

In the cotton stuffing of the shoulder pads, Jaime found a lot of money. He gave half to his partner and with the other half bought a navy blue suit and a ticket to Santiago. The hunchback got drunk, burned the gorilla suit, and began to pelt him with hardboiled eggs dyed black. My father had to run to the train to escape his fury. He reached the capital one Sunday at 6:00 a.m. When he entered Benjamín's apartment, he found him fully dressed, eating breakfast:

"What are you doing here? I've got no need for you. You spent almost two years without writing or worrying about my mother's health. You should be ashamed. If it weren't for the fact that I've gone back to divine

Poetry, I'd be a goner by now. Thanks to poetry, in these immobile rivers, the crutches of long journeys have become baroque chargers. I gallop mounted on a violet blast between the ancient eyes of men who reflect the geometric formulas of this unbalanced world."

"Stop, Benjamín. Stop reciting with that diva's voice and tell me where Teresa is, since she's also my mother."

"She's made extraordinary progress. Even though she has serious cardiac problems, the wandering truths have returned to take refuge in the divine architecture of their demolition."

"You're busting my balls with your babble! Explain it clearly to me!"

"She's become a nice lady. On Sundays, they let her out of the mad-house in my custody. We have a puppet theater, and we put on shows in the hospital for children with tuberculosis. Will you come? Today we're debuting 'The Soldier Who Overcame Death.' A traditional theme, but I've rewritten the dialogue. Art keeps cemeteries alive thanks to the drama of its cadavers!"

The puppet theater stood on the somber patio filled with yellow-ish children, wearing old army jackets with gray blankets covering their shoulders. It was a blue screen emblazoned with the name of the company: THE BOOLOOLU. A cloth with a medieval castle painted on it was the only scenery. The small patients shouted, demanding the performance begin. Stern nurses handed out crepe paper balls filled with sawdust. A bullying doctor waved a Chilean flag, asking everybody to sing the national anthem. Jaime couldn't see Teresa. Benjamín sat him with the mob and said, "Now you'll have to concentrate. You'll see my mother when the show is over. I made the heads of the puppets and she the costumes. I do the acting; Teresa is my helper. We make a great couple." Then he ran to hide himself behind the screen. A cardboard trumpet hooted. Death appeared carrying a young blonde woman with red cheeks, wearing a bridal gown. The girl, fighting to escape the skeleton's embrace, bowed toward the children, asking for help:

"Don't let him take me away. Before I die, I want to see my fiancé, a soldier. He promised me he would return from the war."

The sick children bombarded Death with their sawdust balls. But Death, emitting miserable guffaws, held the girl even more tightly. With great stealth, the puppet master removed his hand from the sleeve. The bride hung empty in the embrace of Death. Inside the little theater, Benjamín extended his left hand toward Teresa so she could slip on the soldier. His uniform was filthy and torn. Meanwhile, my uncle began to act in three different voices.

He made a cavernous laugh as Death: "You are mine, forever!"

He cried as a damsel in distress, "No! Help! Oh my love, come help me!"

He shouted in a romantic soldier's voice, "Oh my bride, hang on! I'm on my way!"

Teresa began to stagger, about to faint. Benjamín whispered, "Quickly now, slip the soldier on tight. What's wrong with you?"

"It's nothing. A passing malaise. Go on. Don't worry."

Death opened the gates of the castle and locked the sagging bride inside. The soldier appeared.

"Old lady Death, open your eight invisible legs and give me back my bride!"

"Too late! Her soul will dissolve into white butterflies."

"Never! If she disappears, you would erase me from all mirrors. Instead, I'll kill you!"

"Kill me? Do you want to cut a sword with a thread? Ha, ha, ha!"

The ragged soldier engaged in a fierce fight with Death. Saber against scythe. Teresa, biting her lips, fell with an unbearable pain in her heart. Benjamín, never dropping the act with his two puppets who battled in silence, looked down to where his mother had fallen.

"I'm telling you not to worry, son. The show must go on."

"But?"

"Whatever begins must end. Go on."

"What's wrong?"

"It's this worn-out heart. My time has come."

"No!"

"Go on, I'm ordering you!"

Amid the cheering of the consumptive children for their hero, the soldier, who dodged Death's scythe by sinking down into the invisible floor, only to pop up like a spring to surprise his adversary from the back. He pierced Death through and through with his saber, proudly exclaiming, "I've killed Death! Here I am, my bride! I got here in time!"

The hero, applauded furiously by the audience but worn out by the fight, made a supreme effort, opened the gate, and entered the castle. The stage was empty. The children asked their frowning nurses whether the soldier was going to find the girl dead or alive. Benjamín, with the soldier on one hand and the bride on the other, kneeled next to his mother.

"Don't quit on me. I still need you."

"Now you see you can't finish the show on your own."

The impatient children began to call to the hand puppets, "The bride and groom! We want the bride and groom!"

Benjamín made Teresa comfortable on the floor, shouted in the bride's voice, "We're on our way!" Then, with the voice of the soldier, "We're enjoying a kiss!" He imitated the noise of a huge smack and sighed: "OOOOH!" General laughter broke out.

Teresa pressed her chest with her open hands. "I'll hang on until the end. All you have left is the dance. Get up. Do it!"

Benjamín, his eyes filled with tears, raised the puppets. The soldier and his bride left the castle. The children received them with a warm ovation. He hugged her in his arms and said, passionately, "Tattoo my chest! Cover it with flames!"

And she answered, "Tiny needles grow on my lips, which for you spurt ink like little squids!"

And he: "Let me introduce the Universe between your lips!"

And she: "I have pieces of gods at the back of my tongue!"

The two papier mâché heads made a tremendous kiss. The children howled hysterically. The bride and groom separated and fell at the edge of the stage, worn out, panting. Then they jumped up and kissed again. The kiss made them spin around. More howls. Laughter. They began to dance a waltz: "We have conquered Death! Children, say it with us!"

The ailing audience, like a single actor, exclaimed, "We have conquered Death!"

"Now together forever!"

The curtain fell. Jaime waited for the sick children to leave, not knowing that behind the screen, his mother, in his brother's arms, was dying.

"Do not suffer, Benjamín. We aren't born, and we don't die. Life is eternal."

"I know it. I'll have to be the soldier who conquers Death."

"You already are, and you have conquered it. We shall remain forever alive. Together forever. We shall go from transformation to transformation, never ending. We lose nothing because we are everything."

My uncle could no longer hold back and began to sob.

"Don't cry. My form is nothing more than an illusion."

"Yes, an illusion but so beautiful."

"Benjamín, I want you to bury my body next to your father's. Under the same stone."

"I promise I will."

"Finally I know peace. How marvelous, how marvelous, how mar—"

And she expired sweetly. Jaime found her smiling in the arms of his brother, who kissed her with devotion. He attempted to come close, but Benjamín made a violent motion of rejection.

"Get out of here. Her death is mine. I will bury her. You never did anything for her. You were born an orphan with no father or mother. You aren't even my brother."

Jaime said nothing. He'd tortured Benjamín when they were small by making fun of his weaknesses, so he understood that hatred. He felt compassion for Benjamín: until the end of his days, he would be married to Teresa's ghost, with no wife, no children, making his language harder and harder to understand until he severed all communication with the world. Poetry would gag him. He left his brother there, clinging to the smiling body, and went to see Recabarren.

He crossed the Mapocho River, which flowed with chocolate-colored water, as if grumbling about the passage of time, stubborn, not wanting to leave the past, denying the city, showing with its mild current the difficulty of passing, going toward itself, dense in its fight not to move forward, trying to turn itself into a liquid lance, seeking immobility without ever finding it, and raging because it had to dissolve in the gluttonous ocean.

He shook his head to break his identification with the river, using it as a mirror, and tried to find number 360 on Andrés Bello Street. It was a modest house with a well-tended garden. A bronze fist at the center of the blue door was the knocker. Jaime began to tremble. Something was telling him that when he stepped over the threshold his life would change. He needed to find a foundation to draw him out of madness, to drop the anchor in solid ground, to find beings without illusions, building on rock instead of sand, to know someone honest on this planet full of crooks and vampires. He made only one knock, which tried to be discreet but sounded like a pistol shot.

An amiable woman with intelligent eyes opened the door: Her hair was cut short like a man's, and her face was mature but without wrinkles. She wore no makeup. Her goodness was clearly the result of her tenacious, direct spirit, which had abandoned the mirages of seduction. Even though everything about her was feminine, the narrowness of her hips showed she'd never had a child.

"What do you want?"

"I'm Jaime Jodorowsky. Mr. Recabarren offered me a job."

"Ah, the young man who speaks Russian! Luis Emilio has already told me about it. Come in. I'm his companion, Teresa."

Teresa! This woman had the same name as his mother. He'd just lost one, and the magic of chance was giving him another, perhaps better, as if the first had been the rough, uncarved stone and this one the geometric form, realized. He knew he was going to love her, without sex, without demands, with an unlimited admiration. All he needed was to see her this way, so complete, to take her as a model for all women. She hadn't said she was the "wife" of the leader, but his "companion." This woman could never accept anything other than love and political ideals to unite her to her man. Marriage for her had to be one more farce in the capitalist system. The house seemed as clean as a warship. The furniture was solid and in the strictly necessary quantity. There were no pictures on the walls, no adornments. Nor were there any crucifixes or other religious icons. But covering the entire ceiling of the living room was a portrait of Lenin painted in tempera.

"You can move in here."

She gave him a room with a narrow bed, a chair, a dresser, a bathroom, and a pitcher full of water.

"I'm going to serve bean soup, bread and butter, and coffee. After you eat, you can begin to put the books in order. They're still in boxes. What with all these sad events, we haven't had time to unpack them."

Was she referring to the betrayal involved in the way the government of Alessandri thanked the people for the support they'd given him? Five hundred miners murdered in the San Gregorio nitrate mine, coal miners shot by the police in Curanilahue, demonstrations broken up by beatings, massacres of workers in El Zanjón de la Aguada, women fired for holding a meeting in Santiago at the site of the O'Higgins monument, peasants from the La Tranquilla ranch in Petorca murdered? The denial of the right to assemble, jailings, deportations, torture . . . Or was she talking about the internal squabbles that broke out immediately after the founding of the Communist Party?

Jaime ate with a good appetite, washed his dishes and silverware in the kitchen sink, and opened the boxes. He was so excited to touch the books that formed Recabarren's spirit that he forgot his internal vigilance, which the Rabbi took advantage of by appropriating his personality. What the Rabbi loved above all things was books. Under Teresa's astonished eyes, he organized the books, capturing the essence of their contents in two or three pages, while emitting shouts of pleasure in Yiddish.

He separated literature from pure philosophy and gave a preferential place to political texts. He put poetry on the highest shelf. He did not order the books alphabetically but by theme, not concerned in the slightest about which language they were written in. He understood everything. He read paragraphs in Russian, Italian, German, and French. Also in Spanish.

Each new idea filled his mouth with saliva, as if he were sampling an exquisite dish. For the pleasure of feeling the miraculous structure of a sentence, he recited it, giving it musical intonations. He sang the books, or rather, he stored them in his mind, whistling their rhythms. He fluttered about with the open books in his hands, looking like a bird.

"The songs of my language have eyes and feet, eyes and feet, muscles, soul, sensations, the grandeur of heroes, and small, modest customs. Mmm . . . Touch her body, touch her body, and your miserable fingers will bleed! Great poet! Oy vey! The signs by which the gods revealed themselves were often very simple: the noise of the sacred oak's leaves, the whisper of a fountain, the sound of a bronze cup caressed by the wind. This aesthetic isn't bad. God appears, man is nullified: and the greater divinity becomes, the more miserable humanity becomes. *Ase méne dermante zir in toite*! When you think about death, it's because you aren't sure about life. These anarchists who grind up God so much make holy sausages."

Making an effort so intense that it used up his energy and he had to lie down for a few hours in bed, Jaime recovered control of his mind. Teresa, making no comments, brought him a glass of hot milk and covered him with a wool poncho.

"Sleep in peace. My companion Recabarren will be here at ten tonight. We'll dine together."

The crowing of a rooster woke him. A soft, reddish light entered through the window. The glass that was on the floor next to the bed projected a long shadow that reached the shoes of Luis Emilio Recabarren.

"Last night you were sleeping so soundly that we didn't want to interrupt. Around here, we get up early. Come have breakfast with us."

Teresa served café con leche, highly sugared, and a little basket of sweet rolls. She offered them fried eggs and ham with slices of fresh tomato. Jaime, timid, ashamed at the Rabbi's invasion, could say nothing. Recabarren calmly read his workers' paper. He folded it carefully, put it in his pocket, and brusquely said, "Well, Don Jaime, what are you waiting for to join the Party?"

My father choked up, spit out some crumbs, and answered without thinking, "If you accept me, it will be a great honor to do so right now."

Recabarren's face opened into a glowing smile. He dug around in a drawer in his desk and pulled out a small red ID book. "We'll have to find you a name. Because of all the persecution, every comrade signs in with a pseudonym. How about a Mapuche name like Lautaro Quinchahual?"

This time the nation was indeed opening a door for him, not with a hook from which he'd be hung by the hair, not through the hallucinations of a plant, not through the cruel womb of a grave, not through a stolen cross or the anonymous darkness of a gorilla suit. He was being baptized a second time, reborn in a homeland that accepted him as a native son, granting him a brotherhood. An official membership card for the Communist Party, signed and sealed by an admirable person, someone who saw the splendorous reality beneath obscure dreams!

"Comrade Quinchahual, I want you to know that the red on this membership card is not the red of violence but of the blood spilled by our martyrs. Today we are few, barely two thousand militants, a small figure if you take into account the total number of people in the working class, but the political importance of a party is not only measured by numbers of members but also by the efficacy with which it is able to broadcast its influence and weight through society. For that reason, you are going to be very useful to me. Teresa's told me how you go into a trance and speak myriad languages. I know some Russian and more than a little German. We'll have to translate Marx, Lenin, and Engels. The degree of illiteracy among the workers is immense. For centuries, the exploiters have kept them buried in ignorance. Better than buying rifles is founding newspapers. Come with me to the press."

That's how the new life began. Jaime had finally found the perfect father, almost the antithesis of Alejandro the shoemaker, the mystic, the madman, the universal victim. Recabarren was an atheist saint whose loyalty to the people was solid, so honest that, in this society of thieves, he seemed a fanatical idealist.

To achieve his objective—a happy, free humanity—he'd limited his imagination, his loves, the growth of his personality. Dry, austere, focused, more than a man, he was a sword. Every night, after his meager dinner (he didn't like to eat meat much and didn't smoke), he reviewed his day out loud, as if it were someone else's life, and criticized even the slightest weakness, incisively seeking the errors in order to discover a lesson. "Let's see now, Lautaro. Let's study what Luis Emilio's day was worth. He got up fifteen minutes late. Careful! The comrade must not let discipline slip. The mattress is the worst enemy of action!" He recalled every sentence spoken during meetings, the details of the international news, the intimate problems of hundreds of militants. My father saw two aspects in him: one, the impetuous, spontaneous, intense horse; the other, the implacable rider, capable of sacrificing everything, even his own life, to get a just world. Standing alongside that man was to stand with all workers: "If you look inside me, all you'll find are other people."

Two years of intense activity went by. Arturo Alessandri did not carry out his program. For Recabarren, the president was a puppet of the oligarchy, playing an impotent revolutionary in order to trick the proletariat and slow its social evolution.

"This is a very well-organized comedy. The opposition Congress keeps the reforms proposed by the government from occurring. The workers think their scarecrow president will get them better days. Meanwhile, there are repressions, firings, and massacres. Today the president and the parliament accuse each other of being responsible. The conservatives sing arias charged with noisy words: 'dictatorial intentions,' 'administrative corruption,' 'incompetence.' Tomorrow, instead of resolving the crisis, his Offended Excellency will resign. A drumroll and a triumphant march, please: the military will arrive. Applause from the ignorant public. The oligarchy will accept superficial changes and will pretend to be docile in the face of what's going on because the warrior heroes, students of Mussolini, will be nothing more than their lackeys. Militarism, Comrade Quinchahual, is the ruthless enemy of the independent and revolutionary workers movement."

Jaime translated articles, printed and sold newspapers, helped foment strikes, was persecuted and beaten. He observed how Recabarren faced up to myriad forms of violence, insidious calumnies, and attacks of all kinds, suffering defeats, winning victories, passing through betrayals and desertions, feeling his efforts were compensated for by the loyalty and affection conferred on him by the workers.

He always tried to conform his actions to the teachings of Lenin, "the genius of theory." At the end of the year, Recabarren announced he was going to make a trip to Russia, where he would stay for several months. Teresa and Jaime saw him off in Valparaíso. The man was very excited. Finally he would see with his own eyes a nation that had completely rooted out the exploiting regime. And possibly, at the meeting of the Congress of the Third International, he might speak to Comrade Lenin and shake his hand.

"You know, Quinchahual, that we love you as if you were our own son. Protect my companion. The enemy can always deliver tricky blows, and it's better to prevent than to cure."

Teresa was so demure she seemed a shadow. She never made even the slightest noise. She was the only person my father ever knew whose footsteps made no sound. She slipped around like a ship in a tranquil lake. Around her, beings and things put themselves in order. She would step out into the garden and, very quietly, would stretch out her hand to offer a slice of pound cake that only she knew how to bake. Soon flocks of sparrows would come to flutter around her body, pecking at the spongy mass and sometimes perching on her shoulders and head.

If another person approached, they would flee in nervous confusion. My father stood still for two hours in the garden with a slice of Teresa's pound cake in his hand, but not a single bird came near. But no sooner did the woman come out and put her hand on his arm, than a cloud of tiny birds surrounded him. If she released his elbow, they flew away.

During those long days when he missed his master's presence, Jaime decided to find a lover to kill his nostalgia. The only female member of his cell supplied with sufficient breasts and backside, Sofía Lam, was a lesbian and long-suffering. She had three or four scars on each wrist, the result of failed suicides caused by married women, who when push came to shove decided not to abandon their husbands. Her long, plump, and flexible body excited him, but her face, with its large mouth and tiny nose, round eyes and sagging ears, seemed as ugly to him as a Pekingese pup.

Nevertheless, he thought, "It doesn't matter; I can have sex with her in the dark, or on my back, or with her skirt pushed up to cover her face. The bad thing is she always wears trousers."

One night, when the meeting was over, he invited her to have coffee, to see what possibilities there might be to found a new newspaper. They chatted for a few minutes, and then suddenly he asked her out of the blue, "You're a virgin, correct?"

"Not a virgin, though my hymen is intact."

"Would you like to have it broken?"

"With a man? Men disgust me."

"How do you know, if you've never tried a man?"

"Men are sticky. Full of vanity. When they penetrate, they insult."

"Do I? Do I make you vomit?"

"I never thought about you in that way. You're discreet. Don't spoil things."

"Now, are we or are we not revolutionaries, comrade? Why do you limit yourself so much? You should yield to noble experiments! You might not change, but you would certainly be enriched! Let me take you in my arms, and just see what you feel."

"All right, but don't get mad if I find you repugnant. I'll be frank."

"Exactly what I'd expect you to be."

Jaime approached her little by little, with the slowness of a dream. He made his spirit neutral and did not embrace her the way a man embraces a woman but the way one person embraces another. He pressed his body to hers, taking the care not to apply any pressure that might be interpreted as overpowering or even as a sexual advance. He offered his physical company, nothing more.

"How strange, Lautaro! Contact with you doesn't bother me. You're the first man to have that effect on me."

"Well then, Sofía. Let me suggest the following: with no commitment of any kind, I can free you of your hymen. You should take it as a simple surgical procedure. We won't mix in desire or feelings. I assure you I will be dispassionate. Nothing will upset you. After, you will be able to move with much more ease."

"Where and when?"

"I have to prepare the 'medical' material. I'll await you tomorrow night in Recabarren's house. I have a separate room there, so no one will bother us."

He bought prophylactics, rubber gloves, a surgical mask and cap. He put the bed up against the wall and the desk at the center of the room covered with a sheet. He placed the lamp at the foot of the bed so the "operating table" would be bathed in light. When Sofía whistled to him from the street, he first sprinkled a little ether and alcohol on the floor so the place would smell like a hospital. Then he let her in and ushered her into his room without saying a word. He washed his hands under her eye, making lots of foam with the soap. Then he dried them and powdered them with talcum powder. He put on the cap and gloves, then he covered his face with the mask.

"Get into bed here, naked."

The girl stripped immediately, with no sensuality, and stretched out on her back, inert, on the desk. Jaime moistened her pubis with warm water, soaped it up, and began to shave the brownish stain. She did not complain. He disinfected the skin on her stomach and breasts.

"Spread your legs wide, I'm going to proceed to the operation."

Sofía revealed her sex, a line like a doll's. Jaime rubbed in some Vaseline, leaned over her and, taking her from below her knees, raised her thighs. Then with extreme care, he pushed his erect sex in and made it touch the hymen.

"The scalpel is in position. Now you'll have to be brave and push. Don't think that I'm penetrating you but that you are absorbing me."

And she, pressing her heels on the sheet-covered surface, applied pressure with her hips toward the root of the phallus. The membrane resisted. Exasperated, she gave a violent push and swallowed the entire membrane. Jaime felt the sticky warmth of the blood running down his testicles. Sofía moaned, smiled, and with inexhaustible energy yielded herself to a series of slips and slides, rubbing her clitoris against my father's curly pubic hair. The rhythm began to possess her. Subtly, slithering like a snake among rocks, Jaime began to synchronize with her, and then, suddenly, both were enmeshed in a furious series of hip-thrusts that ended when Sofía's body contracted until it seemed made of stone and she emitted a hoarse howl. Jaime removed the prophylactic full of semen and, showing it to her, said with artificial coldness, "The operation is over. You can get dressed, thank the surgeon, and go home."

He sent her on her way without taking off the gloves and mask. The comrade walked to the Mapocho River, picked up a stone on the shore, and with all her strength threw it at the moon, shouting at it, "You old bitch!"

At the beginning of 1923, Recabarren returned. A mob of fans went to greet him in Valparaíso. He responded to the applause with modest gestures of thankfulness. On the train, he requested a private compartment and locked himself in with Teresa and Jaime. His smile vanished, and a profound sorrow appeared on his face. He fixed his eyes on those of his companion and, mute, for the entire trip simply stared at her. Teresa, like a blotter, absorbed his sadness. The tears, slipping down her cheeks, fell onto her bosom. A dark stain appeared on her red organdy dress. When they reached Santiago, she hid that damp tarantula with a package.

The master slept for two whole days. When he awoke, and without even having breakfast, he began to write a pamphlet to report the principal traits of the transformation taking place in Russia. A reddish scale fell onto his papers. He looked up at the ceiling. Because of the humidity, the portrait of Lenin was peeling.

Recabarren said to my father, "It may be that reality is not as we dream it, Lautaro. Nevertheless, sometimes our dreams are what create reality. It is of vital importance that Russia continues to be a socialist nation for the sake of the workers movement all over the world. What I saw, or what might have been able to see, you shall read in these lines: 'The Russia of Workers and Peasants.' I ask that you always place your confidence in me. Take Teresa as an example. She realizes I don't want to talk for a while, so she remains silent. Stop asking yourself why I'm sad and do the same."

And silence entered the house like a translucent ghost and filled the rooms with absence. Freed from the oppression of human voices, noises took control of the space. The act of eating—chewing food, the cracking of chicken bones, the bubbling of saliva, the snapping of tongues, the dense act of digestion, the intestinal rumbling—all of that became a symphony. That muteness threw light and shadow into high relief; it opened the way for scents that came from the garden and the kitchen to flutter in the dining room like long-legged birds. It erased the bodies, encrusting them in their absence in the chairs.

One morning, when the rooster was crowing, Recabarren woke him by depositing on his legs a large package wrapped in shiny paper. In his left hand, he held a heavy suitcase.

"We're going on a trip, comrade. I have to take advantage of my position as a member of Congress; they will not dare to kill me. We're going on a tour of Tarapacá and Antofagasta. We're going to distribute propaganda, translated by you, along with my pamphlet on Russia. It is our political obligation to elevate the low ideological level of the Party directors and militants."

Wearing trousers of ordinary cloth, a T-shirt, and an old vest, the representative of the people in the parliament took a third-class seat on the Longitudinal and, joined by Jaime and Sofía as they left the house, he left for the north, subjecting himself to the discomforts of the trip: the heat, the flies, the dust, the anxieties. The lesbian had fallen in love with my father. Even though he rejected her, saying, "That is not our contract, comrade. I was only your doctor. I don't want you to flood me with filthy feelings," she slept every night on a bench just outside the house, contenting herself with spying on Jaime's venerated shadow moving behind the curtains.

In Zapiga, the police, alerted by some unknown informer, forced them off the train and made them sleep out in the open, next to the door of the station, all to keep them from visiting the office of the nitrate mine there. Down from the mountains blew a wind so freezing that Recabarren began to tremble as his fingers turned blue. To warm him, Jaime embraced him chest-to-chest, while Sofía warmed his back. That way they managed to withstand the cold for a few hours. But then they all began to tremble. A cavernous, convulsive cough shook the master's body. His comrades, much younger and therefore much less affected, began to rub him down from head to foot, putting all their energy into the massage.

When the attack passed, Recabarren said to them, "Don't worry so much, children. I've withstood worse things—beatings, torture, forced marches, and hunger. No physical ill can bring me down. And it won't be my age that conquers me. Let's walk to the mine. We'll sleep on foot."

They divided up the heavy propaganda and advanced like sleepwalkers, followed by an enormous moon. Recabarren was muttering a speech to the dunes, taking them for Party militants:

"It's insane to use capital with no other goal than increasing the amount of your capital, comrades. It only leads to the poisoning of the planet and the death of humanity. The solutions offered within society as it is are transitory and fictitious. We should . . . "

The miners received them with profound emotion; seeing them walk toward them was something like a miracle, a National Deputy on the point of death, covered by the dust of the road, almost unable to speak because his throat was so swollen, his tongue dry, and his lips split. Forgetting Marxist atheism, they fell to their knees and began to pray before him as if he were a saint. Furious, Jaime interrupted them:

"Drop these superstitions, comrades. Don Luis Emilio is a man just like you. Instead of prayers, give us a mattress to sleep on."

Recabarren protested, "None of that. There is no time to lose. First we'll do our duty, then we'll rest. Gather the militants and fellow travelers in the gymnasium during their lunch break. We have pamphlets of the highest importance that must be distributed."

Even though he'd walked so far without sleeping, Recabarren spoke with overflowing enthusiasm on the subject "Something of What I've Seen in Moscow." When the siren sounded, calling the workers back, he rushed to finish his speech:

"Workers in Russia have in their hands the strength of political and economic power. There is no one in the world who can strip the people of that power they've already conquered. The expropriation of the exploiters is complete. Never again will a thieving, tyrannical regime of the kind we put up with in Chile return to that society."

The workers were able to lend them a school where they slept a siesta that lasted until the next morning. Recabarren used the principal's office, while Jaime and Sofía slept in a classroom.

Jaime was dreaming that a panther was biting his skull without hurting him, in the way cats play with mice, when Sofía woke him, naked, straddling him and trying to swallow his penis in her sex.

"You are raping me, Comrade Lam. That's not right."

"Things belong to the person who needs them. Go back to sleep, Comrade Lautaro. I'll do all the work. Your instrument has been expropriated."

"But . . ."

"Shut up. Don't distract me. I have almost no feeling, and it takes a lot of work to have an orgasm. Let me concentrate."

And she began to move with deep and regular moist kisses that captured him to the core. Jaime opened his eyes wide and looked at her face, hoping that her resemblance to a Pekingese would deflate his erection.

But her hard breasts and abundant backside added to the woman's energy as she pumped up and down on the axis, giving tail switches like a hungry shark, passing from moans to roars, and ending by hurling out a string of obscenities that would make a saloon drunk blush. It all kept him erect. Amid all this brawling, he tried to say, "Remember, comrade, you are a lesbian."

But a sucking kiss covered his mouth and absorbed his entire tongue, obviating such an important revelation. His will began to weaken, and the vital liquid began to boil. He was chilled by a strange object that began to work its way into his anus. The comrade was trying to give a humility lesson to his manly pride by introducing a rubber phallus to his sanctum sanctorum.

"Here, there is neither masculine nor feminine, my dear. Let's be like snails; let's penetrate each other and simultaneously allow ourselves to be possessed. Equality is born from love."

In a rage, Jaime tried to push her off, but it was then he realized his wrists were tied with a length of chain. Sofía, with insane strength, immobilized his legs and, despite his groaning, begging, and protesting, penetrated his anus with the thick object. To his shame, all that promiscuity brought him closer to explosion.

"That's it, that's it, my androgyne! Come on, give me your syrup! We're going to make a champion child!"

Desperate, Jaime broke his chains, gave a leap backward, shook off the vampire, fell on top of the propaganda, and ejaculated onto "The Left Wing, an Infantile Sickness of Communism," translated from the selected works of Lenin. He pulled out the rubber phallus and in disgust threw it at Sofía's head. He hit her right in the center of her forehead, raising a lump that looked like a bite from a mountain flea.

"The flies have flooded your head, comrade. Too much of a good thing is no good. Your motto ought to be 'Praise Marx but pass the Lautaro.' I'll be a father some day. I feel in my balls a spirit asking me to engender it, but I'll deposit my seed in the uterus of a woman who shines like the planet Venus, not in a dyke like you."

Sofía Lam roared out, slamming the door so hard that three tiles fell off the roof. Then, muttering insults, while at the same time slicing the air with a long, sharp stone, cutting off invisible penises, she headed for the coast, entering the immense pampa. I can't say that I breathed a sigh of relief, because at that time I had no lungs, but I did swing around in joy because there was no way I wanted that woman as a mother.

But I didn't view her as severely as Jaime did, and I thought his way of cutting her off was exaggerated, this sticking the label "dyke" on her. It was denigrating. She was no hypocrite and had obeyed her instincts without opposing them with prejudices or fears. Her authenticity deserved a more courteous separation, but—and this is what horrified me—when I was on the point of landing in her ovaries, I saw that they were already inhabited by three spirits ready to pass through the frustration of miscarriage. They need to be engendered, to accumulate a few months of hope and only then receive the lesson of failure. They were three prophets wanting to view the promised land from a distance without entering it. Souls that in previous, egoistic lives did not know how to sacrifice themselves to themselves.

Without Sofía, my father and Recabarren continued their travels to Iquique. The people received Recabarren like a hero, and a public event was organized in Plaza Condell. When the leader, standing in the kiosk, was giving his speech, the shout Long Live Chile! Death to Communism! rang out and several shots came from the public. One bullet left a red line on the speaker's cheek. The workers dove to the ground to avoid the shots.

Recabarren, unperturbed, remained standing and speaking. Five young fascists wearing military shirts, boots, and riding trousers tried to scare the audience. Jaime detached the sickle from the red decorative screen and, scrambling around the flattened bodies, went up to the aggressors. One of them, fired up by the power of his pistol, tried to empty it at Recabarren's head. Jaime jumped like a cat and, still in the air, cut off the man's hand. A steaming spurt poured out of the stump all over those on the ground. Never fearing the bullets, my father ran toward the other fascists but they fled, scared out of their wits, carrying their mutilated comrade who never stopped screaming.

Jaime picked up the hand that still held the pistol and placed it on the table behind which Recabarren was standing. He interrupted his speech, removed the pistol from the stiffened fingers, and pointed it at the workers. They ducked their heads in shame.

"Comrades, you have to learn to give your lives so you can make a living as you should. No one is separated. We are a group, not individuals. Individuals are mortal, groups are eternal. When we stop fearing death, the gods fall off their pedestals. They tried to stop me from speaking with bullets, and all they achieved is that their shots turned into my words. Each one said Freedom!"

An ovation exploded, and in one voice they sang "The International" at the top of their lungs. Then Sofía Lam appeared, falling down drunk, hugging a prostitute dressed in red:

"Bastards! This long-suffering woman has more balls than all of you, poor he-men who know how to sing silly songs with the voice of a hot burro, but you abandon your leader when a rich boy starts shooting!"

She tore her Communist Party membership card to pieces.

"I'm leaving the Revolution for prostitution, that's my song!" And she fell into the arms of her lover, who picked her up like a baby and carried her off to the bars at the port. Paying no attention, the demonstrators finished singing the anthem, and to keep Recabarren and Jaime from being beaten by the police, who most certainly would be waiting for them at the train station, they gave them two mules and a guide who led them through the hills to Antofagasta. They took the Longitudinal and returned to Santiago. Before they went in, the master passed the revolver wrapped in a handkerchief to Jaime, saying, "Lautaro, you keep it so Teresa doesn't see it. Always keep it clean and loaded. You never know."

The portrait of Lenin went on peeling. By now it no longer had a face. During their silent meals, from time to time they heard the small sounds of the paint hitting the oilcloth table cover. When, in January 1924, the news came from Russia of the death of the great revolutionary, all that was left of the portrait was a white stain, rather like a ghost. Recabarren, without showing his emotions, went to the chamber, delivered a verbal portrait of Lenin, and asked that a condolence telegram be sent to Moscow. His proposal was rejected.

That night, back at home, Recabarren did not eat. He was sitting in the garden until 3:00 a.m. Teresa, always like a ship slicing through water, brought him hot tea every half hour. When the eighth cup came, the man broke his silence:

"Don't sacrifice yourself, Teresa, go to bed. You listen to my silences as if they were screams. Do I have to explain what's wrong with me? You know that ever since I was a boy I've given my life to the people. I'm not even fifty, but people call me 'the old man.' I'm no dreamer; I've only asked for what is right. It's not crazy to demand an end to war and the exploitation of man by man. Those who deny that are the ones who live outside reality, giving the orders, massacring innocents to preserve their power, making themselves owners of the Earth's riches, worsening consumption, leaving the workers hungry. It's insane! I never should have gone to Russia. I saw things. Errors I don't want to remember. Lenin died because he could not go on living that way. Now, Comrade Stalin... terrible... Well... Don't make me speak, woman. I no longer know what man is."

"We don't know what man is when he's asleep, Luis Emilio. The man who is awake is sublime. If you don't believe me, just look at yourself."

They embraced tenderly. He rested his head on Teresa's firm bosom and, without making a sound through his clenched jaws, controlled the weeping that shook his shoulders. Jaime, hidden by the curtain, heard everything from his window, listening avidly to his master's words, and felt ashamed to be spying on such an intimate scene. He stepped away, went to look at himself in the mirror, and gave himself a couple of good slaps.

In March, the master's term as deputy was up. He presented himself for reelection but did not make serious efforts. He didn't get enough votes. In September, a contingent of military men invaded the Senate to express their annoyance, demanding a political and administrative purification. Parliament approved the petitions presented to it. Arturo Alessandri, alleging he'd lost control of power, resigned and left the country. Exactly as Recabarren had predicted! That same month, a military junta met, intent on dissolving Congress and convoking an assembly to draft a new constitution. Public opinion approved enthusiastically, and the conservatives were obsequious and docile as events unfolded. Exactly as Recabarren had predicted!

The master was tired when he came home from the Party meeting. He handed Jaime some money and asked him to buy some pisco. My father returned with three bottles. It was the first time Recabarren expressed a desire to drink. Taciturn, they sat down under the huge white ghost. There was a liter for each of them. Gulping it down, the master began to empty his bottle. My father and Teresa copied him. Little by little they lost equilibrium and began to sweat.

The leader drank the last drops and began to guffaw. Teresa tried to smile, but her face was petrified. She put her head under her arm, imitating a hen, and began to snore, sitting in that odd position.

"The Lion of Tarapacá turned out to be sterile, Lautaro. His reactionary, anti-labor government has been replaced by a junta of generals who are even more reactionary. What a charade! They make promises to the people that go from the human to the divine only so the workers will bend their backs and keep on wearing the yoke. We're on our way to a criminal dictatorship, here and in Russia. All demagogues. Shut up! There's no more pisco?"

Jaime passed him the quarter liter he had left. The master finished in one swallow.

"Would you like to know, Quinchahual, how some young comrades responded when I suggested that it was infantile to believe that the proletariat alone, through its own efforts and a great struggle, could establish a Workers Government? They shouted that I was foolish to think myself owner and master of the Party, that I behaved like an absolute monarch reigning over his servants. I was treated like a rat, and one militant dared to spit in my face! Can you believe it, Lautaro? Within the bosom of the Party there are fights and internecine struggles provoked by those sleeping men. Someday someone has to wake up! Go get the gun."

"But . . ."

"Obey your father!"

Overwhelmed by Recabarren's will—he seemed to have aged a century—Jaime fetched the pistol.

"Let no one say that what I am going to do is the result of alcohol. Let's wait until we're sober."

The master took a notebook out of a drawer and leafed through it. It was covered with his tiny, tortured handwriting.

"These are the memories of my life. Here is what I really saw in Russia, what I think of Lenin and of the future that awaits us if things don't change."

He put the notebook in a metal tray and set fire to it. The rooster began to crow. Teresa awoke and saw the pistol. She dug through the ashes trying to find a legible fragment. The ashes flew around the dining room like a flock of nocturnal butterflies. She said, with infinite dignity, "Goodbye, Luis Emilio. You know what I feel for you. I'll never forget you."

Recabarren brought the pistol to his head and squeezed the trigger. He fell over with a red rose on his temple.

The government didn't dare forbid the funeral procession that would pass on Sunday through the center of the city to the General Cemetery. The coffin, covered with a red flag, was followed by a multitude of workers who filled the streets like a slow, silent, incredibly long river. The union banners paraded with a black ribbon on top of the letters embroidered in the velvet. Delegations of miners, maritime workers, men from the copper and coal mines, peasants, students, railroad men, bricklayers, bakers, and, at the head of the parade, guiding the coffin with a firm step, Teresa. Dressed in workers clothes, she glanced with pride toward the windows of the elegant houses where groups of people gathered to look out.

A barricade of one hundred policemen, armed with rifles and wearing metal helmets, stopped the procession. The human river paused. The master's companion, standing next to the coffin, sang with such intensity that her voice could be heard blocks away:

> *Without fear of sanctions*
> *I bid farewell to the subversive man*
> *Who has known a thousand prisons*
> *Without committing any crime.*

Thousands of voices united in the melody and, repeating the refrain, the marchers once again moved forward. The soldiers didn't dare fire and disappeared as if by magic. In the cemetery plaza, every worker became an orator. Thousands of inflammatory speeches launched in bursts, joined in a chaotic chorus, like the sound of a waterfall, to bid goodbye to Recabarren's remains. As those who were hungry and tired gave up, others took their place. At 6:00 p.m., the ceremony was finished, and the body was left in the hands of the cemetery staff so that on Monday the gravediggers could place the coffin in the family crypt.

The next morning, very early, the sun barely giving a yellowish tinge to the cloudy sky, the gravediggers, asleep on their feet, suppressing with grumbles the ill effects of alcohol, opened the gates to let Teresa, Jaime, and Sofía Lam (who turned up riding a man's bicycle and wearing a sailor suit) enter. The three marched silently behind the four drunken gravediggers who carried the coffin on their shoulders, zigzagging and tripping amid muttered curses. The iron crypt that belonged to Recabarren's grandfather was open. A dark-skinned boy, about twenty-five years old, with short, thick legs; a wide, hairy chest; calloused hands; big teeth; and straight black hair, was waiting for them, leaning on the aluminum cross.

"Yesterday I hid here, Doña Teresa. I forced open the doors and spent the night here, trying to join my family. I am Elías Recabarren."

Surprised, Teresa set aside her painful silence. "You are Elías? Luis Emilio's son?"

"Yes, ma'am. I came because . . . "

"Let's get on with the ceremony. Later you can tell us everything."

The gravediggers tossed the coffin into a niche as if it were a sack of potatoes. The jolt produced a bell-like sound in the metal crypt. They screwed the cover back on, whispering obscene jokes, and stretched out their right hands hoping for a tip. Teresa gave each one money. Grumbling, even though the amount was correct, they demanded more. Jaime kicked them out. They went off to sit on a tomb emblazoned with a winged woman playing a trumpet, where they passed around a bottle of wine as they took turns caressing the statue's marble hips.

At the coffee shop, The Last Goodbye, across the street from the cemetery, Teresa, Jaime, Sofía, and Recabarren's son drank their sodas in silence, not knowing how to begin the conversation. Sofía slapped the table, trying to kill a fly. The others emerged from their stillness to keep the glasses from spilling over, and attention focused on the girl.

"I came today to pay intimate homage to the master and to express my repentance. For obscure sexual motives, I betrayed the most sacred thing, the Party. My vagina and clitoris weighed more heavily than the pain of the exploited working class. Shame made me discover my vocation: I am an atheist monk. Count on me for anything. Are we friends, Lautaro?"

"Friends, Sofía!"

"Now it's time for me to talk, and I'll be sincere. About Communism I know nothing. I've lived far away from politics, no fault of my own but of my father. As you well know, Doña Teresa, he was married to Fresia Godoy, a maid, my mother, an uneducated woman from the south. Recabarren learned to read quickly, developed his intelligence, found the ideal that would guide his life, went north, and never came near us again. His love for the people made him forget his son. He worried about everyone but me. I grew up humiliated, with no education, in the basement of our bosses. My mother died when I was thirteen. I had no money to bury her decently. She disappeared into a potter's field. I hated politics, the struggles of the workers, that world that had stolen away my father. I also detested him. He should have come to find me, to teach me what he knew, to give me the chance to prepare the Revolution at his side. He shouldn't have left me cast aside like a contemptible orphan. I was working for a few days here in Santiago, in a furniture factory. I'm a carpenter. I read the news of his death. I shed not a single tear. To the contrary, I smiled and felt avenged. I asked permission to take a day off, saying I wasn't well, and I walked downtown intent on getting drunk. It was there the demonstration caught me. That human river following the body of the man who engendered me was pressing against my body, clinging to my skin, to my bones, in order to add me to its flow. I dissolved in the mass, and then, without personality, anonymous, one more cell in the gigantic animal of the people, I felt what everyone else felt, the greatest sadness coupled with an immense gratitude. I admired the honor of a solitary and valiant man who gave everything he had trying to get his compatriots out of poverty. I understood that my hatred was egoistic, and I felt proud to be the son of such a father. When the crowd left the cemetery, I hid so I could sleep in the crypt. Last night I felt no cold even though the walls and floor are iron. Recabarren's arms were around me. Also, those of my grandfather and great-grandfather. This iron house is a grave for men. In our family, hearts detach from women and immerse themselves in the struggle. That's the tradition I wish to continue."

"Elías, what you're saying is very beautiful, and I'm sure that if there were such a thing as heaven, your father would be happy to hear you. Luis Emilio often asked himself about your fate. We made inquiries, but we never managed to find your whereabouts. Finally, we reached the conclusion that you were dead. From this moment on, our house is your house."

"Let's not forget Comrade Lautaro Quinchahual. I too want to continue the work of my master and adoptive father. Give us advice, Teresa."

"Often, Luis Emilio talked to me about the importance of developing political awareness among the workers. Despite the fact that in the past few months he was crippled by sadness impossible to explain, he was also very concerned about art. He thought that the best medium to awaken the workers was the theater. He thought about the possibility of forming theater groups of four persons each to travel the country and go to the mines, putting on shows. He wrote several one-act plays. He finished the last one a day before his death. It's a comic drama for clowns, quite symbolic. If you want to be faithful to the ideal of my companion, I suggest the following: I'll sell the house, and with that money buy a truck. There are four of us, and we can travel the country putting on his posthumous works!"

A spontaneous and enthusiastic "Agreed!" turned them into traveling actors for several years.

In January of 1925, a movement led by young army officers staged a coup d'état against the junta of conservative generals and brought

Arturo Alessandri back to finish his term in office. But it wasn't really the president who controlled things. All power was concentrated in the minister of war. Carlos Ibáñez del Campo, who on the one hand tried to attract the workers and on the other tried to destroy the workers' movement. The new constitution had been approved and left almost all power in the hands of the executive. On June 4, at the La Coruña mine, the police and army massacred more than two thousand miners, women, and children. Discontent grew to such a point that Alessandri had to resign a second time before finishing out his term.

After two years of tug of war with the judiciary, Colonel Ibáñez was elected president, creating a dictatorial government that brought with it detentions, exiles, disappearances, executions, and the limitation of civil liberties. Luis Emilio Recabarren's theatrical work began acquiring more and more meaning as these things took place. Teresa, Sofía, Elías, and Jaime slept in the truck, which, chugging and bucking like an angry mule, carried them from one mine to another. The workers to whom the companies gave no entertainment other than the wine from their company stores, filled, with infantile eagerness, the soccer fields transformed into theaters thanks to the stages constructed from tables in the collective dining rooms.

Teresa was no longer the discreet woman who had remained silent for twenty-five years next to her idol. Dressed in trousers and a blue work shirt, she drove the truck through the pampa, overcoming the obstacles along the way by means of her ironclad will. Without her, the truck would have collapsed like an old house. She learned how to change tires and fix flats, to repair the motor, take it apart, put it back together, change parts, and, her face stained with grease, to curse at the mist to make it fade and clear the road. At the end of every performance, it was she who took up the collection. In addition to a bit of money, they were also given some food and a tank of gas. With every change in the government, with every important political event, they reexamined their act. And merely by changing their tones of voice, leaving the text intact, they managed to keep it up to date.

Teresa would announce: "Ladies and gentlemen and children: you are going to witness the grand performance of the International Failure Circus! We shall present on this stage a beast . . . "

(And here Elías, dressed as a bureaucrat, would enter and sit on the floor.)

"and an implacable lion tamer . . . "

(And here Jaime, dressed as a colonel, would enter dragging a chair and snapping a whip.)

"Let the action begin!"

LION TAMER: "Come along! Get up on that chair!"

BEAST: "Grrr!"

LION TAMER: "It's your property!"

BEAST: "Yes, it is mine! I sit on it. Few beasts manage to own their own chairs. I'm happy!"

LION TAMER: "Take a look at this chair."

BEAST: "It's the same as the other."

LION TAMER: "Apparently it is, but actually it's very different. Generations of noble beasts have sat on it. It's an honor to own it!"

BEAST: "I want it for myself!"

LION TAMER: "Impossible. It belongs to the director of the circus!"

BEAST: "I'll trade the one I have for that one!"

LION TAMER: "Yours is vulgar."

BEAST: "I'll give you all my money too!"

LION TAMER: "You don't have enough money."

BEAST: "What can I do? I'm ashamed of living on an ordinary chair."

LION TAMER: "If you kill the director of the circus, I can get it for you."

BEAST: "I'll get the chair, but what will you earn?"

LION TAMER: "I'll get to direct the circus!"

BEAST: "Perfect! I'll rip his guts out! Let's go!"

The bureaucrat Elías and Jaime, the colonel, went over to a corner where Sofía, the circus director, dressed as the president of the republic, was standing. Jaime would give her a shove and throw her to the floor. Elías threw himself on her, biting her stomach, pulling out of the vest a long intestine made of rags. With a tricky sleight-of-hand it looked as if he'd eaten it. Teresa, sitting in the audience, would applaud and shout, "Bravo! Great, magnificent, they killed him! Now the circus will work really well!"

LION TAMER: "Take the second chair. You've earned it."

BEAST: "Grrr. It's delightful to sit in it."

LION TAMER: "Even so, your first chair, despite being ordinary, had a warmth the other does not possess."

BEAST: "That's true. My new chair is cold."

LION TAMER: "The first is so agreeable that other beasts have decided to buy it."

BEAST: "Never! It must be mine again!"

LION TAMER: "But you already have a chair."

BEAST: "I want both of them!"

LION TAMER: "I can get it for you."

BEAST: "How?"

LION TAMER: "First, obey me blindly."

BEAST: "Give me orders!"

LION TAMER: "Fight, shoot cannon, gas them, invade, destroy, massacre!"

BEAST: "Grrr! Ready! What next?"

LION TAMER: "Take the chair you want by force!"

Elías would then leap toward the chair, imitating the attack of a ferocious soldier, and, after liquidating his invisible enemies, would take control of the chair, place it next to the other, and lie down on both with his hands under the nape of his neck.

BEAST: "Now I've got both! Now I'm happy!"

LION TAMER: "This place is full of people in chairs. What are your two chairs next to all these? You've got to expel the audience so that the entire circus is ours!"

Elías would then leap toward Teresa and hustle her around to drag her off the floor. Then he would return and stand on top of his chairs.

BEAST: "We've expelled the audience! The circus is ours!"

LION TAMER: "Stupid beast! You deserve a thousand lashes! Who do you think you are? The circus belongs to me!"

BEAST: "Oh dear! Forgive me! You keep the circus. I'll be happy with my two chairs."

LION TAMER: "Why? Have you got two backsides? This chair where generations of noble beasts have sat belongs to the person who gives the orders. I'm taking it back."

BEAST: "Oh, first chair of mine, I'll find you again. I never should have abandoned you."

LION TAMER: "Delusional beast, not even this chair belongs to you. I've decided to appropriate it. Animals don't need to sit down. Stretch out on the ground."

BEAST: "So what are you leaving me?"

LION TAMER: "Freedom!"

BEAST: "Freedom to do what?"

LION TAMER: "Freedom to eat just enough to stay alive. Freedom to obey me without arguing. Freedom to move around within a square yard. Freedom to receive the blows I might want to give you. Freedom to die for me!"

And Jaime would then take out a rifle and fire at Elías. He would fall down dead with red ink pouring from his mouth. Then my father would lament in anguish:

LION TAMER: "And now what do I do alone in this enormous circus?"

Teresa would pass around the hat, whispering into the ears of the spectators, "Without a beast, there is no lion tamer."

Dressed as miners, Elías, Jaime, and Sofía would appear with guitars to sing a cueca. The public would abandon their chairs and start dancing.

At dawn, March 15, 1927, the Communist Party was declared illegal. Radio Mercury transmitted the high-pitched, penetrating voice of Carlos Ibáñez:

> *The definitive moment for settling accounts has come. The malevolent and socially corrosive propaganda of a few professional agitators, along with a handful of daring outsiders, is no longer acceptable. We must cauterize society above and below. The time has come to break completely the red ties to Moscow. The Communist press will be shut down. All the organs of the Party, beginning with the Central Committee, will be under strong and constant siege by the police. We shall jail hundreds of their militants and leaders, relegate them to the most inhospitable places, submit them to severe torture, and assassinate some of them. After this operation, the nation will be at peace: happy within, and respected abroad.*

Teresa removed the hammer and sickle that adorned the hood of the truck and began to paint it black. They went on giving performances without changing a thing, but with other costumes, more innocent in appearance. Elías would wear a tiger suit. Jaime would exchange his colonel's uniform for a blue lion tamer's costume, and Sofía, the circus director, would wear a tuxedo. Teresa would introduce the show dressed as a clown.

For months, along the roads on the pampa, they passed gray trucks full of soldiers. They passed them by without being alarmed. The truck, now decorated with circus designs, aroused no suspicion. From time to time they were stopped and, after a rapid scrutiny, would be asked to tell a few jokes. Which was something Sofía knew how to do very well; she had a repertoire learned from the whores at the port, so obscene she made those insensitive male pigs wet their pants with laughter. Then they'd be sent on their way. Those same soldiers, if they saw a miner walking the hills, wearing a white cotton outfit, would shoot him just to watch him wave his arms like a dove. The vultures, attracted by the abundance of carrion, began to darken the sky as they followed the army patrols.

After each show, Teresa would invite Party members and, in secret, dodging informers, meet with them in some mine tunnel. For long hours she would recount her conversations with the man she'd venerated. Soon her gaze wandered, her voice would change along with her rhythm and gestures, and she would begin speaking as if she were Recabarren. Calm, profound, she would quote Engels, Lenin, Marx, and others to show her comrades the roads they ought to follow in the future. Elías would sit down near her legs, and she, never ceasing to lecture, would massage his hairy head, always shedding tears. Jaime and Sofía Lam, respectful, their bodies dried out after so many trips in the arid mining zones, would listen to her realizing that through a love that did not recognize death as a limit, that faithful woman kept the thoughts of the master alive.

One Saturday night, so starry that they could see one another's faces without lighting a lamp, forty comrades gathered secretly a half hour away from the Huara nitrate mine, listening with religious respect to the words of the "old lady." They were interrupted by a messenger who arrived almost out of breath, madly pedaling his bicycle:

"We've been betrayed, comrades! We caught an informer telephoning the soldiers at San Antonio. We made him confess; he gave them a list of our names and descriptions. All of us are marked men. He also squealed on our four friends, telling about the subversive labor they were carrying out. Right now, a truckload of soldiers is coming to arrest us. If we surrender, they'll shoot us. If we run away, we'll die of thirst in these arid hills or we'll be shot by the patrols out 'pigeon hunting.' It's better we fight, even if we have to throw rocks and die on foot!"

Like a single man, they all began to pile up stones and dig a trench in the soft soil.

"You, friends, do not have to sacrifice yourselves. Take your truck and run for Arica. If you get there, burn the truck and hide out in the home of some sympathizer—you're all on the list."

Teresa embraced the miners one by one, sat in the truck, and, with painful rage, drove off. Her three collaborators, their eyes lowered, got in too, not wanting to see for the last time those men who would be massacred. Sofía began to cry:

"They're going to die, and it's our fault. We brought them together."

Teresa abruptly changed direction; instead of driving north, she turned onto the road to San Antonio. "They won't die. I can save them. You three get out! I'm going to ram the soldiers' truck!"

"I will accompany you, ma'am. I want to be worthy of my father. In any case, the police know who I am. Sooner or later, it's all the same."

"The soldiers have killed off almost all my friends, of both sexes. Being homosexual in this idiotic dictatorship is a crime. One of these days, they'll tie a stone to my ankles and toss me into the sea. I too will accompany you, Teresa."

"Allow me to sacrifice my life for the freedom of this country, which is now mine. We started out together, let's end the journey together."

And with that my father, seated next to the door, locked it and held on to the seat. Far in the distance, the two headlights of military transportation blinked.

"We'll soon see you, Luis Emilio," said Teresa, pressing hard on the accelerator. The stones from the desert valley began to run backward like rabbits. With savage hunger, the truck ate up the road. Sofía howled with enthusiasm, kissed Elías and Jaime on the mouth, lit four cigarettes and distributed them. They smoked eagerly. Jaime smashed a fist through the windshield so they could feel the mountain air. Their blood was so hot they didn't even feel the biting cold.

The collision was imminent, and the body of my future father was going to be destroyed. I began to protest. All my efforts to get him to La Tirana, where the woman I wanted as a mother awaited him, would be in vain. I might need centuries to find another couple appropriate for my plans. Damn it! This young man was heading straight to his death, AND I WANTED TO BE BORN!

Desperate, I emerged from the hiding place I'd made in Jaime's testicles and sought out the Rabbi. He understood the situation immediately. He was horrified. My father was breaking many of the 613 commandments of his religion. It is forbidden to kill. When He created the world, God ordered men to increase and multiply so it would be inhabited. To destroy others and oneself is to destroy the world. Abstain from all labor on Saturday. Causing a collision is work. It is forbidden for any tribunal to sentence anyone to death on Saturday. The Eternal One has desired, in honor of that holy day, that even criminals and sinners find repose and tranquility on Saturday. It is forbidden to take vengeance. What happens to us, be it agreeable or annoying, has been desired by the Lord. The men who hurt us are instruments in the hands of the Creator. Our faults constitute the first cause of what happens to us. It is forbidden to hold rancor. It is unworthy to fix the offender in our memory and later imitate his conduct. It is forbidden to cut one's own flesh . . .

By now the trucks were so close that the Rabbi stopped enumerating the commandments that were being broken. He gathered strength and, transformed into a transparent spider, seized Jaime's brain, and taking control of his body released the lock, opened the door, jumped toward the dry ground, and rolled away in a cloud of dust.

The two trucks collided. The noise echoed throughout the silent pampa with such force that it seemed the sky had split. The boxes of hand grenades exploded. The pieces of bodies flew through a ball of flames. A herd of guanacos, dazzled, crossed the road, trampling the bloody flesh. The Rabbi, his mission accomplished, returned to the Interworld, and I returned to my genital hideaway.

Jaime, feeling like a traitor, ashamed, limped over to see if anyone was still alive. But the vultures got there first. Nearly burning their feathers in the flames, they stretched out their black spines and began to devour the roasted remains. My father saw one of the raptors perch on Teresa's decapitated head and a haughty gesture sink its beak into her eyes. The order of the world began to collapse. What meaning did a life so short have? Was sacrificing it worthwhile? How could a woman like that end up as food for vultures? Was it true that there was no fucking Destiny that rewarded virtue?

If this sordid Universe was only able to give these heroes a tomb in the gullet of those carrion-eating birds then he, Comrade Lautaro Quinchahual, would take charge of their remains until he found them the sacred place they deserved because of their sacrifice! He took a piece of burning wood and attacked the vultures, shouting his head off. The screeching cowards flew off in a dense cloud, leaving behind a rain of excrement. Jaime looked everywhere, trampling the guts and pieces of soldier that remained in the bonfire. The fire had consumed the bodies of Elías and Sofía. Of Teresa only the head remained, with the eye sockets empty and bloody. He took it by the hair and ran into the pampa, heading for the mountains.

How many days did he walk, insane, under the burning sun, neither eating nor drinking, persecuted by a cloud of horseflies getting drunk on the juices that dripped from Teresa's head? He couldn't remember;

it seemed like an eternity. Forgetting himself in that harsh solitude, he sought a worthy place to bury what remained of his friend. He stuck out his swollen tongue, stared at the sun, and shouted defiantly. If he ran into a stone, he embraced it, kissed it with his cracked lips, leaving red marks. He made it an accomplice, gave it a Mapuche name, and enrolled it in the clandestine Communist Party. He tried to form an army of rocks to help him implement the Galactic Revolution, to shock the planet out of its orbit, transform it into a comet and lead it in a straight line out of this badly made Cosmos where spiders ate flies and newborn children were received by Death, who hunkered down and opened its crocodile maw right between the mother's thighs. He ran barefoot over the surface of the salty earth. He fell face down and licked the dry cracks as if they were the sex of women, trying to give life to the landscape that had become sterile for lack of human love.

"Where there is no heart, drought appears, and for that reason I sink my sex into the sand so that the rain may begin."

His father Alejandro came with a golden halo over his mane of white hair, offering him a perfect pair of shoes that he, his disdained son, had given him one day:

"My son, the wounds on your feet acquire order in my bosom and form letters. They say: HOPE. What you gave me is restored to you. Don't cut me off. Absorb me."

He began to shrink until he turned into a gnome two inches tall. Jaime picked him up, placed him next to his left nipple, and, pushing him hard, inserted him into his heart, where he dissolved.

His mother's body appeared, guillotined, spurting a fan of red gushes from her neck. She looked like a tree. She held out her hands, asking him for the head of Recabarren's companion. Jaime hugged the corpse and, with painful rage, spit a ball of dry saliva into the bleeding wound. The headless woman twisted as if wounded by a bullet, her neck began to suck in air as if it were a mouth, and, moving its edges, spoke in a crusty voice:

"We mothers have an infinite comprehension. Within your forehead are hidden all the stars, lying in wait like lions, to leap aboard the ship of God, when I caress you with my brains."

Jaime took her in his arms and kissed the oozing hole that was her neck. The wound whispered, "Enter into the deepest part. I want you to sink your tongue into my awareness like a blind fish so that once and for all that diamond star that is the child of our dissolution may appear."

Jaime, his thirst satisfied forever, turned into a solitary eye past which events slipped by, as if over a dead whale. After the day came the night, and after the night, another, and there were no more days. Carrying the head, on which a beard of worms was growing, he advanced in the darkness. He knew he was seeking not only a grave but also a woman.

He found himself wandering along the crests of a mountain chain parallel to the Andes. The horseflies, feeding on the rotten soma that dripped from Teresa, had grown to the size of cats, and, buzzing like airplanes, they pierced his body with their stingers, opening wounds out of which his reason poured in a gelatin of letters. His feet, so swollen that they couldn't fit into his own footprints, forced him to stop. Jaime told the head that when he was a boy he had feet smaller than his footprints, which made him run all the time to fill them. Now, expelled from his steps, there was nothing left for him to do but become a statue of salt and die. He collapsed among the ovoid rocks like a marionette whose strings had been cut.

He was grabbed by his mane of hair, which now reached his waist, and with a powerful tug he was set on his feet. It was Isolda, the Lightning Bolt of Limache, the knife thrower.

"Don't be a rube. You're a circus man, free and potent, not a formless mass. Give thanks to your skeleton and the muscles that mobilize you. Thanks to them you can oppose an authority you detest. Recover faith, your feet are the same size as your footprints. And those footprints were made before you were born. All you have to do is follow them.

Have confidence in your bones. In any case, your hair grows straight to heaven."

Lola and Fanny, slithering like snakes, led him to a path where a line of steps was shining. Benjamín, with wings of red cartilage, flew around him:

"On you converge the phosphorescent screams of the enchanted steps awaiting the kiss that will transform them into moon. Share with each one the inexhaustible skin of your tiger and the cerebral roots that make your feet flower. Go give the fish an idea of what water is!"

But Jaime still did not have the strength to advance. Tralaf came:

"Huinca, repeat after me: *Amutan chengewe mapu mew,* I am going to the land where the people become one. Leap toward the Future, put your feet on top of it to make it Present, flee from the borrowed sun, and live in your center."

Eleodoro Astudillo, the gravedigger, also came:

"If you ask me, 'What's going on today?' I'll answer 'Nothing is going on. It only goes.' Let yourself be carried by them and become what takes place so that the poor, who neither see nor know and go around begging, take control of you and turn you into food."

The hunchback, Jesús de la Cruz, joined the group:

"Why did you abandon me when I'm your golden goose?"

He began to honk, his hunchback opened like the roof of an observatory, and out came a big golden egg that, flying before him, led him to the land of "Always Always." Jaime walked and walked along his footprints until he reached the abyss where the aurora is born. He descended from those high peaks, crossed the deep glen, and reached a dry plateau where there stood a church with stone buttresses and towers crowned by wooden belfries. He entered. In the solitary temple, the flames of the candles, transformed into calcareous tears, tore the shadow that came from the glass rose. The floor was flooded with liquid lead, and blind doves devoured the flesh-colored scarabs that nested in the plaster sculptures. Above the altar, a bleeding Christ, with His arms spread but with no cross, was looking at him. Jaime grabbed an iron candelabra, and with one blow, decapitated Him. The crown of thorns remained floating in the air, like an opaque halo. He raised Teresa's head and placed it on the wooden neck. The wounds on the hands and side closed. The chest became transparent. A heart, burning like the sun, filled the church with light.

Having fulfilled his mission, Jaime fell into a chute and, sliding at dizzying speed, advanced toward death.

In the sanctuary of La Tirana, my mother awoke with a deep pain in her ovaries. From her sex ran a perfumed blood, so hot that when she held it in her hands it gave off steam. She put a drop on her tongue. It tasted sweeter than honey. She daubed the face of the Virgin with the red plasma and murmured a melody meaning:

"Today make the unknown man arrive who I've been awaiting for ten years."

I rolled around within her womb and established an invisible bridge between her ovaries and my father's testicles. He was stretched out, almost dead, shaken by fever, twenty miles away. Sara Felicidad immediately obeyed the call. Because of her speed, her steps lengthened, and in twenty strides, each a mile long, she reached the small church where all the horseflies of the region had landed, eager for its interior light, transforming it into an enormous cathedral.

Next to the altar, under the wooden Christ with the fleshy head, lay Jaime, dying of hunger, his skin hugging his bones, his swollen tongue sticking out of his mouth like a white horn. My mother, to keep him from dying of thirst and hunger, spread her legs, brought her sex to my father's mouth, made his hard tongue penetrate her hymen, and absorbing it until her vulva stuck to his teeth, fed him with menstrual blood.

He began returning to life. On his knees before the gigantic woman (she now measured six foot nine), he realized the profound love that had made him travel for ten years on the trail of an unknown woman.

There she was, born from his dreams. Her soul had made a tiger's leap, piercing his skin, and fell before him. He remained there staring at her with inexhaustible pleasure.

They did not feel the passage of days. Once I proved to myself that my mother's ovaries were fertile, I ordered them to couple. They lay down naked in the church. My father's sex swelled with such force that it became purple, and my mother's red-hot oval secreted a white torrent in which the two of them submerged, transformed into aquatic angels. Pleasure transformed their flesh into consciousness, the stars began to travel the heavens, filling them with silver lines, the semen galloped through the canals and surged, bubbling, to fill the magic cavern with foam. I wasn't mistaken. Those two beings, saturated with love, their breath braided together, were giving me the miraculous opportunity to once again possess a body.

During the months that followed, my tranquility grew. Having successfully joined my selected progenitors, I yielded myself to the wisdom of the cells. They possessed the millennial knowledge to form me. Only one task was left to me: to have myself born in the exact geographic site, during the proper month and time of day, so that my Destiny would be in accord with my ambitions.

Jaime was a man of normal height, five foot nine, but my mother's extra twelve inches made him look like a dwarf when he walked at her side. Nevertheless, the strength that emanated from his spirit, granting his body a beast's dignity, and the balanced sobriety of his gestures, complemented my mother's supernatural beauty instead of contrasting with her. When the couple entered Iquique, traffic stopped dead, and the city quieted down as they passed. Normal people viewed them as beings from another world, and the beauty of that love became so enormous to them that they, who knew nothing of the delirious extremes of the soul, became terrified.

A nervous crowd, about to throw stones, saw them disappear into the Six W's (Wonderful, Wholesome, Wise, Wholesale, Welcoming, White), the enormous store owned by Jashe, Shoske, Moisés Latt, and César

Higuera, named in honor of the six points of the Jewish star. Everything there was white, from the food—cheese, milk, eggs, rice, chicken breasts, and fish fillets—to the clothing, kitchen articles, and even the children's toys, transformed into a collection of ragged ghosts that represented all human activities—train conductors, deep-sea divers, pilots, doctors, etcetera.

Not one, not even her own mother, recognized Sara Felicidad. The image she had of her was of a mute, ragged, hunched-over child, who had died lost in the hills. She knew Sara Felicidad was her daughter when she picked up a pencil and rapidly drew, line for line, some of the greater arcana of the Tarot. Jashe suddenly recovered her memory and, whispering, "Alejandro, Alejandro," sank her face into the blonde hair of my mother, who had fallen to her knees. She wept bitterly. The wound had not healed and would never heal. The Russian dancer was still burning in her heart like a sacred fire.

Shoske said to Moisés, "Your wife can't stand seeing her. She reminds her of past suffering. If you don't remove Sara Felicidad from her presence, my sister will die."

They flew a rabbi in from Santiago and had my parents marry. At the same time, they took the opportunity to bless the betrothals of Jacobo the First with Raquel the First, Jacobo the Second with Raquel the Second, and Jacobo the Third with Raquel the Third. They gave the newlyweds a truckload of merchandise, a good amount of money, and the keys to the store they'd rented for them on the central street of Tocopilla, 140 miles away. A good excuse never to see them again.

The store was called Ukraine House, because Jaime and Sara Felicidad decided to pass themselves off as white Russians to avoid political problems. There, among porcelain dishes, cuckoo clocks, and ladies underwear, I developed until the precise moment I decided to be born: ten in the morning on October 24, 1929, a day known worldwide as "Black Thursday."

At the same moment, the economic crisis in the United States exploded and extended all over the planet. Banks closed one after the other, and industry was paralyzed. Chile was the nation hardest hit by the catastrophe. Nitrate mines closed down, and a fourth of the population fell into indigence. The Six W's shut down and Ukraine House, for lack of customers, did so as well. My parents, with me in their arms, suddenly found themselves penniless, sleeping on the beach and having to stand in line outside the municipal office along with miners and their families to get their free dish of soup.

"Great! We've touched bottom! Finally, we've found our land. Now we are citizens of misery. We lost hope and because of that we lost fear. All that's left for us is to rise. We shall baptize our son with the name Alejandro, the name of my father and your father. He is the light we shall burn at the altar. Hoping that one day, forgetting himself and living for the sake of others, he will come to awareness in order to serve in an impersonal form, making known the first word, the one that is the origin of all languages: 'Thanks.' So that toward him converge the phosphorescent screams of the enchanted frogs awaiting the kiss that will transform them into Buddha. So that he will be the illuminated fruit that will transform our obscure tree into a cathedral lighthouse."

While my mother sang a lullaby, feeding me at her breast, Jaime, blowing into my nose, transmitted the Rabbi to me. Happy to find himself in a brain that offered him no resistance, he began to enumerate his new commandments:

You will not kill death. You will not covet the wife of the widower, and you will be faithful to your ghost. You shall not steal that which belongs to you nor speak with the mouth of your fellow man. You will not take the name of God in vain because all names are He. You will sanctify your workdays and transform your parents into shoes. You will make of the Earth an altar where the sheep sing and where finally you will bless yourself.

383

ABOUT THE AUTHOR AND TRANSLATOR

ALEJANDRO JODOROWSKY is a Chilean-French filmmaker, playwright, actor, author, musician, comics writer, and spiritual guru, best known for his avant-garde films including *Fando and Lis* (1968), *El Topo* (1970)—which became a cult hit and inaugurated the "midnight movie" phenomenon—*The Holy Mountain* (1973), and *Santa Sangre* (1989). As documented in the recent film *Jodorowsky's Dune*, in 1975 he began to work on a colossal adaptation of Frank Herbert's *Dune*—which was to star Orson Welles and Salvador Dalí and to be scored by Pink Floyd—that was never made. (A version of *Dune* was later filmed by David Lynch, and the creative team Jodorowsky assembled influenced a generation of science-fiction filmmakers.) Recently, after 23 years away from the screen, Jodorowsky released his autobiographical film *The Dance of Reality*, about growing up in a Chilean mining town. Jodorowsky himself, his first wife Valerie, and his sons Brontis, Axel, and Adan have all appeared in his films.

A circus clown and a puppeteer in his youth, Alejandro Jodorowsky left for Paris at the age of 23 to study mime with Marcel Marceau. There, he befriended the surrealists Roland Topor and Fernando Arrabal, and in 1962 these three created the "Panic Movement," a performance art collective inspired by Luis Buñuel and Antonin Artaud and named in homage to the god Pan. Jodorowsky became an adept in the art of the Tarot and a prolific author of novels, poetry, short stories, essays, works on the Tarot and "psychomagic" healing, and more than thirty successful comic books, among them the Incal, Technopriests, and Metabarons series, working with such highly regarded artists as Moebius (Jean Giraud) and Georges Bess.

ALFRED MACADAM is professor of Latin American literature at Barnard College-Columbia University. He has translated works by Carlos Fuentes, Mario Vargas Llosa, Juan Carlos Onetti, José Donoso, and Jorge Volpi among others. He recently published an essay on the Portuguese poet Fernando Pessoa included in the *Cambridge Companion to Autobiography*.